Segments
and Challenges

Dear Tom and Lonny M. llie.

Previous Publications by the Author

- *Bends and Shades (2014)*
- *Indu (2015)*
- *House of Twenty-Two Buffalos (2017)*
- *Passion and Pathos (2019)*
- *Chasing Dreams (2021)*
- *Reflections (2022)*

Segments and Challenges

Jahed Rahman

Library of Congress Control Number:		2024921849
ISBN:	Hardcover	979-8-3694-3179-5
	Softcover	979-8-3694-3177-1
	eBook	979-8-3694-3178-8

Print information available on the last page.

Rev. date: 10/29/2024

To order additional copies of this book, contact:
Xlibris
844-714-8691
www.Xlibris.com
Orders@Xlibris.com
861898

To Our Dearest only Nati (grandson) so far:

Henry Rahman Tavares

With

All Love, Wishes, Prayers

CONTENTS

Note for Dearest Nati (Grandson) ix

Preface xi

Scenery...1

Storm 33

Shelter 53

Shield 89

Sight..105

Shred..146

Stage 161

Sojourn 218

Shred..236

Stuck..268

NOTE FOR DEAREST NATI (GRANDSON)

YOU ARE NOW about three years old, a toddler, while I just finished eighty-five long years of gracing this wonderful space, commonly attributed as the earth. I have had a fulfilling life, and my only regret, after observing your growing up so far, is that I will miss your long, slanting hair, provocative eye reflexes, mischievous smile, and playing soccer in your abode with Dad Joe shouting encouraging words. With the passage of time, I will not be there to enjoy very much your further growing up with new varied laurels. That is the hard reality. That is the motivating factor for writing this book.

I was all absorbed in delineating a way to let you have an idea as to who I am, the pros and cons of social settings I grew up with having a semblance of idea about values, traditions, and practices of the time. Needless to mention, many of those have undergone rapid changes with the passage of time, enhanced communication and greater mobility, in all their jolts and shades, as well as greater exposure to a wider, tangible perception of the world.

These are being detailed not to measure success in life but to document the likely positivity of having an open and receptive mindset. As you grow up, I hope that you will be safe, secure, and happy, blessed by a matching mindset.

My only other expectation is that you will read this very ordinary writing once you grow up to assess and appreciate various statements from their respective perspectives of time, conditions, and relevance. These are being detailed not to measure success in life but to document the likely positivity in having an open and receptive mindset.

PREFACE

THE THEME THAT premised the book's essence is that in life's journey, there are a plethora of fragmentations, mostly causing frustration and dismay, but some of those also create opportunities for a new start, mostly wiping out initial distresses. That typically depends on the alertness and commitment of the incumbent to respond and silhouette new opportunities. The book is thus titled *Segments and Challenges*.

It epitomizes the entire life of Javed, the principal character of the story, making progress in life in the midst of the frequently fragmented turn of his journey but still making significant strides even though burdened by social and traditional impositions.

This publication is the consequence of the urge of Henry's grandfather to document the surroundings of living and the backdrop of emotional persistence for indicative portal of social conditions and traditional values at the time his Nana (as the maternal grandfather is addressed in Bangladesh) grew up in Bangladesh in settings conditioning his life's progression, encountering fragmentations and related challenges. It is not feasible to authenticate the facts nor the same is intended. Hence, it is written principally as fiction, taking shelter under some illusory characters. The purpose is to lay a perceptional depiction to have a very rough impression of nature, types, and constraints of earlier social practices. Within the bounds of those, Nana made a progression in life to be able to motivate Henry's mother to go to Harvard and Stanford for higher levels of undergrad and post-grad learning.

It is not that the attainments of his mother and her siblings solely had marks on his feelings and realizations. Nana was happy and content observing his progenies having a broad understanding of life and living beyond faiths, practices, and inferences without disputing any of them.

These are being detailed not to measure success in life but to document the likely positivity in having an open and receptive mindset.

Nana nurtured the hope that his grandson would, as he grows up, be safe, secure, and happy, blessed by matching intellectual insight and mindset.

I am conscious of the fact that I am not a natural writer. It all started in 2014 as a response to the loneliness that I felt after moving from demanding social engagements in Vancouver. Soon I decided to leave a documentary evidence of life and living so that my generations hereafter have idea as to what is my root, who I am, and how my life was shaped. Gradually, I continued writing with happiness and a sense of leaving something behind and started enjoying it instead of just idling my retired life. Between then and 2022, I published six books, being marketed through various outlets, including Amazon. I then decided to stop writing.

All those happened before my Nati (first grandson) was in the panorama, and as he was growing up. When he was about two years old, I started enjoying his playful actions and expressions. That motivated the present writing. On that journey, I was often ridiculed by close ones. That heightened during the writing of this one too.

There are, however, a few others who always encouraged me with my passion for writing, and that kept me in my writing endeavor. Not only that, I will be failing in my moral onuses if I do not recognize Ms. Rukhsana Hasib, an intellectual and social motivator of Pennsylvania; Mr. Naseem Rabbani, a businessman, community motivator, and a pseudo authority in religious philosophy and related religious injunctions of Schaumberg; and Mr. Rukunul Islam Babar, a civil servant, a social motivator, and a leading responder in case of community needs of Chicago, for their sustained efforts in encouraging me in this journey.

Jahed Rahman
Evanston

SCENERY

T HAT WAS THE day following a tense and high-stakes midterm elections of the year in the USA. By all counts and as per his assessment, Javed was expecting a better turnout and relatively a more positive outcome. Though the following morning sun was a bright one under a clear blue sky, he was increasingly disappointed by the sheer number of votes the opposition party candidates accounted for in the early count, shading his cogitated expectation.

After a long swaying discourse with his friend, Naseem Rabbani, on the telephone expressing immense disquiet as to the constituencies' inability to make a prudent choice between short-term issues like inflation and cost of living versus long-term policies affecting rights, which, once undone, will affect the lives of the following generations is of no relevance. Javed, from his perspective, got disheartened and exhausted internally. That sort of feeling was aggravated by the apparent loathness of the incumbent party in power to repeatedly emphasize that specific focus in an electoral tradition heightened by voting practice inclined to parties instead of issues. As he fibbed in his reclining chair, he unconsciously dozed off and involuntarily went to a deep nap. And that was a pretty long one too, unlike his normal practice. There was no one in his abode at that time.

As the election results were being unremittingly telecast by different channels, Javed woke up from his precipitous shuteye only to observe the sudden swamping of the sky with a dampening thick cloud, convoyed by precipitous rain unpredictably accompanied by gusty wind. As a diversion from TV, he beheld outside across the vast open space of his home to clinch about a definite slowdown of activities outside as well as traffic flow.

That wind, moving in a spherical fashion, was visibly impacting the surrounding trees with their remaining leaves, quite significant both in terms of volume and their enchanting fall color shades. Javed, as a startling change from the immediate past, started enjoying the movement of branches of surrounding trees and the dancing of their remaining leaves to the tune of strong circular winds, with most falling on the ground. Those on the ground were flashing to the tune of unprecedented wind flow. As he viewed it from his home, this sudden atmosphere spectacle became a welcome diversion and treat for Javed. He, contrary to his penchant, started enjoying it, simultaneously appreciating the fancies of Mother Nature.

To energize himself in that lonely setting, Javed dared to go out for a short drive to get his favorite Starbucks coffee. As he hurriedly stepped inside the store to order coffee as per his specifications (big double cup Pike with about two inches empty top for pouring "half-half" steamed milk with no foam and no sugar, a specification often being difficult to communicate using a drive-through facility), he was astounded seeing a cluster of students chuckling limitlessly, being totally oblivious of what is going on at the national level. Having returned, he concentrated on sipping his favorite drink before it lost its steam.

As Javed was at the end of his drink, the doorbell rang. Opening the door, he was surprised to see his regular therapist, Rick, whom he did not expect to show up from the south side due to the weather and overwhelming election results. Rick was very calm and quiet, and, after exchanging usual greetings, concentrated on arranging his message table, putting associated accessories in their usual places. Neither the weather nor the trend of the election results bothered him at all. Javed tried in vain to initiate a discourse, but Rick was nonresponsive. Being disheartened, Javed took his position on the massage table and Rick started his routine massage therapy having only related homily.

Closing eyes while lying on his back and enjoying the massage, Javed traveled back to his roots in Bangladesh and visualized the scene back home under an identical setting. Everyone, whether a teacher or student, a professional or rickshaw puller, would be engrossed in having election results related to tête-à-têtes. That scene would be repeated in railway stations, bus stops, and bases for ferries, not to talk about tea stalls and the like. What a contrast in approach and attitude! Recognizing the variance and reconciling with divergent realities in the context of societal approach and an individual's commitment to assigned duties, Javed accepted the present realities without hesitation.

Saying adios to Rick, Javed sat down on his sofa and started to analyze his experience of the day. Without being loaded by deviations in features and priorities of the two social systems, Javed reconciled with realities without being bothered as to what is opposite or what is not. That was akin to his longstanding realization that any conclusion about divergent issues is best understood and settled if reconnoitered and assessed from the perspective of the other party. He also believes and practices this dictum in personal relationships, and that made him adorable to a host of others in social settings, at home and abroad.

As Javed was pondering on related issues, the doorbell rang again. It was the mail delivery lady from the US Postal Service. Despite prevailing weather conditions, she was performing her assigned duty without excuses or grievances. She was followed by a heating company's technician who came to service the heating system as per contract. And these, among a host of others, made USA what it is and is known to be. Adherence to commitments and discharging assigned responsibilities silently and diligently under perceivable adverse situations and irrespective of broader national issues are the hallmarks of the social setting.

The prevailing wind was still blowing in a circular fashion. Observing that and taking pity for the arduous challenge the technician was facing, Javed, being a product of Bangladesh social etiquette, politely offered a seat and a cup of coffee. The technician thanked him and stepped out. Standing alone in the front portico, Javed refocused his attention on the trees in the open space. Precipitously, a flow of sporadic blustery wind accompanied by drenching rain from the east end to the north swept the area. Moving inside the home, he continued to look through the window.

Most of the leaves that withstood earlier onslaughts succumbed this time. Leaves having different shades dominated by yellow, dark pink, and burgundy were flowing like crazy butterflies. Dancing to the tune of wild wind, some fallen leaves continued to have sudden changes in their positions while most others that fell remained on the ground with frequent changes in positions. Leaves that soaked heavily lay on the ground and would become natural fertilizers to help grow new grass with the change of season. This possibly is one of the many interventions of Mother Nature to sustain greeneries, helping habitats.

This episode and related thinking took Javed back to his early childhood. While he has had no trepidation of many social practices in Bangladesh, he cannot subscribe to the taboo of totally keeping sex strictly out of bound of social communications and education practices. Bangladeshi girls are relatively better placed in this regard as mothers, aunts, and sisters usually play the role of guide and mentors as the girls grow up. Firstly, it is perhaps due to mutually supportive interactions based on a relationship premised on fear of the unknown. Second, visible physical changes in the physiology of girls are more prominent and obvious. Thus, preparing a girl for womanhood takes precedence in thinking and action.

The same, however, is never the case with boys. Social discussions on sex-related educative matters with or in the presence of growing boys and seniors are not only discouraged but also not permitted. Society imposes various restrictions, compelling growing boys to get information, as their physiological changes emerge, from divergent unreliable sources, more prominent being illiterate male household helps.

Javed recalls an incident when he was about eight years old. Though in his early phase of growing up, he was recognized as a talented and meritorious student. Everyone wanted him as a friend. But he was always very reserved, exercising due care not to hurt anyone. The only exception was a class fellow, Ebad by name. Javed's relationship with him was owing to Ebad being a good student too. By traits of character, Ebad was very friendly, could make fun of everything, and could laugh very vociferously as well.

That was the day before the short school break for spring. Everyone was in a holiday disposition except Ebad. That struck Javed. He took Ebad to a quiet corner and inquired as to what was bothering him. Ebad was nonresponsive, and both returned to the classroom. Javed got out of that thinking and concentrated on his studies, carefully noting the guidance of the math teacher for study during the holiday as the periodical examination is set immediately after the vacation.

Like all previous days, both walked out at the end of routine school time while Ebad still maintained a somber stance. Walking together was the practice of both, sharing a common path while going back home before separating for their respective destinations. That separation point was at the end of the local *dighi* (big pond).

Suddenly Ebad sat down on the bank of the dighi, positioned his school bag by his side, and started shredding grass with rage. Observing that unusual act and recounting the strange behavior pattern of the day, Javed was certain that something exceptional had happened, which not only was bothering Ebad but equally kept him noncommunicative the whole day.

Instead of any verbal communication, Javed quietly sat by the side of Ebad and started throwing pebbles in the dighi water with no expectation. Precipitously, Ebad opened up after seeking a solemn assurance from Javed about the privacy of what he was going to tell. He started saying with care and caution what he held so long within himself.

Ebad, with perceived hesitation, started saying, "You know that my father is the chairman of our Union Council (the lowest level of the local government system). We are relatively well off. That enabled me to have a separate room and bed in the relatively spacious house since I was in class three. I enjoyed that space and freedom. My parents are also happy, observing that my separate accommodation enabled me to focus on study.

"A few days later, my only maternal aunt, since her wedding about a year back, came to visit us with a stipulation that her husband would join at the time of her return. That was a very happy time in our house with mother's happiness in having her sister as a visitor overflowing with expressions and actions. Surprisingly, our father, normally an authoritative individual both within the home and outside, was equally blissful, enjoying the exchange of hilarious frequent comments with his sister-in-law. I did not understand that at all but was pleased to have an enjoyable and happy home ambiance. Similar was the reaction of my sister, and she openly shared that with Mother, occasionally in my presence.

"My second paternal uncle suddenly showed up with his wife for urgent consultation with my father about some real estate matters. That necessitated adjustment in sleeping arrangements, with my sister sharing the bed with Mother, and I sharing the bed with my maternal aunt.

"That was the best arrangement that we could have without significant adjustment in view of the short nature of their stay, as mother casually explained later, and all were happy. My happiness was, however, not that unrestrained. Sleeping alone, I got used to my own way of sleeping. In any case, I too accepted that as an obedient house member. In due time, I placed my pillow near the wall side of the bed and lay straight for the aunt to take her place on the front section of the bed, minimizing her discomfort. I went to sleep straightway while Mother and Aunt were enjoying comments and jokes with Uncle and his wife, while Father was savoring the puff of his favorite hookah (a waterpipe-based smoke) with an impish smile, an omnipresent feature of his post-dinner relaxation. He was somewhat restrained that evening due to traditional practices and local dictates. That was more due to the presence of the younger brother and his wife.

"I fell asleep rather quickly. It was about midnight. As I sensed a hand on my body and Aunt's physical posture being close to mine, an unforeseen happening, I woke up. Both being confused and nervous, I maintained total silence to avoid embarrassment and preferred a static position. In that state, I sensed her breathing heavily with frequent changes in sleeping positions. Notwithstanding this, she maintained a closeness with me. I was both edgy and muddled but continued to pretend to be in deep sleep.

"Then the most bewildering thing happened. My aunt delicately placed one of my legs between her two thighs, gently pushed that upward, and started pressing her thighs. After a while and as I was wearing my usual short pants, I sensed some wetness, as if she was urinating offhandedly. After that experience, she changed her posture, released my leg, freed her hand from my body, and started sleeping while keeping a distance. With a lapse of time, I too fell asleep.

"That perplexing experience of last night made me panicky from two perspectives: Should I take Mother into confidence and frankly state what I experienced last night? And the second one is how do I handle the upcoming night? There will be no problem after the oncoming night as Uncle is scheduled to leave the next morning with his wife.

"I could not concentrate on anything since waking up. More perplexing is the manner my aunt was behaving. She was conducting herself in a manner as if nothing had happened the previous night. That probably was based on her feeling that I was in deep sleep.

"The predicament persisted. As an escape, and to be out of the same surroundings, I went to school relatively early. As you have noticed, that did not work. I wanted to offload the emotional impasse. Hence, I opened up to you. Please treat the matter with due precaution, and do not discuss it with anyone else."

Javed was dumbfounded. He had no understanding of what Ebad detailed. Before leaving for their respective homes, he assured Ebad about confidentiality as emphasized by the latter.

As Javed was walking toward home alone, a neutral inkling dawned in his mind. Their household help, Nazir, was to him the wisest individual around. He used to talk with him about many matters of daily life, some in confidence. Javed had full sureness in Nazir's wisdom.

As per local tradition, and more the practice of their family, Javed used to address him as *bhai* (brother). He convinced himself that mentioning the dampness in the aunt's thigh without specifics on what Ebad experienced would not be tantamount to a breach of any trust. His simple inquisition would relate to whether women mutely urinate when sleeping at night, and if so, why?

He was looking for an apposite opportunity, and had not to await long. It was sunset time. Nazir was engaged in tying two of their domestic cows in the cowshed. He appeared to be in a jovial mood as he was softly singing the popular *Bhawaiya* (local song originating in Rangpur area of Bangladesh), made immensely popular to all and sundry by the most popular late folklore singer Abbas Uddin Ahmed many years back. In a jovial mood, he was singing softly that song with the lyrics, *"Amai bhashae le ray, amai dubai le ray, okul daria ar kono kul nai ray"* (You have swept me away, you have drowned me under, this water stretches on with no shore around [evidently a metaphorical rendering]).

That time was very opportune as household seniors were in the mood to perform *magreb* (sunset time for Muslims to pray).

Javed's anxiety to get needed clarification from his most unswerving source was inexorable. To him and at that age, Nazir was the source of all information and wisdom. Tense within, he took slow steps toward their cowshed and exchanged smiles with his dear Nazir Bhai.

In response to Nazir's usual greeting, Javed opened up with hesitation and said, "Bhai, I need to ask you a question but treat that absolutely confidential." Having said that, he paused for a while as Nazir Bhai remained focused. Then he continued saying, "Do women sometimes have petite urination when asleep?" While pondering about the probable genesis of such a question, Nazir, with an unusual facial expression, inquired about how he came to know about this.

That made Javed panicky, thinking about possible adverse inferences related to his simple query. He fumbled for a while and then responded by saying, "Yesterday, as you would recall, was a rainy day. I was stranded while returning after taking my homework assignment sheet from the math teacher. Some seniors were also similarly stuck. They were talking loudly about the issue of my inquisition focusing on occasional wetness in the upper thighs of women. That was something very strange as I had no inkling about it. I was taken aback. So I decided to talk to you."

Nazir looked around and in a quiet voice said, "Never ever discuss this matter with anyone. If Shaeeb (akin to *sir*) and Amma (mother) come to know about such matter and our discourse, they will be upset, incensed, and probably will lash you while I may lose my job."

After saying those words of caution, he kept quiet, possibly to unearth the premise of my query. Then he said, "Human beings undergo many physiological changes as they grow up. It is more so in the case of women compared to men. While changes in men are more internal, and relate to feelings and sensations, women, in addition, have visible changes like prominence of breast formation and shaping up of hips. As you grow, you will recognize these without being told by anyone. For the time being, you keep your mouth shut for the good of both of us."

Befuddled and indeterminate, Javed started walking back toward home. He was arguing with himself about the real implication of his simple query. He went to Bhai for clarification and understanding of an unpretentious matter and now returned with a greater load of burden. Bhai never behaved like this. He concluded that it is perhaps the convolutions of life and living, and who knows what one has in his destiny.

Time passed. Javed's education persisted with accelerated success and splendor. At that tender phase of life, he was recognized as an all-espousal boy of eminence. Everyone in the family and surroundings was happy and proud of him. To Javed, the only missing thing was the absence of Ebad, his closest class fellow, consequent to his relocation to maternal uncle's house at the district level for more assured and better educational opportunities.

The happiness around was all ubiquitous. The embellishing of that was the precipitous decision of the family to get the eldest sister of Javed married to the only son of an affluent family of nearby habitation, a distance of about five miles. Though of tender age, Javed was reluctant as the groom-to-be did not have much educational attainment. During a family dinner, he carefully articulated that point. Father responded with understanding, mentioning that he too had this in mind. All trustworthy scouting confirmed other related good qualities of the groom in terms of temperament, manners, decorum, habits, and so on. His lack of educational attainment was due to the relative priority of the family. The groom's family was of the view that a much higher level of education would probably cause detachment from the root, encouraging him to have a life in a metropolitan setting, impairing the well-being of the vast parental estate. Father continued, saying, "Daughter Fatipa's staying closer will help her to be in touch with us more regularly." This, obviously, is a great positive stance. That discussion ended there.

The wedding took place with all merriment. Javed's three paternal uncles participated in the jollity with their families. That was equally applicable for relatives from the maternal side. He, however, could not enjoy that happiness fully as his periodical class six school-term examination was set immediately after the wedding. He nevertheless tried to involve himself in all matters to the extent socially and family-wise desirable and feasible on his part.

After the gala wedding of Fatipa and her leaving the paternal home with hubby Fyruz at the end of *firani* (traditional short visit to the parents' home after the wedding) ritual to stay permanently at her in-laws' abode, the ambiance of Javed's home returned to normal. Javed completed his school examination extraordinarily, notwithstanding the side pressures and diversions all around due to Fatipa's wedding, and everyone was happy. Javed was enjoying his winter vacation. That appears to be common in the case of community.

The community exuberance was even more this time as the local administration and the community elders made arrangements for the holding of a *mela* (local agricultural and merchandise exhibition for about a month) for the first time. The mela had multiple diversions and entertainment items such as food stalls, outlets for consumable items not available locally, *jatra* (depicting epic stories in an open space setting), circus, and the like. Normally, people from the locality and adjacent areas visit the mela after sunset and enjoy themselves.

Nazir wanted very much to visit the mela himself. As a side justification, he decided to propose to Amma to take Javed along as the latter had no study pressure. Amma readily agreed, convincing herself that it would be a desirable opportunity for Javed to witness different activities under the care of the ever-trustworthy Nazir. She even gave some money to Nazir to defray related expenses.

Nazir was boisterous apparently for two reasons: first, a much-desired diversion from routine household work; and second, because of the unexpected responsibility he was bestowed with to take and guide Javed as a guardian. This had never happened before.

They had to negotiate a vast open farmland as they started for the mela site, more to shorten the distance. The vastness of the openness and having the responsibility of guiding Javed made Nazir buoyant beyond comprehension. Having no other subject of interest, he unpredictably recalled the discourse that both had, centering the issue of the occasional wetness of women. He initiated the discussion by saying, "Dada (colloquial term for "brother" irrespective of age), do you recall our brief discussion in the cowshed sometime back concerning physiological changes in men and women? About two years have since passed. You are growing up and must have an inkling of some changes within you. But that is where you stand at the moment. In the next two to three years, you will understand fully what I am hinting at.

"You possibly did not have much of a clue of similar changes in the girls. Since our area is mostly Muslim inhabited, it is unlikely that you can observe emerging bulginess in girls of your familiarity. It is more so as you always look down when you interact with female family members. Girls in the neighborhood always place the tail end of their *sarees* on their chest, covering the breasts. Similar is the case for those who use scarves (*orna*).

"The mela site is adjacent to settlements of a minority community. Their growing daughters normally wear long, flowing frocks without orna. So, their physical changes are always visible. You may see some of them in the mela. Enjoy observing those," he said, then laughed.

While waiting for the entry ticket, Javed was delighted to observe the surrounding mela area beaming with electricity and humming with the visitors' presence, activities, and laughter. As he entered the mela premises, Javed was astounded to see the glaring stalls full of merchandise of different types and makes. Then the presence of a series of food stalls enchanted him. As he walked past that setting, holding the assured hand of Nazir Bhai, he precipitously felt hungry due to the sinuous odor of meat kebab (rotisserie). Sensing that, Bhai assured Javed, saying, "We will come back. Let us first get a glimpse of the whole mela."

As a reversal of moving forward, Bhai suddenly turned back, seeing some clusters of minority families emerging through the alley opening of the food stalls. The families had a proportionate mix of male and female folks with the presence of grown-up girls. Bhai's happiness was irresistible as his facial expressions indicated. He tried to redirect Javed's focus to the uncovered chests of those girls. They followed the families but stopped after some time to shun any bellicose feat by the group's guardians.

Javed momentarily glanced through, and with shyness omnipotent, pressed Bhai to move toward the original direction. As they proceeded, Javed's enthusiasm was overwhelming seeing the setting for the circus. They stood for some time as Javed continued to enjoy the bicycle tricks.

To get Javed moving, Bhai this time bought some jal muri—an indigenous preparation of puffed rice with chopped green chili, slices of onion, little black pepper, some cilantro, and a bit of lime juice, and that mix was vigorously lurched before it was put into a makeshift old newspaper ampule. That did the trick. Javed enjoyed it very much, the first such experience outside of home.

They roamed around, but Nazir did not lose sight of Javed's intent to savor the kabab. After completing their sojourn, Nazir repositioned themselves in front of kabab stalls, sat down on two pews, and ordered a plate of chicken kebab.

Javed was taken aback as Nazir Bhai ordered only one plate of kebab. Nazir could note that, observing Javed's reflexes. As the table boy placed two glasses of drinking water and two service plates, Nazir opened his mouth saying, "Order of one plate is good enough for two of us, more as a snack, as it has four kebabs in one service. After finishing Kebab eating, we will leave for home. Otherwise, both Shaeeb and Amma would be worried. Now prepare to eat kebab, and for that, both of us would use a portion of water in the glasses for modestly washing our hands."

They left the kebab stall soon after eating but both evidently were reluctant to leave immediately. In that backdrop, Nazir approached a tea stall and ordered tea for both. That was another exceptional first for Javed as he was never allowed to taste tea at home. Javed relished his first cup made of dark boiled tea, full cream hot cow's milk, and sugar. To his surprise, Nazir, observing the relished way Javed was enjoying his first cup of tea, stated, "If you like tea, I will suggest to Amma to allow you to have tea at home as you are growing up. I think that will be okay."

After that, both happily returned home. Amma was equally happy observing the glee on the face of Javed. But that was more due to their return before Shaeeb came back home from his social interactions with friends.

Javed went to bed after finishing his daily rites, but he could not sleep that easily. The recollections pertaining to his first visit to mela and first going out without his parents enthralled him. That experience was unique and indicative of his growing up. As casually mentioned by Nazir Bhai in the cowshed, he was feeling a sort of unexpected physical sensations in his thinking and reflexes.

Javed vividly recounted what happened when Nazir Bhai abruptly turned back and started following the minority family members, and more so their female ones. Momentarily he slackened his contact with Javed as his focus at that point in time was to be as close as he could to a female member of the group, exercising due caution.

And that was the moment a most unexpected—and equally unique—thing happened. Being momentarily detached from Bhai, Javed was walking sluggishly but maintained proximity with the minority family members. He was conscious that a teen girl from that family was also walking parallel to him. It was just normal. For a split moment, and possibly being unmindful, her foot knocked a full-size misplaced brick on the pathway. As she tumbled, her body dashed against the rear of Javed's body, and he, for the first time, intuited the physical touch of a semibulging female breast, and enjoyed it. The girl repositioned herself easily as falling was not complete due to Javed's proximity. She looked toward him pithily, smiled lovingly, and mingled with the rest of the group. All these happened when Nazir Bhai was busy in his own pursuit.

Javed recognized the privacy of such an incident. He also realized the rarity of such an incident. He recalled all his previous discussions with Nazir Bhai on related matters. Javed realized that as he was growing, his sensation profile was undergoing rapid and equally unpredictable changes, making him think more about women and their physiology.

Nazir's previous indication that he would know about physiological insinuations was coming to reality. Nazir Bhai unknowingly became his closest ally for related discussions. He smiled at himself. Slowly and happily, he fell asleep.

Life progressed merrily. Javed moved to class eight with greater distinction while his immediate only elder sister, Rafisa, moved to class seven with relative distinction. Her slow academic progression was more due to the absence of a girl's school until the present one was established. The eminence of the family was the talk of the community.

Then the most unlikely event happened, shattering the family. Mother Ambia succumbed to unexpected caprices due to sudden diarrhea causing, among others, both acute dehydration and malabsorption. The initial impression was that she was just having a discharge of loose stools, a common phenomenon in the local setting. Her abrupt deterioration with symptoms of nausea, unbearable pain in the abdomen, and deteriorating dry mouth and sunken eyes caused alarm. Hectic efforts were made to ensure available medical interventions. Though overpowering in efforts and actions, those were too much in too short a time.

Ambia's physique gave in to the call of nature. Father Zakir Mia was shattered and shocked beyond comprehension. Though dumbfounded, he was outwardly unruffled, being aware of Fatipa's first pregnancy and the possible effect of that on her health and the baby's life. He was also mindful of the tragedy's impact on the minds of his son Javed and daughter Rafisa.

The headmaster of Javed's school, more commonly known as Hamid Ullah Sir, devoted his time and energy to keep Javed consoled even though the loss was irreparable. Fatipa, notwithstanding her health status, focused her full attention on taking care of young Rafisa.

Mourners' presence and sympathy were prodigious. They consisted of relations and community members from far and near. Everyone was trying to sincerely convey sympathy.

Fyruz quietly took charge of the situation, keeping in-law Zakir Mia to grieve in his own way. The burial was completed on time and with due solemnity. The *milad* (Muslim prayer in congregation) on the fourth day of the death seeking the Almighty's mercy for the departed soul was performed with desirable solemnity and unforeseen participation by all and sundry.

Visitors' presence slowly declined. Relations gradually left for respective places. The core family stayed together though exchanges were far and few.

Since the sad demise of his dear Amma, Nazir took charge of handling the daily necessities of the family without prior consultations. That embraced from food to other needed services. Also, he devoted his time and energy to taking care of his respected Shaeeb.

As family life was turning to some sort of normalcy, and at the silent behest of Fyruz, a core family assembly was planned. That included a father, two daughters, and a son, along with a son-in-law. The objective was to suggest an agreement on how the family moves forward, leaving the past reality in view.

Fyiruz made a brief statement to enliven the depressed father-in-law. Then Fatipa took over, more reflecting her earlier discourse and understanding with Fyruz. She said, "The best respect we can show to our departed mother is by accepting reality and having a customary life notwithstanding our grief and frustration. There should not be any two opinions about it. The issue is how best we can have an arrangement that allows each of us in the family to have a life commensurate to the late Mother's ideas and desires.

"In that context, the most challenging issue is how Rafisa lives here, being the only growing-up female individual. It is not only undesirable but equally problematic. I discussed the issue with Fyruz earlier. Our common position is that the most appropriate arrangement would be for Rafisa to move to our home as our family member. I promise that I will look after her as Amma would have done it."

The father was taken aback. He wore a blank look beyond the faces in front of him. Within himself he was dazed, feeling how soon after her marriage, their loving daughter had grown up as a responsible family member, having the confidence and tenacity to take on a proposed huge responsibility. He was even more amazed by the tone and tenure of conjugal relationship both developed so early in their married life. Notwithstanding that sort of feeling, Father was nonchalant.

At that stage, Fyruz took over. With customary modesty, he, with inherent confidence, said, "Father, I fully acquiesce with what Fatipa just postulated. We discussed the genesis of that proposition last night. You need not have any reservations about what Fatipa proposed. I fully assure and give my unqualified commitment to you that I will take full responsibility of Rafisa's life and progression after having consultation with and guidance from you while keeping Javed involved in every bend of her future life."

Fyruz paused for a while and continued, saying, "I could not make much headway in educational pursuits, and as you are aware that was more due to family's priority and preference. I may not have a formal degree but never stopped pursuing learning. I have a room in our home full of books and journals. I devote considerable time to reading and assimilating knowledge. And that is my private life. I encouraged Fatipa to pursue that habit. We now, most of the time, jointly have discourses after every new reading. Fatipa's present maturity is partly due to that besides her upbringing under the prudent guidance of our late Amma."

He further stated, "I am assuring you, without any inhibition, that Rafisa, under the care of Fatipa, will have complete freedom to pursue education in line and with the focus she would prefer. All decisions pertaining to her life, including marriage, will be taken with due cognizance of her choice and your endorsement, and there will be no pressure on her from our side. The rest is up to you."

Dizziness had been omnipotent in the facial expressions of the father. All that he was assured of so far by his dear son-in-law was beyond his anticipation. Even though he was happy and assured, the pertinent decision had been very challenging for him. He still kept quiet.

Monitoring all that, Fatipa, without any discontent on her part, further said, "Abba (Father), you would recall that proximity of Fyruz's abode to that of ours was one of your significant justifications in support of our wedding. The present catastrophe has eminently proven that to be of relevance. Even if Amma is not with us anymore, I am here by your side and in that proximity that you had in mind. That justification now equally applies to our proposition. You and Javed can see her at any moment of your choice. Likewise, Rafisa can visit you more frequently and at her choice. So our proposition is a win-win option under all perceived settings. Either you or Rafisa can reverse that decision any time any one of you would like. We will be happy with that. Now the decision is at your end. Prior to this gathering, I privately discussed the proposition with Rafisa, and it has her concurrence."

Javed, a quiet participant for so long, nodded his head affirmatively, indicating his agreement with what Fatipa-Bu (elder sister) and Dulabhai (brother-in-law) emphasized. Sitting at a distance on a *madur* (traditional placemat), Nazir conveyed his happiness by his physical expressions.

Father observed all these and especially took note of Javed's nodding and Nazir's reflexes. Finally, he opened his mouth to articulate his affirmative assent. In addition, he added, saying, "Among many probable thoughts that engrossed me, I noted seriously, besides both of your points, the reactions of very neutral individuals, i.e., Javed and Nazir. Being in a growing-up phase, Javed's 'nodding' affirmation is empathetic to support what both of you proposed. Considering our association and his loyalty toward the family, Nazir's silent affirmation also mattered to me. Thus, I agree without any hitch."

Father took a respite and continued, saying, "By agreeing, I am not absolving myself from parental obligations toward you all, more specifically, dear Rafisa. Any time and in case of unforeseen need, be frank with and candid to me as all of you have done today. Further, I give my promise to look after and guide Javed in his journey forward. Henceforth, I plan to minimize my social involvement and undertake to take care of Javed both as a mother and a father. Nazir will be of help to both of us in this regard."

Everyone was silently happy and relieved. Nazir then said, "On that happy note, I am going to make some special tea for all, including Javed Bhai." Everyone laughed and promised to remain in their respective positions until the tea ritual was complete.

Time passed and months rolled out. In that process, Javed became very close and friendly with his Abba. Father and son continued visiting

Fatipa and Rafisa, though Abba minimized that with the passage of time. The inherent reason was the traditional practice the society stresses that discourages any father's frequent visit to his son-in-law's habitat.

Amma's most unexpected demise was the first major tragedy the family suffered, but over time it became a memory. Family members adjusted to that and moved on. The most significant one was that of Father in respect of his social commitment, and that of Nazir related to taking care of the basic and day-to-day needs of the family.

To mitigate the burden that befell on the shoulders of Nazir, a decision was taken to hire another household help with general duties, among others, of taking care of domestic cows and keeping the cowshed clean besides tendering to the decaying front garden, which was very much loved and liked by the late Amma. Also, he had the additional assignment of developing a vegetable plot at the rear, fulfilling the desire of Javed. The new recruit, Moqbul, was young but very energetic and committed. His late father used to work for Zakir Mia's family. Hence, the recruitment process was very easy. Everyone was happy.

Father was surprised to receive a communication requesting his presence in Fatipa's home with Javed and Nazir the next Friday at early noon with the proposition of having lunch together. That never happened before. Father was apprehensive and thought about the reasons, while negativity predominated.

At that point in time, Hamid Ullah Sir showed up. The latter made it a point to visit Zakir Mia more often, both as a well-wisher and a friend. The present situation of Zakir Mia's life equally bothered the revered Sir. More so he noticed a marked decline in Zakir Mia's presence in the popular social setting of the locality.

Hamid Ullah Sir had something specific in his mind to talk to Zakir Mia. The national political scene has taken a distinctly negative turn, and every day it was deteriorating, dividing the nation between patriot and enemy. Their own locality was not immune from that. Even the peaceful school environment had not been spared. The issue he had in mind was to accept political divergence, avoiding any major conflict with undesirable homicide.

Zakir Mia noted the serious point the revered Sir was alluding to. To cut short the discussion, Zakir Mia said, "I have also noted that. I am waning from the tragedy that has befallen my family. So, very frankly speaking and with respect to what you and others are likely harboring in your mind and thoughts, I must be very frank and open that I foresee a very limited role to play. I am very clear about that.

"I am conscious that issues involved and on the table are very emotional ones. It is not a political game focusing on policy issues but access to power. That matters to leadership both at national and local levels. The worst aspect of this phenomenon is that those in command would prefer by choice to clinch to power at any pretext and cost, sustainably propagating imminent danger the country and locality would encounter if they were to leave."

Vindicating his feelings and position, Zakir Mia glanced at Hamid Ullah Sir. The latter did not lose time in responding, "I fully understand and appreciate your thinking and opinion. Nevertheless, we cannot isolate ourselves from the emerging social and political veracities. We need to act, however modest may be our efforts. There is perhaps no qualm that our local civility and institutions are at peril. Over many years and due to the sustained efforts of all concerned, our high school has earned a name and fame, and that is now in danger. Politics is now creeping into our school premises and environment, endangering its virtuous image. That is the reason I have come to you seeking your help."

Hamid Ullah Sir then continued, saying, "Before I came to meet you, I gave a serious thought as to the options we have. It dawned on me that perhaps candid communication without any political affiliation or favor with the community may protect our social amity, and thereby save the school and its related surroundings. I also had preliminary interactions with the elders of the Chowdhury family and Moulabi Bari (house). It is considered a view that the idea I floated with you is worth trying. It was also considered the opinion that you are the best person to take the needed lead, and all of us would support you."

Zakir Mia went into a deep thought in a nonchalant genre.

Hamid Ullah Sir intervened, saying, "All of us noted your gradual distancing from community matters and social issues since the sad demise of our respected *bhabi* (sister-in-law). We also have admiration for your recent focus and attention to family matters. But please bear in mind that Javed is also a son of this soil. Notwithstanding his innate sagacity, he can't remain totally independent of the surroundings we are concerned with. You please give due thought to this too."

The quietness persisted. There was an evident lack of eye contact between the two. Hamid Ullah Sir strained himself to assess what was going on in the thought process of Zakir Mia but preferred not to shove the matter with haste. The apparent reason was his having a full idea about Zakir Mia's personal traits and full respect for his sagacity and straightforwardness.

And then it happened. Looking straight ahead, Zakir Mia opened up, saying, "Hamid Ullah Saheeb (a salutation respectfully used), you do not belong to this community. But your link with this community has been strong and solid since you joined our Ghazipur Kallan High School as a teacher many years back, and now you are its headmaster. Thus, your association with and concern about the school in the context of present social and political surroundings are well understood and thankfully acknowledged. You enjoy tremendous respect in our community. Every word of yours is valued. Hence, I am in full agreement with you. But there are two specific points that I want to share with you, and I need your full concurrence.

"The first one relates to what you highlighted so far. The other one is a personal one, and I need your assurance with a solemn pledge of privacy.

"On the first one, I suggest that you continue private consultations with chosen local elites for a small meeting soon to arrive at a consensus for a larger community gathering under the banner of Shomjota Shonmelon (Assembly for Amity) in the school compound. In that assembly, we can urge the community to maintain harmony irrespective of political affiliations and to keep the school and students (the community children) out of prevalent turmoil for the good of all. In that context, I will do whatever is needed with low visibility.

"The second one is very personal. I moved to this community many years back as a bachelor due to attitude-specific divergence with my three immediate male siblings. In their approach and focus, they demonstrated a very outdated priority. In thinking and attitude, they are very different from me. In my early twenties, I concluded that I would not like to spend the rest of my life with them and would also not like my future children to live in such an environment. That was the reason for my moving into this community under the guidance and stipulations of my late father, and with his concurrence.

"I must admit that all the stipulations my late father had about property and income sharing were honored and acted upon by my siblings. I do not have any qualms with them except those related to attitudes.

"The reason I am detailing this private part of my life to you is that Javed is still very young, and thus someone outside the family should know about this should there be any need in the future either for guidance or for help with decision-making. You are not only Javed's intellectual guide but also his mentor in the broader sense. Thus, I trust you fully.

"My settling far away also meant that I do not have any immediate and enlightened relative in proximity to guide my family in case of need. The sad demise of my wife compounded this problem even though I have a very responsible and equally sincere son-in-law."

Commonly known as a soft-spoken person with prudence and care, Zakir Mia, breaking that image, continued, saying, "I have a wholesome life with no regrets, being blessed with an understanding and intelligent life partner, as well as two appreciative and gifted daughters and a son. The boon is an equally approving son-in-law. I never experienced financial impediments. Though most business operations have had ups and downs, I could manage things as my wholesale operations always generated good money, more so at times of scarcity.

"Moreover, as part of my deal for not being engaged in farming activities and living separately, I surrendered a portion of my farm income entitlement at the suggestion and to the satisfaction of my late father to cater to annual revenue obligations. Irrespective of emotional factors and related impediments, that decision motivated me to live separately and at a distance with the consent and blessings of all. I must admit that all the stipulations my late father had about property and income sharing were honored and acted upon by my siblings. I do not have any qualms with them except those related to attitudes. I never had to remind them.

"The major devastation in my life is the sudden demise of my wife. Since that happened, I have witnessed an ominous feeling within me. And that has increased with the passage of time. Thus, I would request an assurance from you. If something unforeseen happens to me, you will try your best to guide the family, particularly with respect to Javed's future progression. I will keep the children informed about this.

"Hence, you are so relevant to me. The latter thought was the reason why I took so much time to respond to your request. I was thinking of the best way I can do that."

Zakir Mia was relieved after unloading himself. Hamid Ullah Sir was astounded to note the trust the soft-spoken and standoffish Zakir Mia was reposing on him even though not being a local and not having any blood connections.

Before conveying his humble consent without preconditions and postulating that it would InshaAllah (will of God) not be needed, Hamid Ullah Sir, at the departing point, paused before saying, "Probably the best option for recurrence of negativity in mind is to shred it off as much as possible and focus on the positive aspects that life beholds for the future." Then he stepped out.

Hamid Ullah Sir then left for the school after that discourse, thinking all through the probable reasons for Zakir Mia to open up and feel grateful for the confidence Zakir Mia reposed in him. He concluded that perhaps the shock he experienced from the death of his dear wife impacted his thoughts and actions.

Sitting alone, Zakir Mia was musing about the best way to approach the possible mitigation of a negative national portent. His reservations were due to his earlier resolve to delink himself from community-related matters, allowing him to devote time and energy to the desired rearing of Javed in every respect. That to his mind would amount to fulfilling the commitment he stipulated to Ambia many times in the past, and his assurance postulated to his daughters and son-in-law in the immediate past.

In that setting, Zakir Mia recapitulated the just received message from Fatipa, urging him to be in her place, along with Javed and Nazir, the next Friday to have lunch after *juma* (Muslim weekly prayer congregation).

This specific request is a clear deviation from past practice. This message from Fatipa did not indicate anything, nor was there any hint. Zakir Mia was at his wits' end with the multiplicity of possibilities, and they mostly related to negative inferences. His associated anxieties multiplied. Notwithstanding the concomitant anxieties and nervousness, all three showed up at the envisaged time.

The atmosphere in Fatipa's home was a very exultant and relaxed one. Both Fatipa and Fyruz exchanged communications and gestures between them, pressing each other to divulge the information. The pervading sense of modesty, premised on local values and practices, was the main obstacle. As per long-held family tradition and local customs, all significant, sensitive, and private matters used to be communicated to Zakir Mia first through Amma before their public deliberations.

Contrarily, this latest message of Fatipa did not indicate anything, nor was there any hint. Zakir Mia was at his wits' end with the multiplicity of possibilities, mostly related to negative inferences.

As Zakir Mia and all others were sipping their prelunch yogurt sherbet in a mood of silence, the usually less talkative Rafisa spontaneously broke the news, saying, "Abba, your loving daughter and dear son-in-law were in a quandary about the apposite way to convey the news to you. Since they are unnecessarily spending time coming to a consensus, I am taking the liberty to divulge that: it is a son to their delight, based on the image results of the ultrasound test."

Upon saying that, Rafisa resumed drinking her sherbet, amusingly winking at the brother-in-law. Fatipa was delighted with the way Rafisa acted. As the impasse was tackled desirably, Fatipa opened up, saying, "We went to see our gynecologist. At his suggestion, we had the ultrasound performed. We discussed and agreed to break the news with a little bit of surprise to make you blissful in a gathering, as most of the time you have been alone and feeling anguished."

Zakir Mia laughed, and then, in a sudden serious mood change, raised his two hands toward infinity, as Muslims do at the end of each submission to Allahpak, praying for a healthy and long life for his grandson. He then behaved in a startled way, as Fyruz privately envisioned earlier, discussing with Fatipa the fitting way to break the news. Father first lamented the absence of Ambia, with tears rolling down his cheeks, and with no lapse of time laughed, looking at Javed, saying, "I may not be there. It would be Javed's responsibility to look after the progression of our grandson as if he would do those on our behalf and the way we preferred, learning from the way he was raised."

Then he sarcastically commented, saying, "Javed Mia (using the Mia salutation for the first time), you are no more the small guy of the family. You are soon going to reach the stage of shaping up."

Having said all these, Zakir Mia informed all concerned about the substance of his recent discourse with Hamid Ullah Sir, including making a joint effort to minimize current and emerging social and political tensions, more in the context of their community. He also detailed his request to the latter to guide them all with respect to Javed's progression in life if something happens to him.

Before Father could make any other point, Fyruz intervened, saying, "Abba, it is better that we do not countenance negativity to impact our current life. Who knows what is in store in the future? Nevertheless, we take note of your discussions with Hamid Ullah Sir, and assure you unhesitatingly that we, if any such situation arises—or even other matters concerning the family so warrant—will honor each of your wishes, if the event so dictates. We are aware of your relationship with Hamid Ullah Sir."

Father happily smiled and commented, "Please do not misunderstand me. Both you and Fatipa will have full authority to make decisions concerning the family if the future so necessitates. I am bringing Hamid Ullah Sir in the depiction as my three younger brothers, with no malice in my mind, are not like me. They are by nature very self-centered and value everything on their own terms, more so when related to money and property. I will also be honest to admit that they have so far lived up to the stipulations envisaged at the time of Father's death. My proposition is only to ensure that they do not take any unfair advantage in my absence. Hamid Ullah Sir is sort of a security in that perspective."

Nazir, sitting on a stool slightly away, was a silent observer of what was going on even though he noted carefully the essence of the discourse the family was having. He soon diverted his attention toward the dining table and was unable to reconcile the placing of six plates, as the family members were only five. He quietly left the room and went to the kitchen where Fatipa was busy arranging the service of lunch.

Nazir expressed his desire to help Fatipa in lunch service efforts. Fatipa warmly said, "Nazir Bhai, you are a guest in my home and would have all the love and consideration you deserve. Also, this is a special occasion. You are going to have your lunch sitting with us, and we will eat together."

On being advised as such, Nazir was flabbergasted. His immediate reaction was a no. He said, "Fatipa- Bu (sister), whatever you have in mind and say, I cannot sit at the same table where Saheeb will be sitting. I would not be able to swallow my food. If you want me to have a nice meal, then permit me to continue sitting on the stool while having food served by you. You can help me as and when replenishment is needed."

Fatipa smiled and consented. Nazir got involved in arranging the service of lunch and helping Fatipa and Rafisa.

Father-in-law and Fyruz were engaged in discussing the way forward to act warily in carrying forward the inkling of Hamid Ullah Sir in a socially desirable way while Javed was walking in and out of the house to kill time, as he did not fit in either of the discussions Father and Dulabhai were having and activities going on in the kitchen.

After accomplishing all basic work pertaining to lunch, Fatipa, after giving the necessary instructions to her household help, left to clean up and change her attire, leaving with service-related residue tasks for Rafisa and Nazir to finish.

Noting Fatipa's re-entry into the room, Rafisa, in an unusual commanding tone and pointing to Father and Fyruz, raised her voice, and said, "Possibly both of you can talk even after finishing lunch that has been served. But none of you are showing any inclination. The food, so painstakingly prepared by Fatipa-Bu, is getting stale and you have no fretfulness. Both of you are betrothed in solving undefined social problems. Now please move to the dining table."

Father was very impressed by the tenor of Rafisa and was internally happy noting her growing up. Fyruz commented, saying, "My dear, we were waiting for your command, lest we be blamed for unacceptable moves. Here we are following your directive. Food can never get cold so long your warmth is there." All those present laughed.

While having food, Zakir Mia said, "It would have been nice had your parents been here too, sharing the good news and the delicious food."

Fyruz responded, saying, "An urgent message was received the other evening from my sister's home about her health. The message had no details. That made all of us worried. My parents promptly prepared to leave the following morning. That coincided with the appointment with the gynecologist. So all of us went together and ensured their easy boarding of the bus to Raghunathpur, my sister's place. After that, we saw the doctor and had the ultrasound process done. As we are unsure about their return, we decided to inform you immediately. When they come back, we will have another lunch to celebrate the good news."

The sumptuous lunch was relished by all. But the related comment of Javed took all present by unmitigated surprise. Javed innocently stated, "I had no idea that Fatipa-Bu could cook so well. I have not tasted food so much since the demise of Amma."

Fatipa was very happy to note that, and then added, "Rafisa cooks very well too. She probably got it from Amma. Once we have another lunch, it will be the food cooked by Rafisa." Father enjoyed all these conversations, adding, "I had no idea, even interacting so intimately during the last few months, that Javed developed a taste to opine, among others, about the food. I am determined to know Javed better in the future as I plan to disassociate from social settings after having the planned Shomjota Shonmelon per request of Hamid Ullah Sir."

During all these discussions, Nazir was not present. The reason became evident as he entered the dining place with a tray full of teacups for everyone present. Javed twitted amusedly and then, to the embarrassment of Nazir, told everyone, "When Bhai took me to mela for the first time years back, he, among others, offered me my first cup of tea. Since then, especially after Amma's death, he continued serving me tea, avoiding Abba's attention. He really makes good tea."

While sipping Nazir's tea, Fyruz concurred with what Javed stated about the expertise of Nazir in making tea, commenting additionally about the competence of both Fatipa and Rafisa in making that too. He also said, "My father is fond of tea prepared by Fatipa."

Referring to the relativity of various actions, Fyruz, with due reverence, detailed for information all the propositions of Shomjota Shonmelon that his father-in-law discussed with him prior to lunch. He then opined, saying, "Abba (as a father-in-law is locally called), the landscape of social setting has considerably changed in the immediate past. There is a clear signal that the young generation is no more slanting to listen to elders, and most unwilling to share or endorse their views. They are generally more inclined and pliable to authority, power base, and money. So people like you have a tight rope to walk in achieving the objective you and Hamid Ullah Sir have in mind. Care and caution should have priority in any discourse with the present generation. It is more applicable in your case as you would prefer to disengage yourself from customary social complications to devote your time to the well-being of your shattered family, especially taking care of Javed. You should aim at respectful disengagement."

He kept quiet after such stipulation. Fatipa and Rafisa concurred with what Fyruz emphasized.

Father had an admiring facial expression, reacted approvingly after thanking Fyruz for what he said earlier, and assured all that he precisely had those in mind. He said, "In my commentary, I will not either adore any group or deplore any other. All that I will say is time is ripe for mutual accommodation in our journey forward as those who are young today will be in our shoes in no time. So we need to establish a practice of accommodation with respect to each other for having a habitable community and serene social arrangement."

Those discussions, on the initial service of tea and appetizer, took a sudden turn on a subject beyond anyone's anticipation except that of the father. He winked at Nazir, who was ardently camouflaging so long a set of documents that Father handed over to him with instruction that no one should have any inkling about his carrying those.

Father then said, "Of my three children, the first two are daughters, followed by Javed. Two daughters of mine stand out in their own right, while Javed is shaping up as a responsible young man. My happiness about such a family setting burgeoned after having a son-in-law like Fyruz. I have thus no anxiety. But all my confidence was shattered by the sudden demise of your mother. In my carefree mindset, I always thought of life in terms of age and not time."

He tarried for a while. Both daughters and son-in-law ogled at each other while Javed was enjoying the way Father was gabbing—a characteristic he got used to due to their very close interactions after the death of Mother.

Father then, finishing the last sip of his tea, resumed spelling what he had in mind, and said, "My father, though not very lettered, was a practical man. To my mind, his greatest weakness was always to shelve problems instead of facing them. Perhaps that was how he successfully handled his considerable farmlands and related confronts.

"One day in a jovial mood after celebrating Eid Ul Fitre (Muslim happy religious event), he called all of us, his four sons, and said, 'I have all along observed that Zakir is very different from the three of you, having priorities other than farming, and that is causing clatter among you. In my absence, that is likely to exacerbate. That thought has pained me within myself, and I do not like it to be the talk of the community belittling our family. I have thus decided on an arrangement that will possibly protect our property and family the way my progeny prefers.' He then enunciated his proposition, giving no option for dissent.

"Being his eldest child, I had a clear understanding of who I am and my way of life. My late father had candid views of my thinking about life and living. After discussing my preferences with Father further, I moved out of our homestead with his consent after giving him two assurances: maintaining regular contact with the ancestral home, and not dividing our vast farmland. The latter was due to his firm belief that physical divisions of farmland only trigger the decline of any wealthy family based on land holdings.

"I left home with a good amount of seed money from Father on the consideration that I absolve him from all related future expenditures concerning me. I invested part of that in setting up an upscale grocery store with separate wholesale and retail operations. With the rest, I bought this piece of land at that time in the periphery of the township for good reasons: my preference for an open setting and its relatively cheaper price. Now, of course, it is in the middle of our growing community. That also means that I do not have any immediate and enlightened relatives in proximity to guide my family in case of need. The sad demise of your dear mother compounded the problem, even though I have a very responsible and equally sincere son-in-law. Hence, you are so relevant to me. The latter thought was the reason why I took so much time to respond to your request. I was thinking of the best way I could do that.

"Being a practical person, my father handed over to me a complete set of land and property-related documents in case I need those in the future. That is what Nazir handed over to me at my behest. I have brought them not for reading here but to show it to you all. This will always be in the top shelf of Almirah that I have in my bedroom."

On the way back home and sitting in the rickshaw, Javed was very frisky in his exchanges with Father, whereas the latter was somewhat quiet and meditative. Nazir was following them closely while riding his bicycle. Of his many inquisitions, including the approximate delivery month of Fatipa-Bu's baby and that of the astuteness as shown by Rafisa-Bu, Javed was somewhat compliant while at home.

After being rested from the return trip, Father noted the somewhat unusual movements of Javed and called him. Having squinted at Javed, Father, out of blue, started saying, "In life, small happenings often make big differences. That was the reason why I took property documents and showed them to you all. Life's variables are most uncertain and unpredictable. The future by and large depends on how those variables are handled by having access to pertinent information. I would expect you to bear this in mind always."

Javed was flabbergasted and was evidently unable to comprehend what his father alluded to. He was having a blank look. Noticing this, Father said, "I know that what I said is beyond your current comprehension. I do not expect you to understand that. But please try to remember that. It may help you in life."

He further continued, saying, "In the case of Rafisa, it could be that the unprecedented shock of losing her mother and the unexpected change in shelter due to circumstances beyond her caused a prodigious impact on her personality and thinking, making her more mature and practical. Why don't you look at yourself? Think of the way you are talking with me now. A few months back when your mother was alive, it was unthinkable for all of us. Tragic experiences are part of life. Sometimes positive developments are the unbridled offshoot of tragic experiences in life."

Javed still had some points to make and replied, saying, "I cannot fully grasp what you are alluding to. But if I face in life any situation that warrants me to be in another's place, I will much prefer struggling on my own rather than be a dependent."

Father was astounded and looked intensely at Javed. He clinched that the discussions perhaps are going in the direction of unconstructiveness. He thus closed that discourse saying, "I get your point. But bear in mind that Rafisa is a girl and has limitations in choosing options in life. You will understand the related inherent implications when you will have a daughter in life." Father smiled and outwardly focused his attention to the neighborhood they passed. He took the stated opinion of Javed seriously and started reminiscing about it.

Days passed. Zakir Mia, with Hamid Ullah Sir's involvement and efforts, had concentrated consultations with notable community elders. There was consensus about such a dialogue, and the local school field was chosen as the venue. The date was fixed, and regular announcements were made by using the local speaker with a loud buzzer. While doing these, Zakir Mia involuntarily opened up one day and advised Hamid Ullah Sir about his exchanges with Javed while returning from daughter

Fatipa's abode. He not only detailed what Javed hinted and wondered, saying, "I never expected to hear something like this from someone of Javed's age."

Hamid Ullah Sir patiently took note of what Javed said and its emotional upshots that were bothering Zakir Mia. After taking due time, he said, "In your apparition, Javed is a growing boy with infantile thinking abilities. But I have a different assessment of his intelligence and thinking prowess. That is not only me, but generally, the school faculty has the same assessment. In terms of learning and academic prudence, he is remarkably ahead and can, even though in class eight, undeniably compete with present class ten pupils. Unfortunately, our education system has no scope for accelerated learning. We thus can't do much to put him in a challenging genus in optimizing his learning.

"But that is not all. By preference and motivation, he has a self-reliant mode. He abhors help and pursues his goal with his own effort. One does not need to worry about him. He will find his way in life, however challenging it might be."

Both father and teacher were contented with the outcome of their side discourses concerning Javed, with the father returning home with a gratified mindset while the teacher on his way back to school was musing himself for being able to convey to Zakir Mia what he always wanted to do.

As preparations were going on with due care and commitment to hold the planned Shomjota Shonmelon, the local youth wing of the party in power took that negatively. There was consensus that in the pretext of "amity," the whole objective of the proposed Shonmelon was to sabotage at a local level the success of the ruling party in the upcoming election. But there was division as to which action to be taken. While a group of activists was of the view that the immediate launching of grassroots-level, intensive activities would be most appropriate, the militants' preferred option was confrontation denying any opportunity to organizers of the Shonmelon any footing before they became a force to reckon with. The militant faction dominated the decision-making process.

Zakir Mia was in a cheery mood the whole morning. He specifically asked for paratha (handmade flat bread, slightly thicker than roti and made of flour dough and fried in oil) with an omelet. He also said that Javed should join him for breakfast.

After finishing his post-lunch slumber, Zakir Mia got up, performed ablution, changed to formal attire of white kurta, pajama, and tupi (Muslim headgear), and was ready to go to Shonmelon. In a quiet mood, he was waiting for the arrival of Hamid Ullah Sir as agreed earlier.

Along with other selected local elites of different political shades, Zakir Mia took a seat on the makeshift dais and waited for his turn to deliver the address. Within himself, he was gratified by the attendance and conveyed his happiness to Hamid Ullah Sir by nodding his head. As his turn came, Zakir Mia stood up, moved to the microphone, and, waving his hand, said, "Assalamalikum."

Right then, a group of militants supporting the establishment raised their dissenting voices, swinging their bamboo sticks and other cache. Pandemonium reigned immediately, and chaos set in. For safety reasons, Zakir Mia was being escorted out of the scene by some volunteers shadowing him as much as possible. Suddenly a piece of brick hit him on the back of his head, and Zakir Mia collapsed in the arms of his escorts, succumbing to injuries instantly. The propagate of noble efforts became an indeterminate victim of rowdyism.

STORM

THE OFT-REPEATED SAYING, "Misfortune never travels alone," became the harsh reality for Zakir Mia's family. The house was full of sympathizers and fellow admirers. Fyruz, Fatipa, and Rafisa rushed after being informed of the fatal accident, but the reality of death was not divulged to them at that point. When they were on their way, Fyruz was told about that privately by one of his friends.

Being shattered and equally dumbfounded, Fyruz positioned himself close to Fatipa and whispered, "We should be prepared to face any unfortunate reality for the greater good of the family." He then took hold of Rafisa's hand and whispered, "I have full confidence in your ability to handle any unforeseen happening as well as take care of Fatipa in her current delicate health conditions."

They did not wait too long. Seeing them approaching, Nazir rushed while wailing, and the message was loud and clear. Fatipa collapsed in the arms of Fyruz, who took her to the bed of Zakir Mia to lie down involuntarily. Javed stood motionless, holding on to one of the poles of the verandah, and wore a blank look at the assembly of people around them, surrounding the dead body of Zakir Mia. He was unmoving and devoid of expressions and outbursts.

Taking cognizance of that, Rafisa, leaving Fatipa to the temporary care of some sympathizers, moved close to Javed, held him in her arms, and shook him intensely, shouting for an immense reflective reaction. Javed responded, hugging Rafisa, and quietly approached the dead body of his dear father.

Fyruz, who was discussing the details of the funeral arrangements with local gentries, including sending a messenger to Zakir Mia's ancestral home to inform his brothers about the sad happening, noticed Javed's movement. He, along with Hamid Ullah Sir, approached Javed and escorted him with words of consolation. Javed quietly sat by the side of his dead father and slowly put his head on his father's chest, later on standing up and kissing the dead body incalculably.

Javed then approached Fatipa and said, more as a grown-up elder brother, "Fatipa-Bu, you have the responsibility of taking care of Father's *amanat* (safekeeping of something precious, meaning in this case, the baby in the womb) as he stipulated during last lunch in your place. We all are to handle the situation, keeping that in view." He then embraced his dear Fatipa-Bu. Rafisa joined them. Tears were rolling down incessantly from the eyes of all present as they were consoling each other.

The funeral was completed the following day after Johor (Muslim midday prayer). Almost the whole community participated in the *janaza* (the mandated Muslim community prayer before placing the dead body in the grave). The immediate snag was related to recording the death in the local police station as a murder. The police station officials declined to record it, on the grounds that the said death had already been recorded as an accidental one by some people who were present at the Shonmelon. Hence, there was no scope to chronicle another one.

This caused immediate dismay among the family and friends of the late Zakir Mia. However, it did not take much time to find out that a segment of the establishment, that started the pandemonium, took a prompt preemptive action to file a FIR (First Information Report) reporting the death as an accidental one. The whole scheme of things had the blessings of concerned government functionaries.

That was clear to all concerned who assembled to discuss and agree on the future course for the late Zakir Mia's family. The assembled people were family members and the three younger brothers of the late Zakir Mia. The only outsider was Hamid Ullah Sir, being both a very close associate and repository of the former's wishes and desires.

The reality, so long shadowed by a semblance of respect and decency, popped up when self-interest and greed came into play. The three younger brothers made a unified stand, saying, "The house of brother Zakir Mia was an interim arrangement as per the desire of our father, and his real rhizome is the ancestral home at Shetra village. We therefore propose to sell this house while honoring the income-sharing arrangements detailed by our late father."

Discussions continued with no resolution in sight. While the family elders were engrossed in discussions with property and money, Fatipa, Rafisa, and Javed were sitting slightly at a distance with frustration pervading their thoughts from the perspective of their future. Each one of them was feeling frustrated as no one from their paternal side prioritized the future of Rafisa and Javed. Their priority was property and money. In a silent mode, they exchanged looks with each other, transmitting their frustration.

At that time, Hamid Ullah Sir politely raised the issue of Javed and his upbringing while alluding that Fatipa and Fyruz took full responsibility for Rafisa after the sudden demise of Begum Saheeba and during Zakir Mia's lifetime, with his full concurrence. "We now need to be absolutely clear about the thinking of the uncles concerning Javed before understanding is reached about the house," he said.

The response from the paternal side was quick and reflective of being a unified one. The oldest of the living uncles straightaway said, "Yes, we have discussed that among the three of us earlier. Javed is our responsibility, and we have a plan for him. During the interim period and allowing him time to adjust to reality, he will stay in this home of ours until it is sold. As and when the property is disposed of, he will move to his ancestral home in Shetra, finish schooling in the local school, and be of occasional help to cousins in farming activities. Among us, we also agreed that we would establish a grocery store in the local market, and he would be the sole owner of that. The prospect is very good as Shetra is no longer a dormant village. It is bustling with economic activities of varied types, and one lacking facility is a good grocery store. Bhai Shaheb did it with great success. It is our assessment that Javed too can excel in such business."

The response was a bombshell for others. Fyruz, being a son-in-law and having not much interaction with his uncles-in-law, was hesitant to intercede. Hamid Ullah Sir, being an outsider, was thinking about the modus of his intrusion.

He opted not to get involved in property and home-related family matters and took a more neutral stance focusing on Javed's future educational priorities. Hamid Ullah Sir gave his candid opinion, saying, "The school in Shetra has not earned any distinction as an academic institution. Contrarily, our school is famous for its academic excellence and performance. Moreover, Javed has already earned the undisputed reputation of being a meritorious student, and our faculty's considered view is that he will earn a distinction in the Secondary School Board examination. So, and for your consideration, neither his going to Shetra school nor getting engaged with cousins in farming activities, or the proposed grocery shop should be any option befitting his merit as well as the image and good name of the late Zakir Mia."

The three uncles started looking at each other to frame a more appropriate riposte.

To the astonishment of all, Javed moved forward and said, "About a month back and while having dinner, Abba suddenly raised the issue of life's reality when the situation is bleak. Referring to the case of Masud of the next village, he commented, 'Orphans are pawns to be abandoned by the poor and drained by the rich of the family.' In that situation, probably, self-reliance with determination holds the key, as Masud demonstrated."

The seniors of the family—the three uncles of Javed—were staring at him both with surprise and taciturn derision, the unspoken reaction reflected in physical reflexes signposting, "How dare he intervene while seniors are talking." Ignoring those, Javed continued, saying, "My father passed on, knowingly or unknowingly, some values and ways forward in pursuing a meaningful life with purpose, and I very much intend to follow those. You can make decisions about the house and property as you deem appropriate, but I want to retain the right about the course of my life based on discussions with and guidance of my sisters and brother-in-law. Without leaving any room for uncertainty I want to make it clear that I am not going to Shetra as part of any likely deal."

The position indicated by Javed made his sisters very happy and likewise caused crossness among the uncles. They proposed a short break to enable consultations among themselves before they could proceed further.

That break was unexpectedly brief. They returned to the assembly and resumed the deliberations. There were concerns in the mind of Fyruz and that of Hamid Ullah Sir about reaching a consensus.

The eldest of the three uncles opened up, saying, "Our nephew has evidently inherited some of the attributes of our late brother, and we are happy about that. Frankly speaking, we had no inkling about Javed's academic excellence. Our original proposition for his going to Shetra was based on the general assessment of the priorities of a growing-up boy like him in our vicinity, and to assure him of a shelter and pursuit of life. We thought that by doing so, we would be discharging our brotherly obligations.

"We are thankful to Hamid Ullah Saheeb for placing facts before us. We thus fully agree that Javed should stay here, pursuing his education under the most practical arrangements worked out by his sisters and brother-in-law, and with the guidance of Hamid Ullah Sir. We will not have any qualms with that. The joint ownership of this house was repeatedly asserted by our late father. He also stipulated that so long as Zakir Mia lives there, it should be treated as his. What we have in mind and are now emphasizing is what was told to us. We respect the decision of our late father. What we are now proposing is also essentially a part of that decision. Moreover, it is our firm view that the house needs to be sold to avoid depleting its value. An empty house is a liability, from all reasonable perspectives. We understand that it is an emotional issue, but according to our views, practicality warrants the needed consensus."

All were pleasantly surprised by the tone and tenure of those pronunciations. Before they could react, the eldest of the uncles reconfirmed their commitment to continue honoring the farm income-sharing arrangement worked out when their father was alive. He further said, "There was never a single incident of deviation about sharing income and the annual transfer of Bhai Saheeb's share. We will continue to adhere to that. It is a solemn promise. We will discharge that obligation annually under arrangements that our nieces and nephew propose. Moreover, Bhai Saheeb's children, especially Javed, are an *amanat* to us. The Shetra home is also Javed's. He can be there any time as he chooses or needs."

In that contented mood and based on winking from Fatipa, Rafisa got up to prepare a second service of tea before their uncles left for Shetra. The uncles and others present were surprised to see Rafisa walking in with some tartlets, followed by Nazir with a tray full of teacups.

After the uncles left, the reality hit the rest. For so long, they were thinking of and maneuvering to work out an acceptable arrangement about property and income, but now the practicability related to Javed's future living and academic progression has come to the forefront. Everyone was anguished, and the tea was losing its heat and miasma. Of the remaining five attendees, two were the most relevant. They were Fyruz and Hamid Ullah Sir. Both were handicapped as Fyruz was relatively new in the family and Hamid Ullah Sir was an outsider. They were evidently thinking about the best course of action concerning Javed.

Against that backdrop, Fatipa unexpectedly broke the taciturnity, saying, "To enable us to chalk out a viable option, we need to know the views of Javed. It is more relevant since the house will be sold soon for good reasons enunciated by the eldest uncle. Today or tomorrow, Javed will have to vacate the house. This is the reality. The issue is where he goes for the next two years until he finishes his secondary school education. I discussed this dilemma with Javed before coming to this assembly and offered him the option to move to our home. He declined my offer, for the good reasons that Rafisa is with us already and the distance involved in going to and coming from the school. Notwithstanding the unabated support of Fyruz to my proposition, Javed maintained his reservation about that. He was very clear that it, or similar other stipulations, would not befit the values and social standing that Abba enjoyed and left for us to protect. He further said that we should try to honor that, whatever may be the temporary inconveniences or constraints. Javed proposed that we look at other probable arrangements near the school that allowed for modest independent living, possibly in any hired accommodation, with needed support services. He assured us that notwithstanding the proposition for independent living near school, he would be visiting us frequently." That serious setting referred to assurances of uncles regarding the regular inflow of the share of farm income and Fatipa- Bu opined, "The independent living expenses of Javed will only be a fraction of that inflow. Thus, he will have a truly independent living in his quest for learning and fulfilling the dreams of Abba."

Everyone laughed, and both Fyruz and Hamid Ullah Sir were palpably relieved. Nazir continued to have a blank look, and it was difficult to discern what he had in mind. Noting this, Rafisa raised another issue. She said, "With our house to be sold soonest, we do not need Maqbul anymore. He should be told accordingly, with fitting financial compensation. So far as Nazir Bhai is concerned, I will propose that he, being almost a family member, should be retained on payment of his regular salary but will go back to his home."

Fatipa interjected at this stage. She said, "Nazir Bhai can visit us any time of his choice and stay any length of time with us. So far, I have the inkling and can guess his reflexes, my proposition has the blessings of Fyruz."

Fyruz not only concurred but also said, "That will be very helpful in the context of our expecting a son soon. Thus, this is a very positive move. We will be happy to have Nazir Bhai in our home as a family member as he is in this home. The flexibility pertaining to his future stay as Fatipa indicated is also okay with me."

Hamid Ullah Sir kept unexpected silence during the preceding discussions. Fyruz took note of that and inquired about his own assessment.

In response, Hamid Ullah Sir said, "I was wondering how to interact as those matters relate to your family. Before responding to your query, I must honestly say that irrespective of being an outsider, I consider it a privilege to have a place in this gathering and try to understand and appreciate all of your thinking concerning the future course of action. Being a friend, associate, and well-wisher of the late Zakir Mia, I have no hesitation in saying that I am very happy with the way all in the family, notwithstanding age and relationships, have so far expressed themselves and interacted.

"There is a saying, 'Even serious catastrophes often have great outcomes.' The discussions that I witnessed so far confirmed that in my mind, notwithstanding the setting being a tragic one. Javed's motivation for his future independent living, Rafisa's way forward with respect to household matters, Fatipa's concurrence and commitment about Nazir with a humane perception, and last but not least, Fyruz's validation of all those speak volumes. Having the fortune of knowing the late Zakir Mia Saheeb intimately, I can safely say that the latter's noble soul, wherever it may be, must be very contented.

"Having said so, I would like to put forward an idea for Javed that cropped up in my mind against the backdrop of current discourses. A few weeks back, I had some startling discussions with one of our neighborhood gentlemen whom as a fellow community member I had known for quite some time but never that intimately. He is Rahmat Bepari, who is more engrossed with ever-flourishing business doings. We crossed each other many times, exchanged *salam* (Muslim greeting) and smiles, and moved on. A few weeks back, something unexpected happened. We were crossing each other as usual while returning to my abode after a day's work in the school. After exchanging social greetings, he surprisingly stopped, came close to me, and then said, 'Brother, if you have time, I want to discuss some personal matters with you.'

"Palpably, I was taken by surprise and happily consented. He took me to the nearby *ghatla* (steps going down in a pond with a platform on the bank) of the adjacent *dighi*. We sat closely on the sitting setting of the ghatla. Fortunately, there was no one else.

"Rahmat Bepari, without any reservation, opened up on a personal matter saying, 'I am a half-lettered individual and hence always maintained distance with persons of your attributes. Moreover, coming from a very humble background, I focused all my efforts and attention on reversing my life's maladies by succeeding in my present engagement, business. That, of course, cost me my family name, Choudhury. With success in my trading endeavor, I soon came to be known as Bepari (trader).

"'In that progression of life, I married into a modest but respectable family of adjacent Raipur Thana (lowest administrative unit). The all-embracing happiness that blossomed around our married life did not last long as my wife was unable to conceive after her first two miscarriages. All medical, traditional, and religious options and related actions were tried meticulously without success.

"'That was the sixth year of our married life. One distant elder of my in-laws' family, who was always very fond of my wife, unexpectedly showed up. My wife—and me too, later on—addressed him respectfully as Amin Chacha (uncle). Hosting him with all earnestness and exuberance, she broke down before her revered Chacha after lunch, lamenting her inability to conceive.

"'As a pious and respectable person, being unmarried in his rather long life, he always endeavored to be helpful and supportive of people around him. In the case of my wife, it was more so as he always loved her from early childhood.

"'Spontaneous crying manifestly relieved her, but it pained him very much. He consoled her, saying that he would pray for her at the ensuing night, and if he had any impression out of that, he would tell her so before leaving tomorrow afternoon.

"'The following morning and noontime passed. He finished his lunch and got prepared to leave but did not say anything. He was very calm and quiet, and refrained from talking. That pained her all the more.

"'As he stood up to leave, my wife bent her body to *salam* by touching his feet. Right at that moment, two teardrops fell from her eyes on his feet. He remained nonresponsive. He moved forward to leave. With his one foot crossing the lower wooden frame of the main door, he unexpectedly paused, and, without looking back, said, "Ma (mother), this probably is our last meeting. As you know, I do not have a child being a bachelor all my life. From day one I loved you and wished you well. Nothing is more precious to me than your happiness. I prayed for you the whole night but have nothing specific to say. You have tried various options without success. But please try one more. There is a belief in our social setting and faith-related surroundings that adoption sometimes stimulates physiological interfaces miraculously, helping conception. Probably as a last act and the least advice, I suggest you try that. Incredible things do happen in this world. We do not have an inkling about Allah's will and power."

"'Saying those noncommittal words and still not looking back, he lifted his other foot to commencing his journey and only uttered "Fee Aman Illah ([be] with the safety of Allah)."

"'My wife took that very seriously. Because of her insistence and for peace within the surroundings, I eventually concurred and started to look for options and a way forward. That was a difficult task too for me. My preoccupations with business-related daily challenges gave me little time to explore opportunities. Moreover, the twin factor of emotions and responsibilities stood in my way to try the issue of adoption earnestly.

"'One night before we went to sleep, my wife suddenly suggested adopting our niece, Munira. My sister Marina died suddenly when Munira was four years old. Based on solid justification of the need to have someone at home, my brother-in-law hurriedly married a widow hailing from a nearby neighborhood.

"'Then the saga started. His new wife, after gaining the confidence and trust of the husband, started treating Munira with harshness and, with the passage of time, its recurrence multiplied ostensibly, premised on correcting the latter's mannerisms and behavior patterns. The father gradually inclined to what was being told by his new wife and made Munira's life tough and miserable. Gradually, it became the talk of the community, and it traveled to our family too. Against that backdrop, we all were concerned and sympathetic.

"'Pursuing the matter further, my wife, without any pretension, candidly suggested adopting Munira, irrespective of the outcome related to her conception. She said, "I thought through this possibility, and it definitely has win-win upshots: We can make Munira's life a really pleasurable one and we will have someone dancing and interacting joyfully in our home, distracting us from the frustration of not having a baby. The departed soul of your sister will definitely be happy in her infinite locale."

"'I liked the proposition. Frankly speaking, I too had that in my mind but refrained from discussing it with my wife as adoption per se has links with the infancy of a baby, and Munira, being about six years old, does not fit in. I also mistakenly had a misconception of my wife, taking that as an excuse to bring Munira to our home.

"'On hearing what my wife proposed, I not only felt happy but equally was miserable within myself for harboring a narrow outlook. I hugged her and readily concurred. Munira moved into her new home to the delight of the new wife of my brother-in-law. Apparently, he was relieved too.

"My wife was very delighted and started behaving in a way that she found out a new delight. She devoted her best self to molding Munira as a distinct girl soon to be treading into womanhood. As a preparatory step, and in the absence of any girls' school, my wife got her into the only local nonformal girls' education facility, commonly known as Manoshi "Mar" Patshala.

"Then the miracle happened. In about seven months' time after Munira's arrival in our abode, my wife conceived. We were blessed with a son. My wife all along believed that it was the Dua of her uncle and Allah's will that she conceived. We ardently named him Amin too, as a symbolic gratitude for his guidance and Dua (prayer of invocation).

"Amin gradually started growing up under the love and care of Munira. Time passed, and Munira finished her class five study in Manoshi Mar Patshala. Being marooned at home in the absence of a higher education facility locally for girls, she was engaged in helping my wife with household chores besides being a playmate and guide for Amin.

"As Munira attained the age of marriage by local standards, we were concerned. At that time, my manager brought me a proposal. Initiating the proposition, he said, 'The young man is from the Horinkata settlement, completed technical education from the district polytechnic institute, and went to Dubai with a job. He is now back on leave and the family is keen to get him married. I had in my mind your current angst concerning getting our dear Munira married. In my discourse with that family, I tentatively floated the idea of a matrimonial relationship between Munira and their son. They appeared to be very enthusiastic.'

"'In consultation with my brother-in-law, I consented and gave the go-ahead. During our rather long association, Manager Sanwar Ali earned my confidence and trust for his exceptional trading insight. However, I was pleasantly surprised when I observed his hidden acumen to move forward with the proposal. The main handicap was Munira, being our adopted daughter. In such a setting, village politics often play a dirty role. In this case, it was thus not an exception.

"'Sanwar Ali kept me out of these complications and opted to proceed in consultation with my wife. Eventually, everything was settled to the satisfaction of both parties, and the wedding was accomplished grandly. Everyone was happy.

"'That happiness caused a new problem at our end. By this time, my son Amin finished his elementary learning at Manoshi Mar Patshla and was all set to go to a formal school like yours. The absence of a senior in the house to monitor and guide Amin after the departure of Munira for her new home and my preoccupations with business were causing apprehensions for my wife. She is of the view that in this phase of growing up and to ensure safety and security in going to and coming back from formal school, he needs a companion. This is where I am at this moment."

Rahmat Bepari tarried for a while. Hamid Ullah Sir was wondering about the reason for such a long prologue on the part of Rahmat Bepari while anguishing himself about his role in such family worries.

"That haze was cleared soon. Rahmat Bepari opened up, saying, 'My wife requested me to talk to you seeking your support and help. She is of the view that a responsible senior student recommended by you could be a resident house tutor for Amin, taking care of his growing as well as an escort to and from school. This is the backdrop of my long narration before. Because you are a respected person, I am soliciting your help and support without hesitation.'

"In my response, I said, 'I fully appreciate your and your wife's concern about Amin. Both of your anxiety to ensure a proper grooming up of Amin is valued and cherished. Your request is a treasured trust reposed on me. I promise that I will do my best to recommend one to you both, but I need some time. I am to find one who is capable as well as in need. He should be one worth the trust that all of us behold.

"We left that discourse with a clear understanding of the need within a limited time. I was very happy that a family that never interacted with me has reposed that responsibility on my shoulder. I decided to gather private information about the temperament and reputation of his wife.

"More authentic evaluation of relevant information testified that Rahmat Bepari is a sort of an introvert, whose world moves around his business challenges. He has a few friends but no enemies. Further, my initial inquisition gave very positive feedback about his wife. She is loving, caring, modest, and responsible, and enjoys a good image in her social setting. Moreover, their abode is relatively in close proximity to our school.

"All related equivalences with respect to Rahmat Bepari's request and the present need of Javed match miraculously. The burden on Javed will probably be minimal, giving him ample time to pursue his own learning.

"Against that backdrop, the pending request of Rahmat Bepari is possibly a workable match in the present situation considering the unforeseen disaster in which your family is and the will of Javed, even though very young, to pursue life on his own."

The common saying, "Even the darkest cloud has its silver lining," is aptly applicable in this case too. As family members were engrossed in finding a way out to help Javed in attaining his life's goal, the possibility of having a board and lodging near the school with the noble task of looking after a seven-year-old in making progression in the latter's life is nothing short of a miracle.

Everyone was happy while shrouding it under the cloud of apparent reservations. All present were engrossed in thinking about the most appropriate response in view of labyrinthine sensitivity. Both Fyruz and Fatipa were in an arduous situation, more so as the proposition had been floated by one like Hamid Ullah Sir, a revered friend of their late father.

In that melee, Rafisa unexpectedly intervened. She framed her general opinion stating, "What revered Hamid Ullah Sir has outlined deserves our ardent understanding and respectful consideration. While doing so, one should not be oblivious to the emotional ramifications that the proposition entails. I am saying so based on my own experiences. I most unexpectedly had to move to the abode of my motherlike sister Fatipa and brotherlike brother-in-law, Fyruz. I will never ever be able to repay their love and care. But the fact remains that I suffered initial stress caused by that relocation.

"Javed is in his teens. An impetuous transition from a pampered lifestyle and somewhat affluent setting to an unknown family setting as a resident house tutor has definitely startling consequences. That may impact his future growth and potential. These need to be kept in view by us."

This spontaneous commentary of Rafisa made opinion formulation by others a challenging task, more so when available options are limited, and the time is squat.

Hamid Ullah Sir, referring to Rafisa's annotation, observed, "What Ma (affectionately a daughter is so addressed as per local practice) articulated perhaps is in the cognizance of many here. I thus would like to clarify some related matters.

"I am not only an admirer of the late Zakir Mia but correspondingly treated him as a brother. This element of brotherhood was bestowed on me by him spontaneously when he said that you, as a brother, showed a genuine understanding of me that I did not get from my own siblings. It is thus my obligation to help your family in case of need, and I will do so as long as I live. Before I placed my proposition to you all, a few things were considered by me seriously. Among others, I was guided by the fact that our options are limited, and our time is squat.

"After having discussions with Rahmat Bepari, I quietly gathered information about his family environment and had mostly positive feedback. As I said earlier, based on reliable information, the lady of the house enjoys an undisputed reputation in the neighborhood as an adorable human being. Rahmat Bepari, being an introvert, has limited social contacts. The family's only visitor is their adopted daughter Munira from time to time. The family lives happily, with the main focus being the treasured seven-year-old son. So the setting is perfect from all perspectives. Further, Rahmat Bepari's home is in ideal close proximity to our school, with my living place not being farther away. The decision is, of course, yours."

As Hamid Ullah Sir paused, Javed interceded. He said, "Since the death of Amma, it was almost mandatory for both of us, me and Father, to have all meals and snacks together. It was very helpful to have frank discussions with Abba (father).

"To be very candid, it was discomforting for me initially as I never had a friendly chat with him so long as Amma was alive. She was friendly and very open to me. Abba was preoccupied with his social commitments and engagements. As such, he was somewhat reserved, notwithstanding prodding by Amma. I always thus had an unintended distance from him. The table radically turned with the sad demise of Amma and Abba's conscientious efforts to guide me in life's voyage.

"I always tried to introduce lighter talking points to make our meals enjoyable. But that was not to be. My repeated efforts to have joyous discourses concerning his relationship with Dada-ji (grandfather) and the reason for his diametrically opposite personality traits related to siblings were in vain. Equally, I wanted to have a glimpse of his feelings after Rafisa-Bu had to be relocated. That likewise failed to generate any reaction from him. He preferred to discuss life and living-related social issues, sharing his perspective and conveying the essence of those to me. He wanted me to grow faster than my age. As time passed, I naively started enjoying those high silhouette matters and absorbed them.

"It is apposite to recall that one night when we were having dinner, he precipitously raised the issue of 'opportunity' in life. He said, 'Look, son, in every life, irrespective of social and economic standings, opportunity shows up for the betterment of conditions. But we often forget that opportunities always have ingrained challenges. If one bungles in handling those challenges, the lady opportunity withers away. It is imperative that one handles each of life's challenges with commitment, determination, and confidence. Also, always bear in mind, that opportunity and luck are two contrary aspects. While one can shape his life by handling related challenges to optimize opportunity, luck is something akin to a bonanza, easy to get and faster to lose.'

"He also said that the shaping of one's life independently is not only fulfilling but simultaneously also enhances self-esteem. 'I am saying so for you to bear these in mind as you are growing up.'

"Because of these and similar discourses that I had with Abba, I have mentally grown up as an adult even though I am still in my teens. On hindsight, I think he had some sort of premonition about his longevity.

"My earlier stated preference for independent living is premised on similar discussions with Abba, notwithstanding what Rafisa-Bu so ardently specified now. In the absence of parents and enlightened guardians around, Hamid Ullah Sir is our sentinel supported by dear Fyruz Bhai.

"I am thankful to Sir for keeping this option in view. I am comfortable and would like to try it out without any inhibition. In case the envisaged arrangement causes undue sway on my growth, I will be the first person to bring that to Sir's attention and your notice. Please bear in mind that I am not abandoning my roots. I give you all a solemn assurance that wherever in life I may be, I will always remain the son of the late Zakir Mia of this soil, including Shetra.

"Also, my earnest desire is to save as much as possible our farm income over time and, if possible, buy back our home in the future, reflecting all our gratitude to our revered Abba. This is one of my many rationales for independent living, as feasible."

All present were startled by the way Javed enunciated his opinion and laid out his understanding of the current challenge and the way forward. While Sir and Fyruz had in-depth practical understanding, both Fatipa and Rafisa were at their wits' end in grasping the reality.

Against such a backdrop, the uncertain setting of a few minutes earlier lessened considerably but still lacked a consensus toward finality. Marking that, Hamid Ullah Sir proposed an informal visit to Rahmat Bepari's abode before a final decision is taken. Fyruz pungently supported that. So was the case with others. Rafisa strongly said that she would very much like to be included in that sojourn as Fatipa-Bu should not go due to her delicate health status. Moreover, a lady's eye can always assess the family setting better than a man's. All present agreed and requested Sir to initiate the process.

Hamid Ullah Sir left that discussion happily. The outcome of that informal assembly was definitively positive from his perspective: It would enable him to help the family of a reputable and respected consociate no more in this world, and, if agreed to, it would be befitting the trust reposed by an individual with whom he had little contact. He merrily doubled down to achieve the objective in mind.

During the visit, Javed for the first time faced the reality of proving himself among elders. Being an odd member among relatives known and unknown elders, he, on his part, devoted time to interact with Rahmat Bepari's son, Amin—the impetus of all the attention and concern of the family. That was more so on the part of Rahmat Bepari's wife, Tahera. In the fifteen years of married life, all her thinking and expectations centered on their seven-year-old son Amin. It is accentuated by the wedding of Munira, their adopted daughter.

That was the backdrop of her insistence to have a guardianlike resident tutor who can give company to Amin, guide him, and, as appropriate, occasionally play with him besides tutoring.

Tahera was delighted when Rahmat Bepari told her about the proposed visit and shared pertinent information about Zakir Mia's family, their social standing, and the unforeseen catastrophe the family suffered as detailed to him by Hamid Ullah Sir. He also shared with Tahera Javed's acumen, including his academic excellence and behavioral attributes based on his experience and exposure, both as a family friend and head teacher of the local high school.

Tahera was enormously delighted and received the visitors with an open heart. In no time, Tahera and Rahmat Bepari intermingled with the visitors unreservedly. Rafisa, being charmed by Tahera's politeness, frankness, and warmth of interaction, bonded with her easily. The whole formal setting predicating the visit became a casual one as if that was a visit by old family members after a while.

The elders of both families unwittingly observed the brotherly interactions between Javed and Amin. As Javed was probably explaining something related to their setting, Amin devoted all his attention to absorbing those with rapt attention and wide-open eyes. That was a communication scenery reflective of an elder brother, which Amin never had, passing on homily to a younger brother which was missing in Javed's life too.

That affable interlude between the two youngest in that assembly with bonding as brothers was the most unexpected outcome of that visit. The ease and comfort between the two were spontaneous.

The assessment was positive from the perspective of both families. Rafisa, in particular, was very engaged in making her assessment. Tahera impressed her from the beginning as a caring and loving mother. Limited exchanges concerning Munira's life before and after relocation to Tahera's home spoke volumes regarding the amiability of the latter's persona. What impressed Rafisa most was that Tahera always referred to Munira as "our daughter." The fact of adoption was never referred to and a related word was never uttered.

But Rafisa's prognosis was not limited to relationship-related aspects only. She equally focused on material aspects too. On her specific inquest, Tahera said, "The separate frontage structure of our house is a two-room accommodation. Since we are toying with the idea of having a resident house tutor, the spacious one of those two rooms has recently been renovated with an adjacent washroom facility. To minimize the feeling of desolateness, we will have a support staff of our *arath* (wholesale business establishment) live in the other room, with minimal contact with the resident tutor. Both of them will be under my watch as Amin's future grounding will be at stake."

Rahmat Bepari, being an introvert, remained calm and discreet while keeping watch on the facial reactions of others. He was, however, taken aback upon observing Tahera's forthright discourses with others, mostly with Rafisa and Fyruz.

Fyruz was frank and prompt. To close the discussion, he took note of the affirmative lingos of Rafisa and quietly passed that on to Hamid Ullah Sir.

On getting that indication and quiet exchanges with Rahmat Bepari, Hamid Ullah Sir summed up the outcome. It was decided that Javed would move to Bepari's abode at the beginning of the following week, and Hamid Ullah Sir would chaperon him. The day is Friday, and the time is after *asar* (Muslim's evening prayer time). All were happy and mutually supportive.

Reaching that consensus was apparently easy, but its implications were innate, especially the emotional facets. Fyruz, Rafisa, and Javed returned home and reported to Fatipa the positive outcome. Fatipa could not hold back her emotions. She started to cry, recalling their growing up under the same shade with the love and care of their parents. Precipitously everything fell apart. The home is going to be sold by their uncles. Javed is going to be relocated to live with another family. The once compacted family is just on the verge of withering away.

Both Fyruz and Rafisa were speechless and were at bay, thinking of the imaginable apposite way to intervene to redress the emotional repercussions on the part of Fatipa. Everyone present was internally concerned about the likely impact on Fatipa's pregnancy.

Fyruz, after exchanging a taciturn look with the rest, moved closer to Fatipa and started cajoling her, and that had some immediate impact. Noting this, Rafisa drew the attention of Nazir, requesting him to prepare tea for all. As a mark of exculpation for all, Fatipa spoke for the first time, advising Nazir to serve the *pithas* (indigenous pastries made of rice powder) that neighbor Rahima Khala (aunt) had brought in the morning. All were relieved.

Taking advantage of the transformed disposition, Rafisa opened up, saying, "Fatipa-Bu, we all had an arduous feeling like you while accompanying Sir uncle to the house of Rahmat Bepari. It was more so as the identity of 'Bepari' has an inherent negative connotation in terms of social standing. Even uncle Sir was calm and speechless. Manifestly, he most likely had the burden of bewildering responsibility too.

"Our agonizing mindset underwent a quick upturn as soon as we entered the abode. Rahmat uncle is a self-motivated introverted individual, but his wife, as Sir uncle earlier advised us, is a genuine person whose openness and expressions are self-evident. She hugged Javed, introduced him to her son Amin, and then embraced me as if we had known and bonded for a long time. With the passage of time, our bond turned into one of warmth. She possesses many attributes that our late mother had. I came back with happiness even though our decision had the element of sadness and separation from our brother.

"What impressed me most was her spontaneous indication that Javed can visit us anytime he feels like, and we can visit their home any time of our choice. While bidding us goodbye, she hugged me warmly and said, 'Take it as your khala's home, and do visit us any time of your choice. I will definitely visit Ma (mother) Fatipa soon after her delivery.' I genuinely felt her warmth and readily agreed with the proposition that we are to act upon today or tomorrow."

Everyone was enjoying tea and pithas, as Nazir stood nearby, thinking about the most agonizing change the family was going to experience soon. He was oblivious to his own self.

While piercing his last pitha, Javed commented that he agreed with Rafisa-Bu's assessment and opined, saying, "If destiny for me is to live in another house, then it is the one. Also, I liked Amin very much and we bonded easily. He is a responsive and a quiet toddler."

That brought peace to everyone's mind. Fatipa adjusted to the new reality and, after exchanging looks with Fyruz, concurred. Her happiness soon turned into a thrill when Javed started saying, "My earnest desire is to save as much as possible from our farm income over time, including our share of sale proceeds of the residential property and, if possible, buy back our home in the future, reflecting all our gratitude to our revered Abba. This is one of my many rationales for independent living, as feasible. And Amin's home is likely our best option. Also, it will enable me to groom myself well for future independent living when I am to leave you all for higher education. It is inevitable—either now or two years later. So in the absence of Abba and Amma, you all should bless me unwaveringly. That is what I am looking for."

SHELTER

WITH A FEELING of separation overriding and a simultaneous panorama of hope, having a probable concoction of ambiguity overpowering, Javed, in the company of Hamid Ullah Sir in one rickshaw (three-wheeled cycle) and Nazir in another one with belongings, stopped in front of Rahmat Bepari's home.

Hamid Ullah Sir was astounded, noticing Rahmat Bepari standing in front of his home awaiting to receive them. His amazement was prodigious as Rahmat Bepari ushered them straight to the main accommodation, giving the unqualified impression that all of them were being treated as family members. That was accentuated when the wife of Rahmat Bepari, contrary to the local practice of adhering to *parda* (modesty), showed up unreservedly with a platter in hand, having lemon *sherbat* (juice) in glasses. After putting the tray on the sole table of the room, she walked inside and came out with a stool for Nazir to sit. As Nazir was hesitant, she politely said, "Ma Rafisa told me the other day many things, and reference to you was one of them. I have thus full perception of who you are and your relevance to the late Zakir Mia's family. Treat it as the home of Javeed. Always feel free to come and stay with us." Nazir was speechless and hesitantly sat on the stool.

Tahera then moved to Javed with his glass of sherbet, hugged him warmly, and affectionately said, "Amin has a brother from today. We are fortunate to have one like you from an exceptional family background in our setting. Having a resident house tutor was our initial objective as Amin will be going to school from next year. Allahpak has blessed us with you, more like a brother to Amin than a tutor. Teach him, guide him, and monitor him in his growing-up phase as an elder brother. We do not have any restrictive stipulations. The only request is that you treat him as your own."

At this point, Rahmat Bepari opened up and said, "Sir, me and Tahera had detailed discussions during the week. What she said reflects our common position. We are thankful to you for working out the present arrangement. I am relieved too as business commitments do not give me time and opportunity to get involved in family matters. I am more than certain that Beta (son) Javed, even though the object of unanticipated disaster, is a boon for us. But more importantly, we assure you that he will and would enjoy all accommodation and support from us to excel in his life's goal. The late Zakir Mia was extremely lucky to have a son like Javed. Though premised on a tragic outcome, we too are lucky to have him among us, and we hope that this relationship between our family and that of the late Zakir Mia will flourish with the passage of time. Javed will always be a son too of this home."

Hamid Ullah Sir responded, saying, "I did not have much interactions with you before. Still, you reposed on me the onerous task of having a resident house tutor. Providence stepped in. We were blessed to have Javed in an ideal option though in a tragic background. I am certain, based on my assessment after having inclusive interactions with Javed, that he will live up to our expectations. He has embraced Amin as one of his own. The magnanimity of your wife has contributed enormously. In our local surroundings, she is a hidden treasure—a compassionate, loving, and understanding lady much beyond and above local prejudices. I am grateful for having the opportunity to know your family so well and so soon. You have shown extraordinary consideration by bringing me to your private setting.

"Before I leave, I would like you to take note of what I have in mind. For obvious reasons, Javed could not pursue his educational responsibilities in the recent past. The class eight final examination is very close by. Javed is expected to excel in that examination and earn a good name for our school. He therefore needs time to prepare for that, making good of time lost. He should therefore be allowed space to prepare adequately before he could devote himself to tutoring Amin."

Self-restrained Rahmat Bepari nodded his head, signifying his understanding and conveying the needed concurrence. But the real surprise was waiting for Hamid Ullah Sir.

The curtain of the door leading to the kitchen moved a bit, and in came Tahera. She politely said, "As I was going to our bedroom, I heard

Sir Bhai saying that he would leave soon. That respectfully is not to be. I prepared special food for all of us to celebrate Javed's coming to our home. We would therefore be obliged if Sir Bhai stayed back and gave us the opportunity to share food together. It will be an honor for us."

Hamid Ullah Sir was amazed for two reasons—for referring to him as a bhai (brother) and for including him in the family dinner. In a symbolic expression of happiness and consent, he gleefully obliged. That made all present happy.

In that locale, Tahera observed some restlessness in Nazir's expressions, specifically his focus on the belongings of Javed. On a specific query from Tahera, Nazir said, "I would like to fix the bed of Javed Bhai and place his other belongings appropriately before I leave, and before it is dusk."

As he continued to make what he had in mind, Tahera intervened, saying, "We have prepared the bed for Javed during the morning hours, placing the required table and chair, as well a jug of water and a glass. You can go and check for yourself and, more importantly, place Javed's books and other belongings as per his preferences. We also have a makeshift arrangement for you to sleep in the adjacent room. However, if you want to leave early, I can serve food for you early as we normally have dinner after magreb (Muslims' evening time prayer)." Tahera went to the kitchen after saying those words.

Sir was overwhelmed and traced back his association and social contacts with the late Zakir Mia. In that premise, Javeed softly held the right hand of Amin and both started walking toward his living space, followed by Nazir.

Javed was overawed and internally assured about his upcoming living arrangements while Nazir was equally amazed and felt the urge to go back and report to the family. He went straight to the kitchen and addressed Tahera as Khala (maternal aunt), saying, "I need to go early. So if it is okay with you, I would like to have my food now." Tahera promptly made the necessary service arrangements with the help of her household help girl.

With Nazir gone and in a very relaxed commentary, Javed said, "Amin, as we were approaching your home, our rickshaw puller stopped in front of a rudimentary *mudi dhokan* (basic grocery store) to refit his pedal chain. Incidentally, Hamid Ullah Sir met an elderly lady whom Sir addressed as Manoshir Ma. They obviously were known to each other. On her query, Sir said, 'We are going to Rahmat Bepari's house,' and, pointing at me, further said, "I am taking this young man to that home to be the resident tutor of their son."

On hearing that, Manoshir Ma was very exultant and commented, "Their son Amin was in my patshala for the last two years. Though a toddler, he proved himself to be a very nice and temperate one. His mother, whom I visited a few times, is a very considerate lady. I think Amin picked up many good attributes from his home environment even though is very young."

Insensible to the essence of those discourses, the rickshaw puller commenced his prosaic peddling. Javed continued his oration, "As the rickshaw maintained its momentum, I was engrossed in absorbing the new surroundings, and so it appeared that in no time we reached your home. Thus, I had a definite idea as to who you were even before I met you and bonded with you by holding your hand as you guided me to this place.

"Even though definitely overloading, I must convey my loom to form the base of our relationship. The fact is that I am here as your house tutor, but I embrace you as a younger brother, which I've never had. Besides all these, treat me as a friend, listen to what I say, try to absorb those, and be frank and candid. There is no matter that you should feel shy to talk to me. All these I am saying to you are based on my life experiences as I too once was of your age.

"Some of my present sayings may be beyond your current comprehension, but you will understand them as time passes. Always remember that anything one wants to do is mostly half done if the preparation is well thought out and planned. It is almost like the smell of food, which is as good as half eating."

Amin, still in a reserved vein with shyness apparent in his body postures, was intensely observing Javed, arranging his books and other study-related accessories on the table with occasional exchanges of looks with him.

Observing that, Javed said, "Because of my father's sudden demise, I lost many days of study. I need to perform well in the upcoming class eight examination for myself, the good name of my school, as well as to live up to the expectations of Hamid Ullah Sir. I thus don't have time to waste. Hence, I am setting everything in proper order so that from tomorrow I can devote myself fully after attending to your needs."

They returned to the main home to find that the dinner service arrangements were laid out, and all were waiting for their return. The dinner was served promptly, and everyone was enjoying the food, meticulously prepared by Tahera, while having intermittent exchanges.

As Javed was looking around for Nazir, Tahera said, "He finished his dinner early and left hurriedly with the objective of returning to an empty home before sunset. Before leaving, he requested me to inform you accordingly. I sense it was emotionally demanding for him to say goodbye to one whom he reared up from birth."

Hamid Ullah Sir concurred, saying, "Most of the time, it is challenging to face reality. It is more so when the feeling is premised on emotions. In the case of Nazir, it is logically expected. For a man of his commitment and loyalty, this is what is natural. Time will take care of it."

Everyone focused on eating under the careful and congenial hospitality of Tahera. She was enthusiastically offering different dishes and serving copiously but did not fail to notice the semblance of tears in Javed's eye.

Instead of making pertinent comments, she handled it diligently by saying, "Beta Javed is perhaps finding it difficult to adjust himself since he has not as yet directly communicated with me. I can confidently say that I cannot be like your illustrious mother, but I can easily be your khala. Be easy and feel like you are in your khala's home. Knowing your background and being cognizant of your life's objectives, we have embraced you as a son. Live in this home as your own with Amin as a younger sibling. Had I not had health-related problems, perhaps I would have a son of about your age. So please do not hesitate to address me as khala. Also, you need not devote much time to focus on Amin. It can be a gradual one at your convenience. We would like to see you more as his elder brother than a tutor. That is all I have to say and said it in front of everyone present."

There was a lull for a while. Hamid Ullah Sir was overwhelmed. He interjected, saying, "The food was delicious but what made it tastier and fulfilling are the words voiced by Bhabi Sheeba just now. That was my anxiety so far. I also shared that in the recent past with Bhai Saheeb and made a request to him. Now it is doubly reassuring since it has come from Bhabi Shaeeba. I am not only contented but reassured."

He continued, saying, "I will be leaving this house soon with a blissful mindset for being able to take care of my revered well-wisher's son in quandary and being able to respond to the request of a community member in need of help. From now on, this is the house of my brother. The providence of Bhabi Sheeba is making it possible for me to leave this home with enormous satisfaction and reassurance. Javed is singularly fortunate to be in a setting like this. I am more than certain that he will live up to the expectation of all." The dinner was over with the service of tea for elders.

Both Tahera and Rahmat Bepari accompanied Javed to his accommodation ostensibly to be satisfied about arrangements for and the comfort of Javed. They left soon, giving Javed the needed space to settle himself as he preferred.

Javed, with all his emotional stress behind and settlement process completed, rested in his bed and fell asleep momentarily. The presence of Quddus Ali, the arath staff, in the next room was his confidence belt in sleeping in a new place for the first time.

Waking up in the morning, Javed was in a mood of reflection. The oft-repeated saying of his late father "Time never waits for anything or anybody" flashed in his mind. He was wondering about its contemporaneous relevance in his life.

Right at that time, Amin showed up, saying, "Amma is waiting for you to have breakfast and sent me to escort you." As they were on their way, Javed was surprised to notice Amin's going to the kitchen instead of the place of the home where they had dinner last night. He hesitantly followed Amin.

Seeing Javed standing with some hesitation, Tahera said, "This is normally the place of our breakfast. The serving of food in the main house has a semblance of formality. As you are now a family member, I wanted to get away from that sort of procedure early. I hope it is okay with you?"

Javed was not to be undone. He promptly responded, saying, "This is my khala's abode. I am thus with everything of my khala's preference."

As the address "khala" was uttered, Tahera stood up, positioned herself near Javed, and hugged him, saying, "You made my day. This khala of yours will do anything to make you happy without preconditions. Rest assured about it."

The new bond took its preferred shape. Formality was done away with. The spontaneous address of khala by Javed was all gratifying with happiness omnipotent in the facial expressions of both. Similar is the case with Amin but more as a reflexive one seeing Amma and Bhai contented.

It was contradictory to what Javed had in his mind initially. Since the proposition of moving to Amin's home was floated, he conditioned himself to maintain a formal relationship with the family and nothing beyond a "resident house tutor." But the reality was just the opposite, proving the common saying, "One does not know what the future holds for him."

This informality grew imperceptibly beyond Javed's expectations. Two successive visits by Fyruz and Rafisa, and one by Nazir, bonded the two families very quickly, and that too had everyone addressing Tahera as "khala."

In response to Rafisa's urging for Khala to visit Fatipa in her home, Tahera graciously commented, "At this point in time, she does not need a visit from me. I would rather visit her after her delivery and bless both mother and son. Meanwhile, at the end of each *namaz* (Muslim prayer), I will pray for her good health and safe delivery." That impressed Fyruz most. Javed, however, made it a point to visit Fatipa based on convenience.

Notwithstanding the unforeseen family fatality resulting in a major dislocation in his life and living experiences, and as expected by the school faculty, Javed excelled in his class eight examination, topping the district. That happily coincided with the normal delivery of Fatipa, with both mother and son being okay in all respects.

Contrary to the usual practice of waiting till akika (practiced Muslim obligation to slaughter a goat[s] to thank Allahpak for blessing the family with a newborn), Tahera, in the company of Javed in a rickshaw, started for Fatipa's home followed by Hiron, her household help, in another rickshaw carrying gifts and sweets. Fyruz welcomed them and then guided them to the room of Fatipa. The union was complete amid loving words and good wishes. Rafisa's presence was delayed due to her preoccupation in the kitchen. But once present, she made up for the lost time with choruses and acts, including softly placing the newborn on the lap of the khala. Hilarity was pervasive, and interactions were spontaneous. Not for a moment was it impacted by the shocking loss of Zakir Mia, though the feeling of his absence, together with that of Amma Ambia, was in the mind of all present. Life moved on. That was the reality.

While returning, Javed took the opportunity to float his idea to Khala about his planned approach to molding Amin for his future journey. Seeking her consent, Javed said, "Khala, both of you have assigned a major task for me to shape Amin, both in terms of learning and mannerism. I have observed Amin effusively in all respects and thought through it intensely. Thus, besides being his tutor, I would like to mingle with him in every respect of life. The only way one can do that is to become a friend too—playing, talking, and interacting as a friend. This is important as my stay with you is likely to be about two and a half years. I plan to live up to your trust in that period of time. I need your understanding and concurrence."

Tahera Khala was both pleased and happy. Her unqualified response was in total affirmation. She, however, promptly commented, "From day one, I have accepted you as a son. Amin therefore is your brother. Shape him and guide him as you deem appropriate. There is no need to get my permission. Please bear that in mind always. But I am somewhat disheartened by your mention of staying in our place for two and a half years. This is and will always be your home. You should come and stay with us whenever it is possible. I am not trying to delink you from your family. Our home should be treated by you as your additional space where a khala will always be waiting for you. You must promise that to me and now."

With tears overshadowing his eyes, Javed looked outside as a diversion tactic, and then said, "Very candidly, my decision to be Amin's resident tutor was based on my intent to remain formal with you all. As you embraced me at our first encounter, that mindset withered away. I readily accepted you as my khala, one that I never had. You likewise should not have any doubt about that."

Saying those, Javed became somewhat normal and exchanged a passionate look with Tahera.

Considering the relaxed vibe, Javed went on to explain, "After Amma died, Abba started devoting time to guide me in life. Many of his sayings and statements at that time were beyond me, but I tried to remember them always. Through that endeavor, he made my teen mind become that of a young man, which I realize now. Thus, it has been possible for me to take many decisions based on his teachings. I want to repeat that with Amin. I will not be with him always. Hence this is the time for me to try that with Amin too, in a way that he can absorb. I took this opportunity to talk to you, having none present around us, and to make sure that you do not misunderstand my effort."

The response of Khala was brief and direct, saying, "Amin is an Amanat to you. I do not have any worries."

Javed was a kite-flying enthusiast all through his childhood, encouraged and supported by Nazir Bhai. Having Amin in his care, he floated the idea of kite flying, and Amin was equally receptive.

Javed silently bought the necessary strings, string holder, and spool. He also got hold of a broken chimney from the depository of household trash and requested Hiron to crush that diligently so that broken pieces could not be seen but could only be felt by hand. Sharing his game plan with Khala, he got other ingredients like some atta flour.

That was a Friday morning with the sun shining brightly. One needs sunshine for aeration. Amin was sitting patiently to oversee what Bhai is aiming at and to internalize the likely process.

Javed was waiting for his friend, Rafiq, as he needed three sets of hands to complete the process. Rafiq was also to bring a *gaab* (local fruit with a thick skin having grease-type juice used as a coating matter with the scientific name of *Diospyros peregrina*) as an essential ingredient.

Getting Amin involved in the process, he assembled the needed items and positioned them under the big mango tree at the southern end of the yard of the home.

Notwithstanding being cognizant of Amin's palpable uncertainty about what was to be expected, Javed systemically commenced the required mixing process of various ingredients while waiting for his friend, Rafiq.

While waiting, Javed carefully explained the method of mixing up and its rationale.

Javed commenced his commentary by amplifying, "What I am going to do is called *manja*, an indigenous process of coating kite-flying and fighting strings. One needs to prepare a semiliquid constituent by pouring the needed water into the atta flour and coxing that with glass powder. Then, one needs to put gaab juices to ensure early compaction while drying the strings.

"The process entails three people. It needs two *natais* (kite spool string holders), a few rolls of sewing strings (about 500 feet long), and very small portions of used linen.

"You will sit here with the natai (spool) and its holder full of strings, releasing the same slowly and as I indicate. I will sit about two yards away, holding mixture-soaked cotton pieces, enabling the strings to pass through it, and Rafiq, sitting at a distance of about 100 yards, is to roll that back in his natai while monitoring compactness and dryness. That makes the string fit for combat with another kite intruding in your space."

Waiting for Rafiq to arrive, Javed continued his adage, explaining its applicability in a real-life setting. He said, "One has great things to learn from this, which is ordinarily treated as an activity for fun and enjoyment. In pursuing life, one often is to struggle to survive and make concerted efforts to succeed. Sustained thoughts and prudent preparations are the important elements of this. Assembling of ingredients needed for manja to sharpen one's strings is the thought process; going through the process of manja is the preparation; and the ability to fight one's way through in the open sky is the success.

"It is definitely challenging for you to comprehend all these, and I do not expect that either. I would appreciate it if you remember what I am saying from time to time and recall those in rea-life conditions as you grow up.

"My late father told me many things before he died. I did not understand most of them at those times. As I am now facing real-life challenges, these things flash in my mind, helping and guiding me in my progression.

"Also, bear in mind always that learning and knowledge are not necessarily confined within the bindings of textbooks. The whole world is an archive, and one can learn from his or her environment at every moment."

Javed was astounded to note an extemporaneous affirmation from Amin, who focused his eclectic eyes on him. Whatever might be the outcome, that made Javed contented.

The waiting process was over soon. Rafiq arrived with much-needed gaab.

Both the mixing of ingredients and the manja process were completed on time. Most notable was the enthusiasm of Amin.

Observing all of these from time to time from her space in the kitchen, Tahera Khala was elated. In her thoughts, she quietly thanked Allahpak for blessing her home with happiness and joy.

That feeling of joy was multiplied by the unannounced presence of Munira the following day for a periodical visit. Her unstructured and spontaneous discourses with Mother were dominated by matters related to the experience of having Javed as a resident house tutor. Mother's enthusiasm to brief her about Javed and his qualities was thwarted by Munira, saying, "I do not like to hear more about him from you. Let me have the chance to form my own opinion. Then we will share our views." Being confident about the outcome, Tahera readily concurred, and devoted time to prepare additional food items to celebrate Munira's arrival and presence.

It was late afternoon. Both Amin and Javed returned from school, following the drill for the former to stay back until Javed finished his classes. This arrangement was okay with all as Amin could practice his study module before returning home and then enjoy free time for play and fun.

As always, Amin rushed to the kitchen to brief Mother about what he did in the school. Noting his approach, Munira hid herself behind part of the entry door. Observing that his dear Amma was not as excited as before, Amin, with anguish, took turns back toward the main home. Right at that moment, Munira hugged him from the back. Noting her surprised presence, Amin was jubilant, surrendered himself to the embrace of Munira, and started talking about his startling doings in the recent past, including that of manja, and dragged her to Javed's place, stating how good he was as his house tutor.

The much-desired direct meeting was achieved without formalities. Seeing them entering, Javed paused for a few moments, smiled, and politely inquired, "You are Munira!"

On her query how he could guess so, Javed answered straightforwardly, "While I have many things to talk about and convey to Amin, his favorite subject is his Munira-bu, emphasizing time and again how good she is and how much he misses her. The glow on his face as you entered spoke volumes about his happiness. I had thus no hesitation to conclude about who you are!"

Requesting her to sit on the only chair the room had, Javed moved to his bed to position himself comfortably. Observing that, Munira said, "This is your chair. You sit there. I am an ordinary housewife and thus always more comfortable sitting on the bed."

Javed marveled at her wit and openness. He commented, saying, "I now know why Khala always speaks about you and why Amin is so fond of you!"

In that milieu of affability, household help Hiron showed up, conveying, "Amma would like you all to be in the kitchen. She is waiting with enjoyable eating items."

They stepped in together. Neither Munira nor Amma raised the earlier unsettled opinion about Javed. Unspoken words were more than passable for evident consensus.

Days passed with merriment and conviviality. Munira planned a visit to a class friend from Manoshi Ma'r Patshala in the company of Amin. That friend got married recently and was staying at her in-laws' place at a negotiable distance. Tahera suggested that since it was by local standard quite a distance, preferably someone else should accompany them. Subsequently, it was decided that Javed would be the person.

All three boarded a rickshaw with the hood on. Most parts of the secondary road, offshoot from the main road, were bumpy, and for safety reasons, Javed held Amin between his two legs.

Frequent bumps made it unnerving for the passengers. Everyone in that rickshaw was very careful. Notwithstanding that, Munira bounced at the rear side of Javed's back, with her breast smashed against his body. Munira quickly repositioned herself, only to experience a second and successive similar bumps.

While Javed was embarrassed, an unexplained physiological impulse engulfed Munira's reflective manners. She quietly started enjoying those bumps with Javed, who was holding Amin firmly. Since there was no space to maneuver, Javed could do little to avoid those.

While returning home, the same experience was repeated, with Munira being easy with each bump, taking time to disengage. With each dash of Munira's breast, Javed recounted his first experience in the mela when a teenager from the minority community crashed on his back, giving him his first familiarity with the female breast. Recalling that, he too started relishing what Munira was doing. Eventually, they reached the paved main road, and both kept quiet while Amin had some inquisitive queries about the surroundings.

Tahera was pleased to see them back. Both Munira and Amin had ecstatic expressions and responses. Sitting in his room, Javed diverted himself from the occurrence in the rickshaw and concentrated on studying, preparing for the week's next day. Things around the home were very normal and calm.

Javed, as usual, was sitting alone in his space after returning from school the following day and finishing the standard service of snacks in the kitchen. Normally, Amin would have been with him. Due to the presence of Munira, he was spending more time with his dear Munira-Bu.

Right at that moment, Munira joyfully stepped in with a plate full of *ambra* (hog plums, a local juicy sour and tasty fruit) pieces, having separate red chili dust and salt. With all inherent easiness, she offered him that elatedly. Javed took some and relished that intake, more due to chili powder and salt. His thoughts brought him back to the early days when Rafisa-Bu shared similar treats with him.

Without any posturing or mortification, Munira spontaneously started saying what she had in mind. She looked at him straight and said, "I apologize for last night's conduct. Due to unexpected road conditions, I could not maintain my posture. The first bump was unexpected. But then, my physiology overtook my sense of decency and aptness. I thought through this last night intensely.

"I had a physical relationship with my husband for about fifteen nights. The moment I started being open to him and enjoying the conjugal life, he was gone for Dubai, promising me a visit soon. He has now moved to Qatar with a new job and is not likely to be with me anytime soon. His plan is to save enough money to build a house. It so appears that my emotions and physical needs have little relevance to him at this stage. This perhaps was the genesis of the very indecorous gestures of last evening. I lost all control and behaved improperly. I am so sorry and repent that very much.

"We are almost of the same age. It is a fact that you are not my brother, but as Amma has taken you as a son, you are more than a brother to me. That makes me more remorseful.

"I do not know how much you know about me. I am not Abba-Amma's daughter. I am their adopted one. I am the daughter of Abba's sister. My father married a second time after my mother died. My stepmother mistreated me to the extent of torturing me. The upside of that is I learned to live in a disparaging setting.

"To rescue me, and because they have no children, Abba and Amma adopted me. After about seven months of my adoption, Amma miraculously conceived and Amin was born.

"Since then, Abba-Amma never uttered the word 'adoption.' I was always addressed and introduced by them as 'our daughter.' Rearing Amin with all love, Amma meticulously groomed me as an upright person in every respect and in terms of tenets and ideals. Last evening's acts were thus contrary to all those teachings. I am extremely remorseful.

"Without trying to justify, I must say that the occurrence of last evening has a wide range of ramifications, with society being totally oblivious. With many young men living abroad and money flowing in, a newfound affluence has overshadowed the previous value system. While seniors and well-wishers are happy, most of the wives, being young and with physical aspirations, are depressed and easily fall prey to varied allurements, including extramarital sexual indulgences. The society, perhaps, and unnoticeably, is progressing in the wrong direction."

Notwithstanding Munira's dallied static posture for a while, she continued munching on pieces of amra. The nature of grinding and heavy application of chili dust did not escape Javed's attention. He decided that to be the opportune stint for him to interact.

He said, "Thanks for your openness and your elucidation about emerging social changes. Let me respond beginning with your last point.

"It is a fact that the phenomena of affluence are impacting our value systems. Too much money and that too so quickly are giving rise to indiscipline, insolence, and arrogance, and my late father was a victim of this. I am not in the position to pass any specific dictum so far advent of extramarital rapport is concerned. What I understand is very simple!

"With most family elders being illiterate or not adequately familiar with prevalent phone technology, the young wives have the responsibility to handle remittance-related matters, both through official and private sector channels. In short, she is in charge of the purse, with exclusive authority on all matters. In such a locale, men with deleterious intentions try to become friendly, establish a bond, and in many cases cajole her into a relationship. Most participation by housewives is usually premised on newfound affluence, authority, and deprived physical needs. The onus is on the elites and social leaders to act.

"You must be wondering about the contents and nature of my response. My perception of the issue is a recent and unpremeditated one. A few days back, I was waiting for our B.Sc Sir (as mathematics sir is commonly identified) to get some guidance. Due to preoccupations, he was late to meet me. I suddenly picked up a magazine from his table. That had a detailed article on the issue you articulated. Having an interest in social issues, a unique curiosity possibly inherited from my late father, I read that article fully and internalized its contents. That is the reason for my ability to respond to your related narration from a wider perspective.

"Now let us deal with the issue of the lewd experience of last evening. Frankly speaking, I was initially surprised but somewhat enjoyed those bumps when they were repeated. Upon our return, and sitting in a relaxed mood, I treated that as coincidental, parked that occurrence away, and concentrated on my studies. That was not in my mind until you raised it a while back."

Javed then picked up another piece of ambra and started chomping it without chili and salt. Looking straight at Munira, he continued, saying, "Ingredients like chili distort the sweet-sour coalesced test of amra. Likewise, any relationship is always an enduring one if devoid of words and is based on feelings. Hence, I would be straightforward with you. From now on, you are my sister in the truest sense as the ambiance of this abode treated you as our daughter. Though difficult, I understand the adherence of Khala and Bepari Shaheb in always maintaining their intended stance, but at a bay to understand how it is possible for one like Amin to meticulously refrain from saying that you are his 'adopted sister'?"

Munira, in an assured vein, commented, saying, "That speaks volumes about the qualities of my amma. She is a less talkative person. But when she says something, she says that from her heart, without ifs and buts. And that is the essence of the environment of this home. I occasionally come back to recharge myself."

Javed closed that homily saying, "Next time when you come, I will take you to my Fatipa-Bu's home and introduce you to my two other sisters." She laughed and nodded her head.

Right at that moment, Amin showed up with a plate of *pua pitha* (a popular Bangladeshi round-shaped dessert made of all-purpose flour, semolina, and sugar and then deep fried). He said, "Amma wants you both to finish this as dinner service tonight will be delayed." Javed got hold of Amin and said, "Sir, you too join us." Amin responded happily and joined them in crunching pua pitha.

In that cordial setting and fulfilling ambiance, time just flew. Fatipa's son was about two years old. Rafisa started schooling afresh with the establishment of a girls' high school in the vicinity of Fyruz's homestead. The only thing that never changed was the regular visits by Nazir.

Amin was to move to class three, and Javed was preparing for his final secondary school certificate examination. The latter received a message from Hamid Ullah Sir to meet him. The day and the time were indicated.

As he entered the office room of the headmaster, he noticed Hamid Ullah Sir having a friendly chat with a visitor.

Welcoming Javed, he said, "This is Mukles Akram, our new mathematics teacher. Shurendra Babu, our current mathematics teacher, suddenly decided, under pressure from family, to migrate to India. Obviously, for personal reasons, he kept that secret until last week."

Hamid Ullah Sir continued, saying, "I was in a disarray. But as I told you and others many a time, unanticipated and flustered episodes sometimes happen with relatively positive options. In this case, it just happened.

"While going back to my place after school hours that afternoon, I felt like having tea. As I stepped into my preferred tea stall in the periphery of the *bazar* (local market), I unexpectedly met our school board member, Belayet Saheeb.

"In the midst of sociable discourse, Belayet Shaheb told me about a problem he had. He said, 'During my growing-up phase, I received a lot of help and support from a second maternal uncle's family. Their son, who enviably performed in his bachelor of science examination, needs a job. And more pertinent is the need to have a job in the vicinity of his home at Mukhdumpara so that he can conveniently look after his ailing father and aged mother. That was the content of my Mami-ma's (maternal aunt) brief communication with me. I do not know how to respond to one to whom I am indebted so much.'

"As he finished his oration and I was in the midst of seeping my residue tea, it almost trapped in my throat. Recovering from that at the earliest, I could not help but laugh.

"Obviously, Belayet Saheeb was appalled and stood up to depart. Observing that, I promptly said 'Belayet Saheeb, please be seated. Once I tell the full story, I bet that you too would be acquiescent to laughing.'

"Narrating the gist of my unexpected exchanges with B.Sc Sir (Shurendra Babu), I frankly said to Belayet Saheeb, 'Shurendra Babu's sudden notice and my anxiety about preparing upcoming SSC candidates overawed me. Having no option, I felt emotionally stressed and suddenly entered this tea stall to reenergize myself as well as to have a serene thinking as to a way out.

"'Then you tell me about your dilemma. I could not help but laugh due to inherent inferences: what is a problem for you came out as a solution to my problem, even if temporary. I am ready to interview the young man soon and employ him temporarily with the proposition of making that a tenured one if satisfactory.'

"That was the turn of Belayet Saheeb to laugh and he did it vociferously. It made me relieved and relaxed. I immediately focused on early action in consultation with the school board president and prominent faculty members. The consensus was an immediate appointment to facilitate a smooth transition, especially focusing on your class. I specifically discussed with Mr. Akram the prospects you hold both for yourself and the school per se. That prompted calling you to introduce to Akram Sir without loss of time."

As an obedient student, Javed nodded his head, and left the office room of the headmaster, promising need-based interactions with Akram Sir.

That was very swift as Javed had the intent, notwithstanding the opinion of Hamid Ullah Sir, to form his own assessment, not that it matters, about academic prudence and the teaching excellence of Akram Sir. After two informal sittings, Javed was awed: Akram Sir had much wider views of mathematics as a subject, its teaching approach, and smart ways to solve many problems. Moreover, the new sir had an equally good command of English. That made him exuberant, and good words about him spread very quickly.

Javed availed this opening to the fullest extent, getting necessary guidance and help from Akram Sir, more in the case of English compared to mathematics.

The common social dictum is that "good vibration and unspecified anxiety" are twins traveling together making one's life both challenging or depressing depending on the outcomes. That precisely happened during a nonacademic discourse between Javed and his new adorable B.Sc Sir after a few days of introduction

Akram Sir said, "Javed, I like both the school and the way it is being managed, earning a sustained reputation. The community appears to be good too. Everything, including proximity to my home, is favorable for me. The element of proximity is very important for two reasons: the ailing and old age-related parental problem is one known to many, but there is a second one too that is emotionally very germane for me. From that standpoint, the school location is ideal. But I have encountered a significant drawback and that relates to food. Over the last few days, I tried options locally available, and nothing appears to meet minimum expectations. I am thus in a dilemma as to what to do?"

Having said so, Akram Sir looked at the undefined horizon probably either as a chronicling point of his frustration or seeking an elucidation from the divinity. Seeing that and the agony evident in the facial expressions of Akram Sir, Javed innocuously said, "Sir, my late father, after the sad demise of Mother, developed a sudden trait of loading me with heavy words and statements beyond my compression at that stage of my growing up. Nevertheless, as a mark of obedience and display of respect, I made it a point to internalize many of them. That apparently made him happy as I could sense. My occasional queries as to the implications or relevancies of many of his sayings or words would be reflected with glee in his face full of pride. He repeatedly said, 'Son, always remember that problems are part of life, but the most uplifting datum of that fact is that in many situations, the outcomes far outweigh the problems that caused initial despair and irritation.' Most of our theoretical interactions would end with equally puzzling abridgments. With the passage of time, I started living with those while enjoying them likewise. The focus remained to remember them as much as possible."

At that stage, Akram Sir intervened, saying, "Hamid Ullah Sir told me in detail about your family, especially your illustrious late lamented father and your current status. That, as I could understand later on, was premised on introducing you as a bright student to me with a commitment to my special need-based attention in guiding and teaching you so that you can excel in the ensuing SSC examination, earning in the process kudos for the school. Based on his earnestness and focus, I do not have any doubt that he was not just discharging his responsibilities as a headmaster but doing something extra more as obligations emanating from his association and deep-rooted bond with your father. I gave him my word. So whenever you need any help in the process of preparing yourself for the upcoming examination, whether it is math or any other subject, please feel free to come to me, and I will do my best to respond to your need."

Javed thanked Akram Sir profusely and expressed his indebtedness for the former's readiness to help him as needed. However, he had a query about which some sort of clarity was needed from Akram Sir for better understanding before leaving.

Considering the present setting and the informal pattern of discourses both had in the immediate past, Javed, taking time and notwithstanding the innate hesitation, opened up, saying, "Sir, in initiating your oration about the problem you are having in settling down here, mention was made about having two factors that determine your motivation while looking for a place of opportunity. The first one you had already mentioned is understood. I am somewhat inquisitive to know about the taciturn second one if that is not very cloistered or delicate."

Akram Sir was instantly enthralled by that query from a student of class ten, especially as that enormously relates to the course of their exchanges. He was singularly impressed by Javed's attention to his words and statements. Akram Sir had no doubt about the veracity of the superlatives Hamid Ullah Sir used in floating Javed's case for need-based help from the former in preparing for the upcoming SSC examination.

Observing Javed's facial reflexes and restless inquisitiveness in the set of his innocent eyes, Akram Sir instantly re-engaged, and said, "The subject that I have in mind is neither sequestered nor sensitive. It is, in a sense, both personal and public, depending on the location of information sharing.

"About six months back and against the backdrop of subsumed high ambition and plan premised on excellent performance in my latest B.Sc examination, I precipitously got married contrary to my plan and ambition. Moments before that prodigious decision, I never envisaged to get married so soon.

"From my flank, I decided to marry a young (by rural standard) girl to retrieve her from a socially embarrassing condition as the groom party withdrew from the planned marriage setting. That was no fault of the girl—

the daughter of my reclusive father's dearest friend. In that emotionally heightened condition and milieu, I momentarily shredded all my academic and intellectual ambitions and plans and decided to marry that girl to save her from social humiliation. There were two pertinent other reasons motivating me to take that impulsive decision and they were to save her family from gossip-based mortifications and give solace to my father for his inadvertent role in that catastrophe.

"In that chronicle, my ever-reserved, calm, and less loquacious father had a significant role. Being a reclusive personality, he, notwithstanding being a warm husband and loving father, has a few friends. Among the few acquaintances, he is very close to Choudhury Saheeb of Dhakkin

Para, an upscale rural settlement about fifteen minutes' walk from our home.

"The home of the Choudhurys was suddenly engulfed with activities. The premise of that happiness was the ensuing wedding of Choudhury's only daughter with the graduate son of Khan Bari of Bolorampur enclave.

"Both Mother and myself, like some others of the community, extended needed help and support to ensure a wedding event of distinction in that community. Father was most of the time in Choudhury Shaheb's abode, sitting and observing the preparations underway, and quietly passing on some suggestions to the latter. His other preoccupations were chewing *pan* (betel leaf preparation), pupping of the *hukkah* (hubble bubble), and occasionally seeping hot tea while there. He indulged in all these pastimes and enjoyed them, more due to the absence of my mother in that locale.

"Choudhury's abode cogently wore a festive ambiance as the wedding date drew close. Like a few others, that exhilaration traveled to our home too with respect to the preparation of different types of pitha (local victuals basically made of rice powder) and occasional cooking of eating items catering to the need of relations and casual guests swarming that house.

The related exhilaration reached its peak in our house on the wedding morning as Father wanted to be the first person to greet Choudhury Saheeb that early noontime besides having a seat next to him. Putting on his brand-new brocade *sherwani* (elegant Muslim male attire), with the backdrop of light yellow and mild green small leaves, Father was moving with excitement and impetuosity hurrying us up.

"The groom's party arrived about two hours later than the agreed time. The reception nevertheless was all espousal, with the hilarious participation of both families. Enjoyment was all ubiquitous. My ever-reserved father's joy was palpable in the involuntary smile of his facial impulses. Choudhury Saheeb was all jubilant while extending desired courtesies to the groom's party. He was being extra careful about compliance with socially desirable hospitality traits. Then the most unexpected thingamajig happened, even though the start by all standards was an amiable one.

"As official wedding rituals were to take place and the local *kazi* (marriage registrar) took seat on the right-hand side of the groom, the senior brother-in-law of the groom suddenly said, 'Before the wedding is performed, we would like to have a preview of the gold ornaments, both in terms of weight and finish, agreed during *pacca kotha* (engagement).'

"That took everyone by surprise and shock, more so as it came from someone close and relevant as the senior brother-in-law of the groom.

"Choudhury Saheeb, irrespective of the inherent negative nuance of the garish proposition of the brother-in-law, put up a semblance of casualness in his facial expressions and politely said, 'All promises and commitments made during pacca kotha are being and will be honored. Yours is a respectable family. This abode also enjoys an unparallelled good name in this community. Thus, instead of digressing on peripheral issues, let us proceed to finalize the nikha.'

"Apparently, the matter was not as simple or straight as Choudhury Shaheb would perceive it to be. Subsequent exchanges between the groom's entourage and bride's family members made the problem more delicate and complicated with respective perception of prestige at stake.

"At that stage of tension and temper, the paternal uncle of the groom's father, the revered and most senior entourage member, made a fatal intervention saying, 'What we are requiring is very simple. Instances are multiple where the bride's side cheats both in terms weight and quality of ornaments. We have with us a jeweler who will undertake the required assessment publicly, thus putting a permanent seal on probable controversy later on. It is good for both sides. There is no scope for further discussion.'

"That conclusive testimonial of the most revered member of the groom's party was too much for Choudhury Shaheb to handle. He was dumbfounded. A sense of absolute quietness befell and engulfed the venue. Tension started mounting on both sides.

"Taking his seat on the chair adjacent to that of Father, Choudhury Saheeb mildly took possession of the right hand of the former and involuntarily pressed it.

"That unwittingly triggered some disconcerting immediate impulses in my father. Like a lion getting up from a broken siesta, he, in a most uncharacteristic trait of his persona, roared, and said, 'What a relationship we are about to have where trust and sincerity are to be the subject of third party's evaluation. If that is the case, then we better . . .,' and he suffered a stroke with full body dysfunctional. Miraculously, his brain, eyesight, and facial impulses were modestly functional.

"The joy and merriment of Choudhury Bari and those around took a grim look with the quiet withdrawal of the groom's party following the dictum of the senior most in that group.

"Most men were busy in caring for and nursing my father. Some rushed out to get a doctor or a compounder or a *kobiraj* (people traditionally practicing ayurveda) soonest.

"In the inner court of the house, it was a mix of silent crying, some wailing, and a few lamentations with my mother and some like her exerting efforts in consoling the wife and sisters of both father's and mother's side. The bride, Mehruba, shredded off all makeup, changed her ornamental saree into the usual one, and sat by the side of a wooden ornamental post inherited from the grandfather. Resting her head by the nearest side of that column, she surprisingly was in a stable and firm mood directing household helps as necessary, including serving the grieving mother lebur sharbat (lemon drink).

"I was bewildered initially but took no time to recover. Looking at the wide-open noontime blue sky having patches of clouds sparingly, I scanned my life and my priority of living, and unequivocally decided on my destiny. The instant realization of mine was to liberate Father from any mental anguish that he might succumb to having both the feeling and burden that his loud and roaring responses to the dirty utterances of the groom's party caused the breakup of the wedding proposal.

"Considering all ramifications, I promptly decided on my destiny and decided to marry Mehruba on that day and in that environment. I called Mother, took her to a corner of the abode, explained what I had in mind, and sought her permission and blessing in marrying Mehruba. I also opined that this action of mine may possibly be the best antidote to help the process of Father's possible recovery, and early too.

"Mother had a straight look at me and, with a dawdled wink of her eyelashes, drew me close to her chest with flowing teardrops, kissed my head profusely saying, 'I would spare no effort or flout any direction of treatment for his full recovery. The possibility is greater and the physician from the district headquarters opined in favor of such an outcome, taking annotation of the stable status of his brain, face, and eye. That was relieving information against the backdrop of unexpected happenings of the day. And that made me somewhat relaxed.

"But what you just said is beyond any anticipation. More so, I have a clear perception of your ambition to excel in higher learning. I always have been dismayed by your decision to stay close to our setting to take care of us in our old days. But what a turn of events: your present proposition not only helps you to stay on your preferred path without polemic. This is going to help the course of relieving the mental agony of your dear father, save the Ijjat of an innocent girl whom we adore too, and usher a sense of renewed respectability to a renowned house of the locality. What can I do to proclaim that 'this is my day.' I am proud beyond imaginable comprehension of being the mother of a son of your mettle. Your proposed decision and proposition are monumental from all possible angles. My blessings are instinctive, and my happiness is ponderous. But we need to get the consent of Mehruba's parents first before seeking your father's blessings.'

"Mother first talked to the distraught mother of Mehruba. On hearing the most unanticipated proposition, the instantaneous response of Mehruba's mother was to cry incessantly with hiccups and then surrender herself to the embrace of Mother. Seeing that affirmative indication, I hurriedly went to our home, sent my second uncle to get Kazi Shaheb, finished my bath and required ablution, put on a pajama and kurta, and started for Mehbuba's home with my cap in hand.

"During that intervening period, both mothers went to the space of Mehruba, appraising her of the proposition they have in mind and sought her consent. On hearing the most unanticipated proposition, a prospect she always nurtured with tranquility in the inner court of her cognizance, Mehruba was astounded and looked at both mothers forthright. She took her time to absorb the most unexpected reality.

"On being pushed by Mother, Mehruba, placing her hand around grandfather's favorite post she was reclining so far, stood slowly in a shivering stance, placed traditional *ghomta* (veil) by extending her *anchal* (tail end of a saree when put on), and performed salam (traditional way of seeking blessings by touching feet of elders).

"She performed that quietly first with her mother, followed by Mother. The most impetuous feature of that was after finishing the process of the last salam, Mehruba involuntarily surrendered herself on the chest of Mother, clinching Mother's back as firmly as she could lest it too slips away.

"That taciturn pose continued for a while. In initiating the disengagement process, Mehruba slowly opened her eyes and was pleasantly surprised to see me standing quietly with a cap on. Emotionally heightened, she left Mother gracefully and took shelter behind her mother.

"All of us guardedly moved to the main room where Father was lying in the master bed, mostly immobile and uncommunicative. A few youths in the surroundings were massaging his body tenderly as per the advice of the local physician while steps were being taken to move him to the district civil hospital.

"Incongruous was the position of Chowdhury Saheeb. As a reflection of his mortification and displeasure for things happening in his abode, and that too in his lifetime, he positioned himself on the easy chair and covered his face with a pillow. That conceivably was a despairing attempt by him to hide from reality.

"Mehruba's mother cautiously moved close to her father, and softly said, 'Akram's mother is here to talk to you.'

"That instantly caused an impulsive riposte, and Choudhury Saheb promptly removed the pillow, straightened himself with a predominant presence of embarrassment shadowing his persona, and politely said 'slamalaikum' with focus on the floor.

"Mother responded by saying, 'Walikum Salam,' and then went to the bedside where Father was being laid out in a motionless condition. She silently put her hand on his forehead and held that for a few moments. Father closed his eyes, a first-time solo act since the stroke.

That made attending volunteers very contented while no one knew what she communicated and what he understood.

"Mother then approached Choudhury Saheeb saying, 'Bhai Saheeb, I am here with my solemn proposition seeking the hands of Ma (akin to mother) Mehruba for our son Akram. This proposal of mine has the endorsement of all present here. I got the silent sanction of Akram's father.'

"The immediate reaction of Choudhury Saheeb was the spontaneous flow of involuntary tears with hiccups. However, he spared no time in raising his two hands toward the divine authority, expressing his earnest gratitude for all that were happening, so positively and so quickly.

"Choudhury Saheeb then embraced Akram to the delight of all present. Holding the hand of Akram, he moved toward Mehruba, put his two hands on their two heads, and blessed the couple.

"As the second uncle was going to get Kazi Shaheb, the news of Akram marrying Mehbuba spread at titanic speed. Thus, when the second uncle arrived with Kazi Shaheb, a stream of friends, well-wishers, and supportive community members surrounded the *uttan* (akin to a courtyard).

"The religious rite was carried out promptly, and all present were joyfully entertained with a specially cooked early dinner that was supposed to be a lunch with the involvement of different sets of people. The exhilaration of Choudhury Saheeb was beyond comprehension: a mix of joy, contentment, and excitement, being occasionally both steadfast and perplexed. A sense of ubiquitous euphoria was overwhelming in and around his abode. The community at large was in merriment, with kudos showered by all and sundry.

"Concurrently, Akram, along with Mehruba, Mother, and mother-in-law went to the temporary bedside of the father, and the couple silently performed salam, a socially desired act of Muslims. With eyes open, Father spotted their movement and acts and slowly raised the lower end of his left hand, indicating blessings.

"A set of local well-wishers and relations of Choudhary Saheeb were engaged in moving Akram's Father to the district hospital, and they did it smoothly without further loss of time.

"The sun was already set. Darkness engulfed the local conditions and surroundings. Preparations were, undertaken for the prompt departure of the new couple for the groom's home in the company of Akram's mother.

"Since the bride was wearing jewelry and had other accompanying valuables, it was decided that they would be escorted by some friends and relations to ensure safety.

"The two rickshaws carrying the bride and groom as well as Mother were slowly being dragged rather than pulled, having well-wishers around. Soon it joyously became almost a mini procession with prodigious hilarity.

"Getting down from the rickshaw, Mother escorted Mehruba toward the entrance door while Akram and his second uncle thanked everyone for their spontaneous help. They then followed Mother and Mehruba, keeping one rickshaw waiting.

"Positioning herself before the entrance door, Mother paused for a second, got her bunch of keys by unknotting the rear end of her saree's anchal (a traditional way to safe-keep keys), and handed them over to Mehruba saying, 'From today, you are the custodian of these keys—this home, its prestige, respect, and nobility. I am not abdicating but would devote most of my time to taking care of your father-in-law.'

"Saying those farsighted words, Mother, in the company of the second uncle, left for the hospital to be by Father's side. We thus started our precipitous conjugal life in a most atypical fashion and setting.

"You are not expected at this stage of life to understand certain social nuances. That, among others, applied to handing over a bunch of keys. Traditionally, the bunch of keys is the sublime representation of family power and authority. Often it becomes a serious issue impacting family rapport. It was thus significant from varied perspectives, and more so in the case of Mehruba. The relevance of such an unanticipated act from Mother is premised on circumstances the former became the daughter-in-law of this home.

"This long oration is in response to your short but very relevant query. Had my marital status been told upfront by my uncle, it would have been information as getting married after graduation is more than normal. As the said information is now being passed on based on specific queries, people probably could be inclined to look at that from varied angles, as the rural and semi-urban practice normally is.

"I have narrated the details not just to share information but for you to have a clear perception as to who I am, and the values I uphold.

"I am conscious of the fact that what I articulated in terms of choice and value is not applicable in your case as you do not have parents alive. The extent and focus of your priority in life currently center around your own progression and your sisters. As you grow up, this possibly will wane away as you will have new aspirations, and they will have new priorities. I hope that what I said will never be applicable in your life but if that happens, you will find solace, as relevant, from my life experiences and decisions.

"At this point, something is dawdling me internally. I have the inner pressure to share that with you.

"What I have in mind is quite mundane but there are deep-rooted implications to influence and shape a life. I am detailing that for you to remember as you are doing with respect to many sayings of your late father. It may or may not be of relevance in your life, but remembering that will not have any bad insinuation. Always ruminate that nothing in life, for that matter in this world, is static. Factors are likely to change. Implications may be at variance, but the essence remains the same.

"When I took the sudden decision to marry Mehruba, it was obvious to me that I would be her thought guardian and would have significant responsibility in guiding her with respect to connubial relationships, family matters, and social behavior.

"But what a turn of events and experiences in life. Mehruba showed her special mettle pertaining to all earthly and social matters within a short time, and everyone in the family has been looking to her for opinions and decisions. That surprisingly applied in the case of Mother too, who ran the family single-handedly during all the past years. She even had a consultation with Mehruba about Father's treatment, including matters related to moving him from hospital to home.

"I have had been surprised by that initially but soon realized, with the passage of time, that I myself am getting more comfort and assurance having discussions with her even with respect to matters ordinarily considered outside her known competence. It is such a feeling that is molding me to be around Mehruba and be in touch with her.

"The lesson I learned is that it is both folly and unwise to understate women just by age or educational attainments. They are gifted by the divinity with a special sixth sense to reign over family life, besides other attributes.

"I do not feel bad or sad either. Rather, I am happy and proud of such a realization in the early phase of our conjugal life. This simultaneously ushered a relationship between us based on respect and feelings, which in modern open expression one can say not only to be loved but 'true love.'"

That informal conversation between the new teacher and a recognized student of the senior class came to an unexpected closure as another guardian came to meet the new teacher.

The open and unbiased mind of incipient youth Javed continued to be silently roaming around the unpredictable turn of events in Akram Sir's still emerging life and the series of life-related decisions he had taken without hesitation or remorse. Besides academic excellence, about which he already had a grueling insight, Javed was certain of Akram Sir being bestowed with a prodigious mindset of enormous latitude that propelled his young self to take all recent decisions and actions likely to have ramifications in all his future turn of bends in life.

Akram Sir's earlier decision to be around elderly parents to take loving care of them was an emotional one, perhaps premised on surrounding experiences, and needed to be respected. But Javed was somewhat dismayed by his decision to sacrifice his quest for learning in a bend of life full of openings and opportunities.

He recalled what Akram Sir explained in his related preceding query of justification for sacrificing his own endeared focus in life till recently.

Without any pause or hesitation, Akram Sir replied, saying, "I am neither a philosopher nor an intellectual. I see life as it is even though in an intangible form and I am at ease with that. My subsequent narration with respect to your query should be taken and evaluated from that perspective.

"In life, it is very imperative to distinguish between expectation and happiness. The expectation is desire without boundary. Happiness, on the other hand, is a state of mind and realization reconciling with reality, however minimal it may be.

"One can hunt desire, but one should not chase happiness unwittingly. There will always be ample reasons for one to feel shortchanged in terms of desire, but that should not be a reason for being unhappy.

"And that is my position. Even at this young age, I have learned to be gladdened with what I can attain irrespective of my cherished desire otherwise.

"To be by the side of parents and be able to take care of them has always been my cherished desire. Getting married to Mehruba is a fulfilling step toward that. I do not see that as an impediment but more as an opportunity. That makes me happy.

"In addition, a satiating married life is likely to be supportive of my inner quest for learning. My inclination for a teaching career will definitely be of significant relevance relating to that journey for learning. This is me."

While walking back to Amin's abode, he was deeply engrossed in analyzing the varied statements of Akram Sir but was unable to comprehend most of them. He slowed down his walking pace, took some respite near the side of the local dighi, and then slowly resumed his stride. Suddenly, something quivered his thinking. He came to the nippy conclusion that he had the key to solving the irresistible problem that was upsetting Akram Sir.

Because of such thought and realizing that he was getting late for the usual coaching of Amin, Javed enhanced his walking speed only to find that Amin had finished his dinner earlier, having been exhausted from playing various games with friends, and went to bed with the help of Hiron.

Javed was somewhat disorganized and inattentive while having his dinner. Khala noted the same and was worried within herself as she knew that Akram Sir called Javed for a meeting. All sorts of ominous thinking were pervasive in her mind. She could not hold it any longer and straightway asked Javed, "Is everything okay? What did Akram Sir say to you? Is anything bothering you?"

That was the opening Javed was looking for. He looked at his favorite Khala, smiled a bit, and said, "Yes, something is really bothering me. But I am confident that you trust me. With that backdrop, I solemnly assure you that what I have in mind is for the good of the family, more particularly Amin in the long run."

That discourse started when Javed was in the initial phase of his dinner, and resultantly it prolonged.

Rahmat Bepari joined that unfinished dinner and listened minutely to what Javed, detailed based on his discourse with Akram Sir.

After summarily recalling Akram Sir's life experience and actions, including his wedding, Javed referred to the real essence of who Akram Sir is to warrant his highest reverence. He said, "Akram Sir frankly told me that he is neither a philosopher nor an intellectual. To my assessment, he is an ardent thinker, quick in understanding, prompt in decision-making, and absolutely solid in adhering to those. He is a man of principle, a man of commitment, and a man honest to himself and his surroundings."

Rahmat Bepari interjected at that stage saying, "Beta (son), since I joined you for dinner, you are only talking and not eating. If that trend continues, it would mean that I, as the last one to join for dinner, will be the first one to finish. That sort of reality is contrary to our practices. So you may talk but also eat, paving the way for me to have a full dinner. I am quite hungry too." Everybody laughed.

Javed however became overserious in placing a proposition that he had in mind since finishing the discourse with Akram Sir. Drawing the special attention of both Khala and Rahmat Bepari, Javed thankfully and politely said, "Yes, it is a fact that both of you have taken me and treated me as a son. I too respect you both and will do everything to uphold the essence and values of this home. But the reality is, I am physically with you all in this home for another five to six months. Then I am going to pursue higher studies with occasional visits. Thus, I need to find someone who can suitably be my substitute in coaching and guiding our dear Amin. I have been looking for that but could not identify anyone as yet.

"In that setting, I came across Akram Sir and bonded with him very quickly and dearly. In this short time, I have a complete assessment and idea about Akram Sir and his future life focus.

"Considering everything, I have no hesitation in recommending Akram Sir to take my place once I am gone. There are many plus points in this proposition: he is a well-educated, considerate, and well-thought-out person with clarity about his ambition and focus. His goal is teaching and learning with a commitment to be near his home, enabling him to take care of his parents. He has just married and committed to conjugal living. He can be of long-term help to you both and an effective guide in the growing-up process of Amin. If you trust me and agree, this will be a very positive solution to a major problem that we are soon to face.

"The other side of this proposal is equally attractive. It helps Akram Sir to make a positive decision about his job here in close proximity to his home and alleviate the recurring food problem that he is currently encountering.

"By all consideration, he is a family man with remarkable intellect. I am certain that both you and Amin will be equally comfortable and benefitted. And if my suggestion works out, it may be of long-term benefit to all concerned.

"I have not hinted anything to Akram Sir as to my present proposition without your consent. It is thus still a personal idea. It all depends on you both."

Tahera and Rahmat Bepari kept quiet for a while, more as a space to digest what Javed just said. Taking their own time, they exchanged looks with each other, and then Tahera Khala opened up, saying, "The issue of your imminent leaving this abode for much cherished higher studies has been looming in my mind for quite a while. I even raised the issue a number of times with Bepari Shaheb in the immediate past, and his standard response was ' rest assured, Javed will take care of it'."

After saying that, Khala kept quiet momentarily while Bepari Saheeb finished his usual drill of drinking a glass of milk, a post-dinner ritual, as Javed harbored anxiety within himself. That was evident from Javed's whirling of rice and curry time and again without putting that in his mouth.

Observing that, Khala resumed her oration saying, "Bepari Saheeb's prophetic avowal and your most explicit proposition contentedly matched very candidly. Before we articulate our position with respect to your proposition, I would like to restate our most cherished feeling about our relationship: We have taken you as a son devoid of any implications and you will always remain so, wherever you are and irrespective of your all-round attainments for which we will pray to Allahpak after performing daily namaz. And our firm conviction of Amin being an Amanat under your love and care will always bloom. We do not have more to add to this.

"The time period you alluded to in your statement is not that material for us. But your Akram Sir has an immediate problem with respect to his daily food with possible multiple negative implications. To obviate that, I would like to propose that you talk to him immediately suggesting the option you have in mind. On our behalf, you need to request his immediate consideration and action to move to our place.

"We need someone in five to six months to fill up your eventual vacant place. But if it is someone like Akram Sir, we can accommodate him with immediate effect.

"I quickly thought through the likely arrangement. As our son, you would move to the main house and share the room with Amin. We will put a separate *choki* (wooden rudimentary bed) for you in that room with support facilities. In the future too, that will be your place whenever you are here. Akram Sir will be the new occupant in your present place."

Javed responded with a mix of happiness and embarrassment saying, "It is so gratifying but your unequivocal trust in what I assessed and indicated is too much for me to bear. I take the affirmative decision as it is but still would suggest that both of you meet Akram Sir and talk to him before the seal of finality is embossed. That will relieve me of potential burden."

JAHED RAHMAN

With an impish smile adoring his face, and a white flowing beard and scanty salt-and-pepper hair mostly covered by a round cotton cap on his head, Rahmat Bepari said, "Beta, as you are aware, I am in the business of trading. In dealing with people, I have acquired an attribute to read a mind beyond his words. Even though our communications have never been that intense, I know who you are and the quality of your persona. There is thus no need to crosscheck what you are saying or proposing."

Adding a subtle comment, Tahera Khala said, "I fully agree with what Bepari Saheeb just alluded. I also appreciate your concern. In response to your agony and to mitigate any sense of likely burden, I suggest you discuss with Akram Sir the present proposition more as an option that you have in mind after discussing with us his predicament. If he is amenable, then convey to him our invitation for tea next Friday afternoon. As discussions shape up favorably, which we are certain to be, then we will place the proposal for him to decide. That takes care of everybody."

The very thoughtful interpretation of Khala was very helpful but could not relieve Javed entirely. In essence, it implies an additional mouth to be fed for about five months. Being at the center of the equation, Javed suffered from a sense of guilt. On being pursued for his continued sense of uneasiness, he could not hold it longer and spelled out his ongoing reason for discomfort.

While Rahmat Bepari unleashed the puff of his huqqa in a relaxed mood, Tahera Khala took that specific feeling of Javed seriously. She said, "Beta, always remember that when one shares his ability and ingenuity, those never diminish. And we are doing that for a return that brings our one son closer to us physically and the other son likely to grow as a better human being. You are not forcing anything on us. So be at ease."

The resultant progression was spontaneous. Akram Sir happily moved to the Bepari abode, and Javed relocated to the main home under the care and support of Hiron, and somewhat watchful observation of that transition by Amin.

Lying on the bed in his new setting, Javed was both blissful and prying. He was happy that his sporadic thinking paved the way to solve a rambling problem that Akram Sir had and assured a sustained arrangement for the teaching and guiding of Amin, a cause of primacy and prominence, both for himself and Khala's family.

Thinking about his own identity, he could not help but laugh. As life began, he was popularly known as "the son of Zakir Mia." With the passage of about two and a half years, with Father dead, and being in a relatively new setting, he is now commonly known as a bright student in his school and the resident teacher of Rahmat Bepari's home.

In essence, he remained what he was with a new reality predominating. He cherished his past even though loaded with emotions. Equally, he is enjoying the present with copious challenges and opportunities. Life with all its mystics moved on.

SHIELD

EVERYONE REALIZES THAT life's inherent reality is death. Even though uncertain of that mark, individuals wish to live longer irrespective of experience of its quality—premised on power, prestige, or poverty. But the less-talked-about and most silent element is perhaps the fear of the unknown—from the familiar setting to something unspecified.

Notwithstanding that element of fear, people generally enjoy life, notwithstanding the unpredictable nature of its journey and its challenges. In a complicated setting of desires and frustrations, the pursuit of life is generally enjoyed mostly because of inherent improbabilities. That happened in Javed's situation.

In his case and the context of the critical Secondary School Certificate (SSC) examination conducted by the autonomous board, Javed, generally known as a very accomplished student, was expected to earn kudos for himself and his school.

Javed was aware of the impending announcement of the SSC results but was more concerned about the upcoming reality involving his relocation to Dhaka for a better exposition and challenging higher learning.

He took a break from that anguish and started playing Ludo with Amin while sitting under their favorite mango tree at home, enjoying both the shade and breeze.

Right at that moment, and most unexpectedly, Rahmat Bepari showed up in the company of Hamid Ullah Sir and Akram Sir. Most home occupants were astounded. The reactions of Javed and Amin were limited to general inquisitiveness.

Tahera Khala was astounded. Her steel-faced facial expression conveyed an inherent anxiety of extreme implications than any word or inquisition could do.

Noting all these at random, Hamid Ullah Sir promptly stated, "Sister Tahera, there is nothing to be worried about. I came back from district headquarters this noon with remarkable news that our dear Javed topped the district-level SSC examination, and board-wise, his position is seventh. This is a remarkable achievement, and we are so happy and proud of him. Equally, your trust in me and the generosity you bestowed on Javed, giving him a feeling of home, are remarkable. I am personally grateful to you both.

"Because of that feeling, I went to Rhamat Bepari Saheeb in the company of Akram Sir to share the good news. What surprised both of us was that Bepari Saheeb was not only delighted but equally gracious to entertain his staff with sweets and drinks, sending one staff with spare rickshaws to bring Fyruz, Fatipa, and Rafisa, along with the toddler grandson, without divulging the news, and ordering sweets to be delivered to home.

"All these impressed us very much. However, we were taken aback when he volunteered to accompany us on our journey home to divulge the news. No pressure was applied on him. It was a Suo motto decision, bringing out the passion in a Bepari mind for learning. I could sense the genesis of his inherent desire to have a good in-house tutor for Amin. I pray to Allahpak that our dear Amin shapes up akin to Javed under the care and guidance of Akram Sir."

The reaction of Tahera Khala was unique. She moved and bent near Javed, and intensely hugged him, transmitting the sincerest feelings of a mother for the achievement of her son. At that moment, Javed felt like his mother, Ambia, was hugging him.

In the whole process, Javed was in a state of daze—happy for what he achieved; depressed for the absence of his beloved father who had guided him meaningfully even for a brief period; the unqualified love of Tahera Khala; and the most meaningful time he shared with Amin in helping the latter in pursuing his early life. Within himself, he also recalled momentarily the contribution of Hamid Ullah Sir, sisters Fatipa and Rafisa, brother-in-law Fyruz, and that of Rahmat Bepari and Nazir Bhai in his life that far with the inner resolution for a more meaningful progression in the future. Consequently, his outward reflections were relatively minimal.

In response to Hamid Ullah Sir's happy inquisition about his own reflex regarding achievement, Javed regained his senses and stood up courteously, only to bend slowly to salam (showing respect and seeking good wishes for the future) by touching Khala's feet. This was repeated in the cases of Hamid Ullah Sir, Rahmat Bepari, and Akram Sir.

As Javed was about to bend to salam Akram Sir, the latter promptly held the former's hands, drawing him closer to his chest saying, "Your place is here. You lived up to the trust that Hamid Ullah Sir reposed in you, and I promise to live up to your trust reposed in me so far as guiding Amin is concerned."

That coincided with the arrival of three rickshaws: two carrying the anxious family members of Javed and the third one having the delivery of sweets earlier ordered by Rahmat Bepari Saheeb.

As grim-faced family members were alighting from rickshaws, Javed rushed to divulge the news of his academic prowess. While Fatipa embraced him with tears of joy flowing, Rafisa had a mixed expression of joy and sorrow, the latter due to reflecting on the ordained absence of his parents. Fyruz, while holding the baby boy, escorted them all to join the other segment of the extended family.

The merriment was total and complete in all respects with both mother Ambia and father Zakir Khan being omnipresent in that episode. Equal was the expression of gratitude to the family of Rahmat Bepari Saheeb and Tahera Khala by Fatipa for making Javed at ease in all respects in initial unfamiliar location and new way of life. The kudos were unending with gratitude, love, and respect highlighted by Fatipa and responded to by Tahera Khala with equal zest. Khala was determined to stress that even though Javed's location in the Bepari home was the outcome of a very sad episode, it is her home and the family who are the greatest beneficiaries. She insisted on how lucky they were to have Javed in their home, more as a family member. Khala continued her oration, saying, "The process was easy and without stress due to the high tradition and values that were practiced by the late

Zakir Mia's family and unanimously acclaimed by the community." She paused.

Taking advantage of that lull, Fyruz intervened, saying, "In our effort to thank each other, we certainly are bypassing, if not ignoring, the most relevant individual in that game plan. Our two families, expressly Javed, are to be eternally grateful to the revered Hamid Ullah Sir for all his efforts in connecting two ends of respective need, the fruit of which we all are enjoying in this assembly."

Availing that opening, Hamid Ullah Sir interjected, saying, "I always had trust in Javed's competence. We all, including the relevant two families and the school faculty, per se, played our respective roles, and Javed delivered.

"But we should not be oblivious to sister Tahera's significant sustained role from the beginning to the end. It is she who encouraged Bepari Shaheb to talk to me. It is she who had embraced Javed as her own. It is she who, by her sheer sincerity and love, easily won over Javed's earlier focus to cultivate a formal relationship with the family of his future residence. All these contributed to what we are celebrating now in the memory of brother Zakir Mia, who is ever-ubiquitous."

Time passed by. Noting this, Tahera Khala opined that it was already past evening and it would not be advisable for the visiting Fatipa family to return that night. She suggested that everybody stay back for dinner while Fyruz beta (son), Fatipa, and Rafisa would share sleeping arrangements with them, however inconvenient it might be.

That was agreed to, even though some initial resistance and hesitation typified the decision process. All were relaxed. Tahera Khala returned to the kitchen and asked ever-efficient Hiron to slaughter two chickens from their domestic captive setting with the help of Javed. Rafisa unrestingly moved in to help Khala.

The dinner, even though very late by local standards, was enjoyed by all. The atmosphere returned to normalcy with the accomplishment of dinner service.

That satisfaction element was heightened by the simple comment of Fyruz stating, "In spite of the delay, this dinner bears special significance as being the maiden joint eaten by the two families under one roof, cementing the already existing relationship." All present concurred.

As tea and pan were served, and Rafisa joined the group, Hamid Ullah Sir commenced to unleash what he had in mind. He said, "To my judgment, both the setting and the time are apposite to discuss matters of relevance so far Javed's progression is concerned. Being a friend of the late Zakir Mia and a well-wisher of the family, I would like to put forward my two propositions for your information and consideration. These relate to Javed's pursuit of higher learning and his immediate focus on study.

"On the first issue, and to my judgment, it should definitely be Dhaka matching his intellect and opportunity for quality learning. But that has a caveat: Someone from the family should accompany him to settle him properly into his new environment.

"The other issue I have in mind pertains to the focus of his study. He is eminently qualified to pursue any field of study of his choosing. But I would suggest, and to begin with, at the intermediate level, that he opts for science as a field of study. He would spend two preparatory years before pursuing a higher field of learning at the graduate level. That will be years of exposition and experience with a better assessment of his interest and focus. After finishing his intermediate level, he can decide to continue with science or move to other areas of interest such as arts and commerce. But the reversion is not possible. This needs to be kept in view.

"The other reason for suggesting science is rooted in my understanding of who Javed is! Each word of his before the decision is taken for him to be located in this home rings in my years. His utmost desire is to be self-reliant and self-supporting. Academic achievement helps him in that process. He will get a scholarship from the government as well as a merit scholarship from our Zella (district) Council being the acclaimed student of the district. So immediate financing will not be an issue. As I know him, Javed will not stop there. He has an inherent desire to buy back Zakir Mia's home and accumulate the needed funds as soon as he can. He is likely to pursue that, however minimal it may be. I foresee his continuous involvement in private tutoring, and a science background will be very helpful in that regard.

"That is what I have in mind. I just place it before you all, Javed's siblings and well-wishers, for consideration. You can take time and decide."

An unexpected silence pervaded. Surprisingly, it was Javed who reacted instinctively. He promptly said, "While the matter of someone accompanying me to Dhaka is for the family to decide, I fully agree with what Sir has just stipulated about my immediate engagement and involvement in pursuing learning. I am also of the view that probable private tuition will be a positive diversion in a setting that is unfamiliar to me."

Javed's aforesaid stipulations relieved all and avoided unnecessary discourse. Fyruz brought it to a definite closing by volunteering to accompany Javed to Dhaka for all guidance and needed initial support assistance.

Taking note of all these, Hamid Ullah Sir further said, "My very dear university friend, Ajmat Beg, is presently the vice principal of the Government College in Dhaka. Though we do not communicate that regularly, our bond and friendship have remained intact. I will write a letter to him introducing Javed with a request to take care of the latter in all matters of concern and progressions. That letter will, of course, be hand carried by Javed. I am sure that my friend will do his utmost in honoring my desires."

At this point, even the habitual introverted person Rahmat Bepari could not remain silent. He expressed his inner joy by saying, "What a day for this house! We all are celebrating in this venue one of the most acclaimed academic achievements with the participation of families and well-wishers. The extraordinary part of it is that even matters about moving forward were decided with no glitch. I only pray that in years down the drain, we will be able to repeat it, celebrating the attainments of dear Amin."

Akram Sir reacted by saying, "Our dear Amin has all the positive attributes: merit, commitment, and focus. I will put my best efforts to guide him. This is my solemn assurance. But we need to be clear in mind that achievements have many dimensions and should not always be identical. There are different routes to success in life. Its type and nature may not always be akin. In essence, the outcome is judged by its impact on society, its relevance to life, and its influence on individuals."

Preparations for travel to Dhaka went as planned. Javed, in the company of Fyruz, left the Bepari house on the scheduled day after seeking blessings from all present, including Fatipa, Rafisa, Hamid Ullah Sir, Akram Sir, Bepari Saheeb, Khala, and, not the least, Hiron and Nazir Bhai.

As they were to take steps out, an unexpected commotion astounded all present. Jumping out of a rickshaw was none but the ever-friendly and vociferous Munira. Khala and Bepari Saheeb were thrilled, and all present were enchanted. Munira, unmindful of the surroundings, rushed to Javed, stood facing him without any discomfort, and handed over one *ganda* (marigold) flower, symbolic of her good wishes and prayers. She opened up, saying, "This is the first one from the plant that grew out of the seed that I planted. Hold it for some time, at least." Saying those words, she moved to her Amma (Tahera) and happily surrendered to her embrace. All present were elated. Javed and Fyruz commenced their journey.

Javed, having been blessed with an inquisitive mind with matching eagerness to know, has had broad impressions about the economic progression at large of Bangladesh and neighboring countries and that of their metropolitan living. He was conscious always that print and photographs may often cause unreal impressions. With that sort of mindset, he landed at the main railway station of Dhaka in the early hours of the morning.

A sense of despair and dismay immediately engulfed him as he was gazing around. Fyruz meanwhile negotiated a deal with one of the competing porters to carry their luggage. Javed was impressed by the performance of Fyruz Bhai considering the prevalent chaos and confusion. That was a great induction for his future life in this metropolitan.

Stepping out of a privately owned residential place during that noontime on their way to the government college, Javed assuredly followed the footsteps of Fyruz. While Fyruz was alert in monitoring and guiding Javed in the chaotic movements of people and rickshaws, the latter had a sort of relaxed mindset, keeping in mind that the Fyruz Bhai visited Dhaka a number of times before, particularly during the wedding with Fatipa-Bu, and is quite familiar with the locale.

Entering the truncated office setting of the private secretary (PS) to the vice principal, Fyruz, with due reverence, said "salam" as a precursor to explaining the purpose of their presence.

The PS was nonchalant and even refrained from looking at visitors. However, he drew their attention toward the vacant chair and an empty pew in that space and asked visitors to sit on them.

In a subtle, relaxed mood, the PS then reclined on his chair, picked up a small towel from the table, and placed a toothpick in the lower setting of his tooth. That appeared to ease his unexplained discomfort. He straightened up to pick up from his table a glass full of water and drank it smoothly.

After finishing all those rituals, the PS looked at the office wall clock affixed to a side wall due to space constraints. It was 1:31 p.m.

The PS then volunteered to say, "My lunchtime is between 1:00 p.m. to 1:30 p.m. Nobody is expected to disturb me during that time. You are lucky that my personal orderly has gone to fetch a specially made cup of tea for me. That enabled you to be inside. Now tell me who you are and what brings you both here?" He had those two queries after looking at them for the first time.

His authoritative query made Javed edgy but Fyruz, having experienced handling government functionaries at a district level, maintained his cool. He started saying, "Sir, before coming to meet you, we took a break in the canteen more to have an idea about the surroundings. Fortunately, our adjacent table was occupied by a few senior students, and they, among others, referred to your position cum office superlatively, highlighting, among others, how efficiently and effectively you run this office, mitigating the burden on the principal's office. That gave me the confidence to enter your office oblivious of the protocol. I am sorry for that."

The PS, bearing a sylphlike smile, had an affirmative expression and politely renewed his earlier quarry. In response to that, Fyruz stated, "I am carrying a letter from revered Hamid Ullah Sir, headmaster of Ghazipur Kallan High School, for respected Vice Principal Shaheb. I was told that they are good friends. Additionally, the letter concerns this young man, Javed, a brilliant student of his school. At Hamid Ullah Sir's behest, I have brought him here. Now it is up to you, Sir, as to when we can meet him."

Hearing the name of Hamid Ullah Sir, the PS realigned himself on his chair, bore a friendly smile, and recalled a short visit by Hamid Ullah Saheeb about one and a half years back. He further said that he was astounded when his Sir, generally known as a reserved person, accompanied Hamid Ullah Saheeb up to his rickshaw while saying, "Khuda Hafeez." This ordinary person followed the Sir to be available for any possible exigencies.

The PS then paused and said, "Sorry, you will have to wait. It is Sir's lunchtime. No one is allowed to meet him at this time. As soon as the time permits, I will deliver the letter to him, and the rest depends on him."

Fyruz promptly responded saying. "Sir, it is so gracious of you. That vouches for why the students were praising your office management while sitting next to our table without knowing who we were."

Silence persisted for some time while Javed was restless, trying to understand the nature and tone of dialogue that was going on between his favorite Fyruz Bhai and the PS. All the signals he received from Fyruz were tantamount to keeping quiet.

The PS opened his momentarily closed eyes, undertook a gargle with a residue of water in the glass, and inquired whether Hamid Ullah Saheeb briefed him about the Vice Principal (VP) Saheeb. Getting a negative response, the PS took the initiative to introduce who the VP was!

He very happily said, "Our VP was to be a principal sometime back. But having a son with autoimmune disease, he is needed in Dhaka and thus had to forego a promotion for the time. Being a brilliant student himself and equally a very distinguished teacher, he has had many talented students, and some of them currently hold important positions in the civil service. He has benefited from that connection. Thus, though officially he is VP, he, in fact, runs the college from a shadow."

He continued saying, "Our Sir is a restrained communicator and does not encourage the unnecessary presence of anyone in his office, and I hope that this information will be helpful to you."

The PS then looked at the wall clock, and it was just past 2:00 p.m. He then asked for the letter.

The PS entered the office of the vice principal (VP) with all the pleasant reflections that he could muster and said, "Sir, there is a visitor carrying this letter from the respected Hamid Ullah Saheeb, headmaster of Gazipur Kallan High School. He has a young man with him too." He then handed over the envelope. The VP opened the envelope promptly and started reading the letter.

As the PS was about to take steps to leave the VP's office, he was politely restrained and asked to stay put while the VP remained engrossed in reading the three-page-long letter. At the end, the VP attuned a serious posture reflecting outside through the wide glass-framed window, and then requested the PS to connect him over the telephone with the principal of the well-known private degree college nearby.

That attempt failed but the PS was smart enough to leave a message for the principal to return the call of the VP. That was okay as the principal of the private degree college was once the junior colleague of the VP.

The VP then instructed the PS to tell the visitors to wait, and that he would call them at the appropriate time. Meanwhile, the PS should ask the orderly of the VP to serve them tea and cookies. The PS noted those and left the office.

The PS returned to his chair in a sort of cheery mood and advised Fyruz as per the instruction of the VP. He then said, "Sir very eagerly and minutely read the letter of Hamid Ullah Saheeb, appeared to reread that, and is engrossed in deep thought. I have never seen him in such a mood. So we are to wait."

Finally, the call came, and both Fyruz and Javed were ushered in politely. The VP stood up and gracefully shook hands with both, conveying a feeling of affinity even though it was their first encounter. He specifically congratulated Javed for his excellent performance in the SSC examination. The VP went further and opined, "Hamid Ullah has a high barrier and by all standards is an illustrious person himself. It is thus a more significant and singular achievement that you could earn his trust and confidence. I am aware of you and your family background from his letter. Let us come straight to the point."

The VP then said, "The life of Hamid Ullah is a unique paradigm of what balance in life could achieve and contrarily lack of it could impair. During our student life, we adored him for his intellect and always presumed for his distinguished achievements in life ahead. His greatest deficiency, as was apparent from subsequent decisions and actions, was his inability to maintain balance in life. Desires outshone the reality in his life while being unable to handle tragedy with which he had neither any involvement nor even remote connection. He withdrew in life and is now the head teacher at your school. But we have neither forgotten him nor slackened our respect for him even though contact and communication have declined. He continues to be a luminary in our hearts. He is still the same old Hamid Ullah, except for his smile.

"I have read his letter and thought through the way I can live up to his expectations. Javed does not need Hamid Ullah's letter for admission to our college. His academic achievements are good enough. I re-read the letter. I have no doubt in mind that in Javed he is perceiving a self that he could not be. Thus, I ephemerally thought through Javed's setting in life with both parents deceased and his will to be self-reliant in life.

"Keeping all these in view, the best option I have in mind for Javed is to get admission to a reputable private college. Intermediate-level education is more a grounding for subsequent higher levels of education, and so one should waste time at this level.

"Our college being a government one is infested with national and local political conflicts. Whatever way one tries, one cannot escape political involvement. Under the current environment, political affiliation is primary, and academic pursuit is secondary in our college.

"I suggest therefore that Javed gets admission to a reputable private college, completes his intermediate-level education with no loss of time, and then decides about his university-level pursuits. There is one about half a mile away from our campus. Located in a residential setting with boarding facilities, it has earned a name for itself.

"The principal is three years junior to both Hamid Ullah and myself, and he has a definite idea as to who Hamid Ullah is. Besides that, we always have mutually respectful contact. I have already talked to him with reference to Hamid Ullah's letter, and both of us, having full agreement with respect to the validity of his assessment, concurred to assist Javed. Keeping in view the high cost of private college education and Javed's current family and financial conditions, the principal assured me that subject to his exchanges with Javed, he can be exempt from 75 percent of the tuition fee. He further said that the budget of his institution has three support financial assistance programs per academic year for needy meritorious students, and fortunately one is still available. The balance can be met by family support, scholarships, and charitable grants.

"Bear in mind that tomorrow both of you have an appointment with Principal Shahdat Asim at 10:00 am. Now wait in the room of my PS. He will give you all the necessary information and direction."

That was a long day, and that too on tea and biscuits solely. Fyruz Bhai suggested an early dinner that evening after having a brief preview of the private college they are to be in tomorrow. Javed concurred readily but internally was engrossed with some other thoughts concerning urban social ethics and etiquette. He was waiting for a suitable space to raise that issue with his dear Fyruz Bhai.

That opportune moment was the time between placing an order for dinner and waiting for service. Taking note of Javed's reluctance to have any pre-dinner soft drink, Fyruz ordered a Coke for himself and was relishing that with intermittent initial sips.

The setting was ideal with few customers around as that was a period between the usual time for afternoon tea and dinner. The relationship was a congenial one. But Javed was still hesitant. It was because he never had the opportunity to cultivate that friendly relationship due to the unexpected deaths of his parents, and Fyruz played the role of family custodian accentuated by the relocation of the former to Rahamt Bepari's house as resident house tutor.

Fyruz noted the sort of restlessness in Javed and inquired about it. Javed replied, saying, "No, nothing in particular. I am very happy with the outcome of today's discussions. However, one side issue is bothering me. I can't comprehend why you used the address 'Sir' so many times while talking to the PS of the Vice Principal Saheeb. He is a petty functionary and addressing him 'Sir' so many times amounts to pampering him beyond decency."

Fyruz smiled gently and thanked Javed for observing that. Internally, he was both amused and surprised.

The former took his time and frankly said, "Javed, I am astounded by your query. Very few of your age and background would note it. You are blessed with a proving mind. Keep this up, and it will be very helpful in your life's journey."

He continued saying, "You are aware of my deficiency in formal education. That did not mean I stopped my pursuit of learning. I read a lot at home and that embraces all subjects of interest to me.

"Based on that, your simple query, in formulating a response, has two dimensions: one is immediate one based on our social setting and practices, and the second one is deeply associated with undivided India's British colonial history. Both of these were in my mind to share in one form or another with you before you leave the community for Dhaka, but the lack of relevance for making such discourse discouraged me. Providentially, you provided the opening.

"To understand the first one, there are many criteria and elucidations, but I would refer to a simple experience while coming here. As you will recall, we were negotiating our destination on a nice road, occupying seats next to our bus driver. Then suddenly we saw a completed bridge having unfinished small connector portions (probably called 'approach span') between the newly constructed bridge and both ends of the existing road. That unfinished small work evidently was the main obstacle constraining the use of the bridge built at the cost of multimillion taka. That required our bus driver to use a rudimentary diversion road at considerable risk and inconvenience to passengers.

"A position like that of PS, or similar others, in any structured organization of our background is akin to above referred 'approach span.' Perceivably, they have a long-standing career in that or similar structure, are experienced in procedures and processes, and attained competence over a span of time. Outwardly, they tend to be shrewd operators but internally are a bunch of peeved functionaries. They can help you, or make you befuddled, by making the process a time-consuming one.

"I gained this exposure while accompanying my second uncle to various offices in connection with his application for an import license.

"When we started this journey, I was more than certain that the timely and positive outcome of our effort singularly rests on the ability to hand over the letter of Hamid Ullah Sir to the VP on time. I therefore conditioned myself to be respectful and polite to everyone in the process, whatever my reactions and feelings might be.

"With that frame of mind, I consciously used the salutation 'Sir' in having discussions with the PS. Evidently, that pleased him. Otherwise, he would have been within his domain in asking us to stay outside while he was having his lunch during the assigned time.

"In pursuit of life, always remember that in our social setting, these small functionaries play a structural role as the critical link between a proposition and the authority to process or decide on that."

Listening to those words of relevance and wisdom, Javed was astounded. In a neutral setting, he was in the process of knowing a different Fyruz Bhai ostensibly being blessed with knowledge and prudence.

Looking at an absorbed Javed, Fyruz said, "Let us have our food now when it is warm and thus likely to be tasty. A cold service is always distasteful. We will talk about the second part of our discourse when we have post-dinner tea."

As they finished the dinner and tea was being served, Fyruz recommenced his unfinished homily, this time focusing on the rationale of the second dimension of his response in answering Javed's simple earlier inquisition.

He continued, "In the process of life, you will often come across intellectuals and senior citizens referring to old days of good governance during British rule. They could be right from a perceptional perspective but are not so based on reality. The concept of good governance that originated and was being practiced in London (England) ended in Calcutta (India). The Calcutta-based Hindu landlords enjoyed the benefit of good governance. It never trickled down to rural Bengal, the producer of wealth for the absentee landlords.

"This is the most abusive aspect of permanent settlement under which landlords became the owners of land and the farmers for generations remained as sharecroppers. The related culture and practices were consciously developed and adept at keeping powerbase far away from the subjects. Whims and caprices of individual landlords and their functionaries in the field dominated local practices instead of any system, the sine qua non of good governance.

"Carefully nourished misconception gave rise to an administrative culture in the field where entitlements of subjects were treated as prerogatives of landlords and their functionaries for dispensation. Anyone down the ladder occupying a chair of relevance considered him as the designated representative of the royalty. Irrespective of the position, each such functionary expects obedience and sort of submission.

"Our systems, culture, and practices have roots in this setting. Unfortunately, we carry that baggage in spite of two independence. People continued to remain subjects of the old days. It is just that players at higher echelons change. We just can't undo those suddenly and by arrogant practices. We need to follow a process for social change.

"As a group, we failed to use opportunities. The abolition of Zomindari (land lordship) system in the early fifties in then East Bengal was a major missed opportunity. Political luminaries of the time diverted people's priority from much-needed immediate and sustainable economic emancipation to issues of other priorities, even though of critical relevance.

"Against this backdrop, we need to be conscious of the slow creeping in of malice, which very soon became sort of a social parasite and rapidly grew out of proportion. That is the use of the chair (authority) to make money. This has over time maligned our social value system to the detriment of the majority.

"Keep all these in view always while thinking and making sustained efforts for social changes."

Javed was rejuvenated. Internally, he developed immense respect for his dear Fyruz Bhai while renewing his own trust and confidence in the latter's judgments and decisions. Javed also fondly recalled relevant words and statements from his adorable father.

They showed up on time the following day to meet the principal of the private college. The huge billboard in that upscale residential setting initially tickled Javed. More so, the name of the college—"Star Degree College"— charmed him outwardly.

The impression radically changed as soon as they entered the main office building of the college. Cleanliness, friendliness, and efficiency were all pervasive.

Unfriendliness, unnecessary queries, delays, confusion, and other negative elements, which were rampant in most public sector institutions, were conspicuously nonexistent. The overall ambiance was a friendly one.

They were ushered in just in time to the principal's office. The principal, Shahdat Asim, was well prepared and to the point—on admission, hostel accommodation, subsidy entitlement, and, more importantly, the requirement of having an undertaking from students in general for not getting involved with in-campus and off-campus political engagements.

The admission and settlement process progressed as expected under the systematic advice and guidance of the VP, a friend of Hamid Ullah Saheeb. The VP, despite multifarious other commitments, maintained regular contact with Principal Shahdat Asim and Fyruz and was satisfied. During the last courtesy meeting, the VP requested Fyruz to carry his letter to Hamid Ullah Sir and deliver that personally. That was complied with.

SIGHT

AS TIME PASSED, Javed developed an unexpectedly supportive and friendly relationship with the superintendent of the college hostel who was also the professor of philosophy of the college. The mostly unorganized discussions with him were always stimulating to Javed. The latter's principal interest in such discussions was to be aware of superintendent sir's perspicacity about the society, the turn it is taking, and ways of correcting the course if so needed, both individually and jointly.

In one such engagement, the superintendent sir casually asked Javed about his familiarity with Hamid Ullah Saheeb besides being his head teacher. Javed's response was short and straightforward, respectfully highlighting his standoffish persona outside the school campus and about being a close friend of his late father. Javed, after a pause, however, added saying, "Since the demise of Father, he has played a fatherly role in guiding me. My whole family, especially my brother-in-law Fyruz, trust and respect him immensely."

He went inside and returned after a while with two cups of tea, buying his time.

It was evident that the superintendent sir wanted to say something but paused instantaneously. He went inside and returned after a while with two cups of tea, buying his time.

Offering Javed a cup of tea with all the warmth and affection being pervasive, Sir lamented saying, "One, especially like you, has many things to cherry-pick from Hamid Ullah Sir's life in charting your own journey by certainly avoiding inapt pitfalls.

"When I got admitted as a freshman of an honors course at the university, Hamid Ullah Saheeb was a senior in the master's class. He was a talented student who embodied varied qualities and thus was both admired and popular. His special quality was that notwithstanding intellectual prowess, he could interact, talk, and gossip with all and sundry. It was known that because of his all-around attributes, he was very admirable to university women students. On being provoked on the same issue, he allegedly once commented saying, 'It is not who likes me. It is whom I like. I will expose myself to a girl of my choice, and I am certain that she will not be able to say no to me.'

"But the reality was otherwise. At the beginning of the senior year, he exposed himself to a first-year junior lady student in his department whom he silently liked and guided a lot, only to be told that she, by choice and decision of the family, was about to be engaged with a civil servant. That was a negation he neither expected nor could handle properly. Emotions overshadowed him. That all-rounder, who only attained success and glory in life that far, could not deal with that negation. He never prepared himself to handle perceivable negative situations in life.

"That was palpable in the result of the master's final examination. Beyond all expectations and to the dismay of faculty and friends, he was placed second on the merit list.

"Some of his admirers and friends extended holistic support to invigorate the element of confidence Hamid both lost as well as lacked. They opted for a diversionary strategy. Instead of directly suggesting, many of them were talking in his presence about what they would have done in a similar situation. The consensus was that they would have opted for Bangladesh Superior Services Examination (BSS) and proven themselves as more than equal among comparable.

"In that depressed setting, Hamid Ullah Saheeb found merit in that sort of estimation and decided to sit for the next BSS examination. To the delight of his friends, he engrossed himself in preparing for the challenge right from day one. And then the most unexpected thing happened.

"The husband of his abortive love was posted as officer-in-charge, commonly known as sub-divisional officer [SDO], of a northern sub-division. She joined him soon after the wedding with grandeur and recognition that befits the spouse of the SDO irrespective of age.

"Life, notwithstanding being far from metropolitan Dhaka as well as close friends and relations, was exciting and enchanting. They were on

JAHED RAHMAN

their way to Dhaka to attend the wedding of the husband's batchmate. To optimize timing, the couple decided to leave in the early-morning hours of the emerging day of December with the official driver taking the back seat while the husband took charge of the steering and the wife occupying the other front seat of the jeep.

"The northern part of Bangladesh is known for its relatively cold temperature. It was very foggy the early hours impaired visibility. The jeep was cruising steadily and was about forty kilometers away from the well-known Faricha Ghat (Ferry) terminal. The couple looked at each other and smiled. They could not do much to warm up due to the presence of the driver. The husband, Saleem, said, 'In a few more minutes, we will have warm tea at the ferry.'

"The ferry terminals on both ends of the mighty river have their own practices. Those evolved keeping in view the trading imperatives of business establishments located at both ends. The trucks, loaded or otherwise, crossing the river at about or after sunset time for the ultimate northern journey generally take a break at its other end. The driver and his assistant take a break, have dinner, and avail a full rest before commencing its journey in the early hours of the following morning.

"As Saleem was nearing the ferry terminal, gradually the overnight trucks started to cross them with gaps. There was a break in that pattern of traffic flow, and Saleem sped up. In a left-hand drive flow engulfed by river location fog, an opposing truck with only a left-hand headlight on suddenly became visible. Having little space for maneuvering and the speed of the opposing vehicles, they collided forcefully. Saleem was injured badly, only to be told that his wife was grievously injured. Fortunately, the driver was relatively in better shape and could communicate with surrounding people. Meanwhile, most of the skeleton police staff of the terminal outpost rushed and were briefed in a most disorganized manner.

"And that was to be so as each witness had a different time and source of information. Police worked promptly and rushed the injured persons to the nearest district hospital. By that time, the inevitable happened. The wife succumbed to her injuries. The district administration decided not to tell Mr. Saleem about the fatal consequence until he was moved to Dhaka and medically in stable condition. They, however, advised all concerned about the accident and its consequences.

"While Saleem was being taken to Dhaka in a semi-conscious condition in the district hospital ambulance, the dead body of his dear wife followed him in a sort of van with ice spools all around contrary to the hot tea they were talking about a few hours back.

"The news spread precipitously. That was augmented due to a 'breaking radio announcement' about the accident. Inexplicable gloom prevailed with grief, impacting friends and colleagues, and sadness distressing others.

"Right at that moment, while preparing for the upcoming BSS examination, Hamid Bhai (the prevalent culture being to address even a first-year senior as Bhai [brother]) was in a different world of hilarity. Being a student of literature (English), he had not much interest in subjects like history. Since Indian history was a popular subject for competitive examination, Hamid Bhai opted for that and was immersed in reading about Moghul rule in India. As he read about the Moghul conquest, administration, and assimilation with India in high school and intermediate classes, Hamid Bhai concentrated on studies pertaining to art, culture, literature, architecture, music, diplomacy, etc. that enriched India during the Moghul rule. He was reading intensely about Emperor Shahjahan from his romantic perspective.

"In that navigation process, he could not help but laugh, all by himself, on reading that his second wife, Arjumand Banu Begum, popularly known by her bestowed and most adored name of Mumtaz Mahal (the Exalted One of the Palace) bore fourteen children in nineteen years of married life. In her rather stunted married life, she amazed Shahjahan so much that he continued to confer special titles (akin to names) from time to time. Some of them are Padsha Begum (Queen of the Great); Malika-i-Jahan (Queen of the World); Malika-uz Zaman (Queen of the Age); and Malika-i-Hindustan (Queen of Hindustan). She was the only one to be addressed as Hazrat, meaning Mother of the Heir Apparent.

"Life in its essence is governed or induced by certain aphorisms, which, in piloting its journey, ignore or run contrary to current experiences, expectations, attainments, or even distresses. The life of Emperor Shahjahan and Empress Mumtaz Mahal is a classic example of that. Neither the multiplicity of Malika Titles nor fourteen children could ensure lasting love and bond in their lives.

"A queen of eminence, she was exalted as being the sustenance at the time of suffering, glory at the time of success, and inspiring at the time of challenge.

"Being shattered by her untimely death, Shahjahan, spanning over a period of about seventeen years, built a white marvel mausoleum to commemorate their love. Alas, destiny decided otherwise. Shahjahan had to spend his captive life at Agra Fort looking at his cherished sepulcher through a hole.

"Reading and discerning all these, Hamid Bhai was in his own world of entertainment oblivious of the gloomy reality around. As he was about to call the house boy for a cup of tea, the door curtain moved, and his two dear friends, fellow CSS examinees, entered the room. Without pretension, they broke the news of the fatal accident but carefully avoided mentioning the death of his love.

"Hamid Bhai neither talked back nor inquired anything. He quietly pulled his pillow, squeezed it intensely, and placed that against his face. Time rolled on. The prevalent silence was both viscous and taciturn. Friends, simultaneously feeling desolate and inexact, left the room as quietly as they entered.

"The focus of Hamid's anxiety was convoluted per se even though one question dominates: Why did his friends Akash and Koli stop while breaking the news of the accident? Is there anything more?

"Relying on the divinity and all good wishes that he could muster within his depressed self, Hamid took slow steps toward the nearby medical college emergency ward.

"Hamid inanely had a blank look as the stretcher carrying the stale body of Saleem was being taken hurriedly to the operation theater. No one around had time to talk to Hamid. The immediate challenge for staff and doctors was to save the lives of the injured.

"In sort of a disoriented mindset, Hamid found himself in a temporary shelter for dead bodies. He cussed himself for being there and took an immediate reverse turn, only to find the younger sister of his love, along with family members and friends, rushing to the space while howling. The message was loud and clear.

"Hamid was the lone unknown person, except for the younger sister, without identity among many in the disorganized swarm. Reclined on a door frame, he stood in a standstill posture and got lost within himself. He did not have any emotional backlash even when the body of his lost love was pushed through the door to place it in the waiting vehicle for her last journey home, Ananda Ghar (House of Amusement), ardently so-named by her late grandfather.

"With all disenchantment engulfing him, Hamid sluggishly went back to his place of temporary living but promptly decided to go to his bank to withdraw money. Before leaving that place for the bank, he, with an apparent vengeance, packed up all books and other materials, musing that the essence of his BSS venture had lost its relevance with the demise of his love. Simultaneously, he also packed up some clothing and essentials for yet unspecified contingency.

"With related engagements being accomplished, Hamid insentiently reached Ananda Ghar and took his position under the broad crown of the omnipresent kadam (*Neolamarckia cadamba*) flower tree at the center of the huge lawn. During his last two short visits, he spent most of his brief time under this tree with his lost love.

"While most others were absorbed in funeral-related activities, Hamid was engaged in reminiscing the memory of his earlier visits. An unexpected ticklish smile braced his miserable face as he remembered her commenting, 'With your merit and intellect, you will soon enrich our social setting. Always remember that we are talking, standing below the broad crown of the kadam tree whose flower color ranges from red to orange.' In response, and with a solemn tone, Hamid responded saying, 'I should not pass any comment on your avowal but would definitely like you to get a Ph.D. soon in English literature. That is both my hope and desire. You referred to the color of the kadam flower. But more pertinently, and in the context of my yearning, I would refer to the sweet fragrance of the kadam flower and its use in making perfumes. You are that sweet fragrance, and we need to spread it out.'

"The follow-on response stunned Hamid. She commented, 'One needs to have, besides competence, a specific mindset aspiring for PhD. I am not one of them as I have different notions about the preferences of my life. It is not my focus to earn a name in the elite group of learning. I want to be within the masses in helping them in acquiring knowledge and in broadening perception. In that endeavor, even if I could adequately guide a small group of people, I would then consider myself successful. My view is that it is time for this Ananda Ghar to take the lead in converting it into Ananda Mela (Place of Amusement) for the greater social good. However, most of what I have just said is my desire, but being a daughter of this soil and of this Ananda Ghar, many bends of my life would depend on family choice and preference.'

"As Hamid emerged from that sort of reflection, the younger sister, Bokul, came and in a solemn voice said, 'All preparations for the funeral journey have been completed. Very soon, the shroud will be closed. If you want to see her for the last time, you follow me.'

"In a quick reflection, Hamid opted negatively and went farther, not to attend the burial. He also decided to leave Dhaka immediately for an unspecified journey. Rechecking his back pocket to be sure about the cash he had drawn from the bank before coming, Hamid unmindfully stepped out of the Anada Ghar compound.

"Hamid Ullah went back to his place of residence, did not respond to greetings from others, called the person in charge of his rented accommodation and had a brief talk, shunted the door hook, and went to bed. The caretaker ensured that no one bothered him.

"Both hunger and thrust momentarily disappeared from his thoughts and systems. That was not his priority in the backdrop of both shock and prevailing darkness that engulfed the inner and related outer surroundings. The outside lighting systems relevant to his room location were deactivated as per his wish earlier conveyed to the staff in charge while the inner room setting was frighteningly dark. He was in the world of emotions circumscribing agonized self-motivated questions pertaining to life, longevity, purpose, and destiny none of which an incumbent has any role to play.

"He spent the rest of the time pondering about all these uncertainties of life together with sailing through inconsistent and irrelevant issues and thoughts. He did not sleep at all in that darkness. As the early-morning glow of the emerging sun brightened up the outside milieu, his tired mind and physique surrendered to the lap of sudden sleep.

"Hamid got up from that deep untimely sleep in the late afternoon, had showers, finished early dinner, and called the person in charge of his rented accommodation to talk and pay the needed advances for about a month. He then loitered aimlessly, took a cup of tea as a diversion, and suddenly boarded one of the awaiting rickshaws with his earlier packed bare clothing and essentials.

"Approaching the Dhaka railway station ticket counter, he inquired about the next train leaving Dhaka. The railway staff from the other side of the counter said, 'It is Sylhet Mail positioned on platform five and set to depart in ten minutes'"

"Hamid had not had much previous exposition about Sylhet except knowing that some areas of it have partially hilly landscape with many spots having heavy rainfall, and preponderance of tea gardens. Other knowledge he had was its location bordering the previous Assam state of India and the relatively greater presence of the Sylheti (people from Sylhet) population in London.

"He bought the ticket for Sylhet without thinking and approached platform five. Seeing a bookstall on his way, Hamid briefly tarried and bought a pamphlet-type publication on Sylhet.

"That was a quiet travel for Hamid but not for many of the accompanying passengers. Even though unknown to each other, the fellow passengers soon established a link and bond among themselves mostly based on Sylhet derivation. They were engaged in varied types of conversations even if it was going to be late night hours. While glancing at the pamphlet, Hamid, occupying the rear end of a long-drawn sitting arrangement of that interclass compartment, could not help but lend his ears to absorb pertinent information emanating from such unorganized discussions.

"That was significantly helpful for a distressed traveler like Hamid with an overwhelming emotional burden. He was trying to absorb those calmly. Observing him glancing at the pamphlet frequently with unusual attention, many of the co-passengers were certain about that being his maiden one. Suggestions and advice started to pour in, and that ranged from where to go, what to see, how to negotiate places, recommended places to stay, the food to be taken, including shatkora (scientifically known as *Citrus macroptera*, locally cooked as a vegetable along with fish, mutton, and beef to impart a unique flavor), and so on.

"Disembarking from his train compartment at the terminal station of Sylhet, Hamid, for a short while, was befuddled by screams and shouts of competing vendors and other service providers. Recalling the spontaneous comments of fellow co-passengers, he gained back his pause, smiled puckishly, and left the scene as one very familiar with Sylhet.

That pretension worked well initially. As Hamid stepped out of the main arena of the station, he encountered greater chaos and confusion. He decided that in view of the prevailing setting, he has not much option but to seek help. Glancing around, he decided to talk to the vendor of the lone provision shop nearby who, from a distance, appeared to be a friendly person.

Before he could decide his way of approach, another person dressed in semi-Western outfit with a noticeable difference in communication parlance, approached the vendor. From the exchanges they were having, it was evident that they knew each other very intimately. In welcoming him back from London for an apparent short visit, the vendor, in expressing sympathy, lamented saying, "It is so unthinkable that even after five years of the sad demise of our brother Sayeed in that sudden rush of the hilly Piyain river water, you could neither overcome that unfortunate loss of brother Sayeed nor forget Jaflong. You are here every year to organize prayer for the salvation of his departed soul and evidently to register your grievances to the river on the day of his sad demise."

In response, the fellow person commented, "It is a fact that I live in London for sustained living, but all my current feelings and emotions are related to Jaflong, and unfortunately the Piyain river due to the death of my son."

After having relevant other social exchanges as is customary, the gentleman left to catch the bus for Jaflong.

What an ordained opening that was for baffled Hamid. But the inherent surprise was more beguiling. He got what he wanted to know without fretting with the vendor and quietly followed Sayeed's father to the Jaflong bus counter.

Routine local buses have a uniform seating arrangement and tariff except for two front seats next to the driver at a higher price. Sayeed's father bought one as Hamid could hear being next in line and asked for the second one.

As the bus started, Sayeed's father, being sure that the passenger next to him was a nonlocal, opened up with inquiry as to what took him to Jaflong.

Startled but not bemused, Hamid Ullah Bhai responded with all vagueness, wearing a guiltless smile. He was very thoughtful in guarding evolving but very unspecific sudden association to benefit himself pertaining to information related to Jaflong.

For a while, it appeared that the fellow passenger had gone to oblivion. Looking unabatedly from the moving bus, he focused outside apparently in search of the unknown while endlessly trying to keep his tupi (headgear) in its proper place. At that juncture and as the bus was turning left after the airport bazaar, one of its rear tires was punctured. It appeared that their journey was delayed by an hour or so.

Contrary to the negative perception associated with happenings conflicting with one's expectation or causing inconvenience, this tire-punctured incident appeared to be a boon from Hamid Ullah's perspective.

The fellow passenger surprisingly winked at Hamid Ullah Sir with the definite sign of opening and invited, as a general courtesy, the latter to join him for a cup of tea in a nearby tea stall. Hamid Ullah Sir grabbed that without hesitation.

They bypassed the only upscale restaurant of the location and the fellow passenger moved to an adjacent conventional one and took seats in the frontage of that tea shop. Seeing them taking their seats, the service boy rushed in with a stool, placed that in between his customers, wiped the same with semi-wet *gamcha* (a textile piece), usually kept on the shoulder by such service boys, and smiled at his customers. Surprisingly, the fellow passenger responded by smiling too and ordered two cups of hot tea with additional instruction to clean the cups with hot water.

As the service boy left, the fellow passenger initiated a more in-depth discourse contrary to his earlier mien. While tracing the way the service boy followed, he most unexpectedly but without direct eye contact said, "I am sorry for not introducing myself to you so long even though we are sharing our time and agony for the last so many minutes. As a local person, it is incumbent on me to make a visitor like you comfortable in our locale. I am Yusuf Ali from Jafflong and settled in London for the last twenty-three years."

He looked around and then resumed saying, "My uncle was working as personal staff of Gordon Saheeb (locally so addressed instead of mister) of Muthshui Tea Garden. As his time of retirement drew nigh, Saheeb (as European males are locally called) offered my uncle a passage to England. It was difficult for uncle to say no to Saheeb whom he revered. Because of the age of Saheeb as well as being issueless, uncle considered the proposition of Saheeb for him to accompany the former as a stand-by, perceived to be a substitute of a family support, as nonstarter to begin with. He also found it difficult to leave his own growing family. My uncle was caught in a catch twenty-two position. It was equally difficult for Uncle to say no to Saheeb whom he revered. So instead of saying no, he proposed that Saheeb should take the nephew, Yusuf, who is young and has English-speaking ability. He was also of the view that his own proposition to be a workable way out of the delicate quandary without being disrespectful to his boss for a long time.

"Fortunately, Saheeb concurred, and my uncle devoted his time to train me. That effort had a particular emphasis on Saheeb's likes and dislikes and daily routine, particularly the timing of drinks and table settings.

"That was the backdrop of my initial setting in London. Gordon Sir was a kind and considerate person and left no stone unturned to put me at ease far away from home and family.

"As age was catching up, Gordon Sir one morning startled me by raising the issue of his deteriorating health condition and my future sustainable living in London. Out of the blue, he proposed that I consider setting up a restaurant specializing in Indian food and curry. In articulating justifications, Gordon Sir emphasized the absence of one in the vicinity coupled with my capability as a cook having substantive ideas about British taste, etiquette, and practices, including that of drinks and related services.

"That was the most unexpected boom that I ever thought of. Gordon Sir just not floated the idea but took concrete steps guiding and helping me in every step and related effort.

"While scouting for needed property to set up the restaurant in that vicinity, he on many occasions accompanied me. On a particular day and as we were strolling with our objective in view, he noticed a just-listed property adjacent to the local commercial district. There were apparently two odds: first, it was relatively bigger than we were eyeing, and second, it was relatively at the end of the commercial district. I thus politely voiced my reservations.

"Gordon Sir, for the first time addressing me 'son,' observed saying, 'What you see as obvious impediments, I view them as positive opportunities. My age and inner experience tell me that this is the type of venue we have been looking for so long. Remember that one does not always get what he aspires. But one has the ability and scope to achieve any desirable outcome as per the paradigm that one has in his mind and thinking. The related requirements are devotion and hard work.'

"Having said so, Gordon Sir adjusted his hat and repositioned his ambulatory stick, handmade as per his choice and decoration preference out of a branch of an old tea plant of his favorite Muthshui Tea Garden.

"After playing with his favorite stick, Gordon Sir started to draw imaginary lines standing in front of that property, looked at me impishly, and laughed rather loudly by minimal British standards known to him.

He was very happy as he continued to look at me, an unusual act by any of the past behavior norms.

"But his subsequent act was exceptional, and anyone familiar with British etiquette would find it difficult to imagine. Gordon Sir came close to me, put one of his hands on my shoulder, and drawing my attention to a slightly far away but apparently posh coffee shop, said, 'Let us have warm coffee in the serene setting of that bistro.'

"Gordon Sir impeccably noted my body reflex and resultant nervousness coupled with hesitation and surprise. To ease up the situation, he said, 'The main purpose of bringing you here is to make you aware about my feeling and desire of how your future eatery should look like. That should have neatness and cleanliness as you can observe, and a mix of décor reflecting elements of Bangladesh as well as England.'

"As Yousuf Ali's London recollection reached the stage of Gordon Sir's ordering two coffees, the service boy of the conventional tea stall located at Sylhet town periphery came wearing a broad smile and placed two hot teas on the stool. He then rushed out and came back with two pieces of roasted biscuits. Observing our reactions, the service boy promptly said, 'If you do not like it, you do not pay. But one can enjoy the real aroma and taste of our tea when one dips the biscuit in the cup of tea and swallows that.' We happily complied with it and had no second opinion.

"Janab (akin to 'mister' in English) Yusuf Ali resumed discourse to finish his introduction, which started with the puncture of one of the tires of the bus. He said, 'My relationship with Gordon Sir was always very formal and correct. It was always in my mind that he is a *gora* (white man), the boss of my uncle for a long time, and that too of mine for the last five years. So, anxiety and shakiness always predominated my interactions with him even in the coffee shop.

"'Notwithstanding such reality, I must admit that I learnt a lot from him particularly during occasional discourses he had with family and friends. I tried my best to assimilate them in their proper context for an amiable living in England, my new home and identity. In that backdrop, his initial comment about sanitation and décor was a relieving one. But what he observed subsequently made me amazed.

"While waiting for coffee, Gordon Sir continued his annotations by saying, 'I have already told you that the objective of bringing you inside a typical British coffee shop is to orient you properly from the beginning so that both irritation and confusion in the future may be avoided. It is very important. As we embark on the venture with your savings and my funding, our present relationship will undergo some evident change. You, with your unmatched merit, politeness, and confidence, should be up to that.

"'That brings me to your initial two points of reservation with respect to the property we have in mind. Those were very relevant from your perspective, but I have my views on those. Size is a physical element that has its own attributes, and one needs to make a choice. My long tea garden experience convinced me that the success of any enterprise is not in the present alone but holds equally in decisions and actions pertaining to the future. The venue currently is on the side of the market area. But perceive it fifteen years from now with immigration continuing unabated. The venue would likely be in the middle of the market, increasing demand for the location and value of that manifolds.

"'If we opt for that property, we may decide to have a modest but attractive eating place in one part, and can use the other part for storage, temporary shelter, and so on, minimizing current obligations and expenses. Thus, I suggest that we go for this property without any reservation.

"Now, we face your second concern having the location relatively away from the mainstream swarm of the market. The answer to that is very simple and straight, and that primarily depends on you. Unlike many other business operations, the eatery one principally depends on quality, taste, aroma, service, and more importantly, consistency. Unlike other settings, people here drive happily miles for good food. To be successful, restaurants need not be positioned in the midst of the crowd; rather the customers tend to find that out. And the availability of easy parking space is a boom.

"'You are an excellent cook with consistency ever preeminent. In that respect, you excel over your uncle significantly. Moreover, you demonstrated an ardent penchant to try out new menus with incredible success. Let us now think positively and proceed prudently.'

"Something strange overtook my psyche in that setting of the coffee shop. The persistent feeling of master and obedient aid has dominated our relationship ever since I joined him at the behest of my uncle soon evaporated. My sitting on the other side of the same table and in an identical chair unknowingly steered a new sense of identity within me. I started talking with Gordon Sir more as a potential acquainting without hesitation and reservation. We talked about likely challenges as a timely decision was of the essence. It prolonged and we decided to finish our dinner of the night by having toasted sandwiches and a second service of coffee for me and drinks for Gordon Sir.

"Things moved steadily. But one problem emerged as both difficult and delicate. That was the apparent shortage of reliable helping hands, both to help me in business and more importantly to take care of Gordon Sir as needed even though he recruited a lady help to take care of him during the day.

"In related discussions, he readily agreed with my proposal to sponsor my younger brother who was doing his second-year intermediate course (twelfth year of high school education) in Sylhet.

"I was very happy with the outcome, but his subsequent suggestion took me by surprise even though internally I was delighted.

"Out of the blue, Gordon Sir recalled that when he proposed to my uncle for the latter to come to London with him, the latter, among many points of concern, highlighted that he has an eleven-year-old daughter for whose matrimonial relationship in the near future he needed to stay back. Recalling further, he said that to his best awareness, that girl is still unmarried. I nodded affirmatively.

"Without lapse of time, Gordon Sir booked an overseas call to my uncle, a telephone set and connection the former gifted the latter as an element of informal separation package, among many others of material benefits.

"Ever since that discussion, our world and actions focused only on materializing the restaurant proposition. Things progressed rapidly, and every piece of needed accomplishment followed an organized pattern and in quick succession to the delight of both Gordon Sir and me. With his continued help and my own efforts, I got my second brother to immigrate on a timely basis.

"Our dream Indian curry restaurant was fondly named by Gordon Sir as 'Mithshui,' an easier version of Muthshui tea garden. It was opened as planned with my past savings, the liberal funding support of my boss, and some financing from a local bank.

"I rented a modest accommodation about a quarter mile away from Gordon Sir's abode. So we have my own living place, Gordon Sir's home, and the restaurant, Mithshui, all within a distance of half a mile. The stipulation was one of us would stay at Gordon Sir's home during the night.

"I got married to my dream cousin, Lyela, got her immigration, arranged for her two-year elder brother to join the family, and soon was blessed by a beautiful baby boy whom I happily named Sayeed, after my grandfather. It so appeared that Lady Luck unleashed its generosity in making my life a pleasant and blissful one. In this process, and as in the past, Gordon Sir was omnipresent in my life and in all its bends.

"My happiness was overflowing in all respects. In Lyela, I had a wonderful life partner who was sympathetic and supportive of all my wishes and determinations. So was the case with my younger brother and brother-in-law. All exhibited unparalleled ability to adjust in the new setting.

"The presence of the brother was a boom for Lyela. But what impressed me most was her eagerness and response in taking care of Gordon Sir from the time of her arrival in my life, during pregnancy, and even pushing the stroller with baby Sayeed to be with him. Nothing diverted her focus from the unbounded respect and care for Gordon Sir.

"In view of age-old-related deteriorating health conditions and in consultation with Lyela, I planned a surprise for Gordon Sir. We got Lyela's father to London, driving straight from Heathrow to Gordon Sir's abode where Lyela was meticulously preparing to make the most unexpected union between a boss and his longtime trusted subordinate, a memorable one.

"That precisely happened. The unexpected presence of the uncle not only thrilled Gordon Sir but rejuvenated him manifestly. They started spending their time merrily complimenting each other. They even on occasion visited Mithshui.

"After two emotionally triggering deferments, Uncle eventually left for Sylhet. We adjusted our life, centering on Gordon Sir, Mithshui, and my initial involvement with works of the London-based Sylhet Association.

"Since Sayeed had a temperature on a particular day, I decided to take care of Gordon Sir and went to his residence. All of a sudden, Gordon Sir desired to have a cup of tea made of Sylheti-grown tea leaves, following the process and practices trailed in Sylhet. I was happy and promptly complied with it.

"In that moment of joy and contentment, I was struck by what he had to say. Gordon Sir asked me to pull a chair and position that by the side of his bed. As desired, I took my seat on that chair as he was possibly relishing his last intake of that tea. After keeping quiet for some time, he then started ruminating saying, 'There is a segment of my life which by precipitous determination I refrained sharing with anyone. That decision did not bother me all through. However, I think that the time has come to share that with someone of your altruism. There is an emotional incident that impacted my life beyond normality.

"'As a young carefree man, I was deeply in love with one who was apparently much above all the benchmarks I was endowed with and what my expectations were. She was not only gorgeous but equally talented, with a noble background. There were obvious oppositions from her family, but she was singularly focused on drawing me close.

"'She ardently was an aficionado of nature and greens. At her behest, we traveled to the western bend of England and enjoyed the cloudy cum breezy nature while crossing farmland. Suddenly, nature took a gusty turn with roaring airwaves starting to magnify its intensity. In that setting, I was scared but she was euphoric while holding my left hand and dancing like a pre-teen girl. Then the most unexpected happened. A huge lightning, with a thin-edged precision landed, killing her instantly and partially affecting the muscle tone of my left hand and lower body.

"'I was traumatized. That lightning not only took my lady love but crippled me in terms of physical attributes. I lost all normal urges for physical relationships and started finding happiness in solo commentary with her. That was by all contemplation and proclivity a very personal and private experience in my life all through. That was the reason why I, in spite of repeated assertion of your uncle, practiced locking the door at night. She may be physically away from me, but we are, and continue to be, part and parcel of oneself. Every night since then, I have had my solo discourse with her. That did not derail me at all. More specifically it helped me to be on my own.

"'After some time, I developed an urge to escape from my familiar setting and subsequently, with tries in many places, joined a luxury liner. During one such voyage, I was taking care of a guest who had companies trading in India. One of his companies was looking after his tea garden business operations in eastern India and they were looking for young, energetic, and enthusiastic Englishmen to fill up managerial positions. He offered me a job as assistant manager in one of his gardens.

"'Emoluments, benefits, including overseas holidays, and freedom to operate were all very attractive compared to sailing in the sea, but my dilemma was that I do not have any experience in such a business. Over a drink, the gentleman guest explained that the tea garden operation is generally managed by local supervisory staff.

"'Usually they are known as Tila Babus, reflective of the elevated location of their residences in their assigned blocks (locally called Tila) and their supervisory role and responsibility. Babu is a trivial expression for local supervisors. Their numbers vary based on the size of a garden.

"'The workers originally were brought from varied areas of the then India but mostly illiterate poor inhabitants of least developed areas/ administrative provinces by the East India Company, and the present workers are mostly their descendants.

"'And managers' immediate responsibility is to manage this group of Tila Babus. Managers do not have much direct supervisory responsibility involving the plantation, and over time, one gets familiar with the nitty-gritty of garden operations.

"'That is how I landed in your Muthshui tea garden. The undulating topography, the greenness, the spectacle of tea plants, the nearby flowing convoluted river, and so on all embedded immediately in my mind and thoughts. I immediately recalled my lady love, Rose, who occasionally talked to me about a similar setting in Kenya based on what she learned from her grandfather. I immensely felt Rose in the breeze of the Muthshui tea garden and its surroundings.

"'That was the reason why I, despite repeated assertions from your uncle, practiced locking the door at night. She may be physically away from me, but we are, and continue to be, part and parcel of oneself. Every night since then, I have had my solo discourse with her. That did not derail me at all. More specifically it helped me to be on my own.

"'That is why and how I stayed back happily and spent all my productive life here. Your uncle's care and tenderness helped the process immensely.

"'Within a short while, Gordon Sir's health started to deteriorate, and within weeks he died. His death made me feel that Gordon Sir, in the context of Mitshui, left an *amanat* (safekeeping) for me to take care of. Overcoming the initial shock and gloom, I doubled down my attention and efforts to live up to his trust. The process became easier as Lyela, in spite of three follow-on pregnancies, extended her hand in helping Mitshui's business operations, more particularly its take-out one.

"'All round attainments with a thriving restaurant business, a family of four children, a brother and a brother-in-law getting married constituting a support family egis elevated my standing within the family and even the status in the broader milieu of the Sylhet Association. Things could not be better even with the sad realities of my parents' demise.

"'Notwithstanding this happy backdrop, an unwarranted anxiety started dominating my contemplations. That engulfed sustained worries within me were about evident parting from my root. As a proactive intervention, I started talking with our children about our roots but soon realized their general lack of interest. But I had no desire to give up and changed the strategy. I decided to concentrate on our eldest son.

"As Sayeed was growing up, one of my regular pastime passions was to tell him about Sylhet, my parents, how I grew up, and so on, all with the inherent objective of sustaining a link with the root. Having that in mind, I planned to take Sayeed, a reasonably grown-up child among the four, for a familiarization visit to Sylhet. He demonstratively was receptive, liked Sylhet very much, and assimilated with our relatives easily. But his special interest was always rolling stones from the upper hills in India to Jaflong through Piyain River. I could never think that this liking would be the cause of his death. That brings me back to Jaflong every year. In prayers and submissions on the bank of the river and around that locale, I have the feeling of Sayeed even though he is physically no more with me.'"

Janab Yusuf Ali went into hiatus once again, a behavioral feature that was noted by me in that short span of our familiarity. I did not like to flummox him and thus kept quiet.

However, that silence did not prolong. The ever-energetic service boy of the tea stall reappeared with the good news about the bus, and said, "The bus is all set to depart. You should board it now."

The bus started its roaring journey while an all-pervasive silence prevailed within the front section of the bus except for the occasional coughing of the driver and his release of puffed smoke from his local smoke known as *biri*. I just could not bear that taciturnity anymore. Consequently, I point blankly asked my fellow passenger about how Sayeed died.

Janab Yusuf Ali looked at me for a while and then redirected his focus to fast disappearing outside. In an array of ruminating, he said, "Sayeed liked Sylhet very much. Its lush green surroundings, undulated topography, numerous rivers and watersheds, and presence of various mentionable natural features, even though in a small scale, like Ratargul Swamp Forest, Bisnakandi, and Shimul Bagan besides the ever-enchanting tea gardens impressed him most. But flashing of rolling stones from uphill India to Jaflong on a sustained basis attracted him most even though he observed them from a distance. Sayeed appeared to be intrigued by the name of the venue as Bichanakandi.

Numerous fountains of hilly Khasi region in Assam formed a lake, locally known as Boirala, in the vicinity of Indian side of the border having a natural connection with Piyain river of Bangladesh. The sloping topography of adjoining Khasi mountains and force of downstream water flow move sizeable rocks from the upper hills to the Piyain river where many layers of the mountains constitute a flatten bed with moving stones piling on each other. The word "Bichana" is the Bangla language synonym of that flattened riverbed, and the resultant piling is called "kandi," also in Bangla. That was the popular rationale for naming the spot as Bichanakandi. A visit to this site is a unique experience. If luck so ordains, one can see a limited flow of rocks and, in some cases, of boulders. That in essence was the interest of Sayeed.

Related school commitments in London and due to s tight travel schedule, he could not make that to its most enchanting location. His cousins invited him back with the assurance of playing in flowing river water simultaneously and witnessing the slow but steady movement of surrounding stones reaching the flat river surface.

My trivial objection was recoiled due to Sayeed's strong eagerness, the enthusiasm of his siblings, and the tacit endorsement of Lyela. Sayeed was off for Sylhet to witness something both very special and unusual. My cousin Rakibbrother assured me of all care and attention.

Everything proceeded as per plan. We got a call from Sayeed conveying his first visit to the stone resting site. He was excited and very much enjoyed observing an occasional slow movement of stones in that flattened riverbed as well as the pressure of water from upstream. He also indicated the plan for a second full-scale visit the following day in the company of cousins and their friends.

Being conscious of the enthusiasm and excitement that a fresh as well as unique experience may trigger, I repeatedly urged Sayeed to be always near the bank of the river. He assured me about that.

I was not satisfied with that assurance. I then called my cousin, Rakibuddin, who is also the chairman of our Union Council (the lowest tier of representative local government structure) and requested him to take care of the visit planned by the children. He not only assured me but also said that he would join the group monitoring their safety.

Anything can happen at any time and at any place without a perceived reason. Concern, care, and caution are therefore basic elements of human thinking governing progression in life. But those are not a guarantee. There is something called ordained. And precisely that happened in our life.

The following day's expected telephone call was inordinately delayed, causing restlessness at our end. As I was about to call Sylhet, there was a call from my cousin Rakibuddin conveying the most unexpected grim news. He said, "Bhai Saheeb (as elder brothers are addressed in Bangladesh), we have sad news to convey. While playing with cousins and their friends in the midst of Piyain riverbed jumping from stone to stone, something unexpected happened. Due to the sudden release of Boirala dam water in the adjacent border location for emergency repair, a sudden gust of onrush water from the other side of the border overwhelmed all on our side including the youngsters giving company to Sayeed. Being unfamiliar with such suddenness and unversed in the handling of evolved challenges, Sayeed lost control and was swept away. There was another local causality too. He, son of your school friend, Molla Bhai (brother), also succumbed even though attuned to such happenings and slightly senior to Sayeed. We retrieved Sayeed's body about a kilometer downstream and took steps to cleanse the body and wrap it in a white shroud with ice around it.

"I am sorry to convey all these in a blunt form, but we need to act first as the situation demands. I will wait for further instructions from you."

It is explicitly the first precipitous calamity that befell me and my family in the background of efficaciousness that we so far experienced in terms of successes and achievements. This most unexpected happening caused a sharp plunge in family life and my emotional paradigm.

I tried to reconcile with reality but failed. That was the reason why every year since Sayeed's sad demise, I just could not help but be on the spot for submissions encompassing something that is unknown. I am unsure about the rationale of that. The resultant peace of mind has always been very transitory.

I am a firm believer in my faith though not a practicing one. With that backdrop and in searching for reconciliation and peace of mind, I started going to our neighborhood mosque to say the *asher* (night) prayer occasionally. In that process, I developed a propensity for an emotional reflex of weepy entreaty while raising my two hands in submission to Allahpak (the Lord) for the peace of Sayeed's soul.

The imam (Priest) of the mosque noted that. One night when the mosque was almost empty after formal asher prayer, he suddenly came and sat by my side without my knowing.

As I finished my prayer submission, the imam wanted to know why I always cry in performing my submission to Allahpak. Since the query was related to my emotions, I was at a bay in formulating my response.

The imam then said, "I am very much aware of your mental condition. But please bear in mind that it is futile to search for a reason to justify Allahpak's will. Our son Sayeed played his assigned role in our life. The ruh (soul) has now returned from where it came. That soul perhaps does not need our grief. As a Mu-min (believer), we should accept that. While remembering a dear dead one, especially during prayers, is okay, it is perhaps not right to grieve for the dead one, making the life of surrounding dear others pitiable. You have three other golden children. They are Allahpak's amanat (safekeeping) to you. Do justice to them.

"Moreover, possibly the best way of remembering a deceased is to think positively showing respect and love to a departed soul. Perhaps the finest way is to cherish and be mindful of the ideals and values of the deceased in the inner thoughts and actions of living ones. That is true love. That is a genuine feeling.

"One can bang one's head in expressing grief but will not get the dead back. But one can harmoniously live by replicating dead's dreams and aspirations in day-to-day activities with needed variations demanded by changes in emerging social dictates and time horizon."

The imam Shaheb, in concluding his brief counseling, further alluded saying, "Since the soul is infinite, one can pray for its salvation from any place and time of one's choosing."

Janab Yusuf Ali paused for a while and then continued saying. "I listened to all that Imam Saheeb had said without any invocation on my part, assessed them from a neutral perspective, and understood and accepted most of his words and opinions. Against this backdrop, I decided respectfully and carefully to reshape my thinking and actions befitting the greater good for myself and the rest of the family. I thus also decided to discontinue the practice of the annual journey to Jaflong to pray for Sayeed.

"Notwithstanding those reawakening homilies, I had to undertake the present journey as that was planned and arranged much earlier. Any last-minute reverse decision would send a mixed signal to larger family, friends, and associates whose part and parcel I am still despite living in London for many years. This relationship and feeling are unexplainable. It was amply demonstrated during the sudden demise of dear Sayeed. Known and unknown walked miles to share my grief, and that is what makes our social system very special. I could not thus avoid it even though I accepted most of the advice and opinion of Imam Saheeb."

After a relatively long narration of his personal life to a new acquaintance, probably feeling relieved by sharing the burden of assimilated agony, Janab Yusuf Ali went again to a reserved mood with which he started the journey. He appeared to concentrate on passing side sceneries as the bus was heading roaringly to its destination with breaks and bumps, ironically akin to one's life journey.

My very penetrating conclusion was that Janab Yusuf Ali, being a product of the traditional Bangladesh social system until his early youth and growing up in the liberal and open social setting of Europe, is perhaps slightly confused. He was unsure about the appropriateness of what to say, how much to share, and what needed to be withheld in conversation with someone unknown. But the burden of emotional pressure was compelling him to release his excruciating pain. It is possibly the reason for him to talk sometimes and to withdraw on other occasions.

That ironically proved to be consistent when the bus stopped at its destination point. Janab Yusuf Ali just disembarked without any salutation or even adhering to informal leaving etiquette. I too disembarked, positioned myself under a shade with competing confusion as to what I do and where I go in this unknown locale.

At that point, I was dazed to see Janab Yusuf Ali approaching my position. He stood by my side, glanced at me fully, and then asked me about my destination. I forthrightly said, "I have never been to this part of the country, and Jaflong is totally unknown to me. I just want to stay a few days and do not have any inkling about where I can stay."

He then said that one of his friends in London has a motel-type modest residential accommodation with dining facilities, mostly aiming at transiting visitors from abroad and outside the locale. He named that Amar Ghor (My Abode). Janab Yusuf Ali then said, "If you like, I can take you there. It is not that impressive from the outside, but reasonably well decorated and finished inside. It is equally very safe and secure." That was a great relief to me.

As we approached and entered Amar Ghar, each word and statement earlier uttered by Janab Yusuf Ali proved to be authentic. But that was not all. He appears to be well known to staff, and the manager rushed in hearing about his presence.

We were ushered in with startling decency and decorum. There was no discussion about the choice. I just nodded my head and everything, including the welcome tea service and other service-related assurances, was complied with in silent mode. What surprised me was that I was given the most prestigious room at a standard rate.

Against the background of initial worries and the relatively odd behavior pattern of Janab Yusuf Ali, I was bemused by what I was experiencing subsequently. But that was repeated during his departure time. A rickshaw was called in and he quietly boarded it saying, "Have a safe stay," but refrained from even looking back once.

My maiden entry to the assigned room was a startling one sheer by its positioning. The motel was built on a hilltop, having a diamond shape. My assigned room was at the edge of diamond-shaped plot with a narrow rear opening with a small lawn, a big tree, and a nominal sitting arrangement with an overhead umbrella and three chairs. But the most attractive feature was its opening to the Piyain River just before it took its sharp turn toward the east. Other accommodations are deprived of the view emanating from river flow due to the size of the hilltop, the sharp turn of the river, as well design imperatives.

As I was in a relaxed mood enjoying the setting and all unexpected subtleties, the manager reappeared with all politeness and said, "Sir, before Yusuf Bhai (as Janab Yousuf Ali is locally known) left, he instructed me to ensure your comfort and safety, especially as it is your first visit. By all connotation, you are a special guest of Amar Ghar.

"Complying and being consistent with that, we have arranged a snack service for you as it is late for lunch and too early for dinner. I also took note of the fact that you did not have much to eat most of the day. So please finish all cleansing requirements and join me in my office room. I thought that my office room, with a better table and cushion chair, would ensure privacy. To my assessment, it is a better proposition. This will also enable me to know you and your choice preferences."

After a while, I joined the manager. He was a very friendly and jovial guy, spontaneous in words and actions. We clicked with each other right from the moment he extended his hand to shake saying, "This is Akmal. I belong to Jaflong proper and am conversant with local conditions and caprices. You should not have any worries. Just relax and do whatever you feel like but just keep me informed about your whereabouts."

As we were talking like old friends, the motel staff placed food on the table. The arrangement, variety, and quantity of food were beyond my ingenuity. I was awed.

Noting that, Akmal took the initiative saying, "Since I have had no inkling of your liking and preference, we took the safe route of preparing some mixed items. The sandwich, with pieces smaller in size, is the local version of the internationally popular double-decker one. The fillings include, among others, standard ingredients like onion, cheese, tomato, and chicken—the latter obviously is halal. Our crispy samosa (local fried pastry) with savory feelings is very popular among guests and local gentries. We have a sample of that too for you. Both pineapple and orange are grown in Sylhet, and are in high demand all over the country. I hope you will like our preparations. Now, please start."

I was overawed. The efforts made for culinary preparation at an odd time and the earnestness so exhibited overwhelmed me. To his urging, I said, "Akmal, in order to enable me to enjoy the food so specially served, I will expect you too to join me. Let us share the food together, and exchange perceptions for better understanding."

In continuing parleys, Akmal implied that he would be happy to accompany Hamid Ullah during the former's maiden visit to Bichanakandi. In continuation, Akmal also very broadly highlighted the topographical uniqueness, even though on a small scale, of Sylhet, and suggested that before leaving Sylhet, Hamid Ullah Shaheb should at least visit Ratargul as part of the area is a swamp one and is considered a mini-Sundarban in Sylhet with its rare singularities. In explaining further, Akmal elaborated saying, "There is a pronounced wetland in Sylhet, and the area is known as Ratargul Swamp Forest. Most trees of the swamp are of Dalbergia reniformis type (locally known as Koroch tree). But there are other vegetation like cane, bamboo, and straw whose strips are used to make pati or rata (mattress). Hence, the adjacent area is known as Ratargul."

He further stated, "This swamp forest, unique by its nature, is located about twenty-five kilometers from Sylhet proper and around Gowain river belt. This river is connected to a lake-type water formation nearby through a link known as Chengri Khal (Chengri Canal), more relevant as a discharge outlet for waters from India.

"The forest is evergreen by nature even though it remains under twenty to thirty feet water during rainy season and about ten feet water during dry season. The significant variation in water level during the rainy season is due to heavy seasonal rain caused by tropical air and the accelerated rush of water from river links of the adjacent border areas of Assam in Eastern India. Ratargul is at its best both during rainy and desiccated seasons."

This trip undertaken by Janab Hamid Ullah with unclear schema more as a escape from unbearable tragedy of his intended life has all positivity so far in diverting him from many agonies that were tormenting him. In contrast to what has happened in his life in the last few days and dramatic emotional burden it caused, unnerving him totally, Janab Hamid Ullah amazingly started to relax and reflect.

In his reflection, the thought that dominated Janab Hamid Ullah was the magnanimity manifested in general discourse among unknowns binding them briefly as near and dear ones in an unparallel uniqueness. That simplicity has no other bearing except spontaneity in expressions and views wishing unfamiliar others the perceived best one could imagine. The foregoing perception is the offshoot of his Sylhet Mail (train) journey with a viscous heart.

His initial conclusion about the broader relevance of learning beyond a formal education system, as experienced in earlier dealings with Fyruz Bhai, was strengthened manifold. Based on instant experience, Hamid Ullah absorbed the relevance of learning as a certain way forward and a guide for his future life.

Hamid Ullah's interactions with Akmal, the manager of Amar Ghar, were unique and noteworthy. Akmal was not intimidated due to his new guest's association and contact with the friend of his employer. He talked freely and openly. That portents in pertinent homily array impressed Hamid Ullah significantly. Akmal's ingenuousness caused a sort of multifaceted organic reaction within the mindset of Janab Hamid Ullah. For the first time, he started feeling somewhat relaxed, coming out of a depressed emotional burden.

That recouping process was greatly helped earlier by having exchanges with a downcast but equally frank and honest person like Janab Yusuf Ali. Hamid Ullah, by sheer coincidence, encountered Janab Yusuf Ali as a co-passenger during his bus travel to Jaflong. Being aware of that as Hamid Ullah's maiden visit to Sylhet and in an effort to live up to the reputation of traditional Sylhetie hospitability, Yusuf Ali started talking to him with intermittent gaps. Recognizing the similarity in the mental agony between the two due to the loss of dear ones, Hamid Ullah was attentive to what this semiliterate but successful immigrant to England had to share and say.

In that process, Janab Yusuf Ali referred to the advice given to him by the imam of his London mosque. Hamid Ullah listened to them carefully and internalized them, fully agreeing. As a byproduct, he started valuing counseling, both spiritual and psychological, in shaping life.

That was the time and that was the setting that mesmerized the inner feeling of Hamid Ullah. The locale of Amar Ghar on a hilltop, endowed with contiguous undulated topography and a moving snakelike flow of numerous waterfalls flowing steadily over the uneven base of the downhills on the other side of the border, baffled him, raising natural questions about the rationale of a division of Sylhet, akin to many other points of undivided India.

Rivers and water bodies of Sylhet, though perennially dependent on capricious decisions of authorities on the other side of the border, undulated lush green forest surroundings, man-made and equally enthralling eye-catching scenery of numerous tea gardens contributed to uniqueness of Sylhet in the backdrop of pale and flat topography of Bangladesh.

In that mindset, Janab Hamid Ullah was enjoying the freshness of Sylheti tea (tea grown in Sylhet) without the standard ingredients (thick whole milk and sugar) commonly used in Bangladesh. That nevertheless emanated real tea flavor, creating a wanton urge and enhanced liking for it.

Having that melee dominating his thoughts at that moment, Janab Hamid Ullah had a refreshed assessment of happenings in his life thus far and thought about what was in store for him in the future. In that quest, two scenarios engulfed his mind: Janab Yousuf Ali's reconciliation with the most tragic death of his eldest son, and words of conciliation uttered by the imam of the latter's London mosque.

That follow-on in-depth inquisition hit the bottom line incessantly, confirming that individual experiences, however tragic those may be, must be acquiescent to ordains that the future holds. There is no alternative. There is no option.

Against that backdrop, Janab Hamid Ullah found a lot of solace in the aphorisms and words of Imam Saheb and absorbed them internally without hesitation. For a man of his intelligence, it could either be a surrender to faith or an escape from actuality. In any case, he firmly adhered to the present reality and decided not to deviate from that, come what may.

His solace was that he was not writing off Bijli, his lost love, from his thinking and life. Rather, his present decision would enable him to live life through the ideas and ideals of Bijli as enunciated by her during their fleeting discourse under the Kadam tree of Ananda Ghar.

In that thought process, the inherent intellect within Hamid Ullah recalled verbatim the relevant words of Bijli: "It is not my focus to earn a name being in the elite group of learning. I want to be within the masses in helping them in acquiring knowledge and in broadening perception. In that endeavor, even if I could adequately guide a small group of people, I will then consider myself successful."

The precipitous recollection of those words laid the foundation of Hamid Ullah's way forward in life. He committed himself to dedicate his life to fulfilling the mission that Bijli venerated in her thinking.

After a few more days of easing and visiting places of interest like Bichanakandi and Ratargul swamp forest and saying intermittent prayers in the Mazar (shrine) of Hazrat Shah Jalal (Peace Be Upon Him), Hamid Ullah left Amar Ghar in the quest of his mission. That mission per se was very ingenuous and straightforward, having roots in the words and desires of Bijli. The real challenge was to find a place of aptness and bearing for the optimization of inherent impact and intended benefits.

Consistent with Bijli's desires, Hamid Ullah decided to focus on the elementary school setting as that is a proper time and phase of life to influence and shape the thinking of those growing up. He also wanted to be sure about the community's preference and support for enlightened education progression.

The first two attempts failed for reasons much beyond any meaningful intervention and manipulation. That was his assessment in each of those two efforts encompassing about a year. Under duress, he made a third effort focusing on Ghazipur.

The unexpected introduction to Ghazipur was just fortuitous. Hamid Ullah Sir incidentally met an eminent resident of Ghazipur at a social gathering. He was a community leader bearing the name

Zakir Mia. In conversations, expressions and social concerns, he, in a short span of time, impressed Hamid Ullah Sir immeasurably. The former's apparent lack of interest in political engagement and involvement, and ostensible aversion in life for position and power became prominent in such discourse. Notwithstanding these features, his ardent interest in social changes and the challenges inherent to that enthralled Hamid Ullah Saheeb. Zakir Mia's unqualified reference to the earnest involvement of elders of the Chowdhury family and Moulavi Bari (house) of that enclave with respect to emerging social issues made a dent in Hamid Ullah Saheb's mind and thinking process. He quickly formed a fair-minded impression of the Gazipur settlement.

Hamid Ullah Saheb took that interpersonal discourse to an in-depth oration about the dual role and responsibility of education efforts and social responsibility to achieve the desired outcome. He opined that the lack of or unawareness of the relevance of social mobilization is impeding the desired progression in social amity. Contrarily, the negative features of disjointed politics are affecting the attainment of desired impacts.

Against such a backdrop, the two unknowns clicked with each other with ease and grace. While continuing the banter, Zakir Mia elucidated that the Gazipur school management committee, without disclosing his own identity as its chairman, is looking for an assistant headmaster for their Ghazipur High School and would be thankful for his help and support in the process.

Hamid Ullah Saheb made an indicative decision within himself to try the option of Gazipur Kallan School for the vacant position it presently has and casually shared his willingness with Zakir Mia. That was how he landed in Ghazipur. He loved the community as well as the way the school was run by the management committee and, over time, became one of the communities.

He worked hard not only for the school's academic excellence but also to create awareness among community elders and guardians about their supportive roles in this regard. His very common assertion was, "The guardians' responsibility does not end with the sending of pupils to school, but they have a responsibility to monitor their progression.

At the minimum, guardians should maintain periodical contacts with teachers and get feedback on a timely basis."

In this context, he started the practice of visiting the homes of senior class students, keeping guardians informed of the progression of their children and steps needed to be taken for better performance in the board-conducted Secondary School Certificate examination.

All these academic and non-academic initiatives started yielding positive results, and the name and fame of the school spread rapidly.

Hamid Ullah Saheb soon became the school's headmaster. His intellectual probity was generally beyond the community's understanding and assessment, but his social efforts to link up management, guardians, and faculty earned commendations from the community, and in no time became one of them besides transiting from Hamid Ullah Saheb to all respected Hamid Ullah Sir.

In the process, Hamid Ullah Sir bonded easily with other gentries of Ghazipur and surrounding communities. That was the outcome of the reputation he earned in a short time both as a teacher and an individual being blessed with a higher level of intellectual prudence even though, on his part, he remained nonchalant.

His relationship with Zakir Mia stood the test of time even after the latter's voluntary retirement from the school management committee, paving the way for new leadership. At the time, that eventual customary social relationship between them got strengthened, devoid of focused interests or designed intents.

In his vacant mind and lonely life bearing the memory and intensity of the emotional relationship with his lost love Bijli having been slowly fading away with the passage of time, Hamid Ullah Sir found supportive solace in the company of Zakir Mia and the well-being of his family, while remaining equally decent to others. Simultaneous supportive roles and actions to augment the social values of the Gazipur community made him content.

It was the afternoon of the following day that Javed finished his board-conducted higher secondary examination. He enjoyed his lunch of the day even though the menu was almost the same and the taste, known for being stale, remained unchanged.

Ever since moving to Dhaka two years back in the quest for higher learning and germane educational attainments, Javed was never at ease with the surroundings appositely conflicting ones in which he grew up. He consciously isolated himself from prevailing milieus, and concentrated ardently on studies, always bearing in mind his ardent objectives of life, the teachings of his late father, the focus of Hamid Ullah Sir, and the love and trust of adorable Khala.

In this process, Javed was often ridiculed by some, being one from rural scenery while many others praised him for his inherent erudite qualities. He was oblivious to all these and remained focused on pursuing his objectives.

The journey was made easier due to the constant encouragement and guidance of the hostel superintendent Sir. The evolved relationship between the hostel superintendent and his new boarder took a startling positive turn beyond normal criterion.

The foundation of that was Javed's being a student of Hamid Ullah Saheb, a genius pupil of his time. The latter unknowingly carried that positivity down the drain, enabling even four-year junior students like the Superintendent Sir (commonly addressed as "Super Sir") to respect him with due reverence even though they had no personal contact or association. Since he willfully withdrew himself from a known social setting because of very personal but emotionally burdensome imperatives, Hamid Ullah Saheb gradually went to oblivion except for those who knew him or heard about him. In that reclusive life of limitation, he came to be known more commonly as Hamid Ullah Sir.

The initial liking for Javed was premised on the letter of Hamid Ullah Sir that was passed on to different authorities until it reached the table of the Super Sir. The contents of that brief introductory letter, passed on from hand to hand, were more than any conceivable academic certification, and were valued by everyone who knew Hamid Ullah Sir. That was the case with the Super Sir to start with. But a few brief exchanges with Javed convinced Super Sir about the innards of Hamid Ullah Sir's letter and he developed an impulsive liking for that young guy from a remote rural backdrop. It did not take much time for him to conclude that Javed is a real diamond stone in the rubble of a diamond mine.

This realization of the superintendent sir perhaps had another taciturn dimension. A potential boarder of Javed's cerebral ability and prudence would definitely contribute to the fame of the hostel as being a residential place endowed with academic excellence. Being an entity of competitive private sector initiative, it is of utmost importance both to the college as an institution and the reputation of the Sir as a superintendent. He instantly decided to allocate the only room with twin occupancy favoring Javed as all others were four-bed accommodations. He also explained that the other occupant of that room is one year senior to him and is a bright student. That will ensure Javed focuses on his studies.

With the higher secondary education examination process behind, it was time for Javed to leave the residential accommodation of the college. As the time drew close, Javed, for motivations not precise, yearned to have a cloistered meeting with the hostel superintendent sir, more to express gratitude for all his care during the latter's assimilation process with the impulses and challenges of a metropolitan setting. The other longing was to get guidance as to his academic move and priority in the immediate future.

As Javed was marshaling thoughts about the most respectful way to convey that desire to the Super Sir, the former received a brief handwritten note from the latter inviting Javed for lunch at his home on the following Friday. That made Javed ecstatic. Instead of spending time on other matters, he concentrated on matters that he would like to discuss with the Super Sir.

Contrary to the thinking and preparations of Javed and his preferred points in mind, it was Super Sir who took the initiative to set the initial tone of their ensuing dialogue.

Commanding Javed for his academic motivation all through the last two years, which he was certain would be replicated in just concluded Board conducted higher secondary examination, the Super Sir recalled the decision of the vice principal (generally addressed as VP Sir) of the neighboring government degree college. He, with full endorsement, stated, "The VP Sir was right in advising Javed to choose the private college over his own government funded one as realities so proved. With national political sceneries increasingly slipping out of the domain of recognized political leadership to emerging and pronouncedly rebellious student leaders, the much-valued didactic excellence per se was relegated to secondary relevance. Devoid of a sense of history but more propelled by emotions taking prominent priority, the issues of academic parlance, the genesis of the protest movement, started rapidly slipping out of the hands of experienced and enlightened leadership. Non-academic national political demands started dominating the movement and so did the streets. Once that rein was unleashed, it was difficult to contain the upsurge. Repeated strikes and frequent closures of public-funded educational institutions in support of nonacademic issues and demands manifested in its turn to lack of progress in designed academic progression and deferment of regular tests and examinations. Somehow, the private institutions escaped that blitz and could maintain designed advancement. Students of private institutions are immediate beneficiaries. And it was more relevant in the specific case of Javed potentially being vulnerable because of his very conspicuous rural background. The letter of Hamid Ullah Saheb was very helpful in bringing your case to the attention of all involved and concerned. Proper timely decision by VP Sir, his sustained monitoring through me sheer due to respect he, like many others of his time, had for the former, and your earnestness all combined created an expectation of excellence pertaining to you."

Having made this acclamatory remarks, Super Sir recalled his first informal interactions with Javed saying, "I remember asking you how much or in what details you know about Hamid Ullah Saheb. After asking you that question, I realized the gaffe I committed. That question was not appropriate in that setting of discourse between us as you did not have any idea as to who I am. I soon realized my slipup and withdrew from the setting, employing diversionary tactics of bringing tea for both of us. That strategy paid for: neither you dealt with my query nor did I follow that up. But I remember that question with lessons learned that time is of the essence for pursuing any query.

"We have spent the last two years in proximity, had many interactions on varied subjects, and thus know each other relatively well, having confidence in our relationship and respect for each other from different viewpoints. I would therefore like to know your perception about Hamid Ullah Sir and his personality traits."

In his response, Javed plainly said, "I do not have any specific view about him besides being an ardent admirer of my late father, an intellectual of eminence, and a very dedicated teacher. He had proven all these in my jolted life since the demise of my parents. Sir has been very reclusive in his dealings with people except in education and social issues but specifically has no interest in the lives of others. But he remains a father figure to me."

Super Sir was very enthralled by the straightforward response of Javed without manipulating facts either to praise or deride the persona involved. What he stated were facts not warranting any scrutiny.

But his objective is different. Super Sir wanted to share the life and events of Hamid Ullah Sir in a way that Javed, a very talented student who grew up in the shadow of the former, learns some lessons in advance and does not undertake similar missteps in life.

There was a brief pause in their discussions as Javed was wondering about the reasons for this topic while Super Sir was thinking of the right way to convey his message to the former without maligning the image of Hamid Ullah Sir in any way. The providence intervened. The call came from inside as to the service of lunch.

The lunch was a simple one but evidently more delicious than the hostel one and Javed relished that hugely. He was, however, surprised to notice both quantity and variety of dessert items, such as traditional pittas (made of rice powder), sweets made of custard cream (milk), stir-fried semolina with a heavy dose of ghee (clarified butter), topping it with slices of pistachios, nuts, and raisins.

Javed for sure was overwhelmed with the lunch intake. He relished every item, remembering his mother and Khala Tahera.

It was the proper setting for enjoying the traditional preparation of Bangladeshi tea after an overindulged lunch. Tea made of dark liquor (liquid of over-simmered tea leaves) with liberal service of natural full-cream (whole) milk and a gracious input of sugar is generally the most relished drink item in varied conditions of daily life in Bangladesh. Javed and the Super Sir did not have to wait long for that tea.

To his amazement, the wife of Super Sir entered the small seating space, bringing in two cups of tea emitting vapor. That was Javed's first encounter with the wife of Super Sir. Before Super Sir could say anything, the wife spontaneously said, "I am Rohani, and you can address me as Chachi (aunty). Your Sir was very upset as I kept the menu for lunch very simple. I deliberately opted for that as your hostel had its monthly feast only last night. Thus, the appeal of rich menu items will not be that great. In this backdrop and to my assessment, a simple lunch will enable you to taste and enjoy the dessert items that I painstakingly prepared. These are not commonly available and will remind you about family back home. So relish the dessert items."

While Chachi was making her points, Super Sir was deeply engrossed in his own mind. He concluded that whatever he had to say to Javed would preferably be communicated directly so that the message was straight and clear, and the rest depended on Javed.

Finishing his first sip, Super Sir commenced his discourse saying, "There is no hesitation to affirm that you are a remarkably focused student entering the most critical phase of your academic and growing-up life, with the potential of being limitless. This was the phase of life in that Hamid Ullah Saheb succumbed more to emotions than recognized the realities around him. The VP Sir holds the same view. In one of my recent discussions concerning you, a periodical practice he followed since you were assigned at his behest to our institution, he expressed his anxiety about your future for being under the direct guidance and influence of Hamid Ullah Saheb. With VP Sir's authorization, I plan to let you frame about the life pattern of Hamid Ullah Saheb and the decisions he had taken solely based on emotions contrary to realities that other options or avenues beheld.

"Related subsequent avowals are not meant to malign him. VP Sir, as a very close and dear friend, holds Hamid Ullah Saheb in highest esteem. My adoration for him, though from a distance being four-year junior, has been of utmost sincerity and respect. That has been augmented significantly since my close relationship with VP Sir over the last four years and since Hamid Ullah Saheb accidentally re-emerged in our social orbit briefly.

"Hamid Ullah Saheb is a typical paradigm of where and how emotions wedged alternative options and multiple avenues that perhaps a life harbors. Responding to a startling and equally intense incident during his emerging life, he consciously decided to withdraw and took refuge in the setting of rural Ghazipur to pursue the implied preferred desire of his lost lady love, Bijli. At that time of inchoate youth dominated by the intensity of feeling and sense of commitment, Hamid Ullah Saheb saw only one path in life: adhering to the path of a pledge he harbored for her, even though silently.

"You are evidently the most shining outcome of that decision with probably equal susceptibility in life. It should not be doubted that in the absence of parents and the young age of your current guardian, brother-in-law Fyruz, he wields immense influence in the decisions of your family and in guiding your progression.

"In that backdrop, the life and journey of Hamid Ullah Saheb inadvertently is very relevant. But that has one catch. Both VP Sir and I committed to Hamid Ullah Saheb to ensure strict confidentiality of his life's journey."

Surprisingly, neither coercion nor coaxing was necessary to know his mindset during all these years of seclusion. Hamid Ullah Sir was forthright in indicating that of late and with a gradual waning in feelings and emotions, an emerging rethinking about his life is shadowing his current mind. Notwithstanding such remorse, he is otherwise very comfortable with the present stage of his life in the Ghazipur setting. He would not like that to be tarnished in any way. Ghazipur seems to be his new love after Bijli eluded from life.

He initiated the discussion by saying, "The VP Sir is convinced that even though he has no role in guiding you, he has an obligation to make you aware of pitfalls that many of us, including Hamid Ullah Saheb, faced in life. That awareness might help one like you in being equipped with the ingenuity to handle or overcome the entraps, ensuring a steady journey in life."

On being assured of commitment from Javed predicating the confidentiality of information that was being shared, Super Sir scrupulously narrated Hamid Ullah Sir's enchanting academic entitlements and equally charismatic university life full of extra-academic laurels, related incidents and exposers, emotional pressures, and subsequent adherence to one path decision in charting his life's journey. In that process, his emotion-laden mindset was triggered and sustained, more as revenge, a secluded lifestyle devoid of friends and well-wishers. He also opted to sacrifice the inherent future possibilities. Hamid Ullah Saheb consciously sustained leading a life of a singular path. Without a second thought, he abruptly delinked himself from surroundings that adored him and had the highest expectations of him.

That emotional grimness was so definite and conclusive that even the detailed description of the backdrop of the loss of a teenage eldest son of a fellow bus passenger from London, Janab Yousuf Ali, the sudden loss of the girlfriend, Rose, of Gordon Sir of Muthshui Tea Estate of Sylhet, the pious philosophical assertions of Imam Saheb of the London mosque, and many more incidents of life around could not make any dent in his mind and thinking. He singularly pursued the preferred way of life that Bijli indicated to him under the shade of the kadam tree of Ananda Ghar.

With the passage of time, two realisms hit him hard. He became conscious of the fact that what Bijli articulated in that romantic setting was her wish but not the way of her life. In her related homily, Bijli always referred to family decisions. Eventually, she honored that family tradition, and happily became the wife of a civil servant.

It took time for Hamid Ullah Saheb to assess this reality of life. He felt a vacuum of unimaginable insinuation but had no one to share with. The surroundings were not congenial at all. The emotionality is beyond the comprehension of his current associates.,

In that locale, his solitary admired well-wisher was Zakir Mia. With contrary feelings and opposite conjugal life experiences, he was a total misfit in this regard. Notwithstanding that, Hamid Ullah Saheb became close to him for the latter's undemanding but equally delicate handling of social issues without being involved in politics.

What impressed Hamid Ullah Saheb most was the way Zakir Mia handled the sudden demise of his wife and concentrated on the upbringing of his residue family without lamenting, playing the dual role of mother and father.

Hamid Ullah Saheb was both impressed and curious. However, he could not hold back the latter for long and one day asked Zakir Mia candidly how he could do so without lamenting and grieving as he had a very warm and caring relationship with his wife.

Zakir Mia was not taken aback. After having an explanatory look at Hamid Ullah Saheb, he refocused himself on the emptiness of the sky, kept quiet for a little while, and then said, "Bhai, I am a very ordinary person and equally a firm believer in my faith. Notwithstanding that, my mind's searching reactive windows are persistently engrossed about life and death issues. This has been accentuated ever since Ambia left me. I am confused about our existence.

"When one ascribes existence as life, it may be nothing but a make-believe assertion of an ongoing journey of a soul with ambiguity engulfing both stages of its beginning and termination. That abstruseness is the root of fear within the human mindset, giving rise to faith premised on belief. The fact perhaps is that we either do not know anything or have the capacity to comprehend that.

"As a faithful Muslim, I subscribe to the dictum that the Ruh (the soul) goes back to Allahpak, the creator. But the inborn fear of the unknown among living fellows created the impression as if the departed soul, somewhere on the horizon, is monitoring what his kith and kins are doing for him. This is where I disagree.

"To my assessment, death signifies a new journey for the Ruh as designed by the creator. Thus, the preferred way for the successors is to perform earthly duties that would have made the soul happy. Remembrance and respect are best performed through deeds, not through lamenting.

"These prompted me to devote my time and energy to the desired upbringing of the children. I am of the opinion that it perhaps will solace the Rhu of Ambia and will help in ensuring the peace of her soul."

The instant word "opinion," akin to many other similar expressions uttered by Zakir Mia from time to time, reinforced a major mark in the assessment process by Hamid Ullah Saheb pertaining to the nature and value of their relationships. Premised on similar discourses before and after, he became very close to Zakir Mia and selectively with a few other chosen people in that community.

The surroundings and the community of Ghazipur became his identity for life with Zakir Mia being the focal person. This was where he precipitously came to the limited circuit of his current life until having a sense of remorse of late with the passage of time.

Hamid Ullah Saheb unequivocally aligned his mind about the undefined phenomenon that influences, and in some settings, regulates the existence of species on this earth. Contrary to being humbled despite acclaimed academic excellence, he felt honored to have learned the greatest lesson of his life from an ordinary person in this remote corner of the country. A new thinking emerged in his mind with an urge to harbor this remarkable opening in learning. Life and death with transformed lucidity about their meanings enfolded him afresh. He thus continued his divisive journey with assumed larger objectives for social harmony and learning excellence.

SHRED

JAVED'S CONVOLUTED LIFE pattern in Ghazipur since his return from Dhaka after his HSC examination drew the notice of many of the locality besides immediate and extended families. Some ascribed it to adjustment insolence while others related it to possible poor performance in the examination and so on. Nobody, however, confronted him directly. Even Hamid Ullah Sir was also confused as Javed's current demeanor was totally opposed to the feedback he used to receive periodically from his friend, Vice Principal Ajmat Beg of the government college in Dhaka.

Occasions were numerous and talks in the community were plentiful to cause concern at the end of Hamid Ullah Sir about Javed's current behavior. Being coherent with his own specific social behavior array discouraging others from indulging in his personal life, Hamid Ullah Sir refrained from raising the issue of concern about Javed's current glumness with anyone. His assured safety bulbs were knowing Javed intensely for many years, the latter's family background, current contacts and relationships with both immediate and extended families, and the absolute authenticity of regular updates from his friend, Ajmat Beg. Notwithstanding all these, he had the inapt uneasiness within observing specific emerging reserve tones in Javed's behavior pattern.

Time elapsed. The results of the HSC examination of the Dhaka board were announced with Javed earning a coveted third position as per the merit list. The persistent angst disappeared from his surrounding social setting with glee ubiquitous. Some gentries recalled with dismay the dream and aspirations of the late Zakir Mia centering Javed. Hamid Ullah Sir was enthused observing that, especially in both the abodes of Fatima-Bu and of Tahira Khala.

Javed, as per prevalent social customs and traditions, met some local gentries as well as friends of the late Zakir Mia, seeking their continued blessings before leaving for Dhaka to pursue higher education. Hamid

Ullah Sir was the last but not the least one where Fyruz accompanied him.

After initial exchanges of pleasantries, Hamid Ullah Sir, while conveying his utmost good wishes and paramount consecrations, unhesitatingly stated, "I do not like others to talk or probe about my life. On my part, I do adhere to that norm about others. That sort of equation became palpable in our conversations when I first met your father, and we clicked easily with one another. During my initial years in Ghazipur that generally was the norm. With the passage of time, that is waning gradually with ramifications unbounded. The sad demise of Zakir Mia, an ardent social service pioneer, is evidently an upshot of related social and value changes even though with different insinuations. Thus, my foremost advice to you, as you are entering the real phase of life and learning, is that irrespective of your attainments in life, never ever forget the ideals that your illustrated father upheld. Your response may not be identical, but the essence of your efforts should always have the same focus and objectives."

He paused for a while and then said, "I do not have any specific inkling as to your future field of study. Our common estimation of the time is premised on keeping your options open until you have sort of definite semblance about your preferred priority. Hence intermediate science was the right choice. With that, one like you would have an unobstructed opening for any higher path of study in any discipline of preference with a relatively solid grounding in mathematics. This will also be of help in your preferred desire and commitment to continuing with private tutoring.

"Future field of learning priority of yours should be premised on your goal and interest in life, and advice of your teachers. I suggest that you consult with VP Ajmat Beg in this regard. He was a brilliant student of my batch. Sheer bad luck has him in the present stage of life with limited progression prospects. His entry into the coveted, and much sought-after, civil service was thwarted due to medical reasons. But most unfortunately his merited progression even in the current field has been handicapped by having a son with Down syndrome. He is needed to stay in Dhaka for the treatment of his ailing son. His current standing in the public education administration system is thus far below his intellectual excellence and capability."

After saying so, Hamidullah Sir paused for a while and then went inside his two-room modest accommodation and returned after a while with a sealed envelope. Handing over the same to Javed, he specifically desired that Javed should personally hand over the closed envelope to VP Ajmat Beg of the Dhaka Government College. Javed will not have to do anything as the letter is a self-contained one seeking advice and help with respect to Javed's academic progression based on current reality and likely prospects.

Javed, being in a mesmerized mindset recalling each word as Super Ahmed Farid detailed about three months back related to Hamid Ullah Sir, was awed observing the same person, mentally shattered and emotionally miserable, trying to help him discharging responsibilities akin to parental one, almost parental responsibility. During that brief process of measured deliberations, Hamid Ullah Sir was stable, confident, holistic, and farsighted in his reserved expressions, suggestions, and opinions.

Javed affirmatively decided to follow up directly with the Super Farid on the authenticity of all that was told to him earlier.

As Javed was about to step out, Hamid Ullah Sir, unlike all previous engagements, called him back, and said, "Against all my preferences, I would like to tell you something which is of relevance to all but seldom is kept in view by many.

"The timing of saying so to you is also appropriate as with attaining excellence in learning while pursuing education at the university levels and beyond, this ordinary headmaster of Ghazipur Kallan High School may not be relevant in your thinking frame. By no chance, I am hinting at the possibility of your being disrespectful to people like me, but the absolute reality is that by that time your mind will absorb what it encountered, and your persona will take a definite shape.

"Without elongating, I would just say that be always conscious of the fact that everyone has two facets of life: one is his inner self and the other is his outer self, i.e., social face. Assessment of any individual in real life situation should therefore be from these both perspectives."

In a get-together lunch of the family, including those of Tahera Khala, Rahmat Bepari Chacha, and Nazir Bhai, in addition to the revered participation of Janab Hamid Ullah Sir and the resident teacher of Amin, Janab Mukles Akram, matters related to Javed's ensuing departure for Dhaka were discussed in a glee setting. While overall happiness was all-pervasive, Fatipa-Bu, at whose behest that lunch was arranged in her home, was markedly downcast. Tahira Khala noticed it and could read the mind of Fatipa being depressed remembering her deceased parents. She went forward and drew her close saying, "Ma (mother), this is the moment of happiness. You are doing exactly what they would have done had they been alive. Their souls, wherever they may be, must be at peace because of your actions. Precisely because of that, please relax and be a part of real happiness in the achievements of your brother. We too definitely, even though had no interactions, miss your illustrious parents while enjoying equally the achievements of their progeny. So be happy."

Prelunch consensus was that the field of study would be decided by Javed based on his preference, discussions with Super Sir, and the considered advice of VP Sir. Similar will be the option for the institutional preference between public and private ones, considering the pros and cons of each choice.

Javed added that Super Sir, during the farewell call, offered him a temporary stay in the hostel when he comes back to pursue university-level studies, obviously being aware of the absence of relations and other connections. This, the familiarity of the setting, care of his Super Sir, and the guidance of the VP Sir, obviously obviate any need for one to accompany him this time. All presents were impressed by the confidence genre of Javed and kept quiet. Hamid Ullah Sir interposed, saying, "I entirely agree with what Javed just stipulated. He should be allowed to explore his future under the careful and sustained guidance of his mentors in Dhaka. One needs to learn how to swim despite the initial risk of being drowned. My brother, Zakir Mia, if he were alive, would have been enormously happy witnessing such self-confidence in Javed."

As the gentries present were in a mood to leave as was evident in their taking the residue of sophisticated pan (the betel leaf service being the most ardent exhibition of love and respect under Bangladeshi culture) service, Javed suddenly requested them to stay for a few more minutes. He then said, "Most of you are aware of my resolve to buy back my father's house. First, there was a very good base money that we inherited. Due to the extra graciousness of Fyruz Bhai and Fatipa-Bu, that remained intact. I was self-reliant during the later years of my school life due to the kindness of Khala and Rahmat Chacha (uncle). I exhibited my determination during college life, maintaining the same standard. And I hope to continue the same focus during the ensuing years of learning. All I am trying to convey is what I articulated years before remains my priority, and I need your continued help and support in this regard. In addition, we need to consider that it is time that we keep in view the emerging need for the wedding of Rafisa-Bu. That's all."

As related discussions continued with passion and possibility, Rafisa, out of modesty and a sense of decency, withdrew behind the curtain. That discourse ended with the assurance of utmost efforts by all present. Rafisa was internally happy in noting that her younger sibling was talking like a grown-up guardian. Fatipa and Fyruz were equally delighted. All were pleased being treated as a family with obligations to be discharged. As an immediate reaction, Khala moved closer to Javed and hugged him, assuring full responsiveness. That was followed by a big smile and embrace by Fatipa-Bu, simultaneously saying, "Wherever Abba is presently, he ought to be very ecstatic and rewarded." Rafisa was mutely happy. Nazir Bhai's expressions were all fulfilling and gratifying as he raised his two hands, aiming at the divine.

On return to Dhaka and having no other option as well as recalling the earlier assurance, Javed unhesitatingly walked into his previous hostel, informed Super Sir about his arrival, and got permission for a temporary stay.

Not only that. Because of the arrival without advance notice, he got an informal indication from Super Farid to have dal-bhat (a humble local expression for food) at the former's residence. That indication was an expression of love and care, but to his knowledge, it puts pressure on his wife occasionally.

Though he respects and likes Super Farid for his perfectionist attitude, he has always been constrained to be in an awkward position when inadequacies related to hospitality, especially the food, were mostly linked to his wife. The couple, though a childless one, are otherwise very adorable, and Javed was determined to keep them happy during the upcoming engagement.

Javed, forgetting other issues, spent time preparing himself to make the upcoming dinner get-together more as a celebration of his performance in the HSC examination, keeping the expectation of Super Sir in view. But his additional focus was to ensure that Chachi (Sir's wife) remains equally delighted.

As Javed entered Super Sir's accommodation and was about to bend to salam (showing respect by touching feet), the latter held the two shoulders of the former and drew him close to his chest, saying, "This is your place with all my dua (blessings). You not only held your head high but equally proved that our trust in you is worth it. Our college and this hostel are glorified by your success. VP Sir is equally happy and would like to meet you soon. After the publication of the results and even in your absence, we discussed your future. VP Sir even sent a letter to Hamid Ullah Saheb."

Javed was both pleased and gratified in reckoning the essence of goodness in people like Khala, Hamid Ullah Sir, VP Sir, and not the least, Super Sir that make the society what it is despite prevalent enmity, cruelty, and jealousy.

With Super Sir being in the inner court of the accommodation to say his magreb (early evening Muslim prayer), Javed was alone in that setting with no option but to be engrossed with the thought of beguiled ingenuity that the divinity has bestowed on him so far after taking away the parents from his life. He was thinking of the common saying that "if one door in life is closed, the divine opens up a hundred more."

The return of Super Farid coincidentally happened at the time his wife was entering the sitting space through the opening leading from the kitchen end. The thick cotton curtain was creating some inconvenience for Chachi, but she managed to enter with the tray having two glasses of lemon juice (sherbat) intact.

Javed, following earlier inkling, spared no time in greeting his Chachi and convincingly stated, "My two sisters and Tahera Khala were amazed to know about your competence in cooking. I told them that even the preparation of ordinary dal (lentils) becomes super tasty with your preparation mode and the touch of your hand. I still remember the taste of dal that I had in your place before leaving for home. I am certain that the sherbat and the food of today will equally be the same."

Rohani Chachi was evidently pleased and said, "Thank you, Javed. Not many people in my life," obliquely hinting at Super Sir, "ever commented favorably about my cooking competence. Your kith and kins back home must be very good in cooking, enabling you to appreciate even ordinary food." Saying those words, the ever-polite Chachi left for the kitchen.

That impressed Javed very much. Chachi was appreciative of the limit in pursuing any emotional or controversial matter. The essence implied in fewer words is lost when a matter is dragged on. That was an important learning lesson for Javed.

While sipping sherbat, Super Sir, thanking Javed for his extraordinary performance in the HSC examination, dealt with recent discussions with VP Sir concerning his future focus. He said, "VP Sir had a presentiment about your success. He also alluded that for better learning and sustained progression, notwithstanding the risk of vulnerability apparent, Javed should enroll himself in the prime public sector Dhaka University for the sheer reasons of experienced and quality faculty as well the richness of the library. Let him try that way. If the situation worsens, he could as well get a transfer to a prominent private one, and we will help him in that process."

On Super Farid's exploratory query as to why he is interested in Javed's progression, VP Sir frankly detailed his reasons: "First, by all criteria, Javed is a meritorious student from a remote area, having less experience and exposure. Being in a teaching profession, it is imperative as well as our moral obligation that we guide him in every respect; second, and more importantly, I do not like to see that being under the definite influence of Hamid Ullah, we have in Javed another Hamid Ullah being emotionally vulnerable. I would be happy if we could guide him adequately to become a complete and successful person fulfilling his father's dream. The rest obviously is his destiny."

Super Farid was relieved by having the earliest opportunity to convey what VP Sir wanted to ensure: a clear outline before they meet, discussing a way forward. The whole objective of both was to remain neutral and explicit while Javed would have options for decision-making.

Javed was equally happy within as he had the specific indication of opening for meeting VP Sir earliest, enabling him to personally hand over the letter of Hamid Ullah Sir being carried by him. In his enthusiasm, Javed informed Super Sir about the letter of Hamid Ullah Sir and his instruction to hand that over to Ajmat Beg Sir personally.

As the thinking configuration of Javed was taking the shape of contentment, the disquieting issue of authenticity concerning what Super Farid earlier talked to him about the life and living of Hamid Ullah Sir reemerged in his mind.

In that momentary quiet setting, Rohani Chachi entered with paiesh (a local dessert item made of milk, fine rice, and sugar) and tea for all three. The wife and husband exchanged a charismatic look for a trivial moment, which Javed was unable to conjecture. But he was certain that to be the most ideal moment to pursue his inquisition concerning the life of Hamid Ullah Sir.

Javed carefully supped his tea and then politely framed his inquest, saying, "Sir, as you are aware, I have the highest of respect for you as an educationist and intellectual. Also, I firmly believe that both truth and authenticity are the focal points of your all deliberations in being a teacher.

"With this backdrop, I listened to every word you uttered in detailing the life of Hamid Ullah Sir, a reclusive person upholding utmost privacy. But most of the parts of what you said concerning him are distinctly very private. His quoted description and related emotions are very special. Equally strange is his current desire to share elements of his life and feelings more to unburden him.

"I have observed Hamid Ullah Sir during the last two months of stay in Ghazipur very intensely. Discussed social, family, and personal issues but not his private life. I was happy to know in detail about my father and his qualities. I was almost on the brink of highlighting segments of what you told me about him, but I refrained as that could be treated as a breach of trust, or that may even impact my relationship with him, forgetting about other parameters.

"Keeping the above in view, my most simple and respectful query is about the authenticity of personal and emotional details of Hamid Ullah Sir that you told me earlier."

Super Sir looked straight at Javed wondering about the depth of his query, had an inquisitive exchange of looks with his wife, and then picked up his teacup for a relaxing sip before saying, "I am glad that you enquired about the authenticity of what I told you before. That is the right thing to do in all bends of learning and life with the respectability that you exhibited.

"Before I respond, I would like to emphasize that any inquest-seeking authenticity must have a corroborative backup. Fortunately, I have that in support of my response to your inquiry.

"My source is the 'horse's mouth.' What I told you or divulged to you verbatim were the words and expressions of Hamid Ullah Saheb in a private setting of my residence in the place of my previous posting at the district level. They were told to us in confidence and with full trust in the presence of VP Sir, me, and Rohani. Rohani is my corroborative support of that experience of words and expressions of emotions, although she had some brief occasional absences.

"When VP Sir enquired about his uncoupling during all these long years, Hamid Ullah Saheb initially appeared to be confused and dismayed. The natural query of most dear friends during youth and university student life provoked something in his mind. He slowly started opening and ended with expressions and details we never expected. Once the emotional barrier nurtured for so many years in the privacy of his own heart and mind was cracked by the emotional query of a long-lost dearest friend, Hamid Ullah Saheb's determined mindset gave in. And literally, it gave in unconditionally.

"There were perceptively two reasons: first, VP Sir's initial elaboration of the veracities of the lives of those present in that assembly still having a life joy and happiness tackling ordained distresses in best possible ways. Life, a one-time journey, needs to go on meaningfully with all its limitations.

"To make his point more convincing, VP Sir sympathetically stated that life is not a bed of roses. For example, each one of us has his delicate personal and/or family problem, and we are still pursuing life.

"To be specific, and to my judgment, I did not have any plausible reason to be medically disqualified for a much coveted civil service opening. For me, and personally, that was the end of all expectations and hope that I cherished. An opinion, supposed to be an expert one, crippled my life's journey, whereas I am still physically fit and medically healthy. But my divine destiny never paused there. Healthwise, my only son has been impaired since early childhood for which Dhaka is the only place for prolonged treatment with the outcome being uncertain. I am still talking, laughing, and attending social and family events besides performing official duties.

"Look at our most gracious host and hostess. Notwithstanding being blessed with the most aspired attributes of life like a reasonably nice job in preferred areas, loving conjugal living, upbeat social standing, and adorable family support from both sides, their life remains unfulfilled due to the absence of a child. None of the couples has any problem, but they are genetically not compatible to have a positive outcome. Still, they have decided to have a life as ordained. The only irritating factor is the propensity for sporadic unfriendly social scrutiny by some so-called well-wishers. In this narrow setting even, we have multiple unexplained problems impacting our lives. And it is universally true.

"Having said all these, I have my right and reason to know about your life and living during all these long years totally detached from known settings and absolutely disconnected from contacts. I am not aiming to know why you did so as we always admired you for your judgment. I want to know about your life. Do not hesitate to share anything. This is a family, and privacy is our utmost asset."

It is in this convivial setting of the modest home of Ahmed Farid that the window of elongated segregation and that of accumulated emotions spontaneously opened wide and unleashed itself. Hamid Ullah Saheb was no more in control. He impulsively detailed what he wanted and even those that he did not. And that was all that I told you. And those are datum and precise.

Even though Hamid Ullah Saheb appeared to be contented and relieved, anxiety continued to overwhelm him. He concluded his discourse with an earnest closing request. That related to the "privacy" of what he detailed. In a simple and impetuous but sweet submission, he said, "Years have rolled out with passions gradually sliding away. Decisions that were premised on the poignant impulse of the relevant time may appear to be debatable. I am conscious of that and would like to live with that happily. Whatever destiny would have given me as a possible alternative has no meaning in my life anymore. I am happy with myself and with the place that embraced me. Ghazipur is my new identity, which has given me respect and love together with privacy. I will continue working hard to ensure the sustenance of the first two, but to ensure the maintenance of the last one is equally very pertinent for me. The last one likewise is equally momentous to ensure the maintenance of self-esteem. Thus, my most humble request to all three of you is to ensure that."

In drawing emotional pebbledash to his narration, Hamid Ullah Saheb had an intellectual scanning of the facial expressions of all three and rested after being satisfied.

With that backdrop, Super Sir observed that "one can fittingly presume as to what is going on in your intellectual mind and related thinking process." For the sake of ease and convenience, we can group them into two, that is, how Hamid Ullah Saheb was identified, and what prompted Super Sir and others to swerve from the pledge of privacy.

The answer to the first one was genuinely a prodigious happenstance. The government was aiming at a meaningful school education reform, and in that context, launched a trial program to get field-generated reliable feedback in finalizing the proposed program. A needed separate unit, to be headed by a senior educationist, was established. The trial was launched in one selected district of each of the five civil divisions (a division is comprised of a few districts).

That was a temporary respite for well-wishers of VP Sir in the education ministry manned by many ex-students of the former. His posting as director general in that high-powered program unit was a desired bypass for those linked to the chain of progression while temporarily enabling VP Sir to stay in Dhaka.

Among many innovative plans, the consultative process with stakeholders was an important one. Coincidentally, the first one was scheduled for the district where Ghazipur is located, and I was in charge of the district planning unit (DPU) of that district. Being a maiden one, that activity received intensive attention from all concerned, and the minister himself expressed a strong interest in being present in the whole deliberation process to directly assess the thinking and priorities of stakeholders. All related actions were undertaken as per plan, but a last-minute hitch, though kept confidential, impacted the enthusiasm of key actors including Super Sir. The minister's participation appeared to be uncertain due to the scheduling of a meeting of the economic council of the planning ministry, a meeting chaired by the prime minister. The worst was the indication about the DG's possible nonparticipation.

Super Sir was determined to make the consultation process a fully successful one. He focused on stakeholders, their concerns, expectations, and suggestions. He jokingly said to trusted few that the presence of the minister is akin to ornaments. The essence is the body. We thus need to pay attention to the presence and participation of stakeholders while maintaining pressure on the DG to ensure his presence. At midnight, Super Sir received a call from the staff of DG that the latter would leave for the conference by road in the wee hours of the morning.

The conference started with all earnest the following morning with the news of DG's impending arrival.

Mr. Hamid Ullah was the main speaker on behalf of the teachers of rural areas. Even though not known to many, he impressed organizers and other participants by in-depth scanning of problems of education in the rural setting besides needed financing and shortage of quality teachers. Hamid Ullah Saheb, a literally unknown figure among known luminaries of that gathering, roused the feelings and expectations of stakeholders when he highlighted the imperative need for an alternative approach to broaden the access and relevance of education. Expanding his thought, Hamid Ullah Saheb decried total dependence on textbooks and emphasized the vital need to include supplemental learning from society and nature in the process of measuring attainments.

That was the moment the DG was about to step on the stage. On being told that the speaker is the head teacher of Ghazipur Kallan School, Janab Hamid Ullah Sir, DG Saheb stopped spontaneously.

DG Sir decided that he would not like to distract that remarkable oration for reasons of ceremonial entry. He also said neither his identity nor his presence would be told to the speaker until he was brought to the makeshift office room of the conference where he would be waiting.

As Hamid Ullah Sir completed his forward-looking assertions amid affirmative thumping and clapping, one staff of DPU came close to him with the indication that he was needed in the backroom.

At the desire of DG Sir (concurrently used for VP Sir earlier being the same person in a different setting), the back room was earlier emptied except for the additional presence of Super Sir). While Super Sir was monitoring the arrival of Hamid Ullah Saheb from the entrance point of the temporary office room, DG Sir was standing behind the lone office table looking outside through the wide window. Obviously, and as admitted later, he was at a bay in sorting out the best way to greet the dearest friend after so many years of beholding inevitable emotions.

There was a mild commotion around the entrance door of the office room. DG Sir turned back, and Hamid Ullah Saheb, being energized after delivering the most relevant speech since leaving the university years back, was dazed and bemused seeing the stunned person standing across the office table. Moments passed with both Hamid Ullah Sir and DG Sir being unmoving. Super Sir, the only other person in the office room, winked at DG Sir, who slowly moved forward with emotionality beholding. Both embraced each other passionately, with a total absence of verbal exchanges, and that prolonged for a while.

On being disengaged, DG Sir took the initiative to ease the situation. As a diversion, he started to introduce Super Sir, saying, "Hamid, you may not recall this gentleman. He is Ahmed Farid. He was a freshman in our department when we were seniors. In the university canteen setting, and mostly exhibiting reverence, he usually used to be at one of the nearest available tables listening intently to social and political matters that we used to discuss and debate. I noticed him as we were from the same residential hall. In the process of a few months, I developed a very affable rapport with him and then got disjointed. His initial professional life was full of unexpected challenges and impediments, including family cataclysms. During the recruitment process for DPUs, we came in touch with each other afresh and bonded affirmatively based on previous contacts and exceptional performance in the recruitment drill.

"During my previous two visits, I stayed with him and enjoyed the magnanimous hospitality of his exceptionally nice wife, Rohani. This time also, I will be staying with them.

"A message has already been sent to Rohani about you and your having food with us. Ahmed Farid will stay back and escort you soon after the first day's events are accomplished. Now let us move to the conference venue."

The sporadic arrangements for receiving an unknown and equally eminent visitor were meticulously done by Rohani under the very warm guidance of DG Sir. That unplanned setting shaped an unexpected congenial ambiance for reflective and recompensing exchanges between lost friends. Privacy in that perspective was a nonissue as there was none to be there besides the four. That is what can be said in response to your plausible discerned inkling.

With emotion neutralized, camaraderie renewed, and the old feelings recommenced, the whole ambiance of that private gathering in the abode of Rohani and Ahmed Farid unexpectedly turned into a reflection of unqualified affinity. Witticisms and side commentaries started dominating. Both old friends rediscovered themselves, of course, from variable perspectives.

During that short encounter, Hamid Ullah Sir briefly dealt with you, your family background, and your adjunct rural social setting requesting DG Sir to guide you until you attain the desired level of maturity to take care of yourself.

Hamid Ullah Sir's anxiety and concern about the future academic challenge that Javed is to face in a totally different setting and resultant intreat bonded them more pungently. That renewed friendship got a boost, mostly because of this factor.

The second issue has already been touched on in my earlier elaborations. To be precise and recall briefly, the pledge was not broken but twisted to ensure that you do not commit the same mistake as Hamid Ullah Saheb did.

With variables apparent, VP Sir had occasional interactions with Super Ahmed Farid about the future trajectory of Javed while monitoring his progression. For certain and without any doubt or hesitation, VP Sir, time and again, emphasized the nature of vulnerability for someone coming from a rural setting to a metropolitan way of life and living. Maintaining a balance between perceived priorities of life and diversions and allurement of an urban setting is the most challenging one with ramifications of unbounded magnitude.

Both of us considered and agreed that sustained monitoring and guidance is to be a solemn responsibility for an exceptionally meritorious one like you for the greater benefit of society.

VP Sir's admiration and feelings for Hamid Ullah Saheb were genuine and sincere. He believed his reunion with Hamid Ullah has an ordained reason, and the centerpiece of that is you. Occasional communication between the two with matters concerning your progression is ample proof.

STAGE

SUPER SIR, NOTING the eagerness of Javed to meet VP Sir soonest to show respects as well to personally hand over Hamid Ullah Sir's letter, said, "In the given backdrop, I will try to have our meeting with DG Sir on the upcoming Friday, and you should be prepared to hand over the letter to him personally." He had a side observation too, saying that "perhaps the letter, among others, dealt with matters pertaining to your future university-level education decisions."

Super Ahmed Farid always believed in sharing background before any discussion or meeting. Thus, he continued by saying, "Being cognizant of your roots and background as well as the open-ended nature of the future university life, it is considered imperative to make you aware and prepare about snags and the inventiveness to handle or overcome them, ensuring a steady journey in life.

We had a clear perception of our thinking concerning your future and discussed that often between us. It was the considered view of both of us that while the choice of the field for higher studies would be left to you, we would like you to enroll yourself in the public sector Dhaka University with options for a change to private institutions if so needed.

That was what VP Sir communicated with Hamid Ullah Saheb for concurrence. It was also made clear by VP Sir that in all bends of university life, he will ensure the sustainability of Javed's focus on self-supporting life.

I have detailed all these upfront so that you have the impression of what to expect when we meet VP Sir.

Also, note that our monitoring of you will gradually wane as you gain more exposure and self-confidence with your challenges and surroundings." Both showed up at DG Sir's residence for most pertinent discussions and related guidance about Javed's future progression. During that travel, Super Sir observed "that our upcoming discussion though would have the primary focus on the field of study and the institutional options. Other matters of common concern and interest could have related priorities too in shaping and sharing allied thinking."

As DG Sir entered the sitting place of his modest home, both visitors stood up while Javed instantly moved forward to salam (paying respect by touching feet) him, mostly an unknown personality having a direct bearing on his higher study progression so far.

Without sparing any time, Javed politely referred to the letter he was carrying from Hamid Ullah Sir with the directive to hand it over to VP Sir personally. He then handed over the letter, which received immediate attention and consideration from VP Sir. He finished reading Hamid Ullah Sir's letter which, among others, was loaded with desire and request to guide Javed appropriately.

VP Sir, being a standoffish personality, prefers to remain aloof from the visible site of any responsibility, more particularly in personal matters, and prefers always to discharge his responsibilities from behind the scenes.

With that sort of overture, the reticent VP Sir raised the issue of the future education premise of Javed. He said, "What I have in mind has earlier been shared with Ahmed Farid. He informally concurred with what I have in mind. He has my full confidence to guide you accordingly. And more importantly, what Ahmed Farid will tell you has my authority and Hamid Ullah's concurrence." Super Sir nodded his head, affirming what VP Sir just said and had in mind.

The related affirmative prompt outcomes on the part of VP Sir perhaps were premised on all the following three or any one of the reasons: Hamid Ullah Saheb's articulation about Javed's merit and excellence, the acknowledgment of the imperative need to guide and take care of one in unknown mega city like Dhaka, and the inner urge to do something for Javed which he would very much like to try for his ailing son had he been healthy.

As VP Sir has an apparent trust in Ahmed Farid, he pleasantly delegated to him right from the beginning the delicate responsibilities inherent since Javed became a reality within their domain with reference from VP Sir's best friend, Hamid Ullah.

With that backdrop, Super Sir said, "Thus, I got involved in monitoring and taking care of you on a sustained basis since your location in Dhaka after college admission and reported to VP Sir regularly. I have been doing that so far contentedly with the encouragement of Rohani, who harbored a soft corner, knowing you lost your parents early in life.

"VP Sir also considers my taking care of you in the immediate future as a continuous obligation flowing from the last two years' involvement in monitoring you at the entreat of Hamid Ullah Saheb."

Super Sir then continued by saying, "For one as intelligent as you are, it is obvious that you have a definite idea of our monitoring your general conduct and educational progression during the last two years even though not being a relation or other associate. The background of that was the most unexpected reunion between DG Sir and respected Hamid Ullah Saheb after many years of seclusion.

"Being cognizant of your roots and background as well as the open-ended nature of the future university life, it is considered imperative to make you aware and prepare for the snags and the inventiveness to handle or overcome them, ensuring a steady journey in life.

"We had a clear perception about our thinking concerning your future and discussed that often between us. It was the considered view of both of us that while the choice of the field for higher studies would be left to you, we would like you to enroll yourself in Dhaka University with options for a change to private institutions if so needed.

"That was what VP Sir discussed with Hamid Ullah Saheb for concurrence in due course. It was also made clear by VP Sir that in all bends of university life, he will ensure the sustainability of Javed's focus on self-supporting life.

"I have detailed all these upfront so that you have the impression of what to expect when we meet VP Sir. Also, note that our monitoring of you will gradually wane as you gain more exposure and self-confidence with the caveat that our doors will always remain open for you.

"My upcoming involvement was premised on an earlier understanding between VP Sir and me during an informal exchange of views concerning you. Both of us considered and agreed that taking care of you, an exceptionally estimable and intelligent young man, is an academic responsibility for the greater benefit of society. The bottom line is that we would hate to harbor any possibility of a repetition of Hamid Ullah Sir's episode.

"The above approach and arrangement were discussed by us before your current presence. During all such discussions, I always observed a sense of remorse within the thinking of VP Sir. That became clear to me when VP Sir once alluded by saying, "During Hamid Ullah's time, my reflexes were dawdling, losing him for many prime years of our life, and the society has been deprived of his probable contribution and wisdom. In the case of Javed, I am in control of time and events due to delegation by Hamid Ullah. I thought through that challenge and came to a conclusion that possibly, this is an ordained opening for me to pay for the past lack of timely intervention. However, due to my personality traits, I cannot do it alone. I can live up to Hamid Ullah's expectation to discharge this onerous responsibility with only your help and involvement. You lived up to that trust during the last two years of his college life. I will expect a similar commitment from you for about the next two years of his university life. By that time, Javed will be mature enough to judge between right or wrong in charting his way forward."

After a pause, VP Sir referred to the onerous responsibility that he is assigning to Super Sir, acknowledging the exertions inherent as Javed will be staying in a university residential hall and will be involved in pursuing learning in a totally separate higher educational institution. To lighten the burden of that responsibility, the VP Sir observed, "I am not expecting anything like the previous one when I stipulated your commitment for about the next two years. It would not be similar in terms of monitoring. But you have your contacts in the university. Some of your classfellows and friends are now midlevel faculty members. It is through them that you can have a conceivable assessment of his progression. That will be enough for me.

"In addition, I have a request for your and dear Rohani's consideration. Encourage Javed to maintain a relationship with both of you as sort of a family member. That will provide a personal touch so far as monitoring is involved. It will also help Rohani to have a motherly feeling and responsibility which she would very much like."

That epilogue ended with the affirmation by both VP Ajmat Beg and Super Ahmed Farid.

Around this time, two important changes took place in our surroundings. DG Sir had to decide concerning his professional progression—accept a promotion and leave Dhaka—or stay back in his earlier position of vice principal foregoing promotion. He opted for the second one and returned to the previous position, ensuring uninterrupted medical attention to the needs of his son's health.

Because of the cabinet reshuffle, the minister for education was changed. The school reform program unexpectedly lost its high priority. The involvement of the private sector in education suddenly boomed. As per the advice of VP Sir, I left a government job and accepted this position with much more financial benefits and less political interference.

On their way back and among others, Super Sir, more in a friendly tone, referred to that evening's dinner. He casually said, "Your Chachi is planning for a sumptuous dinner on your ensuing last night in this hostel, and that will be a very private one."

That dinner was the most enjoyable one for all three, but Chachi was somewhat unusually active and expressive. While enjoying the traditional sweet item, roshgolla (made of milk byproduct known as chhana and sugar) that she made for me, I was thinking of how to thank her for all her love and care during the last two years.

At that point in time, a security personnel came suddenly and reported about a tension that was boiling up near the hostel boundary main entrance. Super Sir hurriedly left with them, promising an early return.

Being unexpectedly in a lonely setting, with Chachi the only other person present, I was in an inane mindset and was absorbed in playing with the residue of roshgolla and its syrup to kill time.

At that unsettled stint, Chachi took me by surprise when she alluded to uttering the most unexpected philosophical premise of life to be pronounced by a housewife, saying, "You are leaving us tomorrow for greater challenge and learning in life. Though we would look forward to contacts in the future too, that obviously would not be as intense as of now. As a well-wisher, as I would have been for my son had I been fortunate to have one, I would like to emphasize that life is an indeterminate and unclear existence in a staging of yonder beyond comprehension. Its persistence and concentration are premised on irrepressible portents of yearning and expectation. Inadequacy in either way or unpredicted deleterious outcome shatters a life being pursued with dreams and aspirations. The possibility of wrecking in such a situation is omnipresent unless properly guarded and guided during its formation. One precisely needs to have hopes and dreams to motivate oneself. That is only one part. The other part is the most crucial one. All hopes are not to be attained. All dreams are not to be achieved. And that is the pathway. That is how life is ordained.

"You must be wondering as to what happened to your less communicative Chachi this evening. That sort of logical inquisition is positively normal, as being engrossed in practical life, we seldom have time and energy to relate life from its philosophical perspective.

"The philosophical orientation of life is what my revered professor of college used to repeat frequently in those selective words, and that became a topic of joke to many of my class fellows. I, however, took that with some earnestness, tried to memorize those, and made efforts to internalize them in terms of implications and applicability. I unwittingly thought during the last few days to pass that on to you, hoping that the said mantra may be of some relevance in your upcoming life.

"Based on the information that Farid shared with me about you from time to time, I admire your determination to excel in life and remain a self-reliant individual.

Life, with all its beauty, has its unexplainable peculiarity. It grills as well as it glows, with frequency and timing remaining uncertain and unspecific. But we need to live a meaningful life in any case. Look at me. After losing a younger brother due to the capsize of his regular boat for going to and coming from school, and even being told that I would not be able to bear a child in life, I am still talking, laughing, cooking food, and made roshgollas today for you. I have not given up on life. I am moving forward to enjoy the residue with others like you."

As Super Sir returned, apparently exhausted, Chachi got up to make chai (tea). That evening ended with joy and hilarity.

Javed got into Dhaka University with a focus on doing double honors in economics and sociology. The admission process was easy, but the first requirement of getting one in a residential hall before getting into the department of preference stuck with him. Later, he understood that such practice has its roots in its being a residential university.

Things moved with ease and comfort. Javed was particularly happy with the quality of the faculties and study focus. The management of the halls and their respective houses through a structure of provosts and house tutors impressed him to begin with. That particularly pertained to overall discipline, general upkeep, and food service, both in terms of quality and quantity.

After about an initial few days, he decided to visit Rohani Chachi and Super Sir. Both were happy to note that Javed is comfortable in his new setting, except that his room, like most others, is a four-bed one. He accepted that reality after the initial reservations, signifying the willingness and ability to adjust to reality.

In that jollity, Super Sir observed that with the most deserved scholarships and grants and significantly much lower tuition fees, Javed would not need any private tutorial assignment and refrained from looking for it. But only yesterday, he accidentally met one of his old friends and university batchmates in a shopping place where he went to pick up a few blouses of Rohani. The friend was with his family and introduced them to me. My friend's wife appeared to be very smart and alert. As soon as my friend's spouse came to know about my professional competence in the academic field, she did not hesitate to narrate the problems they are encountering in finding a good private tutor for their two school-going sons—the elder in class nine and the younger one in class seven.

She unhesitatingly sought help from me, addressing me as a brother. Javed's face sparked momentarily, and I assured her of my best efforts.

The friends separated after an exchange of respective addresses and telephone numbers.

"Now, young man, the ball is in your court. If the affirmation is the response, then I will negotiate a monthly fee adequately compensating you in terms of compensation and transport costs."

Javed responded by saying, "If the family is okay with you, I would like to avail the opportunity even if I am comfortable with my present status. But who knows about the future? I may be required to change universities, making an unexpectedly greater charge on my resources. But I have one stipulation for your consideration. To begin with, my commitment will be from Monday to Thursday evening. Necessary adjustment can be considered based on need."

Super Sir's friend is a senior-scale central government functionary living in a reasonably large rented private house enjoying all the luxuries of life one can think of. The ambiance is reflected in all its manifestations in the setting of that household. And worse this can even be smelled.

The first day's engagement of Javed in that tutorial assignment had more to do with food rather than study. As he took his seat, the two boys showed up with priorities other than study. They were in a rush to detail what they have and how they are enjoying life to the dismay of close relations and animosity of acquaintances.

Before Javed could even initiate the process of knowing each other to facilitate cordiality in the relationship within the bounds of teacher and pupil, the household help entered with a tray full of varied sliced fruits and three sherbat glasses. The whole attention is diverted to eating rather than talking.

Javed was amazed, observing the attention of his pupils to food compared to books. He decided that if he was to succeed as a house tutor, he should gradually try to reorient focus from food to books, from physical things to learning, as well as from earthly possessions to intellectual enrichments. In the process, Javed realized that all mothers are not like Khala Tahera and all pupils are not like Amin of Ghazipur. Being a teacher, more as a house tutor, one has the responsibility to keep his pupils on track by talking and teaching things and values beyond texts.

Thus, shelving the immediate decision to quit the job, he decided to stay put and attain his objectives quietly. This was a challenge that he took upon himself, realizing that social orientation is an essential part of learning and thus should have equal priority. He instantly recalled Father Zakir Mia and his intellectual guardian, Hamid Ullah Sir, thanking the Lord Creator for blessing his life with their involvement in his life.

Javed did not say anything explicitly but preferred to send weighty signals. He explicitly conveyed by gestures and actions that food per se is not that relevant in the efforts of learning and eventually displayed that by having minimum intake for himself. This pattern continued during the following few days.

This explicitly caused commotion even in the kitchen, and the household help unpretentiously remarked casually by saying, "Perhaps our new sir never had such good food in life and thus reluctant to have them." She wanted to say something else but was shut up due to the negative facial reaction of the house lady.

During a dinner conversation, the father, Mr. Rakibuddin, wanted to have a tentative impression about the skill and competence of the new sir. The feedback was very positive. Mr. Rakibudding closed the discussion by observing that time would take its course, and things would settle down soon.

The eldest son, Rashed, noted all that was happening and raised the issue with Javed during the next discourse. The premise of that query centered around his upbringing with food being the priority of life. Farhad, the younger brother, nodded his head in affirmation.

Javed took that query with good grace. Instead of any snappy response, Javed, calmly and with due consideration of the inherent nature of the question, responded by saying, "Rashed and Farhad, I am so happy that you observed my reactions to food, tried to analyze that, and raised your question upfront."

After due thinking and an exchange of looks, Javed observed by saying, "Please be aware that we eat to live and not live to eat. Prioritization of various earthly needs is a protrusible way to move forward. My job here is to teach you, enlighten you, and shape you within and outside texts to groom you both as ideal young persons, fulfilling the hopes and desires of your parents. I am doing that precisely and firmly believe that if we can pursue that path, both of you, being inherently intelligent, will perform very well in school. Keeping that frame in mind, I confidently believe that I am within the bounds of my terms."

To ease the situation, he quietly took two slices each of apple and guava and started politely masticating them. The pupils followed suit and contentedly started partaking in the food. What however was observed by Javed is a relatively slow approach to food and intakes being smaller in size compared to earlier few times. Javed was happy noticing that. He was pleased to note that his approach is yielding results, even though slowly.

That soon turned into a pleasant surprise when the mother of his pupils entered the study room on the following day with a usual tray but having modest food quantity and items. That amazed Javed, more so as her existence was never referred to in varied talks about the family during the last few days of his induction. He was taken aback when she sought his consent to have a break of about fifteen minutes as she would like to share some of her feelings for a better appreciation of her son's upbringing. Javed, notwithstanding being dumbfounded, maintained his cool and consented readily.

The mother commenced her soliloquy by stating, "I am Binnita, the second daughter of a modest government functionary, having five children. We were groomed to live with hopes but not necessarily have matching means to harbor simultaneous expectations. A middle-class but value-based family had a tightrope walking but sacrificed a lot of desires and amenities to ensure my graduation from the government girl's college in Dhaka. That was the dream of my parents and treasured hope of mine."

"Soon thereafter, I was married to Iskander Mallick, a master's degree holder in economics and was a professor in a private college of Badaripur district headquarters. Our modest mini family had a contended life with the support of a part-time household help. Then the sudden happenings twisted our lives.

My father-in-law was living in a village home taking care of his ailing wife with his farm income and some financial support from my husband and his elder brother living in Chittagong.

The traditional but equally sporadic and unspecified downpours of late April, commonly known as kalboishaki, lashed our village, including some neighboring ones. As usual, that was accompanied by severe gales and hails. This annual storm associated with dark afternoon clouds on the northwest horizon by nature is area-specific and destroys and demolishes most things on its way. Mallick's ancestral home did not escape the wrath even though his father tried desperately to save whatever he could. Worst was a flying saucer of CI sheet, pushed by the directionless ravaging wind, hit the shinbone of his right leg, causing instant bleeding. Proper medical attention was lacking and was delayed until both sons reached home. That injury turned into gangrene, soon needing immediate surgical intervention, making the father-in-law dependent on a crutch for the remaining part of his life.

Both brothers considered options and ruled out any proposition to relocate them to either abode. The elder brother has three children ranging between six and one year due to his early marriage. The dependent mother-in-law is an addition to the family soon after his marriage. By conceivable urban standards, it was a large family caught between constrained space and fixed income.

Facts about us were known and hence not raised as an option by anyone except the mother-in-law. She persistently said, "My son has so much learning and even received money from the government when he was a student. I do not believe that he lacks money now to take us along."

The elder brother had suggestive eye contact with the father while Mallick focused his attention on the ground. The father closed that insolent dilemma by clearly stating, "We are not going anywhere. However, I need money for reconstruction. This need will gradually decline, and the related burden will diminish. For local needs, our long-time sharecropper, Abdul Ali, has assured me of all his support and assistance."

Once back to Badaripur, Mallick narrated all that was discussed and informed me of commitments made, more to be assured of my understating and concurrence.

Except for monthly rent, we acted to cut costs on every conceivable facet of living. That included everything, including consumables and basic marketing needs. We failed to achieve that in one field. When I told the household help about our decision to lay her off, she refused to leave. Her clear position was that even if we do not pay her, she would gladly work for us. That was not tenable to me and more to Mallick. A compromise was reached for her to work for us on a stand-by basis.

We continued to have an apparently happy life socially and constrained daily living internally. There were occasions when we had nothing to eat except soaked boiled rice, green chili, and naked onion.

With all my shortcomings and deprivations, I had a wonderful and very happy conjugal life full of love and passion. We came very close to each other, and I conceived.

It is very natural for women to develop at this phase a liking for food, especially a few selected comestibles. But I had no access to or means of tasting them.

In such a situation, I opened the southern window of our modest home to note that our neighbor couple was eating their lunch at a table having liberal service dishes. I felt hungry afresh.

Hiding myself at the side of an open window and taking shelter behind the nearest vertical board, I absorbed myself in their eating. They were not only having fun but seemed to caustically be enjoying every move and every gesture. A senior assistant in charge of contract bills processing in the engineering outfit of Zilla (district) board, he often comes for lunch as told by his wife sometime back.

I not only felt hungry but developed an inner pressure to eat everything they had on the table and around them. Whenever that scene dawned on my mind, I had the vigorous urge to eat. The simultaneous reflection of pieces of green chili and naked onion in the water-soaked rice heightened my urge to eat everything. I became obsessed with food, and that continued to the exclusion of family teachings and educational orientations.

The most disturbing aspect of that recollection was the scene of the wife tossing a piece of fish to her favorite Minnie, the pet, while I, being the wife of a professor, chomping the green chili and onion. I decided to settle the score with him that day.

At the scheduled time, there was a big crank on the door as if the incoming person couldn't wait a minute. With all the preserved anger and anguish irritating my mind and physio system, I opened the door and, without the usual greeting, sat on the bed with emotions overpowering me.

Happy and exultant Mallick was astounded initially and shocked later on to see flowing unending tears from my eyes. Nervous and confused, he sat by my side, took possessions of hands, and affectionally enquired about the reasons for apparent consternation. This caused a reverse reaction within me with a sudden upcharge of anguish, doubting his ability and maleness. I forcibly disengaged myself, and forcefully said, "If you do not have the ability to feed a wife and the baby in her womb, why did you get married at all? How long I am to live witnessing the next-door bhabi (sister-in-law) throwing fish pieces to her cat while having another life within, I am to chomp chilly?"

Having said those harsh words for the first time in our relatively short married life, I felt both ashamed and nervous. Contrarily, Mallick had a pleasant bearing, took hold of my hands again, pressed them softly, and gently said, "I came to share the good news, and you, due to irritation linked to fish pieces, spoiled that. That exciting news lost its relevance perhaps."

I was still tensed and retorted by saying, "Is it now about the big chili?" and then rested. I realized that perhaps I was crossing the line and made a desperate internal effort to calm down. I sent a signal by putting one of my hands on his clutch.

Mallick moved closer to me, hugged me, and kissed my hands before opening with developments that are all tuned to positively influence our life's onward journey. He said, "I never had known you before, and did not have much idea about your upbringing and family. My elder brother, working in a large British company based in Chittagong, had to go to Dhaka frequently for official purposes, and your dad was his contact person in the relevant government outfit. They interacted positively and liked each other. They clicked with one another.

"That, to my judgment, was the premise of our relationship. I was initially reluctant to marry at that stage of life as I had other ambitions. But in our family culture, it was unthinkable to disagree on such matters with my father and elder brother. So I agreed with an inner idea in mind to test you as a person to be clear about, and possibly assured, of my future life.

"As matrimonial matters were making headway, I applied for a job under the Export and Import office of the Ministry of Commerce. During that time frame, I undertook a written examination and appeared for an oral test just before the wedding. My definite intent was to keep that and the process secret.

"Immediately after the wedding, I was advised that I topped the examination and was being considered as the principal staff officer in the office of the chief controller (CC) of Import and Export. You landed in Badaripur after about a month of our wedding as the spouse of a young professor.

"In the absence of any job opportunity for any graduate lady in the Badaripur setting, you were destined to be a pure housewife. You passed that test successfully as you never complained. You succeeded in the second silent test of managing a home with limited income, even sharing a part of that with parents in the village.

"The crucial test was after the kalboishaki. Since then and during the last three months, you willingly sustained all difficulties and deprivations, except this afternoon when I was almost running to share life-changing good news with you. I fully understand your responses and reactions. By this time, I really knew your traits and qualities. I consider myself extremely lucky to have you as my wife.

"During this period of crisis, my candidature for the job passed all investigative requirements, and I got the job. Here is the letter of appointment.

"My colleagues at the college were jubilant, thinking about a relatively well-off life of mine in the near future with the inherent prospect of progression. Some mentioned the known side pecuniary benefits associated with the job. You can say goodbye to chili for life as I sense money in this letter of appointment."

Binnita had the predicament of being caught between apparent embarrassment and sublime happiness in relation to her behavior and the good news shared by Mallick. Keeping her posture nonreflective of either, Binnita took diffident steps, more mentally recounting what she has in her mini store to even modestly celebrate the surprising turn in life's horizon that is beholding for them.

On a specific query from Mallick, Binnita responded in a relaxed mood, saying, "I am planning to have an improved diet to celebrate the astounding news. That will be your favorite traditional khichuri rice and lentils cooked together with the usual green chili and naked onion."

Mallick quietly walked out to return after some time with two eggs, explaining that the news was so overwhelming that "I did not spend my usual lunch money. With part of that savings, here are the eggs for the omelets to make our celebratory dinner a really improved diet."

Frankly speaking, we spent a good amount of time prior to moving out of Badaripur, though in a shush manner, exchanging varied options for our temporary living in our new place of residence. I was very happy observing that Mallick also shares my anxiety. The options we were circulating included sharing a few days with common friends or general acquaintances and at the least residing in a modest motel or rest houses.

As no common position was on the horizon, my anxiety multiplied to the annoyance of Mallick. He unobtrusively told me to stop rambling on the subject with words like "We will tackle the problem when we face it."

We moved to Dhaka by train, proudly as a second-class passenger as per entitlement. That was the first for both of us. We generally traveled as a third-class passenger, occasionally as an interclass one, when we were accompanied mostly by uncles.

We had no feeling of what was waiting for us at the Dhaka railway station platform. A semi-elderly person with salt-and-pepper modest beard and hair, wearing an embroidered Punjabi (long flowing shirt), and carrying a symbolic cane (stick) came forward, bent slightly, and politely introduced himself, saying, "I am Siddique Ahmed, liaison officer of Mobin International, the most notable export-import firm of the country. People generally know and address me as Siddique Bhai.

"Our managing director (MD) yesterday went on a routine visit to the CC's office and came to know about your arrival this morning. He promptly called concerned people and stipulated all arrangements, including assigning the responsibility to me for your comfortable reception and pleasant stay. I will take you both to the company's guest house, and you can handily stay there until you find reasonable accommodation.

"Please do not take it otherwise. This is a tradition. This is a practice all of us in this business try to perform for all outgoing and incoming officials based on access to information and contacts.

"Now let us move. The car is waiting outside."

As Binnita lounged in the cushion-based rear car seat of the sedan, she naïvely closed her eyes and got lost in a convoluted thought process as the vehicle negotiated cautiously and steadily toward the guest house in Chayabitti township of modern Dhaka.

During that process, Binnita recalled their mutual affinity for witnessing movies that they tried to enjoy even by cutting costs on other accounts. One preference they mostly availed of was walking to a movie theater after dinner and enjoying potato chips and soft drinks by spending rickshaw fare so saved.

Now, Binnita is cruising in a sedan pampered by an escort and respected by the driver. She vociferously laughed at the sudden turn of life's journey. That drew the attention of all and the reaction of Mallick who, by facial expressions, conveyed restraint.

The vehicle stopped in front of an architecturally simple but functionally well-designed relatively new construction. Ahmad Siddique was prompt to get out with an impulse to open the rear door by the side of Binnita while the driver was equally prompt to open the other door for Mallick.

As Mallick was conveying his sincere thanks, saying "Siddique Saheb," he was promptly stopped by the latter. While exhibiting genuine politeness, he said, "Sir, please do not embarrass me by addressing me as

'Siddique Saheb.' Saheb is an address of high reverence in this culture. You can address my boss as 'MD Saheb.'"

He continued by saying, "If you so choose as many do, you can publicly address me by my full name and privately call me 'Siddique Bhai.' Whatever your preference, I will be happy with that and will always be at your service."

Stepping suddenly into the controlled and managed economy with a focus on profit and income orientation from the rather simple world of teaching and learning, Mallick was impressed. That was positively enhanced when Siddique Ahmed showed up briefly in the afternoon to present two sarees with matching blouses and petticoats.

While presenting those, he said, "When I first met Begum Saheba at the railway station, she reminded me of my deceased niece who succumbed to death during her first delivery. But her very ordinary outfit pained me. That was augmented when the driver later commented about her outfit. So without any idea of her choices, I decided to bring this humble gift for Begum Saheba. In due course, she is likely to have many. But as an interim, these will help to command respect from guest house staff at the least."

Saying those words, Siddique Ahmed left promptly with no chance for Mallick to react, to thank him, and/or to seek related clarifications concerning the stay in the rest house.

While handing over the gift from Ahmed Siddique, a jubilant Mallick said, "Bangladesh television regularly telecast movies, especially Bangla ones. There is no need to go to a movie house anymore. We can conveniently witness movies while lounging in the bed.

"But I am having a longing within me to celebrate today about many things that you had concerns and anxieties about since we started the travel. All your worries just withered away. Now relax and let us go to have a Chinese dinner to celebrate our new beginning."

Binnita, having a precipitous realization of her long-held expectations being realized, got excited and cheerfully complied with them.

The first day in the office was a very pressing one. The day commenced with a series of courtesy calls on senior officials, including the CC, unending briefing by colleagues, and an exaggerated show of competence and loyalty by subordinates. Many of the representatives of other trading houses were winkling for the opportunity to pay respects as Ahmed Siddique was relaxed and enjoying the pressures others were undergoing.

With eyes open and ears alert, Ibrahim Mallick realized within the next few days the reality. By saying those pleasing words on the first day and subsequent interactions, Siddique Ahmed calculatedly was undercutting compatriots of other business houses and making efforts to have a space of his own in Mallick's area of responsibility.

Mallick, even though new in the game, was smart enough to have a tentative overall view as to the norms of the relationships in the export-import business and their link with the administrative office of the CC.

Simultaneously, he soon became perceptible about the role and responsibility associated with his position even though of monomial in type. His chair's imperative relevance in reaching the CC became clear in no time. He soon became cognizant that each action or move in this office has a price, and most people are involved in it. Nobody minds about it so long as the demarcated turf jurisdiction is honored. It is therefore futile to oppose that. He aligned himself without hesitation. Gifts and other gestures became the norm of life.

They soon moved to a rented place, bought a piece of private land in a posh residential area, constructed a three-room accommodation, moved therein, and that modest one soon became a two-storied house with all up-to-date fittings and finishing.

In this process, Binnita soon became the much-desired lubricant to reach Mallick. She was endeared by scores of brothers and brothers-in-law, all endeavoring to please her. Life moved on without burden and blame.

Binnita clarified, "It did not mean that I was oblivious of what was going on around us and why some stakeholders are always so nice and kind to us. Siddique Ahmed was not the lone character. There are scores like him, and they surround our purlieu."

Settling in the new accommodation and being pestered by comments and sort of criticism by known entities about their way of living, one day and at opportune contextual, "I frankly enquired about legal implications of his actions in the office!"

That sudden query was just not an ordinary inquisition. It had deeper implications and relevance. Mallick noted that with a straight look at Binnita, he wore a mischievous chortle and commented by saying, "I was always apprehensive and expected a similar query from you a long time back. To be candid, what I am doing is not illegal but may be ascribed as profligate. I am not sitting on files that are awaiting critical or immediate decisions. I am not asking money for doing something. I am not harassing people.

"My position in the office is a sensitive one. With my economics background, I developed a competence soon to read between the lines of various submissions and summaries, and form an indicative but mostly reliable idea about the way any policy is going to be modified and adjusted in the future, both in terms of export and import. In a controlled economy, such information is vital for advance action. Depending on relationships and contacts, I shared that information, enabling advance action by trading houses.

"In this process, I always exercised a cautionary approach not to align with any group, and benefits were distributed among larger bodies, keeping most satisfied if not totally happy. That perhaps is the reason why I command respect from most concerned stakeholders both within and outside the office. As I said earlier, I do not ask for money for doing something or expediting the movement of files involved.

"Most trading house representatives dealing with us are trusted staff of their owners and have had unique operating abilities either sharing ideas for favor or channeling money as a reward. From my exposure, while dealing with them, I was most of the time dumbfounded by the clever and circuitous way they pilot their offerings. Most of the time, those initiatives have no immediate conflict with morality nor have a semblance of apparent corruption.

"What I am saying will be very clear if you recall the smooth way Siddique Ahmed got into our world. Not for a moment we doubted either of his intention or honesty. It is a reality that behind those words of sympathy, and even compassion, the business interest of his MD has been paramount. As we have developed a relationship, he is now reaping the benefits and at the least has access to me anytime.

"But he is not alone. I had visitors who would say sweet words while conveying their points and would often depart the office calculatedly leaving behind a closed envelope. The rest you understand.

"Frankly speaking, I, too, became used to such practices. But the most startling thing happened a month before Ramadan of last year. A crisis was in the offing relating to the sugar shortage. Opinions were diverse as to immediate remedial responses. After having a clear idea of what CC had in mind, I drafted a very convincing summary to be sent to the Ministry of Commerce. He called me and congratulated me.

"I got the signal and was convinced that the government would soon be announcing sugar importation by the private sector. I called the representative of Moon Merchandise Ltd (MML), a very friendly and amiable person, and quietly passed on the information, giving them a critical time advantage in terms of shipment.

"About two months passed and our house construction was slowed down for want of liquidity as what we were aiming at was much bigger than what we planned. That did not remain private. People had related hunch from my utterances, telephone talks, and sporadic visits of some contractors. All of a sudden, the representative of MML showed up, and after enquiring about your health, keeping in view your second pregnancy, he bluntly pushed toward me a stitched cloth bag, saying 'The bag contained taka fifty thousand. This is not a bribe. Consider it as a loan. If you can, repay us any time of your choice. If you can't, forget about it. The oral account will be settled automatically.'

"Saying those few words, he left hurriedly without giving me any chance to react. I was relieved. I took that as a friendly deal: I did not ask for that; I was not favoring him over others on anything competitive at this stage. Perhaps that was their way to pay back for the information I shared with them months back. I do not suffer from any emotional pressure for that.

"My ingenuity as well as drafting competency soon drew the attention of CC, who would mostly delegate working on sensitive initial drafting to me. This evidently has had at least two plus points from my perspective: scope for sensibly articulating policy focus as I have in mind and access to information. I utilized this advantage to augment my financial status. I do not suffer from a sense of moral degradation. I think I have been able to respond to your query to some reasonable extent."

Saying those words, Ibrahim Mallick, with a piercing look at Binnita but equally maintaining his cool, politely floated queries like, "Where were those people, the self-asserted protector of values, when my parents at home struggled for life, and at our end, we had to sustain life with the barest minimum, even spending a night with an empty stomach, when you had to chomp green chili to swallow your soaked rice?"

"The simple truth is that they are jealous. They envy us. Our improved lifestyle is a cause of pain for them. So ignore those. Even if it is proclaimed that human beings are the best of creations, it is still a fact that the human mindset has the inherent character of covetousness. Those people are a part of our life. Recognize but ignore them. Focus on our two sons so that they can achieve laurels in life. That will be the best recognition and reward."

Javed was astounded by the sheer depth of frankness and kept quiet to avoid any possible distraction. That is, among many others, he learned in his association with Hamid Ullah Sir and Super Sir in earlier years.

Binnita, after a pause, started saying, "This is our life. The deep-rooted deprivation of food entered my system, my mind, and my thoughts. Your symbolic gesture in handling food service and your, as I listened and observed from the other side of the curtain, other manners and pronouncements were eye-openers for me. I undertake to refocus our priority in a subtle manner. My only request to you is to guide and teach our sons properly so that they can stand in line with heads high."

That did set up the congenial setting for teaching Javed was looking for. The learning aspects were inducted into the teaching process, and the outcome was self-evident.

About three years passed. The news came about the promotion of Ibrahim Mallick as an assistant controller of imports and exports with a posting in Khulna, the second most important commercial township of Bangladesh. All concerned were very happy except his two pupils and their mother.

A sense of separation anxiety was evident. I convincingly impressed upon them the reality of life in which they would have different ports of call and different sets of issues to be tackled with divergent sets of people.

In this world, it is futile always to look for like-minded people to deal with. It is more meaningful and appropriate to acquire competence to deal with divergent people and be able to carry most of them with oneself by sheer dint of logic, justification, and appropriateness.

My departing advice, based on initial experiences and continued efforts to the contrary, to them in front of Binnita was to "argue your way forward with politeness, respect, logic, and conviction. Your aim in life should not be to defeat the other parties but prevail upon them with prudence and appositeness. In the extreme case of disagreement, it is always wise to withdraw rather than confront."

Javed paused for a while, thought of a wide range of options, and then decided to keep his homily simple and straight for his pupils.

He said, "I am unsure of the possibilities of such a discourse in the future, but I would like to leave the following for you to remember and act in the future as you both grow up: To my mind and priority, learning is a means of spreading all that is good for society.

"In pursuing learning, besides contextual texts in prescribed books, make it a priority to focus on social issues. That would preferably be a mantra for a way forward to sustained social progression, helping you and others uniformly. And in following the process, never confront opponents. The pragmatic course is to carry opponents with changes, having in their mind a seeming feeling of being a partner of that change."

With thanks and appreciation predicating, that farewell conversation came to an emotional culmination with all the participants taking their advances.

Having been disengaged, Javed concentrated on preparing for his ensuing double-major honors examination.

He spent two and half months after his honors examination with elder sister Fatipa and her family, got actively involved in the planned wedding of sister Rafisa, and coincidentally bought back their home from the new owner as certain unexpected catastrophe compelled them to relocate their business in its old place.

But he was equally attentive to visiting Tahera Khala and family, spending many days with family. Among others, he had exchanges with Janab Mukles Akram, the house tutor, discussing the progression being made by Amin.

He also continued visiting Hamid Ullah Sir, specifically enquiring about his sudden failing health, planning for related medical care, and ensuring other support services to help the general living conditions of the former.

Javed was very conscious of his other obligations too, including assigning a small piece of land to Nazir Bhai within the boundary of the homestead just repurchased and helping him to build a small house with an apparent commitment to look after the house of Zakir Mia.

The results of his much-cherished honors examination were published as scheduled, and Javed achieved the highest laurels.

The eclipsed political sentiments in the country hitherto subdued by the control and authority of the administration busted unexpectedly when the administration resorted to indiscriminate baton charges, tear gas assault, and finally firing on the bewildering protest march opposing higher tuition fees. The march, starting from Amtola (underneath the mango tree) of the main piazza of the university, without proper planning and preparation, soon swelled up as smaller processions from nearby educational institutions and community strongholds joined the prime one.

The determination of the administration to contain the protest and ever-propelling reactions of activists resulted in a pandemonium of unprecedented scale, unfortunately resulting in the death of a student activist and a roadside rickshaw puller waiting for a likely passenger. They soon became shaheeds (martyrs). The size of the processions on subsequent days, in their names and for their alleged causes, became larger. Quiescent political and labor entities availed the opportunity, and the movement soon lost its initial focus on tuition fees.

As the days passed, the protest centering tuition fees evolved around divergent issues like curriculum reforms, better academic facilities, workers' right to strike, and so on. In such a melee, three major political parties called for a joint protest assembly in the Paltan enclave, and that mega meeting suddenly turned the focus of the movement to a one-point demand envisaging the resignation of the government.

Though unrelated, it rejuvenated the protesters on the simple rationale that the government in power is a repressive and equally unrepresentative one. Hence, it must go. That one pointer became the pivotal mover for sustaining the protest movement.

Although being totally emerged in family and other social matters of his favorite locality, Javed kept himself abreast about the happenings in Dhaka and increasingly became concerned about his progression. He took time out to drop a brief "thank you" letter to Super Sir as well as conveying his concerns about the future. He indicated the date of his arrival and requested a meeting with him on the following day, and a subsequent joint meeting with VP Sir.

Javed reached Dhaka as scheduled and chose to spend day one in a private boarding house near his previous residential hall, enabling him to have a consultation with Super Sir and VP Sir about his future move to pursue a masters in view of the prevailing political and academic backdrop.

Both Super Sir and Javed went to the residence of VP Sir at the appointed time that was earlier indicated by the latter.

Welcoming both with all their gregariousness, VP Sir joyfully conducted them to his family lounge. Contrary to his usual personality traits of being reserved and sober, VP Sir was open, happy, and hilarious in that setting while initiating the conversation. He started his homily with the most unusual laughter, saying, "Javed, you have relieved me. Your double-honors examination results erased the despondency that eared me all these years since Hamid Ullah disappeared from our orbit.

"Everything in society is susceptible to change in its perennial journey. So is the relationship both in its broader and contextual senses.

Unlike the present time, friendship in our time was among the fellows of the same sex as free mixing was a taboo at that time.

"Our friendship was always premised on unqualified mutual feelings, concerns, and care beyond the present, even though from wombs of different mothers. It has been usually very strong and pulsating.

"Do not misunderstand me. I am not opposed to changes inherent in the current demeanor and charisma but consistently adore the values that our generation has.

"In this context alone, I emotionally suffered a lot, a burden one cannot share with others. I had the feeling that my inaction not being by his side at the time the news of catastrophe concerning Bijli was in the air had given a feeling of loneliness within the thinking and reflex of Hamid Ullah. By the time my senses prevailed, he disappeared from our locale and got lost. But I carried the emotional burden all through silently blaming myself for the loss of a genius in our setting.

"What you have achieved so far is yours, and full credit is due to you. My happiness is for being able, with the silent help of Super Sir, to perform intangible acts in caring and guiding the genius Hamid Ullah referred to me. By doing that, I feel much relieved that my debt for failing in a critical moment of friendship is at least partially compensated. That is why I am so relieved."

Then there was an unintended break. It, however, coincided with the in-house tea and snack service. That was the exalted one due to the personal act of service and supervision by VP Sir's wife, a middle-aged dignified lady of grace and civility.

While partaking the tea, VP Sir referred to his preliminary discussions with Super Sir and said, "We are in an indeterminate segment specifically of your life's journey. Nothing can be said or detailed about that journey with certitude. The known premise of authority governing a society just collapsed in our country. History is self-evident with experiences that show that it is somewhat easy to topple a government, but it is far more difficult and challenging to replace it with a stable and functional one. In most such cases, the issues and demands that were at the root of a movement mostly remain unresolved, or partly addressed, being submerged by grander political priorities.

"Assessing the ramifications of predictable choices, both of us acquiesced that while considering the charting of a way forward for you, one cannot avoid taking risks. No immediate and or even medium-term, forget long-term, assessment can be made presently, considering the perils inherent due to the nature of current social imperatives. The only option that we have is to make a pragmatic decision based on the best current analysis and understanding.

"It is thus our considered view that notwithstanding the uncertainty that typifies the immediate future, it will be advisable for you to pursue a master's degree from your current public university even though its teaching plan and academic course are easily vulnerable to external political manipulations.

"With that premise, we are of the opinion that since the government in power agreed to resign, the main momentum of protest has lost its steam. In case of any deviation, another protest movement would be certain. But that will take time and preparation for an organization. By that time, your masters will likely be completed.

"The other reason is that notwithstanding all other concerns, Dhaka University does still have a noteworthy faculty and an outstanding library to ensure optimum learning. Your academic mission will largely be reinforced by these two."

Continuing his oration, VP Sir said, "Due to protests and resultant disruptions, the demand for admission to private sector universities multiplied even though the related admission fees have been raised ominously.

"In view of what you detailed in a letter to Super Sir, it is our opinion that the option of a private university for your masters will definitely be a challenging one, diverting your attention more to private tuition opportunities to meet increased demands."

He concluded his address, stating, "I am not used to long speeches. Today's one is an exception in complying with my commitment to Hamid Ullah and the resultant obligation. You have grown up since our first meeting and are intelligent enough to assess what I said. That is not only my opinion. Super Sir also shares the same. You will have our blessings in all your endeavors whatever may be the outcome.

"And finally, we most certainly will not be in the same posts and positions indefinitely. But wherever we are, our doors will always remain open and welcoming for you."

Unexpectedly, and amid warm departing salutations, VP Sir appeared to have lost himself in something very personal. Super Sir also noted the same and exchanged looks with Javed. After a while, VP Sir drew the attention of Javed and reminisced a piece of memory from his university life.

Even then, he paused for a while and said, "Our provost of the hall was very fond of debate, and he used to invite luminaries to talk to hallmates on current social issues of relevance.

"One such evening, and after having the scheduled debate and dinner, some of the rejuvenated hallmates were probing the points made by the two respected speakers of that evening's debate, one being an admired sitting justice of the Supreme Court and the other being a controversial but equally esteemed editor of a popular daily English newspaper.

"That small group's friendly discourse started with civility but soon turned to agitated exchanges, with one group endorsing the views of the justice speaker and the other group aligning themselves with the opinion of the editor.

Right then, Hamid Ullah precipitously intervened, saying, "Even though you all are mostly supportive of this debate, I for one am reluctant to endorse it. We should be very clear about what we learned from history, and that summarily is: that debate per se is not conducive to a solution. If not properly streamed, being the most challenging element, it more aggravates an issue or a problem."

He then continued saying, "If I were the speaker today, I would opt to say a few words, inducing the audience to think more deeply rather than taking a side."

On hearing this, Nabi, one of our classmates and ardent supporter of such debate, pointedly asked Hamid Ullah, saying, "Assuming you are the speaker and we are the audience, what have you said to us this evening?"

Not to be undone by such rhetoric, Hamid Ullah smiled and said offhand, "I can think of two points to deliver. First, in deciding on anything or in evaluating any person, inherent relevant thoughts and characteristics should adequately be assessed. As a very rude example, I can say that when we observe an individual constructing a house, we summarily ascribe him as a rich man. But the real test of richness is not at the beginning but at the end when finishing is to be done. If the cash flow is smooth and finishing is accomplished on time and as per plan, one can rate him as a 'rich man.'

"As an additional response to your query, I would like to highlight the experience of riding a vehicle. If one rides in a WWII type of jeep, the vehicle roars as if it is running at a speed of forty miles while the speedometer indicates twenty miles. Contrarily, if one rides in a modern sedan car of any make, the drive is noiseless, and one has the feeling of twenty miles while the speedometer would probably indicate about fifty miles.

"Based on such examples, I would urge my audience to think and to nourish a perception based on inner thinking of related ramifications."

After detailing that experience, VP Sir concluded his unexpected oration by saying, "I was not sure of the impact of those offhand but equally concise philosophical homilies on others, but I internalized them in their totality. I did so not only in terms of words uttered but in the context of a greater frame in terms of implications and have immensely benefited in life so far. In any deliberations or engagements, it has had been easy for me to identify gems from among raucous voices by simply relying on Hamid Ullah's vehicle-related summation."

VP Sir further avowed, saying, "The Hamid Ullah I know is quite a different person than your Hamid Ullah Sir. He perhaps does no longer remember those words and the incident, but I do. I thus think it as my obligation, being a mentor, to pass on that to you for carrying and spreading the mettle."

While shaking hands prior to departure, VP Sir suddenly recalled a request by a close friend to help the latter with a private tutor for his only daughter doing her first-year intermediate course.

He casually commented, saying, "Ashraful Alam has been a very dear friend of mine since university residential hall life. Lady Luck has all through been very generous toward him. From the Get a Word competition of premier English newspaper to miscellaneous local lotteries of our student life, he, most of the time, was a winner. That is being continued in practical life too. Shariful Alam is presently very well-off, opulent in cash, and copious in connections with most at higher levels.

"Your brief letter to Super Sir, among related matters concerning the family, also indicated a debt to your brother-in-law. I, therefore, feel that this tuition option will be very supportive for you.

"If I have your concurrence, I will mention you and possibly his office will contact you. The plus point of this proposition is that I can very convincingly tell him to pay you befittingly, and he will adhere to that."

Javed showed up on the following day in his previous hall of residence, and the provost was delighted. Admission and settlement matters were completed smoothly.

Mr. Ashraful Alam's office in due course contacted Javed through the telephone of the Office of the Provost. Javed had a brief talk with the secretary of Mr. Alam, and it was agreed that the office would send a vehicle to pick up Javed for the initial meeting with Mr. Alam on Friday next.

It appeared later that the scheduled meeting was more of an introductory one for the family to know Javed and for the latter to have his comfort with the vibe of the former. All material elements that normally dominate such a meeting had already been discussed and agreed upon between Mr. Alam and VP Sir.

The understanding so reached between the two was beyond Javed's expectations. That among others includes number of days, absence during major academic holidays, and monthly remuneration. What however surprised Javed was the agreement pertaining to transport support for bringing him in and taking him back.

The courtesy exchanges were over soon. That included the introduction to daughter Lolita and the service of European-style snacks by a uniformed bearer adoring himself with a crisp cap and befitting hand gloves. Javed noted the diffidence and courteousness as the hallmark of his service trait.

Javed roughly formed an idea of what was expected from him, but that did not bother him. His last five years' stay and interactions in Dhaka made one thing clear to him. That is the relevance of money. He concluded that as he would be getting a remuneration much beyond expectation, other constraints would not matter.

Both Mr. Alam and Javed were sitting in the sizable living space as abandoned elements waiting for the lady of the house to show up. They spent time in trivial talk and minor inquisition. From the other inner room of that magnificent home, the intermittent soaring laughter of Lolita and her maternal cousin was prodigious.

Mr. Alam was very open, joyful, and gregarious to begin with. As time passed, he was looking at his wristwatch time and again and became somewhat impatient. Seeing Aiya (lady household help) passing by, he conveyed his anxiety, about being late for an appointment, asking her to tell Begum Saheba to hurry up. Aiya instantly responded, "Begum Saheba finished dressing up and now has gone for a final check about her readiness. She will be with you soon."

Hardly Aiya finished her response, the house lady entered the living room having all the unspoken elements of reason and rush. Looking at Javed, she introduced herself, saying, "I am Kahdija, mother of Lolita. You should address me by my name. I do not like Chachi or Aunty and so on, or even Mrs. Alam. So outmoded and retrograde." That rhetoric of the house lady came out without hesitation.

Being tall, light-complexioned, and having a proportionate build with some portions of her physique more proportionate and visible than others with palpability, Khadija easily draws the attention of others. That together with the affluence of her husband gave her more confidence than apparently warranted. That was proven when she started saying, "I am tired of this life. My husband Sharif is more sharif (gentle and accommodating) when it comes to sponsoring or donating to charities. Thus, there is rarely a day when I am not to attend events as president/sponsor of NGOs, sports clubs, cultural organizations, and so on besides meetings of women empowering cooperatives. There is no time for me to attend to the needs of a growing-up daughter. We were thus looking for one who would both be a tutor and, in that process, would have the qualities of guiding and mentoring our only child, Lolita. Ajmat Bhai recommended you, and we are so relieved."

Saying those words, she monitored the time on her watch and, looking at Mr. Alam, hurriedly said, "Let us go. We are getting late."

That made Javed nauseatingly startled. Known interactions among family members, such as parents, elder sister, Tahera Khala, as well as Super Sir, flashed in his mind, concluding that perhaps this is the exposition of lifestyle among higher echelons in the society. What struck him the most was the words that Madam Khadija uttered, implying that they were being delayed and most of that was due to Mr. Shariful Alam. The fact was that the latter, being suited and booted, was sitting with Javed for about half an hour while exploring miscellaneous matters to kill time.

Like an internet antiphon, Javed recalled immediately all that Father used to tell him about society and individuals during discourses about life after the death of Mother Ambia. But that recollection promptly reminded also what Hamid Ullah Sir told him during the last departure encounter. The essence of that advice pertained to two faces of a human being, both needing careful and cautious assessments at each bend of life.

While sitting alone waiting for his transport as part of the arrangements worked out by VP Ajmat Beg, Madam Khadija rushed in to say, "Javed, I came back just to tell you that this is a warm home, and we are an open family. Relations and well-wishers are always welcome. And all of them love Lolita.

"Badsha, my nephew, has a special place in our family setting, and his probable departure for the USA soon has an emotional insinuation. Of late, he comes frequently to spend time with Lolita. So be considerate to give her breaks as she desires."

Saying those assertive words, Madam Khadija left as hurriedly as she came, ostensibly to minimize the delay by her standard.

Soon thereafter, the lady Aiya of the house showed up with all modesty, having a little tray with simple eating items, apparently within her competence, a cup of tea, and said, "As Badsha bhai was not feeling well, Appa, with Amma's permission, went to drop him. She was supposed to be back by this time but possibly got caught by the traffic. I have sent the reserved driver to get gas for the idle car, and he will be back within minutes. Please have the tea even if you do not like it. It will minimize the pressure that is bothering you."

Javed was bemused and soon came to the conclusion that possibly high-end super social family homes are managed this way as the lady of the home has no time to pay attention to details. A trusted household helps discharge responsibilities within the demarcated boundaries.

Javed was impressed by the politeness and confidence of Lady Aiya, especially her reference to the emotional pressure one is likely to have in such a situation and an unfamiliar setting. He recalled his Nazir Bhai back home.

In that untaken moment, Javed's thought turned to the personality trait of Lady Khadija. The snapshots of her in and out endeavors and vociferous avowals preoccupied his thoughts. That reminded him of VP Sir's statement relating to riding experiences in a WWII jeep and a modern sedan. While a negative inference would possibly be the natural outcome, Javed restrained such a feeling. Madam Khadija is on the trajectory of name and fame, and thus being propelled by forces outside her thinking, consideration, and control. Once one is on such a path with lady success smiling most of the time, looking back is not a choice as neither power nor authority, unfortunately, has any permanency in their calls.

While having a ride back, the vehicle was caught in a traffic impasse, and, as a diversion, Javed, unwittingly went back to the thought relating to his preliminary visit to Mr. Ashraful Alam's abode. Though seemingly dissimilar from all his earlier experiences, Javed was inclined to rate that positively. He also concluded that perhaps this tuition assignment may be a way forward for him to have a proper exposition of life's array and priorities of rich and leading, an arena totally anonymous to him.

Javed revisited his previous private tuition experiences and decided to exercise greater care and caution in the instant case while discharging tuition responsibilities. He also aligned himself to follow a slightly different path in efforts to motivate Lolita with respect to continued interest in studies and focus on learning.

With that impression and milieu, Javed started his tuition assignment to the delight of both Mr. Ashraful Alam and VP Ajmat even though Lolita's academic year had about two weeks to commence.

In related subsequent discourses, Javed always kept that strategy in view. He devoted an initial few days more to explaining and emphasizing the relevance of learning as a way forward to quality education. It was possible since the college reopening after summer vacation was to take place a few days later.

Time and again, he tried to convey that academic progression should aim at altruistic finesses of significant social relevance as well as artistic and literal competence and recognition in life. Teaching, in that parameter, is a means of spreading what is good for society in a sustainable way.

In that process of thinking and self-evaluation concerning the challenge premised on the trust VP Amjad had put in him concerning Lolita, Javed was singularly certain of the need for a modified approach so far his teaching assignment in this household is related.

Javed thus took every opportunity to communicate to Lolita that social progression can only be meaningful and sustainable if opponents of changes are given a space in the process, making them a seeming partner of the change.

His other focus was on articulating the imperative need to manage facial expressions in every sphere of life. The reserved expression was a trait common to his father and Hamid Ullah Sir, but the real relevance he could comprehend when he was in college and benefitted significantly during honors studies.

Javed availed all possible opportunities to impress upon Lolita the benefits to be derived from managing one's facial expressions. He candidly told Lolita on relevant occasions, "Facial reactions should never be a response to what others are talking about. In any discourse where words are being uttered or statements are being drifted not to one's liking, it is most likely to be a safe and rewarding course to be under the shade of calmness with a trifling smile to keep the other party engaged. It is generally advisable to keep impulses within self and remain rheostat, keeping others in quandary until one makes up his mind."

Moreover, the repeated statement of Super Sir sparked his thoughts. On Javed's specific query relating to a particular hostel management incident, he calmly said, "Anguish is a better alternative to anger, though maybe derided in the interim."

But one thing unceasingly bothered him. While Badsha's presence is not a matter of his concern, the frequency of those visits and that too mostly during tutoring time were experiences of uneasiness for him.

Javed opted to handle it in his way. The strategy he thought of was to make the tutoring time more attractive and interesting to Lolita. He decided to enlighten Lolita with enchanting aspects of art, culture, and literature besides values and practices in making life more meaningful and purposeful.

That strategy slowly started bearing fruits. Javed was happy with that. As the college reopened after summer vacation, Lolita started showing heightened interest in academic matters and issues.

Something suddenly happened in that reassuring setting. Lolita, so long behaving to be shy and sober, unmasked herself all of a sudden and enquired from Javed without hesitation as to why he was so expressionless.

Javed, on his part, had a straight look at Lolita, more trying to read her inquisition from a broader perspective. He then looked down and said, "While I admire your sudden inquisition, let me digest that first, and then I will respond. I am uncertain about what you have in mind, but I am sure about the implication of that query. I, therefore, need time to answer properly, and it will be the next time.

"Bear in mind the lesson you are learning at the instant moment. All questions in life do not warrant spontaneous responses. Conversations in life are not like proceedings in a court. So one can take time, if one so chooses, to respond more correctly with clarity so that one is not needed to take a back step."

Lolita, though got the message in its entirety as evident from her facial expressions, reacted rather unusually as she took off her orna (scarf), made a bundle, and placed that on the side of the study table.

Javed was perplexed and equally annoyed but refrained from showing that. He recalled and followed the mantra that "anguish is a better alternative to anger" in the case of orna. Javed decided to digest that for the time being with the hope of unearthing the root in due course.

He knew for certain that orna in the local culture is a symbol of reticence and reflective of reverence. Any other treatment is befuddling. Even then, he ignored it, hoping for a self-induced reflection of Lolita conveying a more accurate understanding of its treatment at a higher level of society.

On arrival at the beginning of next week, Javed received a note from Mr. Shariful Alam requesting him to stay back that evening for an informal dinner with the family. The note briefly states that "the couple's formal dinner engagement was canceled due to an unexpected incident, and both have time for a family dinner. The two outsiders would be Javed and dear friend Ajmat. The note concluded, hoping that Javed would join and that Ajmat's participation has been confirmed."

Javed was delighted but kept his usual reserved posture as Lolita stepped in.

As they settled in around the study table, Javed briefly had exchanges with Lolita about her second-year study priority and focus as he would like her to excel, matching her intelligence and acumen.

Even though Lolita was wrapped in the usual orna setting contrary to the last engagement, Javed was seemingly in an uneasy mood. Being somewhat concerned about the reason for a sudden dinner invitation, he would not like to commit any speciousness and was navigating carefully.

In the absence of designed academic assignments to focus on, Javed opted to take the safe course of channeling that afternoon's discourse to the usual and favorite social priorities and etiquette issues.

As he was about to take that safe route within the broad framework of learning being a meaningful constituent of the education process, Lolita intervened, seeking a pending response to her direct queries of last time about his traits.

Javed, amazed befittingly, was equally happy to note the ingenuousness and alertness of Lolita. He spontaneously developed a feeling of both competence and assurance within himself about the pronounced enlightenment and guidance that he pursued during the last few days in shaping Lolita's thinking and priority.

He had a passionate look at Lolita and said, "In a limited gamut and locale, my growing up was both joyful and hilarious too under the love and care of Mother and sisters. Father's adoration was there equally but not as visible due to his preoccupations with social work. The height of that happiness was the sudden wedding of my eldest sister. Joy was overflowing. Then unexpectedly, I lost Mother. Father disassociated with most social commitments and devoted time to mentoring me.

"At every opportune moment and instance, he would utter philosophical assertions conveying life-related maxims. And most of the time, Father would say, 'What I am saying now is not for your instant understanding. Remember those, and you will find their relevance as you grow up.'

"Notwithstanding losing mother that early, mirth and glee dominated my growing up being blessed by the ardent love of Father, indulgence of brother-in-law, attention of sisters, and sublime vigilance of trusted household help, Nazir Bhai. Then misfortune befell on me. Father was the unfortunate victim of rowdyism. I lost my childhood in the twinkling of an eye. I stopped laughing and joking. Practicality and challenge of life ahead overawed me overnight, and I started thinking like a grown-up.

"The significant determinate of that experience was a firm decision within me to be on my own feet in pursuing a life of competence. I decided not to touch the inherited fund and the annual inflow from ancestral property. The foreseen outcome of that decision was resorting to private tuition income, including a residential one, supplementing marginally my scholarship inflow. Besides the money part, I learned a lot from private tuition efforts in terms of life and related compulsions and priorities.

"In my college life, my hostel superintendent, Mr. Ahmed Farid, commonly addressed as Super Sir, by sheer coincidence, became my mentor in adjusting to metropolitan life and way of living. Like Father, he developed the habit of repeating avowals as a guide to move forward.

"Frequently stressed one related to facial expressions. Having grown up in a rural setting, I developed the habit of calling a spade a spade right at the beginning. In the metropolitan locale, that was a nonstarter. Super Sir identified that and insisted that I should develop the habit of being calm and quiet in expressions even while any conversation is taking a flouting route. One like me should only intervene when the opposition exhausted their stock of points."

"He further maintained that 'in the current social pattern dominated by complication and competition, it is prudent to have neutral face ad-interim at least and in disparaging situations and settings.'

"Super Sir further insisted that 'One should consciously give a long rope before hanging the opponent.'"

With that, Javed took a break. He had a bit of a beguiled smile before saying, "I hope I could explain my position with respect to your query clearly. But that is not all. May I enquire the reason for your taking off the orna on the last occasion, and bundle up the same before putting that on the study table?"

Without any hesitation or embarrassment, Lolita smiled comfortably and said, "My response is simple and straightforward. In regular interactions among cousins and friends, we talk everything about life and living, and that includes physical matters and relationships. I have been very frank with Badsha and discuss private matters without hesitation. My family's dispassionate policy of openness is conducive to that. Badsha very often refers to my physical attributes, and that includes the size and shape of my breasts. I take that as being normal.

"Generally, I do not wear orna at home. I am wearing it before you at the behest of Amma, who specifically told me about your rural upbringing. That perhaps was more a cautionary step, lest they miss a private tutor of your mettle so profusely praised by otherwise standoffish Ajmat Chacha (uncle)."

That was a submission based on facts and reality within which Lolita is growing up and lives. Taking off orna in that upbringing culture was not something to ponder about. She did not take excuses of religious injunctions or social compulsions to justify it either.

Javed happily noted the emergence of a truthful and straightforward Lolita but was not fully satisfied with the answer. He was concerned about unmindfully committing any gaffe in the past.

Observing Lolita being wrapped in the usual orna setting contrary to the last engagement when she threw that off, Javed was pondering a way to reason out earlier action. He was seemingly in an uneasy mood. Being somewhat concerned about the reason for the sudden dinner invitation, he would not like to commit any speciousness and was navigating carefully.

The ever-vigilant Lolita marked that and started saying, "I have only detailed a part of the response, and I need to tell you the whole. On the first day of your assignment in our home, Badsha, referring to your age and youth, jokingly stated that your new teacher would spend more time scanning your physique compared to teaching you. On repeated negative feedback to the contrary, Badsha commented adversely about your manliness. That annoyed me very much. As an immediate reaction, I threw off my orna to provoke you on the very first chance. I was upset observing you are not only expressionless but equally apathetic. So in a rage, I bundled that up and put that on the table."

Javed appreciated the guilelessness of Lolita and likewise acknowledged her forthrightness in formulating the response fully and completely. He reconciled comfortably with the two negative attributes used by Lolita in describing his persona.

Being unruffled, he, as usual, steered to create a comfort zone within the thought process of Lolita to carry forward the dialogue having innate sensitivity.

Javed did put up a simple question expecting a gratifying riposte from Lolita. The latter was dumbfounded with that simple inquisition seeking her perception about why human beings wear attires.

In order to have a more friendly and warm discourse prior to family dinner, Javed opened up, saying, "My inquest has no philosophical overtone. So do not be burdened by it. Mankind started wearing outfits for possibly, and among others, either of the two reasons: to hide likely discomfort or to protect privacy.

"Either of these predominate when one uses orna. The protruding part of the female body is covered in some social conditions for either or both two reasons articulated. Also, wearing orna over time became a social or faith-related obligation.

"In my understanding, the whole gamut boils down to what one feels about it, especially in the context of one's surroundings.

"As such, one like Lolita is and will remain an acolyte to me whether she is wearing orna or not. My job is to mentor her intellectually. I am happy with that frame. That is although having been attributed as both expressionless and apathetic."

As usual, Javed smiled. Lolita, as an exception, was evidently embarrassed for using those two words in ascribing his traits. She thought of escaping from that scenery but hesitated least that would amount to committing another error by leaving him alone. In her variable mindset, the size and space of their magnificent home while vivified in many respects became a burden at that point in time.

Lolita's attention centered on the nice and sleek ledge, mostly full of family albums in a corner of that room along with other bookshelves. She took steady steps, got a hold of random albums, and placed them on the study table. While taking steps to escape from the current sense of embarrassment, she turned back, saying, "I need time to freshen up even though dinner is a family-focused one. My mother prefers that. You will have to be alone for a while. Hence, I have placed some random family albums on the table. You can, if you so choose, glimpse through some of them to avoid perceptible boredom. It might be a good orientation for forming an idea about the family you would be sharing dinner with after a while."

In welcoming Ajmat Bhai and Javed to the family dining table, Khadija, dressed in an elegant tater saree (English term tant sari woven from cotton threads) with minimal trappings, a contrast to her normal outfits, said, "I am embarrassed for the simplicity of the dinner menu. Contrary to the cherished meat-based food items for which this house is famous, we have tonight various types of mashed items and fish curries. Lolita insisted on that, and I had to agree. So please bear that with me."

At this point, Mr. Alam interjected, saying, "I am very happy with what had happened. I have two solid reasons: first, dinner items that we are soon going to taste ought to be very good as suggested by our very dear Lolita; and second, I am tired of eating greasy food night after night. So that is a good departure."

That was followed by a professorial observation by VP Ajmat. He stated, "It is not what we have on the table matters. More appositely, it is important to be able to enjoy the company of guests present. In an akin situation, even good food may taste bad and vice versa. In the present setting, we have the most desirable august company. That has been augmented with simplicity epitomized by bhabi in that traditional cotton saree and minimal accessories. We are certain to taste a good dinner. I would also like to thank dear Lolita for suggesting traditional food items. I have been tasting our traditional food items for numerous numbers of years prepared by the same chef following her familiar recipe. I do not eat food anymore. I swallow them. I am looking forward to savoring a good dinner of traditional items this evening."

He continued, "As is evident with the laid-out food items, Javed would enjoy the food too. Any homemade food is much better than the feast of the hall dining facility."

Javed nodded his head with a side comment that he had been enjoying the variety of eating items of this house for the last many days. He then opined, "Thus, I am certain about the taste and quality of the food that we all are about to take."

The dinner, despite two nonfamily participants, ended in a real family ambiance. The unexpected sound caused by the sudden burp of VP Ajmat caused a silent joviality.

To escape that, VP Ajmat, relying on his professorial competence, initiated a conciseness discourse related to burp and opined by saying, "For anything in life, one needs planning and preparation. Our dear Lolita has done an excellent job on both these counts: in selecting the items for our dinner and in having a congenial service plan following a desired pattern that ensured the flow of taste and desired craving. My sudden burp was a sincere acknowledgement of that." All present had a big laugh.

Life in its respective trajectory was moving rather smoothly. Back on the home front, things were progressing consistent with Javed's preferred expectations: the ancestral farm income steadily increased with the most sincere compliance of income sharing as spelled by the grandfather notwithstanding the sudden demise of the eldest uncle, the Zakir Mia home was rebought with some bridge financing from brother-in-law Fyruz Bhai, Nazir Bhai was allocated a modest piece of land at the rear end of the homestead. Rezina accompanied her husband to Australia, where the latter got a job in an engineering outfit, and Tahera Khala's family and Hamid Ullah Sir were doing well.

With respect to self, things could not be better: his private tutoring assignment in Mr. Ashraful Alam's home settled satisfactorily, with Lolita showing maturity and earning academic kudos as Badsha's influence on her was waning steadily; while preparing for his double master's examination, Javed simultaneously started communicating with a few noted U.S. universities for much-cherished doctorate studies.

So far as Badsha was concerned, much certain, and equally assumed expectations, suffered unexpected hiccups as his planned travel to the USA for education was thwarted twice within a year. It was first due to deficient documentation. The reason for the second rejection was a derisory one.

Communication from the U.S. reflects the date with the month first, followed by the day, and ends with four numbers of the year. Like other communications, the one related to Badsha recorded the date of the interview as 12/02/2004. The private secretary of his father was the designated staff to open and read all communications other than family ones. He read that as February 12 and kept it on his side drawer with hilarious laughter as the U.S. embassy staff, according to his judgment, committed a major mistake in writing the year, which ought to be 2005.

On the third attempt, Badsha was successful, though missed an academic year. Neither he nor his family was bothered by that. For them, the much-desired U.S. visa is what mattered and the loss of one year is of minimal relevance.

Badsha's happiness was prodigious, to begin with, and that multiplied as the departure date of early September was drawing near. He was super busy calling on family friends, relations, and associates of parents invoking their doa (supplication). That was the public face of Badsha.

Within himself, he was being tormented by two probable apprehensions: being away from Lolita and emerging fear of losing her. That was very brooding and agonizing.

The first apprehension was sloped due to the indication from Mother of their plan of a possible visit to the USA coinciding with his first summer vacation. But that was not the whole. The mother also indicated their desire to bring Lolita along with them. That made Badsha euphoric. He literally rushed to Lolita's home to share the most exultant news.

As Lolita was with the private tutor, a message was sent to her about the presence of Badsha. Contrary to previous practices, there was no sign of her coming. That was exceptional. Sitting alone, Badsha was revisiting his recent experiences of meeting Lolita. He concluded that, unlike in the past time, Lolita presently appears to lack enthusiasm for meeting him promptly. That was very frustrating for Badsha, especially that evening when he had the most pertinent information to share. That agonizing feeling was more intense thinking about his prolonged absence and the impact of that on mutual feelings.

Right at that moment, the lady of the house stepped into that space on her way to the kitchen to supervise the preparation of zinger-lintel paste to apply on her face before preparing the skin for high-end make-up. She believes that the application of zinger-lintel paste well ahead of make-up time enhances the glow. Since the couple has a dinner engagement with visiting business associates from Italy, she was preparing herself to be in her best form and likewise in super self.

Seeing Badsha sitting alone in a penitent mood, Lady Khadija was astounded, came closer to him, and affectionately enquired, "Beta (son), why you are sitting alone? Did not anyone tell Lolita about your presence?"

Without responding immediately, Badsha stood up, moved slowly, placed his head on the shoulder of his Fuppi (paternal aunt), and kept quiet.

Lady Khadija was surprised and wanted to have an idea about the reasons for his reflexes.

Feeling the much-desired warmth in her cuddling and noting the cushion of assurances in her murmured words, Badsha, tactfully avoiding his reasons of current dismay, responded, "With time knocking on the door for my departure to the USA, all, except me, are logically happy. The reason for my dismay is the transient but inevitable separation from Lolita. I will remember her at every bend of life in my new place of living. Though my parents' decision to take her along during their planned visit next year to the USA in tandem with my summer vacation, I am not certain of her feelings and liking for our relationship that I and my family value so much. I am still here and at her beck and call. But seeing how she is behaving presently, her previous enthusiasm to be with me and spending time involving gossip and laughter has waned of late and that too rapidly. I started having an inert feeling of losing her."

Lady Khadija drew the emotionally laden nephew still close to her, saying, "Beta, life is not what one expects it to be. It is what it turns out to be. In that situation, one does not have guardrails. One may like it or loath it, but one is to be a part of the process that generally is ascribed as destiny.

"But you are an exception. And you are not yet in that challenging course. Try to avoid emotional backlash. Be positive and trust us. Lolita is my daughter. We have a very open and cordial relationship. Sureness is subduing as I talk about her feelings.

"Present occasional delays that you have noted and earlier indicated are due to her eagerness to learn as much as possible from her tutor. Your probable apprehension about Javed has no basis. He is an ambitious young man from a rural setting, and frankly speaking, is no match from the family background and financial standing. Moreover, he is planning to go abroad soon for his doctorate attainments."

The outside exposure and interactions taught Lady Khadija one thing for certain: where to pause, when to stop, and how to read the minds of others.

Unswerving in her ability to convey emotional paradigms, she gently drew him close, cuddled his hair, and then stood up to leave, saying, "I will send a message asking her to see me."

Taking a few steps, Lady Khadija came back, saying, "Next Friday will be the last one before you leave for the States. Fortunately, Lolita has no tutorial class on that day. Why don't you take her out for more personal and emotional interactions in a cozy setting? There could be no better and safer place than our guest house at Monindrapur. It is away from Dhaka but fortunately close by. The caretaker is a very loyal long-time employee of us. As I hear from Lolita, I will take immediate action. You need not worry.

"Take Lolita along with unobstructed openness, express your unrestrained feelings, and convey your desire and aspirations in the setting of nature. Relax under the shade of big trees, play with the water of the pond, observe how the water lily swings and dances with waves, and then draw her close to convey what you want to."

Badsha was both amazed and amused. His Khadija Fuppi was always nice and friendly but never as open as she was in that scenery. He had a puckish smile.

Khadija Fuppi noted that and quipped, "Your Fuppi once was young too, harboring unregulated dreams and aspirations. What I stipulated just before is akin to what a young heart aspires with adjustments called for. In that context, especially in our ambience, you are not out of tune for certain."

Advising others, especially juniors and less successful in life, is a passion in our culture. The parties involved narrated their wise words with commitment and compassion. The party at the other end mostly listens to those with all intent and attention. But then there is the inevitable gap. People take part in that advice that serves their purpose and ignore the rest of that.

Though not identical, that happened to the cherished stipulation of Lady Khadija. Badsha listened minutely and was delighted to have the opportunity to spend time exclusively with Lolita in the clannish setting of the Bagan Bari (garden house) of Moindrapur.

Seeing the elegant Bagan Bari consisting of two self-contained exclusive suites, a common sitting area, and basic utilities and arrangements for tea and drinks, Badsha was thrilled. His delight was multiplied by the prompt service of snacks and drinks. That snack was more than breakfast as it consisted of parata, chicken curry, omelets, and a garden-grown small banana. Lolita was pleased to note the service of her favorite coconut water with its white, soft, and creamy layers floating.

In a tranquil mood, Lolita praises her mother's alertness, attention, and related actions in all matters of family and her father's business and social world. She could not help but observe, saying, "Even having a short window of time, she did not forget my liking of coconut water with its white layer, and your liking of spicy chicken curry, whether with parata or bread."

Badsha's mind at the time was immersed in thinking on a different track. He was trying to assess the rationale for his Fuppi to send young Lolita with him to this secluded place. She also indicated uninhibited expressions of feelings for a solid foundation of a loving relationship between them. Within the frame of that license, Badsha's thinking got distracted. He took the present state of cordiality as his last chance to bolster the relationship before he left for the States.

All loving and innocent stipulations of Fuppi to enjoy the shades of trees and dancing of water lilies were parked in the trajectory of advice by elders. Badsha's thinking concentrated on the possible strategy for a binding and compulsive culmination of bonding. Such thinking of Badsha got a boost as that would neutralize any possible inroad by Javed, more so during his absence.

The intake of that sumptuous snack in the privacy of setting and preponderance of emotions and cordiality was making steady progress when suddenly, Javed complained of a shooting headache and the associated discomfort. Lolita was taken aback.

As she was about to call the attendant of the property, Javed hurriedly stopped her, saying, "You, more than a doctor, can treat me better at this stage." Responding to the repeated anxiety of Lolita, Badsha stated, "This is happening recently off and on, and possibly a symptomatic outburst of my agony for being separated from you for such a long time. You are at the center of this phenomenon. And it is you who can give me comfort at this stage."

Lolita, for a while, was befuddled and then took her first move to soothe the situation. She slowly stood up and extended support help to Badsha, enabling him to stand up. That was the first time that her bulging breasts came into physical contact with that of Badsha. She slowly delinked her while helping him to lie down on the bed.

Pretending an excruciating headache, he, in a quivering voice, requested Lolita for a head massage. She acted on that without any hesitancy.

Badsha took that as an affirmative indication, maneuvered his body, and placed his head on the lap of Lolita as she was massaging his head and sitting at the edge of the bed's header. As the intensity of the massage increased, Badsha started pressing his face against the lower base of Lolita's body. And that's it. Two young souls got engaged in physical interplay without thinking of the consequences.

Surprisingly, that did not continue for long. As Lolita started enjoying the unexpected contact, Badsha, contrary to his bigmouth oration of performance, discharged and withdrew. He was initially embarrassed but justified that due to the intensity of prolonged exhilaration.

Lolita remained motionless on the bed, being both ashamed and frustrated. She started thinking about the unfulfilled nature of that passion, trying to reason out the inherent inkling for that.

The timespan available rejuvenated Badsha for a second go, but the result was similar. He nevertheless tries to assure Lolita that nothing is wrong with him and eventually, it will stabilize.

JAHED RAHMAN

The unbounded energy that propelled Badsha's Bagan Bari travel was in reverse gear on the way back. He was both uncertain and confused. Tangled Badsha was relatively calm.

The reverse was the emotional orientation of Lolita. Frustration was pervasive due to the experience of maiden physical involvement, but the guilt feeling was more intense as it that tantamount to a breach of trust that the family reposed on her.

Despite all those, Lolita's relative inquisitiveness was spinning around the rationale of physical contact if the end outcome was like what she had experienced. That continued to bother her frequently.

The following few days were super busy for the family with happiness and parting looming concomitantly. At the final moment and just before emplaning, Badsha managed a space near Lolita and whispered, "See you next summer. I assure you of an enjoyable time and fulfilling experience."

There was a fulfilling mindset around relations, though the parents of Badsha had a peculiar feeling of emptiness. Noting that, and at the behest of Lolita, a proposition was floated and agreed to. That entailed her parents taking the parents of Badsha to Bagan Bari next Friday, having friendly and unbiased recollections and reflections, and rediscovering themselves away from the daily hassles of life and beyond children. On their return, they would have dinner in the posh five-star hotel of Pulshan to enjoy tasting food beyond standard preparations. Lolita's parents indicated their strong firmness to host the event, and that was happily agreed to by Badsha's parents. It was also the consensus that Lolita, being an oddity and extraneous in the game plan, would stay back under the loving care of ever-vigilant Aiya. Moreover, it will be helpful for her to have some meaningful extra time to recoup with Javed on issues of life that suffered due to commitments related to Badsha's departure.

As planned, all four parents were in Bagan Bari enjoying the day as it unfolded with bright sunshine and pleasant breeze. Back in Dhaka proper, life was usual with Javed's presence and designed oration as tutoring assignments are drawing neigh with his final academic year at its end and his preparation to go abroad for higher learning is closing in.

Unlike the Monindrapure settlement enclave, areas encompassing greater Dhaka unexpectedly have very high temperatures. The surrounding air itself was abnormally warm, making uneasiness worse. Around late afternoon, the airflow suddenly ceased. A dark thick cloud on the horizon was ominously visible.

Both Javed and Lolita were preoccupied with their discourse concerning the advent of Bangladesh. Javed narrates socioeconomic and political perspectives of the partition of India, and the war of liberation against West Pakistan establishment resulting in East Pakistan emerging as an independent country to be known as Bangladesh.

Lolita was immersed in that narration. Some elements of political strategy for retrieving due rights and facts related to the War of Independence as narrated by Javed were significantly so contrary to current documentation that those engulfed her total attention. She was relatively oblivious to rapid changes in Mother Nature's configuration outside.

The focus and concentration of those exchanges were uniquely so unconstrained that they warranted total attention. That was more so as Aiya had gone to fetch some provisions from the stores and that huge house was just empty except for other male household helpers who were busy with respective responsibilities outside.

Right at that moment, Mother Nature unveiled its ferocity, lashing the greater Dhaka territory with frequent thunders, wild winds, torrential rains, and so on. All the covered spaces, including shops and stores, were full of people. The busy streets soon became empty with passersby and different modes of transport taking needed shelter in whatever was available nearby.

Lolita, like most inhabitants of houses and apartments in and around Dhaka metropolitan, was busy at about the same time in closing windows and doors, and in the process got wet due to the ferocious splash of rains.

Low dark clouds accompanied by squalls of driving rains, intermittent loud and frequent thunders, sporadic lightning, and circling storms had a direct impact on the wind flow making the outside slothful while nervousness and tension made inside settings excruciating.

Realizing that no tea or drink was served to Javed since the arrival both due to the storm and Aiya's absence, she felt embarrassed and apologized. Javed, wearing a polite smile, commented, "I have enjoyed the hospitality of this home profusely since day one of my engagement as a private tutor. One day's inadvertent lapse, more due to nature, is of no consequence. One has something to learn from this experience too. If I was not in your abode sheer by chance, it could as well be that I am one of those stranded people in shops or other shelters. By all consideration, I am in an enviable position. But one thing is certain. Since the narration of that historical episode has elements of emotions, I could not or did not, pause at all. My sole focus at the time was to carry the essence of its historical perspectives without breaking or distortion. Now, I feel that I am thirsty. I will thus be happy to have a glass of water to drink."

Lolita went inside, picked up the needed dry outfits for changing and, on the way back, got a hold of a glass of water. Having replacement clothes in her right hand, she put the water glass on the side of the table and was preparing to pick that up for offering to Javed by the right hand, a symbolic gesture of respect and politeness and much expected behavioral norm.

Right at that moment, the surroundings had scary sparks of lightning followed by a series of huge thunderstorms causing a general brownout encompassing the distribution grid system. Shaken and scared by such precipitousness, Lolita, for a moment, lost all senses. The changing clothes fell on the ground, the glass with water tumbled, and she had her escape of assurance on the chest of Javed. The more Javed was softly trying to achieve a disengagement, Lolita was trembling and clinching his back. Eventually, they got separated. No physical reflection was monitorable as pitch darkness prevailed.

Standing in that darkness, Javed recalled a much-repeated avowal of his dear Fatima-Bu. To get out of any unpleasant happening, she always used to say, "There must be a good reason for that to happen." We used to laugh at such edicts, but she was relentless. Ironically, something akin happened.

A few days back, there was a limited load shedding in and around Dhaka city. At that time, Aiya promptly brought a candle and lit it.

Everybody was surprised. She contentedly stated that having a rural background, she has the habit of keeping adversity in her mind and actions. She thus kept a candle and a match in the first drawer of the kitchen cabinet.

Recalling that, Lolita cautiously stepped into the kitchen, got a hold of the candle and the match, and returned to the earlier place. With Javed's help, she had the candle at a standstill position after warming the base of the candlelight. That was okay that far.

It became increasingly challenging to keep the candle aflame because of the windiness associated with the lashing storm. After repeated efforts, Lolita had the idea to put her both palms around the dancing light of the candle. Observing that, Javed supplemented that effort, placing his palms on the top of Lolita's to form an additional barricade.

Lolita's face was glowing in that setting of luminous candle flame. Her recent wet face while closing the windows and disorganized hair flow made her more attractive. To Lolita, Javed was looking more manly and alluring than ever before.

The palms got disengaged. Lolita surrendered on the chest of Javed while the latter's fingers were intensely caressing the upper back of her physique. They lost their senses and involuntarily undressed themselves. The marble floor base momentarily felt like a heavenly bed setting until she had her orgasm and he ejaculated.

As they stood up, Lolita hurriedly retreated to her room while Javed rapidly looked for his clothes. He strained himself to calm down and, in that process, dressed up. Those were easy, but the sedulous pressure of succumbing to temptation continued to perturb him.

In that messy setting and even with pervasive darkness, the glass of water earlier brought by Lolita remained intact. Renewed thrust overwhelmed Javed, and he finished the water instantly.

He was standing near the candlelight having a feeling of gradual slowing down of the storm's ferocity. His mind was preoccupied with the immediate future: what happens if the storm continues to rage or the restoration of electricity is delayed? His feet in the shoes froze instantly. He was more concerned about the likely turn of his life.

Amid such agonizing internal agitations, Javed was pleasantly surprised to notice the startling stepping in of Lolita with a smiling bearing. But what surprised him the most was her wearing a saree for the first time since he was teaching in this home.

That thinking simultaneously took a scary turn when he was trying to assess what Lolita had in mind, especially as her parents returned. With all ease in her command, she winked at him, conveying a silent query as to how she was looking.

Javed, in his quest of not prolonging any discourse regarding the saree episode, smiled and said, "Why saree?" He was overburdened by the possible reaction of her parents seeing her in a saree!

Lolita joyfully responded, "Just for a change. Nature can change sporadically. People's opinions can change rapidly. Behaviors and reactions may turn the course anytime. So is my liking."

She was smart enough to read what was going on in Javed's mind. She pointedly observed, saying, "This part of the night is all that life means to me. It also epitomizes both the beginning and end of our physical relationship. It reflects my understanding as to what gender-oriented relationship entails. You have given me that feeling and understanding. I am thankful to you even though it was never a part of my thinking. I enjoyed it. But take it from me that you have no obligation for this. I will handle it the way it needs to be.

"You may have an unspecified query as to the reaction of my parents. I also thought about it and have a convincing response. That is very simple and straight. I will say that 'being splashed by rainwater while closing the doors and windows in the absence of Aiya, I was deranged and in need of change. In pitch darkness, I took what was handy and accessible. Hence, the saree.'"

Javed was impressed and complimented her with a common axiom that there is definite truth in saying that women's minds travel in multifarious ways. I now believe in that.

Lolita retorted, "You can have your deduction, but I am very clear about the design that prompted me to oft for a saree. This is a physical manifestation of my emotional transformation from a young girl to an evolving woman. And in that, you had your unintended role. I hope you get the answer."

Javed would have liked to escape from this setting and situation soon, but could not do so for obvious reasons. Lolita was alone. The darkness was dragging on. The night's prolongation was lengthening. Uncertainty was pervasive even though the intensity of the storm mellowed down.

In that mixed situation of natural constraints and pressures of moral compulsions with the sole candle at its lower end struggling to continue emitting light, a common teaching of his late father, a principled life focus of his esteemed schoolteacher, and persistent precautionary avows of Super Sir of his college life flashed in his thinking. Every one of them, in their respective time and role, cautioned him about vulnerability in life. They insisted on extra care in pursuing the path of life, minimizing emotion as much as possible and optimizing prudence as required.

Javed was super confident in that respect having needed orientation at every bend of life that far from a revered father, respected teacher at school, and selfless guide in college. With all that in his mind persistently, he somehow totally forgot a simple cautionary saying of his half-lettered Tahira Khala. That happened on a day when he was feeling depressed for getting involved in a family-related matter against all logic he had. Javed just succumbed to temptation.

Noting that during lunchtime, Khala offhandedly stated, "Mankind's worst paleness is succumbing to temptation. Learning, knowledge, and preparedness have less relevance when temptation triumphs. There is a plethora of advice concerning that, but perhaps persistent alertness is a precautionary strategy possibly to circumvent that."

As a follow-up, Javed said, "I valued that always. As I was growing up, I kept in mind what Khala said casually and practiced that to avoid snares. But all went in vain this evening. The glow in your face with the dancing flash of candlelight created within me a pleasant feeling. I slowly stepped into the trap. The darkness, the thunders, and intermittent flashes of lightning accentuated the process. I forgot all the teachings and guidance.

"Whatever it is, I am the one who is responsible and should remain accountable for that."

Lolita, more due to being saree-clad, looked like a lady in that setting of concerns and conviction. She had a deep adoring look of admiration at Javed with a comforting smile, and said, "You, despite your brilliance and urban living of last six years, are still an innocent and simple guy of a rural setting. If a blame needs to be ascribed, it is me and by no chance you. You forget that observing the formation of a black cloud on the horizon, you wanted to leave. I insisted that you stay back. I had no other intent at that stage. I just did not like to be alone. When I was allowing Aiya to go grocery shopping, I thought it would be for a while. To frankly and honestly affirm, you were never in my thinking process as one with whom I would like to have a physical relationship.

"Since we are an open and free family, we, among cousins and other compatible relations, were very exposed in terms of feelings and relationships. For certain, you were never mentioned.

"You must be wondering about the motivation for our bewildering as well as unpredictable physical encounter. There is a reason." Having said that, she went on to detail the recent happenings in Bagan Bari in the company of Badsha. "Being muddled and confused, I was reactionless in the private setting of Bagan Bari, with the caretaker giving instructions not to disturb us. During that time, Badsha moved closer to me with a supposed headache and evidently pretended to be emotionally intense gradually. I was confused. but my physique slowly started giving in. I experienced startling horripilation. We unwittingly got involved in my maiden relationship. It was a short and totally unfulfilling experience. That short and frustrating experience caused me to think persistently about a physical relationship. I decided to test that experience in an appropriate setting. It was to be an opportunity and occasion with anyone I like. But you were never in the periphery of my thinking. Trust me.

"Whatever happened this evening was at my behest. I am responsible for that and no one is. At this stage, I am not concerned. Meanwhile, and at a suitable time, I will confess to Mother. She is a very understanding and considerate mother. Moreover, our relationship is premised on frankness and friendship. So do not be concerned about it."

There was a pause. An absolute silence prevailed against the backdrop of darkness with the candle being fully exhausted.

Javed thought that to be the most appropriate time to divulge the exciting news he was holding for so long, just hoping to share that with all at the same time. With that backdrop and since time is running out, Javed decided to share with Lolita the exciting news before leaving. He thus said, "Sitting in this darkness, I want to share with you very exciting news about me with a request that you should keep your parents informed about that as soon as they return."

It was well neigh impossible to assess the facial reaction of Lolita due to the prevailing darkness, but her vocal expressions conveyed unhappiness in clear terms. She commented, "If it is about you and the news is so prodigious, why you are holding that within yourself for so long? Perhaps you think that I do not have the maturity to appreciate that. But you are wrong. About the last year, besides focusing on my academic attainments, you spent innumerable hours enhancing and enriching my social concentration and excellence. I am thus a different Lolita now to the amazement of my parents. So even belated, please tell me what you have up in your sleeves."

Javed replied, "You have a very pertinent observation, and that deserves a factual response. But before reverting to that, I would like to react to your observation of considering you not mature enough to share my beholden good news. That is not factual at all. I have been in tutoring engagement from my eight-level class and in the process have handled different students of varied backgrounds. I thus acquired an impeccable ability to judge the intellectual competence of students. My first few days of interactions with you convinced me about your intellectual prudence.

"In our social setting, there are few God-gifted individuals. They are born with intelligence and acumen. They shine with and, even in some cases, without effort. But then there is a group of people who are gifted with the ability to absorb and enrich knowledge and information on a sustainable basis. You belong to this group.

I devoted whatever time available to a culture that capacity in you. I am happy to note that you are up to that actuality and mark. You are now on the prudent track of learning and education propelled by self-will and self-effort. You do not need a teacher anymore to monitor you on this path."

Javed continued his oration stating, "You mentioned spending many hours by me to enhance your social skills and competence. That assertion of you is indicative of my doing something voluntarily and as gratis. The fact is that the same was neither voluntary nor free.

"VP Sir, your Ajmat Beg uncle, negotiated lumpsum monthly emoluments for my services. It has no day stipulation. Neither does it have any time mark. But the sum so agreed with your dad's office was significantly beyond prevailing ones. I utilized that flexibility to enhance your overall social understanding and enhance needed skills.

"On your more pertinent comment concerning maturity, you clearly are not on the proper track. It was not maturity that mattered in my thinking process. I just thought that sharing something good with many enhances happiness. I was just waiting. The persistent storms and darkness diverted the focus. I hope that you trust me."

It was about 9:00 pm. Certain things happened almost simultaneously. The storm was on its definite wane. Aiya returned, and the vehicle to take Javed to his place was in position. And the best part was that the power was restored.

Against this scenery, Javed narrated the essence of the good news, saying, "My avowed aim in life is to pursue educational excellence in a prestigious USA university. You are aware of my application process. The day before yesterday, I got a firm affirmative communication from the university where I wanted to be but had marginal expectations. The other pertinent part is that the acceptance has a full financial support proposition. I am now to complete related processes soonest and to be in the university within the next three months for timely induction in their PhD course. I will be here for about another ten days to complete the necessary documentation requirements and other prerequisites. After that, I will be spending the rest of the time in Ghazipur with family and addressing present and likely family matters.

"My coming today to your abode was in my immediate plan but became a certainty when I received the request from your father's office to be in your place to address some of your academic impasse."

Saying those words and with full endorsement of Lolita, Javed stepped out when the cell phone of Lolita rang. He just rushed out, boarded the waiting vehicle, and proceeded to his place.

On reaching his destination, Javed became engrossed with pressing dares, sidetracking the early evening's incident as a nightmare for the time being.

Lolita was excited to hear the voice of her parents and more so knowing that they all were in the designated hotel of Pulshan enjoying dinner as planned.

Badsha's parents and Lolita's dad were hilarious in their exchanges while having dinner in the hotel despite the bad weather, enjoying the food choices of Lady Khadija. However, the latter was surprisingly subdued. That did not draw the attention of others.

While the parents of Badsha were excited between them in symbolically interpreting that day's experience as a positive signal for binding future relationships, Mr. Alam took the less enthusiastic reflexes of Lady Khadija as the natural offshoot of being tired.

Returning home and finding Lolita joyful with her saree on, both were happy and relaxed. After a while, all three sat together, sharing experiences and challenges of the day, including that of the storm.

In that hassle-free mood, Lolita shared the positive news of Javed's acceptance at his preferred and highest-ranked U.S. institution for higher learning located in Boston. Everyone was happy. Lady Khadija, however, could not hide her anxiety. She observed, "That means we will have to look for another tutor. What a hassle!"

However, Mr. Alam confided, "Yes, from our perspective, this is somewhat bothersome. But we ought to be happy that someone of our acquaintance got admitted to such a prestigious educational institution with funding. The positive side of scouting for a good tutor is that, unlike the previous time, we now have two sources: Brother Ajmet Beg and Javed. Instead of being downcast, let us explore those. Who knows what we have in the store."

Saying those soothing words, Mr. Alam enquired about Javed's immediate plan. On being so advised by Lolita, he proposed to have him over the following evening for dinner. Lady Khadija consented, and the ball started rolling. Javed happily showed up the next day and was warmly received by the family.

While having snacks and soft drinks, Lady Khadija raised the issue of a replacement tutor. Javed scanned the couple as well as Lolita. In a tranquil mood and courteous expression, Javed stated, "The major problem in our upbringing is that we often fail to acknowledge what we have. In Lolita, you have a gem. What she needed was proper stimulus, impetus, and buoyancy. Based on my relatively long tutoring involvement, I discovered that within the first few days. That resulted in apportioning one-third of the time for academic exigencies and the rest on learning and exposition on assessing information, broadening knowledge, and solidness in understanding, giving one the capacity to view issues and problems in broader perspectives. Over time, I am convinced that Lolita has gained that. She is now capable of having her road tramp. She no longer needs a tutor.

"There may be occasions when she is unclear on something or may need guidance. In that situation, you may touch base with your friend VP Ajmat Beg. He has a very dear associate by the name of Ahmed Farid, a professor too but junior to him. He mentored me as my hostel superintendent at the behest of VP Sir. If VP Ajmat requests him any time, Prof. Ahmed Farid would always be obliging. And, more pertinently, he is a genius on matters like counselling and guiding. I am saying so from my own experience."

With such assessment and assurance, the whole ambiance of exchanges became a reposeful and supporting one. Lolita surprisingly maintained a very serene posture, but the unqualified tension of what and how yesterday's happening could come up to the surface was internally pumping the systems of Javed. Fortunately, nothing of that sort happened, and Javed left Lolita's abode, giving assurance of a visit before leaving for the USA.

Tension-free and looking forward to an enthralling immediate future, Javed reached back to his residential place and enthusiastically prepared to leave for Ghazipur.

SOJOURN

JAVED REACHED GHAZIPUR on the date and approximate time indicated earlier. The first person to greet him was his favorite Nazir Bhai. But that happiness was short-lived. Nazir told him about the illness of Hamid Ullah Sir. He also indicated that in the absence of adequate support, sir's health status was deteriorating gradually.

On being so appraised, Javed immediately decided to go to Hamid Ullah's place first. Before he could bend to salam (by touching the feet), Hamidullah Sir extended his fragile arms to embrace him, saying, "I am so proud of you. You have more than proven the trust I have in you." He continued saying, "Fyruz came a few days back to tell me about your fully funded acceptance by the most prestigious university in the USA. I am so happy that the trust reposed by your late father in me to guide you is becoming a reality. Ghazipur is proud of you. So I am."

Exchanging a brotherly look, he asked one of sir's current favorite students present at the time to go and get munshi doctor Chacha, conveying a special request for him to come soonest. He then sent Nazir Bhai to Fatipa-Bu's abode with luggage, and to inform her that he would be home soonest after Dr. Chacha's visit.

On hearing about the presence of Javed, the munshi doctor showed up immediately and undertook a thorough examination. During the period, Javed recalled his conversation with the late father about the competence of Dr. Chacha in the absence of adequate educational attainments. The backdrop of that discourse was the ailment of the late Zakir Mian and his reluctance to go to the district hospital. In support of his aforesaid position, the late Zakir Mian elucidated, saying, "Baba (meaning son), I appreciate your concern. But I decided otherwise based on my feelings about my health and the immediate availability of the munshi doctor. In the absence of a qualified doctor in our area, he has always been the first responder. He has a magic hand. Most of his past diagnoses were correct and endorsed by district hospital doctors. Moreover, he has good professional contacts there. His referrals were mostly attended to promptly. I am comfortable with that. More so he is at my beck and call." That in essence was the reason why Javed thought of Dr. Chacha immediately.

After a thorough investigation, including questions related to the beginning of the current ailment including that of urinal and stool-related constraints, Dr. Chacha, with a smile, said, "Beta (son), as per my judgment, he has no major ailment. Persistent fever and other health-related impairments are mostly due to prolonged malnutrition and symptoms of urine infection, causing weakness and loss of weight. I am prescribing the needed medicines that are locally available. My only request to Hamid Ullah Saheb is to touch base with me in case of any need. If so required, I will refer him to the district hospital physician, and as needed will accompany him."

With that sort of findings, Javed started to proceed to Fatipa-Bu's home and returned to say, "Nazir Bhai will soon come with some food as well as prescribed medicines. Sir, please try to eat as much as possible. Nazir Bhai will help you and will stay the night in your other room.'

Hamid Ullah Sir had a passionate look following the body frame of adorable Javed and was in tears recalling the absence of his respected brother like Zakir Mian.

Seeing Javed entering the abode, all awaiting rushed out, and the first one to hug him was nephew Ameen. Happiness was abounded. Observations and comments were inexhaustible. The surprised presence of Tahira Khala pleased him very much, but he was overwhelmed seeing Munira with her two-year-old progeny. The reaction of Fatipa-Bu was copious. As usual, Fyruz was glad and embraced him before proceeding to set arrangements for the service of food. That was a gala reunion with everyone being uproarious. The only exception was the feeling of Fatipa-Bu remembering her parents after the initial exuberance. At the request of Fyruz, everybody agreed to stay overnight, more as a mental support for Fatipa.

The first two days were full of recalling stories and events by Javed, including recounting his interactions with Binita, the love and care of Rohani Chachi, and the gregarious encounters with Lady Khadija with respect to the lifestyle of the rich and famous. While respectfully narrating the help and guidance received from VP Azmat Beg, the batchmate and good friend of Hamid Ullah Sir, he summed up that his above experiences and exposure enabled him to comprehend life patterns of divergent segments in the society, making him more enlightened and appreciative.

His main emphasis was related to the values and practices of people like Ibrahim Mallick without being familiar with their life challenges and experiences. But his story about upscale society, as epitomized by Lady Khadija, amused everyone. Equally, his description of feelings Rohani Chachi's life being childless drew the sympathy of all adult attendees.

As things settled down, Javed opened his mind on the third morning after a sumptuous breakfast to narrate what he had up in his sleeves. In a family setting, he said, "Fatipa-Bu and Fyruz Bhai, I have some matters that are up in my thinking more in the context of my scheduled long absence, and I want to have your understanding and concurrence on those matters."

On hearing that, Fatipa-Bu and Fyruz Bhai exchanged a reciprocal inquisitive look with each other and kept quiet with full attention.

Javed took a breather more to organize his thoughts and detailed those in an easily understandable manner. Those were:

- The upkeep of the parental home without any intrusion
- Taking responsibility with respect to the living and health care of Hamid Ullah Sir
- Establishing a technical training facility for deserving girls with a focus on stitching and basic technological expertise, and name that Ambia Institute of Technology (AIT)
- Renewing contact with uncles and cousins at Shetra

He went detailing what he had in mind. As Fatipa-Bu and Fyruz Bhai remained silent, Javed continued, "What I am going to say is not casual. I thought through them during my university life and more so after I got confirmation of my admission with full funding.

"My proposal is Nazir Bhai should explicitly be made responsible for taking care of our parental home, and in return, we would assign the title of the small piece of land on which his present home is located.

"Nazir Bhai is to be deputed for taking care of Sir on an intermittent basis during daytime but requiring him to stay in Sir's place at night, and in return to be suitably remunerated.

"We need to have an arrangement with munshi Dr. Chacha for a periodical check-up of Sir and his treatment as needed. Dr. Chacha will be paid out of our family fund, and Fyruz Bhai to have full freedom in committing resources in this regard."

Coincidentally, right at the moment, while going to attend a call, munshi Chacha suddenly stepped in as a courtesy visit and was involved in discussions with respect to the care requirements of Hamid Ullah Sir. Everything was discussed threadbare and agreed to, making all happy.

After munshi Chaha left, Javed resumed his discourse specifying his plan for the proposed AIT. He said, "You are aware of my yearning to buy back the ancestral home. Due to your support and Fyruz Bhai's bridge financing, I could achieve that. But that generated a new desire within me.

"In our social setting, men dominate. We seldom recognize the contribution of female folks. That applies to father Zakir Mia and mother Ambia. In the given social system, Father was glorified and recognized, rightfully so. But his silent partner and galvanizer, who spent all her time and energy raising the children and looking after the family, was seldom recognized and mentioned. Our social system forgets as well as is reluctant to recognize that contributions that enable male folks to pursue their focus and ambition in life even though they are mostly dependent on womenfolk's alertness and help.

"Small soft words, small guidance, and small encouragement that I, for that matter my sisters also, received from her still ring in my years and guide me silently. I sense her presence in every move in my life. Neither father could contribute to society that much nor we could achieve in life whatever we have attained so far without mother Ambia being in our lives. That is the rationale of my proposition.

"To begin with, I, subject to your concurrence, would like to have focus of AIT on training related to stitching expertise and that of internet technology. Based on need and demand, AIT may be upgraded gradually to focus on learning and training, including enriching spoken English capability. In Lady Khadija's home, I met one of her relations who has a readymade garments factory in Jordan with workers mostly from Bangladesh. That gave me the idea of equipping workers with basic English language proficiency. This will partly enhance their confidence to interact and open opportunities in professional life."

Fatipa-Bu was glowing in her silent facial expressions. Fyruz Bhai was evidently impressed by the depth of his proposition.

Javed continued, "I thought through the options we have for the site. My considered view, and for your consideration, is that the proposed AIT may probably be located at half a mile northeast distance on one of our farmland plots at the crossroad location of Zilla Porishod (district council) and the union council roads. To begin with, it will be a modest one, and based on experience and demand, it could be upgraded suitably. I also gave serious thought to its financing. I have some savings out of tutoring that I did for many long years. There are also some funds available from various grants and fellowships. I am conscious of the fact that all these are small money in the context of AIT but would be sufficient to start. We may agree to sell the plot of land at the southeast corner of the intersection of the main road. Fatipa-Bu may recall that while having dinner during one of the good days of our full family, Abba indicated his desire to buy that plot of land in a very important location of Ghazipur. Though Amma generally was not supportive of buying any more land, she readily agreed and suggested registering that deal in my name. So being the sole owner, I have decided to sell that piece of land to meet the likely financing needs of AIT and that too in the future. The other point I would like to state is as the surrounding land prices are growing phenomenally due to all-round development activities and as there is no immediate need for large financial commitment, I propose to defer selling that land sometime next year."

He concluded his proposal, indicating a joint visit of Shetra, including Nazir Bhai in the early part of next month.

Breaking the silence, Fatipa-Bu moved close to hug Javed and innocuously said, "Look at my little brother. How soon and how diligently he has grown up. Parents, wherever they are, must be very happy about his thoughts and plans." She then winked at Fyruz and started crying, a trait she had unknowingly developed since the death of her father.

Fyruz, in addition to supporting all that Javed proposed, suggested keeping Rafisa in the loop fully when she calls next time.

Javed made it very clear that Fyruz Bhai would have full authority to work out the aforesaid understandings and manage the family fund and all financial and other matters of the family until otherwise decided.

Days rolled in and days rolled out. All that was planned was smoothly worked out, including a visit to the family home in Shetra reconnecting with uncles and cousins.

Javed gleefully was preparing for his travel back to Dhaka en route to the USA soonest. It was agreed that Fyruz and his family would be in Dhaka to see Javed off.

The culmination of all these arrangements was the hosting of a big lunch by Tahera Khala in her place, including all those of Ghazipur that were involved with Javed, especially Hamid Ullah Sir.

All of Tahera Khala's home worked inexorably to make that lunch a striking one, both in terms of food and warmth. Among others, Amin was happy spending time taking care of his little niece, daughter Rosy of Munira-Bu, whom he fondly and affectionally started addressing as Moon.

Even the reclusive Rahmat Bepari made special efforts to arrange green coconuts for service as drinks.

The family members and guests were in a hilarious mood, enjoying green coconut water as a welcome drink. Their discussion topics ranged between general social issues and other matters like Javed's ensuing sojourn to the USA and his matrimonial plan. Right at that moment, Hamid Ullah Sir, the quiet man of that gathering, unexpectedly intervened to inform those present about the latest development concerning the school. He said, "You all are aware of my recent illness which incapacitated me for a reasonable period. I managed to run the school, maintaining its reputation pertaining to academic imperatives with the outstanding help and support of dear Mukles Akram, the recently promoted assistant head teacher. However, many of the organizational matters were either postponed or delayed.

"One such matter pertains to two delayed consecutive meetings of the school management committee and the related pending agenda. The combined delayed meetings finally took place last evening. That meeting went very well. Just before the meeting was to end, most elderly and senior committee members introduced a resolution proposing to rename the school as Hamid Ullah Model High School in recognition of my services to the school over the last so many years, bringing it to its present position and standing beside contributing to enhance and sustain social amity in and around Ghazipur. It so appeared that the entire process of tabling the draft resolution was a byproduct of previous discussions and consensus. As the outcome was evident, I intervened, expressing my profound gratitude and appreciation for tabling the resolution. I also took the opportunity to politely but firmly dissent with that."

He then continued stating, "I paused for a while, taking time to absorb the most unexpected development, and that too derisorily related to me. I started thanking them for the trust they reposed in me as is evident from the essence of the resolution and for their consideration of recognizing my contribution. But I made one point very clear. My presence in Ghazipur and my engagement with the school are essentially outcomes of my relationship with the late Zakir Mia. I was in a very depressed state of my life when, by sheer accident, I first met him. His apolitical approach to life and surroundings, concern for sustainable social progression, ability to listen, politeness, and patience overwhelmed me right from the beginning. He mentioned the paucity of qualified teachers for local schools in and around rural settings like Ghazipur. He also articulated his perception of the impact of that on emerging social settings. Mr. Zakir Mia carefully avoided mentioning that he was the president of the school management committee at the time. That was very uncommon in Bangladesh, more in the rural milieu. Notwithstanding my quasi-urban background, the emphasis of Zakir Mia on quality teachers and his pragmatic awareness about the need for social progression impressed me forthwith. I liked the person impulsively and eventually followed him to Ghazipur. We bonded very well, and throughout, I treated him as an elder brother, one I did not have. The hallmark of our relationship was respect for mutual privacy which contributed to my aligning with Ghazipur. But all your support and contribution to ensure that element of privacy are respectfully recognized."

The committee members exchanged looks with each other, wondering about such a long prelude to the contents of the draft resolution from a notoriously famous taciturn person like me, which otherwise would make any one ecstatic.

Sensing that, I continued my nonassertive submission with respect to the school and general silent contribution in augmenting social amity. In doing so, I categorically emphasized my role as being a channel only. Even though not involved in day-to-day affairs dictum, here I am, the byproduct of Zakir Mia's vision, proudly identifying myself as a Ghazipurian (an inhabitant of Ghazipur). Whatever way you observe me now and whatever may be the assessment of the community about my contribution in making Ghazipur enclave a relatively better place for living and more for education are the outcomes of late Zakir Mia's unspecified but quiet vision about the community, and he always viewed the school as the engine of that change. I always sought, and he unhesitatingly responded, at every bend of my inquisition concerning the school. The same applied to his penchant for sustainable social progression. His dedication to social upliftment will always be manifested, notwithstanding his sudden and shocking murder in that abortive Shomjota Shonmelon years back. That surprised and shocked the community intensely, resulting in a reversal of the then-prevailing social impairments heightened by prevailing aggressive political undertones.

His silent, noninterfering vision and apolitical approach during all critical times enabled him to frame solutions to related problems without bias and what was good for the school and the community. And I was the single most beneficiary as being the public face of those decisions.

So what prompted the idea of changing the proposed name of the school evenhandedly relates to the late lamented Zakir Mia.

Moreover, there is another dimension that needs deliverance. Think of the time frame many years down the drain when some people may question, on sheer considerations that have nothing to do with academic relevance, the naming of the school after someone who has no root in the community being totally oblivious of the contributions being relevant now. There may be a demand for renaming the school after a local luminary. None of us will be present at that time to defend that decision. The renaming of the school after Zakir Mia forestalls that possibility.

The chairman of the SMC, who is known for the authoritative conduct of its business, apparently appeared to be mesmerized by the structured and logical oration of its nonvoting member who commonly keeps quiet unless the issue has academic implications.

As Hamid Ullah Sir finished his unprepared passionate submission, unconditionally sacrificing his elevation of a rare occurrence for one who is no more in this world, the chairman of SMC glanced at the faces of all present irrespective of membership and voting eligibility, and then closed his own eyes for a few seconds.

While opening his eyes, he concentrated on the draft resolution reading that from all possible angles of social ramifications both present and likely context and future school management challenges. Having an approving reflex, he congratulated the most senior member of SMC for drafting such a complete document and thanked Hamid Ullah Sir for his visionary assessment of the proposal. Based on such an affirmative conclusion, he penned through the name on the draft substituting by that of "Zakir Mia" and proclaimed its unanimous adoption.

Hamid Ullah Sir was in tears while approaching the chairman to convey profound thanks for honoring his opinion and suggestion in a pragmatic manner, ensuring sustainability.

The response of the chairman took Hamid Ullah Sir and all present in wonderment. He glanced at the nonvoting member of his committee and politely said, "Years back when I proposed, even though reservations were visible, for the head teacher to be a nonvoting member of this committee, there was trepidation about the idea. Thanks to social elites and members of the committee, that affirmative decision was taken promptly, and the benefits emanating from that proposition are now evident with respect to many positive academic decisions we took, more pertinently the present one relating to the renaming of school.

"Mr. Hamid Ullah has always discharged his responsibilities selflessly, and today's decision about school renaming epitomizes that. It is now up to the community to think through the appropriate response to reward and recognize this golden individual in a befitting manner."

That narration relating to renaming the school after the late Zakir Mia was the most unanticipated one and proliferated happiness and conviviality of all present. The only exception was Fatipa, whose happiness was so personal and overwhelming that she had to cover her face with the anchal (tail end) of her saree. Observing that, the ever-alert and sensitive Tahera Khala took small steps, drew Fatipa's head to her bosom, and slowly caressed her back, expressing sympathy and compassion sharing overwhelming happiness.

That rather late lunch became an early afternoon one to the amazement and happiness of all present.

That element of happiness was all-encompassing in his thought and reflexes even on the following day as Javed was on his way to Dhaka to complete his final leg of preparations for a much-cherished travel across the Atlantic.

Completing all formalities, Javed was in a relaxed mood and thought of visiting Lolita's home for a final call prior to leaving for the USA.

He was in a playful mood while preparing himself for that visit, attired for the first time in a formal outfit. He was having an irascible walk as he was approaching Lolita's very distinctive home, known for its architectural finesses together with its size. Lady Khadija fondly named that as Anandadhara (abode of happiness).

While approaching Anandadhara, his physique unknowingly slowed down, his steps were sloppy, and varied anxieties engulfed his thoughts.

Half-open entry door, a feeling of quietness within, and lack of usual activities for which the living area is celebrated stand contrary to "open house and happy home" adjectives Lady Khadija used in welcoming Javed as a tutor months ago.

The precipitousness of that experience took away from Javed's thinking that it could as well be due to his involvement with the yearning of Lolita on that night of the storm and temporary power outage.

Hesitatingly with related nervousness, Javed took cautious steps, seeing the housemaster Ashraful Alam sharing a two-seater sofa with Lady Khadija.

Both were wearing grim faces, with flashy chandeliers, normal decorative features glorifying the happiness and affluence of the house, being substituted by two table lamps. Mr. Alam was affectionally and assuredly holding one of Lady Khadija's hands, a sight of rare occurrence because of their professional and social commitments. They were always preoccupied with individual efforts to climb their respective social ladder premised on financial success.

Slightly away, there was a couple occupying a three-seater. During his last few months of teaching assignments in this "happy and open" home, Javed met scores of friends, relations, and social workers but not them.

They looked tired and exhausted, but their facial expressions and limited body language speak of a deep emotional link with the problem the Alam couple is confronting presently.

Responding to the usual greeting of salam from Javed, Mr. Alam softly responded with walaikum, not completing the reply as dictated by traditional Muslim salutation.

He looked around and then introduced the guests, saying, "The guests sitting there are Dr. Mobin, brother of Khadija, and Nusrat, his wife. They live in New Jersey and arrived this noon. I need not introduce you as your name is familiar to them."

Those last five words made the otherwise solid Javed nervy for a short while. Javed stood motionless but managed to greet them as the tradition dictates. He then, after looking around the space, started proceeding toward the study room when Lady Khadija, contrary to her well-known demon, yelled, "There is no need to go to the study room as Lolita would not be studying anymore."

That curt statement, in the setting of apparent gloom, aggravated the shock and anguish within the thinking of Javed, more apparently relating to his discourse about months back in soothing the emerging anxiety of Lady Khadeja concerning the tutoring of Lolita due to his impending departure for the USA. What a contrast!

While Javed was trying to rationalize that specific issue in a standstill position concerning the relevant context, the voice of Lolita from the shady setting behind took him in both shock and relief.

Lolita said, "I am sitting in the dark corner of this otherwise posh sitting space, which has had the distinction of being the place of connection and contact, paving the way to influence and the ladder for power and social ascending."

She continued, "I am pregnant. This obviously is the offshoot of what went on between me and Badsha in our Manindrapur Bagan Bari (guest house) prior to his living in the States and between you and me on that stormy night in this house.

"The parents decided to take Badsha's parents out for an outing as they were apparently depressed, missing their only son. What else from security and comfort points of view than our guest house at Manindrapur? Your unusually long stay in our abode was due to an unexpected storm and significant blackout."

Apparently conscious of Javed's possible uneasiness on matters of embarrassment during time spent in the last few months of tutoring, Lolita reassured the former, stating, "Do not feel shy or embarrassed. I just have informed all present everything that happened between me and Badsha in the guest house and between you and me in this house during that stormy night. This frankness is the way I have grown up to be always truthful to those who love me and care about me. That made it an open and happy house.

"These premise the backdrop of our dissenting discourse when you were about to enter the scene. My parents and uncle are strongly in favor of a secretive abortion as I am not certain who fathered the child in my womb as both physical involvements were in proximity and my inability to recall the experience. They were of the view that it was the only way to uphold the name of this house and the social status of parents for which they worked relentlessly spending time and resources. But I am absolutely opposed to that. At that point, you entered."

She continued stressing the points that influenced her thinking. In view of the proximity of the dates of our inadvertent physical involvements, I cannot indicate any specific feeling about conception. Our focus was on the suddenness of action that had no prelude. My aforesaid inability has no bearing on the life in my womb. It is my baby and would definitely be my responsibility. If it is so needed, I may disappear from the current panorama to give the space needed.

"I have been loved enormously by my parents despite other obligations, and I would not like to deprive my child of the uniqueness of that experience."

She paused for a while before resuming her oration, stating, "My stated position has other very compelling defenses. Both sides of our family have the unique distinction of having less or no children. Mother and Mama sitting in front of you, and my uncle, the father of Badsha, are living examples.

In light of the foregoing and being fully cognizant of implied repercussions, I just cannot consent to sign the death warrant for my upcoming child. I may not have another one."

Javed, being one of the presumptive culprits, broke his silence and moved forward to face Mr. Alam and Lady Khadija. He glanced at the other couple too to assure their due relevance in what he was about to articulate. Javed exercised due diligence and deserved politeness before saying, "Though my presence at this setting is a brief one, I have had a fair understanding of what is going on. Besides, being a purported perpetrator, I have my right to articulate opinion and to be cogitated."

Stating those words with inherent firmness, Javed politely suggested to "get Lolita by my side so that all of us can have a perception about her reactions to what I would be saying."

He then continued saying, "I am fully appreciative of the need for the newborn to have an identity (in the form of fatherhood with nonavailability of other options). I am supportive of the preference of Mr. and Mrs. Alam for a fresh beginning of Lolita's life and then have a child. Having said so, I do not find any justification for abortion to be the way out. There are obviously other options that we can discuss once the parameter is agreed."

Listening to those words, Lolita had a brash facial reflex noted by all.

"With respect to parental identity, the issue is relevant both from traditional, social, and legal perspectives. But the related response is not beyond us. It is either Badsha or me by choice or default. Since Badsha is not here and his parents being closest to the family are significantly away during these challenging hours, that option, from the present perspective, has no relevance. The other option is me.

"In terms of name and fame pertaining to access to power and connection in influencing decision or action even at the highest level and resource base, my family is no match with yours. Even then, my family commands respect and influence in our setting along with a reasonable financial base. There is a girl school in the name of my mother and a very well-established and famous area high school has been named after my father recently, a long time after his sudden and shocking untimely demise.

"My aforesaid narration of a brief family background may raise a question in your mind as to why I had to opt for private tutoring. The answer is a long one, but briefly, the summation is: when Father died about a year after the sad demise of Mother, I was a class eight student, and out of sheer anger and frustration, resolved to trail the future life on my own, preserving parental resources for noble purposes aiming at greater good for society.

"Along with academic excellence, I achieved all that I had in my mind, but more importantly, that focus gave me rare opportunities to assess and understand the pursuit of life from a divergent perspective. This house, fondly named Annnandadhara by Lady Khadija who introduced the abode to me as one epitomizing 'warmness and openness.'

"Recalling all that and considering my involuntary physical involvement with Lolita, I, without any hesitation and reservation, would like to marry Lolita right now. This has many positive aspects. Among others, the following two concerns will be shelved: your family prestige will be protected and the newborn will need parental identity. I am not at all concerned about the parenthood of the progeny. I solemnly undertake that it will be a nonissue in our family life.

"Do not think that I am articulating these significant decisions without my family's knowledge or of my volition as a response to obviate the current problem.

"Since the demise of father and in the absence of any enlightened relations in proximity, brother-in-law, Fyruz, though very young, took that responsibility with close consultation with Hamid Ullah Sir, the headmaster of our high school and a close associate of Father.

"What happened on that stormy night between me and Lolita was an unbearable burden for me. That was contrary to all the teachings and guidance that I received so far and consciously acted to preserve them. So in the first opportunity, I confessed to Fyruz Bhai to unburden myself.

"He listened carefully and then opined, stating, "Being correct and honest in pursuing every sphere of life as per dictates of morality and teachings of faiths are good goals but difficult to adhere to in real life. Mostly absence of opportunities or other constraints influences decisions and actions. There are many deviations of related sceneries that are germane. The purported action is normally the product of passions contrary to teachings and values. The correct response is to opt for appropriate sanative measures without contesting or denying. You should be prepared for that. What you confided in will be kept secret except. If you concur, I will allude it to Hamid Ullah Sir.

"Thus, concerned family elders are in the know of my onuses, and by articulating the present position, I am acting within that frame."

Ashraful Alam Saheeb was stumped. Lady Khadija was overwhelmed. Both Mama and Mami were speechless seeing a young person with free and frank values willing to uphold responsibility without any pressure.

Briefly, a sense of calmness prevailed in that gloomy setting. That was augmented by easy actions by Lolita arranging two chairs for herself and Javed Sir.

But that was very brief and subtle. After taking a seat, she exchanged looks with all present and then opened up by saying, "I listened carefully to each word and related statement and have to let you know my antiphons. I am thankful to Javed Sir for volunteering to give my progeny much desired parental identity. Regretfully, I cannot accept it. Children are the upshot of the love and feelings of the parents. In our case, it is just the reverse. Agreeing with what Javed Sir proposed would amount to taking advantage of the goodness of a person.

"You paid him for tutoring as per academic assignments, but he spent many hours enriching my knowledge and understanding of many aspects of human life. One he always stressed is not to take unsolicited favors from anyone whatever the warmth of the relationship. That tickled in my mind listening to what he proposed. Moreover, I have a fair idea about the life he would like to lead, including sharing life with a Caucasian girl of his match. I do not like to be an impediment in that process.

"However, if you can work out an arrangement for adoption in a known or confidential setting, then I would be willing to foster the life of my child, but under no circumstances I would be a party to the decision of abortion."

Unexpectedly, the ball landed in the court of the seniors. Noticing a suggestive wink from wife Nusrat, Dr. Mobin stood up and left, pretending to guide his wife to the washroom who was new to this house. Outside the space, both had brief exchanges pertaining to the coincidentally common position of adopting the child, one they do not have in fourteen years of conjugal life.

They returned to the ambivalent setting, first exchanging looks with Ashraful Alam and Khadija and then focusing on Lolita. Being assured of a sort of empathetic reaction, Nusrat laid the proposition from their side, stating, "I have a negative image in the family being generally secluded. And frankly, that is what I am. Having a married life without children aggravated that. Even then, we have a happy and contended life.

"We intensely followed Lolita's position on abortion and respect that. But considering the social status and other local parameters of Ashraf Bhai (brother) and that of Khadija, both of us refrained from commenting.

"We firmly believe that efforts to find fault will not take us anywhere. What beta (son) Javed alluded to holds the key. What happened to Lolita is the consequence of time, setting, and emotion. It just happened. The way forward is to move with prudence. Fortunately, Lolita's latest stand provides us with the desired window.

"Keeping that in view and our pursuing a life without broods, we, without reservation and hesitancy, are willing to adopt Lolita's child. There are many plus points of this choice: the adoption will be within the family; the child will be exposed to family values even if be far away; since we are settled in the USA, the premise of adoption will not be of any likely vulnerability; and both Bhai Shaheb, yourself, as well as Lolita, can have access to his or her growing up seeing photographs from time to time. But be advised from now about two imperatives: that the family linkage will be cloaked and he or she will grow up as an American who will be told about adoption when he or she is of age and intelligence to digest the reality.

"The aforesaid depends on the arrangements and secrecy of Lolita's living from now on to the delivery period. Needless to emphasize, the entire stipulation would require relative indiscernible living of Lolita until the baby is in my lap and our home."

As Azima was articulating her thinking and likely way forward, the ever-outgoing and viviparous Khadija was shredding unrelenting tears while seeking support and comfort from her husband Alam. Lolita surprisingly was stable, considering the proposition of Mami (maternal aunt) to be the God-gifted one even though it has the most perspicuous stipulation about future contact.

Breaking prolonged silence, Dr. Mobin put a seal on the issue, observing that adoption under U.S. law is a very convoluted one, and he would forthwith like to discuss the proposition with his lawyer in New Jersey.

The matter was temporarily shelved at that point, giving an opening for Javed to get blessings from all present before taking leave. On his way out, he felt relieved and assured.

His comfort felt suddenly skewed, noticing the unannounced presence of nephew Amin, sister Fatipa, and brother-in-law Fyruz. On ostensible but silent inquisition, Fyruz Bhai stated that it was the family's surprise reflecting the desire of Ameen. They spent the next two days in joy and gaiety besides spending time showing Dhaka to the loving nephew.

SHRED

WITH FAREWELL WISHES from sister Fatipa and family, Javed boarded the plane to New York en route to London. Since that was his maiden long-range air travel, Javed was both confused and worried. That was short-lived as he found eventually that the next seat had no passenger. He brought out all the papers and rechecked and organized them as suggested by the airline's ground staff, who was a friend of Firoze Bhai. He was the one who helped him in the check-in and boarding process and perhaps was instrumental in assuring the empty seat next to him.

Relaxed and dreaming of a life of excellence in academic achievements, he was in his future world of distinction: achievements, altruistic finesses of significant social relevance, and artistic or literary competence and recognition.

Impulsively, he recalled the response of Lolita with respect to his avowal to marry her, giving much-needed cover to pregnancy and giving the life in the womb much desired parental identity. Javed did not see any nobility in that proposition as he was involved too, even though fortuitously. Lolita's disapproval of that, among others, was based on the earlier assertion of Javed focusing on his life and ambition.

After the first few months of tutoring, Javed sensed that Lolita, being a lone girl in that magnificent home, was trying to take more interest in him than normal. He thus decided to make up a story, indirectly redeploying his life with a sense of pledge. That was the genesis of his aspiration that Lolita ascribed about his marriage plan with a Caucasian girl, a hypothetical one even though. That bailed him out of the most delicate situation of his life.

Javed took the first opportunity to share that with Fyruz Bhai and Fatipa-Bu. Fyruz enjoyed it thoroughly, while the reaction of Fatipa-Bu was more feminine. But she availed the opportunity to raise the issue of Javed's wedding. She was serious, somewhat authoritative, as well as emotional in pursuing the matter underscoring her responsibility in this regard in the absence of the parents.

In this regard and before raising the issue, she discussed the proposition with Hamid Ullah Sir, Rafisa, Tahera Khala, and Fyruz. She continued, "What I am now alluding to reflects common position of all. It is time for you to get married. The onus is on you."

Surprisingly, nephew Ameen quipped, "I am not concerned about the reasoning others have, but I am demon serious to have a mami (wife of maternal uncle) in our family which or like what most of my friends have. They have so many nice and indulgent experiences to share, but alas, I do not have any."

On hearing all what others are thinking about his wedding, especially what dear nephew lamented, Javed drew nephew Ameen close to him, saying, "Okay, I get the message and give you word that when I will be back in about three years for data collection, I will have plan to get married at that time. But I would not have time to be involved in scouting for a life partner. I will delegate that responsibility to my all well-wishers, especially to Fyruz Bhai and Fatipa-Bu."

All present burst into laughter. They were excited and decided to celebrate it by having a nice dinner in a nearby Thai restaurant.

The long air journey ended with a much-needed break at Heathrow Airport with plane changes.

The JFK Airport of New York, from the context of the volume of traffic and number of flights, was surprisingly efficient and friendly.

Javed's connecting flight to Boston had a reasonable layover time in New York, allowing him to have his first glimpse of the USA from cross-cultural and divergent racial perspectives.

After landing in Logan Airport and collecting luggage, Javed was taking cautious steps for a local cab service when he suddenly noticed his name on a banner. That surprised him. As he approached them, the hosts embraced him and individually introduced them. They were James Astate from the Philippines, Binte Rasool from Jordan, and a Bangladeshi one by the name of Humayun Ahmed. As they were driving to their dormitory, Javed was astounded, noticing that Binte was driving the car. It was unthinkable for Javed to expect a lonely lady in the entourage to receive him and more so as she was having control of the steering wheel. The assimilation process was smooth and friendly, and soon Javed became one of them.

Time, a combination of uncertainty, discovery, concentration on research besides acclimatization, and adjustments with local conditions and requirements, flew with a gleam of eye and elapsed very fast.

For Javed, the research reached the most critical phase where assertions in the text of the evolving research paper need to be authenticated by supporting data. Thus, he spent time and energy to frame relevant questioners and to get academic endorsements of assigned guides—a task made more challenging in view of the involvement of two sets of guides—for the formation of a database in support of the main theme of the paper with proportionate-linked focus on economics and social challenges.

Back in Ghazipur, efforts were being made and connections were being explored to find a suitable match. The initial slackness on the part of Fyruz was partly responsible for the dawdling start. As the time was drawing near, necessary efforts were doubled down, but the task appeared to be more challenging than normally thought. And that partly was due to the high standard of expectations of the sisters—one in Australia—with respect to the social standing of the family, academic excellence of the siblings, marital connections of the siblings who got married, financial affluence, and others, each proposal needing vetting of Rafisa, who is living in another continent.

Among such competing priorities, Fyruz was successful in getting the consent of both sisters with one, by the name of Azeefa, of Mia Bari of the Ronokpur enclave. Happiness pervaded as the date of Javed's arrival drew close. As a precursor, Rafisa arrived from Australia in advance, with her husband to follow as the marriage-related events were worked out.

In the midst of related high expectations, news trickled in about the visit of Azeefa's first maternal uncle. He, Ahmed Rouf, is very affluent, wields a lot of power, and is well-known as a member of the parliament. Mr. Rouf happened to be the first most senior relation from Mia Bari to visit the home of Fatipa-Bu, the current address of Javed. The social dimension of that visit accentuated the expectation level, and Fyruz arranged a mini but grand lunch. To ensure a somewhat equal level of conversation, Fyruz sent messages to Hamid Ullah Sir, the suo moto guardian of Javed, knowing him from childhood as well as a trusted friend of Zakir Mia, to attend lunch. He likewise also requested the presence of Rahmat Bepari Chacha for a better exchange of ideas.

Ahmed Rouf exhibited his political probity by praising Fyruz with superlatives, to begin with.

While awaiting the opportune moment to unleash the bombshell he had up in his sleeves, Mr. Rouf was relentless in digressing on unrelated issues while Fatipa was super busy arranging entertainment obligations.

Sensing that the call for food is a matter of time and exhibiting his uncanny maneuvering ability, Mr. Ahmed Rouf suddenly quipped, "The aroma of food being arranged for service smells the richness of the relationship our daughter is going to enjoy. I will convey this good feeling to Azeefa's parents."

Preceding those soothing words, he unleashed the bombshell, saying, "The time has changed. The mobility has multiplied. Previously, people going to Bilat (as England used to known) were few and were respected. Now, the reality is just the opposite. Our foreign ministry is full of complaints about the misdeeds of immigrants from Bangladesh. The most common complaint is about an alleged higher level of educational attainments for pursuing a marriage proposition, which eventually proved to be bogus. Many families' lives were ruined. I am in no way suggesting that to be a likely case with Javed. However, as an abundant precaution, Azeefa's family requested my help in getting the information pertaining to Javed and his stay in Bilat. I accordingly requested our High Commission in London before coming here. Even for a moment, we do not believe that the related information is not correct. However, on the safe side and to avoid future misunderstanding, I reluctantly acted on the request of the family.

"In light of the forgoing, I most humbly request your consideration and gracious concurrence of Azeefa's family position, requesting deferment of the marriage by two months. This will enable us to finish the process and have the wedding in an exultant manner."

Fyruz was thunderstruck and exchanged strident looks with both elders from his side. The serving spoon fell from Rafisa's hand in the kitchen area with Fatipa being dumbfounded.

Ubiquitous calm overtook the setting.

Mr. Ahmed Rouf, being a politician, sensed that. Subsequently, he articulated the whole conversation, keeping himself neutral but making it clear that he had to yield to the family's pressure, or otherwise he would be misunderstood to the peril of his political life.

"Situations like this often stand in the way of a politician's life, but little understood by outsiders."

Rahmat Bepaeri Chacha (uncle), taking advantage of such an indulgent tone, opted mildly, saying, "After a satisfactory level of voluntary exchange of information and dependable verification of those, both families agreed to the proposition. You voluntarily agreed to have your daughter be the daughter-in-law of the late respected Zakir Mia's family. What happened in between? I find it difficult to comprehend!"

In his melodramatic response, Mr. Ahmed Rouf observed, "Rahmat Saheeb, what you articulated awhile back perhaps has relevance, but in this case, we need to take a broader view. True, you have given our side all the information about Javed. We affirm that we are fully satisfied. The postponement we are now requesting is to enable us to have a complete and comprehensive assessment of Beta Jaeved's stay abroad. That is our main concern against the backdrop of the current reality. We need to act in keeping with the present reality."

Hamid Ullah Sir, sensing an apparent tensed feeling in the kitchenette area, finished eating quickly, went inside, and returned forthwith. Allowing time for others to finish the lunch ritual, he opened up for the first time. He took a pungent look at Ahmed Rouf Saheeb and politely observed, saying, "Azeefa's family is well known and well settled in Rokunpur, and you yourself is a very prominent person in that setting and now nationally being a member of the parliament. What you said so far is well taken, and whatever learning we have, we understood that clearly. Our son is a gem by any consideration and yardstick whom I had the fortune of observing growing up as his father's close friend and as a teacher. We have our most valued trust in his acts and deeds. To our best judgment, Azeefa's family has possibly a misplaced concern. I will thus request your consideration and efforts of detaching that concern of the family."

Taking that clue, Fyruz intervened, saying, "I am not only his brother-in-law but a trusted friend too. I can assure you that there is nothing in his life that can cause concern to Azeefa's family. He is a determined young man whose sense of self-respect is beyond any skepticism. We are not inclined to your proposition of deferment. If Azeefa's family so agree, we may proceed as we have a few days in hand. If not, alternatives may be explored. As abiding Muslims, we believe that marriage is something where divine involvement is indispensable. Whatever the outcome, we will take it as a divine one and will move forward without whining."

Observing the lack of contact and communication from the side of Azeefa's family, all involved from Javed's side in the lunch for Mr. Ahmed Rouf reassembled at the initiative of Fyruz. The only exceptional addition was Tahera Khala.

In the follow-up homily, both sisters were very open and vocal, with Rafisa excelling and others taking the point of discourse to snap off the proposition. Initially, there was some disinclination, but the force of Rafisa's barney made everyone agree—get out of the proposition where their brother, to begin with, will have a perceptive downside.

The stand of Rafisa was significantly strengthened when Hamid Ullah Sir stated, "I had that in mind to begin with, but I kept quiet, giving others the benefit of the opportunity to express respective unbiased views. To my mind, Mr. Ahmed Rauf is not a lone case. He, without any inference to Azeefa, represents the mindset of others in the family. His side motives perhaps could be strengthening his hold on Azeefa's family and keeping a highly educated son-in-law in a perpetual negative stance. He was playing with his political acumen."

With the decision so reached, the logical question was what next? Fatipa precipitously recalled a not-too-distant visit by the younger cousin of Fyruz when she lamented about the treatment meted out to girls by society, especially when one opts to pursue higher education and learning. Her in-laws' family is endowed with positive attitudes to life. Among others, the family is presently blessed with a pretty young girl who pursued her masters in Bangla. She finished her MA about six months back and has no marriage proposal. Interested parties backed off because her education attainments or age as a marriageable age by local setting is assumed to be between fifteen and eighteen years. Anything beyond that is perceived to be overaged. Fatipa recalled that discourse verbatim.

As she finished her linked recollections, the ladies present looked at each other. Without wasting a moment, Tahera Khala proposed an immediate visit to the in-laws' house of Fyruz's cousin. The handy availability of Khala's rickshaw with another two from a nearby bazaar (market) facilitated that travel by ladies forthwith in the company of Fyruz while other men were exploring the options.

Before Javed left home to settle and finalize AIT-related organizational and management issues with local elites and well-wishers, he was advised by Rafisa-Bu about the visit of Mr. Ahmed Rouf, second ladder uncle of Azeefa, the proposed bride, to talk and finalize wedding details as the time available is very short.

Keeping that in mind and envisaging a home setting of jollity, he looked at his wristwatch and speeded up his walk. He was certain about a happy outcome with Ahmed Rouf MP on the one side and wise well-wishers like Hamid Ullah Sir, and Rahmat Bepari along with the presence of Fyruz Bhai on his side. With all initial reservations, he felt to be very happy giving his consent to the proposed wedding proposal. That sense received an unexpected jolt as he drew close to the abode of Fyruz Bhai.

While drawing close to home, Javed was astounded to note a home of uneasiness, devoid of laughter and mutual happiness. He slowed down involuntarily and looked around for movement and noise.

With hesitation domineering, he entered the seating area and exchanged a tender greeting with Rahmat Bepari wearing a morose look and Hamid Ullah Sir looking disjointly to the pathway outside through the half-open entrance door indicating negativity without words. The lack of a normal warm greeting took him by surprise, and that was indicative of an evident lack of progress. Total quietness inside the house and privation of vociferous chanting of Rafisa-Bu were sufficient indications to someone like Javed that things are not usual and definitely beyond repair.

Javed silently walked inside, went to his temporary bedroom, and threw himself on the bed clasping his night pillow. While in that position, Javed seriously tried to disengage himself from current worries and refocus on something more pertinent. But all attempts failed. He had a recurrence of the same unanswered question: "Why me? Why it is to be me?" Mother Nature snatched my biological mother at a tender age, followed by the same divine decision about Father within a year. In the frame of a growing-up boy, I started behaving like a mature one, making decisions that had far-reaching implications.

When the current marriage proposal with Azeefa was being weighed, I could sense the positive inclination of Fatipa-Bu, who, apart from other positivity, referred to Father's strong desire for his son, irrespective of professional excellence to be achieved, to get married in and around Ghazipur. Information obtained through his sources helped Javed to make an affirmative decision about the proposal for marriage with Azeefa.

During such agonizing thoughts and being exhausted, Javed unknowingly went to slumber.

The two rickshaws that carried the ladies and Fyruz to the latter's cousin's home returned. Rafisa jumped out of her rickshaw, hurried inside, and loudly narrated the experience, finding and positive outcome of the visit. That was supplemented by the summations of Fatipa complemented by Tahira Khala.

After that, two senior ladies went to the kitchen to prepare a proper dinner after the day's hassle. But restless and ecstatic Rafisa was continuously engaged in delineating her exhilaration. She even went to spiritual height when she said, "The religious maxim stating 'as Allahpak closes one door, he opens hundred more' is very true, and in our case is most applicable. It is only because of the disagreeable experience of this forenoon that we got the window for evaluating Zarina and her family. We must remain thankful to the wife of Fyruz

Bhai's cousin for leaving a meaningful but unintended hint about dear Zarina. In fact, I am so excited that I would like to address her as Zarina Bo (wife).

"Javed has been very blessed by both of our parents, and I am certain that he will enjoy that in life. Irrespective of the outcome, it is absolutely certain that Javed will not have to lead a life of surveillance in a family who could not agree with the local assessment of the character of a gem like Javed."

Saying those disjointed words, wearied Rafisa turned to go inside and screamed, "Oh my God, see who is standing there!" Straightening from his reclined posture, having the support of a door frame with all predictabilities, Javed, even though a junior sibling, mastered all bearings and requested Rafisa's presence in the bedroom for a free and frank exchange of positions.

Maintaining a somber stance, Javed firmly said, "Rafisa-Bu, on the return home, I was greeted by a chilled welcome by two of my revered seniors. Resting in a makeshift reclining arrangement on the bed, I unwittingly dozed off, only to be awakened by the noisy entry and excited loud words of you conveying the sequel. Since then, I have been standing here unnoticed by all.

"I have heard every word that was articulated since then and absorbed them. Looking back to all that happened during the last few days with respect to the proposed matrimonial relationship with Azeefa's family, I fully concur with your assertion that when one door of opportunity in life is closed, Allah Pak opens a hundred more. Thus, listen carefully to my avowals: The snapping of proposition with Azeefa's family is final and absolute. Prayers and blessings of our revered parents saved me from lifelong ignominy. The girl you have just seen and endorsed is okay with me and there is no need for further follow-up. But the time is a major concern for me. As a realistic approach, the wedding will have to be a small one for the time, and we can have a big wedding gathering when we return next befitting the good name of the family and the reputation Abba (father) enjoyed. More important at this point is to have all marriage-related documents, educational certificates, nationality-related documents, and so on. I will take them with me, prepare a visa application, and apply for her visa as wife and dependent."

On the critical issue of the passport, Javed was informed that Zarina's sister-in-law said that she has one, explaining the backdrop. In her last year of university life, four close friends including Zarina had an abortive plan to visit India with a focus on the Taj Mahal. Hence passports were processed and visas were obtained. But three days before the planned journey, the mother of the main organizer passed away suddenly, resulting in the cancellation of that planned trip.

"You can inform all seniors accordingly and take follow-on steps. Time is of the essence. No need to think about formalities."

Even then and notwithstanding time limitations, both sides made efforts to ensure that the mini event was memorable to the new couple.

Despite multifarious responsibilities and commitments, Fyruz made sure to send one of his ardent juniors to Dhaka with a letter to his dear friend, Afzal, requesting help in the smooth departure of Javed. He also explained that due to the latter's sudden marriage at the behest of the family, Javed could not be physically in Dhaka earlier. Neither he has the option of rescheduling the travel due to his university commitments. As Afzal was working in the same airline as Javed had his air travel booking, follow-on actions were standard ones. The request to Afzal was a safety bulb in view of the summer-end travel rush coinciding with one of the two Muslim religious festivals, known as Eid Ul Azha.

Most wedding ceremonies were carried out with largely full participation of both families despite time constraints. The marked downside was that the couple did not have their customary but equally cherished *Bashar Raat* (nuptial night) when traditionally in a very private but equally romantic setting, the couple have their first intense look at each other as conjugal partner, being generally for life. The consolation for Zarina was the assurance of Javed to reenact the *Bashar Raat* once together in Boston.

Occupying the assigned window seat, Javed was thinking about the apparently fully loaded flight, more specifically about the conditions around the facilities area like the washroom after some use. He was equally engrossed, more focused on the empty middle seat next to him, about the behavioral pattern of his likely co-passenger, with most certainty being the flight a fully booked one.

As the aircraft was on the runway being readied for takeoff, the middle seat remained empty. Javed was certain that it was a genuine gift from Mr. Afzal in response to Fyruz Bhai's request.

Once afloat and the cautionary signs were removed, Javed opened his briefcase, took out basic documents related to Zarina, rechecked them, and happily relaxed after rechecking them.

Once in Boston, he was congratulated by the principal supervisor for getting married. Simultaneously, the supervisor shared the good news of the extension of his research period by one year as per a proposition jointly mooted by his team and that of the sociology team. The team also offered help in facilitating the visa for his wife.

It was about the end of the seven months of their marriage that Zarina was in the warm embrace of Javed at Logan Airport, to be greeted additionally by some friends from his economics research team. Merriment ended, the friends left, and Javed was preparing to have a long chat. But Zarina was in a dormant mood with apparent reasons of fatigue and sleepiness. Javed, both out of pity and related disappointment, blessed Zarina with an affectionate kiss on her forehead and went to sleep soon.

That sort of happy day, time, and tensed night alternated for a few days, and Javed reasoned the phenomenon in various sympathetic shelters, including the sudden separation from family and preoccupations with organizing her own mini family, including that of the kitchen, without making that an issue. He was patient, and his research-tainted mind waited for time to respond.

And that unexpectedly happened on the seventh night. Being engrossed with the relating data outcome to the current focus of his thesis, he came out of the study and found Zarina lying on the bed, looking lustrously dressed in his preferred negligée. Javed quickly recalled his experiences with that nightie on their first night in Boston. He very lovingly brought out the most carefully made packet from his dresser and desired that Zarina change, discarding her saree and wearing the nightie to look more beautiful.

But her response on that maidén night took Javed both by surprise and shudder. Her ostensible quick reasons were that the outfit was too transparent, visibly seductive, and thus in conflict with modesty.

Javed remained nonchalant and let it go without losing poise.

Thus, the present scene and experience took him by equal surprise. He kept quiet to know the real answer. In that process, Javed proceeded slowly and softly. He, without any expressed word, started moving his right-hand fingers on her forehead and slowly to her chicks and lips.

With assurance so mastered, he leisurely released his feelings, saying to the closed-eye and immobile Zarina, "You must have wondered the reason I did not react to your lack of enthusiasm for marital intimacy even after seven months. The response has roots in my being groomed in a unique family setting and by a very wise father, a remarkable fatherlike teacher, and a social aunt. I was taught to have time and patience in understanding life-related issues instead of rushing for answers. Impatience often misdirects one, and conclusions so arrived often are inadequate or misleading. So I was taking time. Your current stance is a replication of that teaching.

"I am certain that though in a sedentary posture, you are listening to each word I am uttering. Human life is both complicated and uncertain. Complications often are due to social imperatives. Uncertain fragment causes emotional impulses even when in conflict with upbringing, training, and education, or irrespective of consequences. These are the perils of human life mostly under the shadow of privacy, ensuring a clean image for climbing the social ladder. Generally, no one is possibly immune from that.

"One such incident happened in my life too that belies all that I was taught, all the training I was imparted, and the positive image for which I was known continued to bear in my present social standing. Itemizing all that happened on the fateful stormy night between Lolita and myself, and her decision to absolve me from related responsibility without waiting for time, I once again started floating in normal life. That relieved me, against my expressed decision to take responsibility, enabling me simultaneously to chart a normal life after the bump. It caused within me the fundamental realization about the most unbearable aspect of life—a journey being an uncharted one with a destination always undefined.

"I would have told you about this incident, but tonight is not the one I had in mind. I was propelled to divulge the most private part of my life to convey to you my deduction that life generally is not immune from pitfalls. One should not forget that but needs to move on guarding oneself.

"I am not conjecturing that you have some or similar experiences which you are beholding within, pressuring yourself. But if that is the case, you can open without hesitation or reservation. I am not only your husband but also a friend and a well-wisher. I am not only responsible for your physical well- being but have an equal role and responsibility for your mental well-being and emotional animation. That sort of approach and understanding will certainly make our conjugal life worth having. A sense of calmness together with inner inquisition prevailed."

Zarina's symbolic reaction and reflexes remained static. But her facial complexion turned redden pink against the normal base of her skin tone which is fair. Javed took that as a positive indication and ventured to put his two hands under her vertebral to lift her upper body. She responded favorably, opened her shy semiwet eyes, looked at Javed intensely, and then surrendered on his chest crying like a child.

Javed remained calm, allowing her to release grief, shedding as many tears as she needed. He recalled an avowal of Hamid Ullah Sir, stating, "Tears are unique gifts of God, allowing living entities to handle and overcome grief."

As he allowed her to be in the same demeanor for quite a while, many sections of his top shirt and part of his bare chest were wet by the time she stopped crying. Javed, with all tenderness he could master at the time, lifted the full face of Zarina, drew that close, and bequeathed a loving kiss. Zarina impulsively participated in the process, and that surprised Javed by the sheer extent and nature of her response after such a long period of sluffing tears.

That state of thinking was short and subdued as he was reminded of the saying of the superintendent of the college hostel, Prof. Ahmed Farid, in the initial phase of his Dhaka life. The backdrop of that was

Javed, being a favorite boarder of the hostel and a prominent student from a rural setting having no parents, who had frequent access to Super Sir's residence. He became close to the family, as the couple had no issue. Because of such a setting, Javed was often exposed to irritating exchanges between the couple. Super Sir initially ignored Javed's reactions. Possibly, he was waiting for an appropriate time.

That time suddenly emerged on a Friday noontime. While sharing lunch, Super Sir inadvertently committed an err in passing a negative comment on the taste of big fish curry. She could not take it, especially in the presence of Javed. Perhaps it was more so as she put her best efforts to ensure a proper curry preparation, bearing in mind that Javed was invited by his favorite Super Sir.

Chachi's reaction was prompt, saying, "I have tried my best. If that is not up to your taste, then from tomorrow, you cook." Saying those few words, she left for the kitchen with a rage. Super Sir, exchanging looks with Javed, observed, "Ladies cannot take any negative comment. Their response is always prompt and full of fury. But the best part of this is their reaction is always temporary and transitory. When she returns after a few minutes, she will have the stance of a loving and caring individual." With a smile in his mien, he philosophically added, "That is the charm and challenge of married life. You will appreciate it when you reach that phase of life."

After a few moments, the curtain moved again, and here came the adorable Chachi of Javed with a tray full of sweets and seasonal fruits. Super Sir exchanged a look with Javed and silently asserted the authenticity of his earlier contention.

The emerging hilarity suddenly evaporated due to unspecified subtleties. Obviously, Javed was bemused. He was rescued from that muddled mindset by the uncluttered trust and passion of Zarina. While amorously wiping the segments of Javed's chest due to her unrestrained shedding of tears moments earlier, Zarina had an ardent look at Javed, kissed his upper left chest solicitously, and enquired about his commitment to a previous avowal of being a friend and well-wisher.

Referring to that, Zarina said, "I would be totally honest in detailing my life to you. But before I commence that, I am obligated to keep you informed about an overseas call that I made to a friend in Dhaka Arshi by name. She is my course fellow in masters and, unlike most others, was married. She has been very kind and caring about me. I, too, admired and trusted her. She got a promise from me before I said bye to her concerning a prompt update about the initiation of our conjugal life. I promised to keep her informed, and as per that request, called her this morning.

"Arshi Appa (an urban version of *Bu*) listened carefully and kept quiet for a while. On being goaded by me for the unusual silence, she opened up, saying, 'You are committing a great blunder. In married life, irrespective of the duration, the romance, feelings, and performance of the first few nights are all-pervading and persist throughout life. It is a one-time chance and experience in life. So reverse your attitude and approach. Be an active partner in the process. Shun all pretension and shyness. Remember, sex is the foundation of a matrimonial relationship. All subsequent facets are only additions. The structural strength of additions depends on the quality and strength of the foundation. Act as per my advice and I will call you after seven days.

"Contrary to the preferences and practices of other friends, I decided to follow up the advice of Arshi Appa.

"Symbolically, I opted to put on your favorite negligée and was charmed with the feeling and look I experienced. I felt miserable and wanted to antipodal approach to make you happy."

Having said so, Zarina went on detailing her fostered prewedding surreptitious. She, without hesitation and reserve, plainly started saying with ease, "Our home is a big one with many rooms, but not pitched to specifics in terms of use. The one on the southern side was being used as a study for me. The side use of the room was also to accommodate temporary house guests. And for that purpose, two beds (chokis) were placed between the eastern and western sections of the room. In between those two beds, there were three almirah-type bookcases with glass fascia. My grandfather had a special fascination for the history of the Mogul rule and the British occupation of India besides the partition of India. The bookcases have selected prints of copies he liked, and one of them was on the harems of the Mogul Empire. I was aware of these books because of a duty I voluntarily undertook to keep the cases neat and clean.

"It was time to prepare for a test examination prior to my secondary school certificate examination. That night, I was reading my history lessons. I was charmed by the life and traits of Princess Jahan Ara, the eldest living off springs of Emperor Shah Jahan. That reading was invigorating, but I was tired too of sitting for long. So I lied down temporarily on the second *choki* adjacent to the reading table for transitory relief. I ignored the other one being occupied by the second maternal uncle (revered relationship addressed in local culture as Mama) visiting parents with respect to family matters."

As Zarina was reading, the pages of history turned from ordinary ones to intriguing others like "Was Jahan Ara the real daughter of Shah Jahan, was there a romantic relationship between Shah Jahan and Jahan Ar, or the account of Jahan Ara's romantic involvement with an amir of Shah Jahan's court? Accounts written by some nobles mentioned Shah Jahan having the largest harem (reserved domestic space in a Muslim household for wives, concubines, and female servants) during his reign.

The harem's description, arrangements, and management enchanted Zarina. She was captivated by that reading and finished a few pages before she fell into a yawning sleep without design.

That narration of life in the harem mesmerized her, even in a dream following that sleep. She started dreaming in that episode as an active participant, enjoying every bit of harem life. With the fall of hot saliva from the mouth of visiting *Mama*, she instantaneously woke up to find *Mama* on top in erotic engagement, with her being a passive participant influenced even in dreams by lingering liking of harem life.

She was shocked, surprised, and speechless for a while, and then threw him off her body before ejaculation. Zarina, in a state of bewilderment and edginess, slowly retired to her bed and woke up relatively late in the morning. By that time, Mama left their home to the dismay of mother as he left early morning without having even breakfast.

She thought through the whole incidence and decided to keep the matter within as their disengagement was timely with no evidence.

That far was good and managed. But with the passage of time, a new sensational feature emerged.

Zarina started experiencing a peculiar physiological change in her emotional impulses relating to sexual sensation, and that became worrying when confidential conversations with college friends revealed something contrary to her recent experiences.

She frankly, and without hesitation, exposed herself before Javed, saying, "Before that undesirable incident with Mama, I used to experience exudation after each period or occasionally when I had thoughts or reading something concerning sex or matters related thereto. But it is no longer happening. While my other impulses concerning sexual advances are still okay, muscles around my basic organ tighten and dry up at the time it is to open. I am thus both concerned and afraid of penetration. I have a lot of interest in physical doings, but as a possible consequence of the shudder and precipitousness of that experience, my systems are impacted. That was one of the reasons why I always avoided marriage proposition until that with you suddenly floated. I had no time to think. It moved very past. But knowing you for the last few months, communicating with you, and listening to your words, I am convinced that I am blessed to have you as my life partner.

"This is what is me and everything about me. I am encouraged to be free and frank because of your assurances. I am emboldened by the sure and specific advice of *Arshi Appa*. Now the rest is with you."

With those few words, Zarina laid what she wanted to and bent her head with an earnest expectation of a supporting response. Javed, being charmed by her confidence, raised her full face with the support of his two palms, drew her close, and bequeathed a loving warm kiss. He then said, "Thanks for your free and frank avowal. I have minutely listened to each word, digested them in their applicable paradigm, and assure you once again about civility in my future conjugal engagements."

That was perhaps too much for Zarina and too soon. She collapsed on the bed under the embrace of Javed. Both momentarily reacted with meekness. Javed sensed the essence of frigidity that Zarina alluded to earlier and took unalloyed care and caution in achieving what he wanted after about seven months of marriage. Zarina, with all apprehensions

JAHED RAHMAN

domineering since that unfortunate incident in the study setting, sustained the pain and discomfort with the twin objectives of enabling Javed to have his pleasure and the ardent hope of gradual easiness as Arshi Appa forecasted. Both were contended and happy from their respective perspectives.

Overcoming the personalized moments of concern and happiness likewise, Javed turned toward exultant and relaxed, as epitomized by the displaced nightie frame of Zarina, and drew her close to his body while fingering her equally misplaced shaggy hair. Zarina liked and enjoyed that enormously as was evident from her warm breathing.

After some more time, Javed initiated the process of introducing his family more in terms of background and the broader values it upholds, initially related to immediate family and then the wider objectives of social wellbeing.

Narrating what happened after the sudden demise of mother Ambia, he detailed father Zakir Mia's transitory efforts to take care of the family. "Though his sudden demise too brought an unforeseen end to that effort, the teachings and values he left behind guided us enormously in moving forward. His one practice made an undying mark on my growth and shaping up.

"He had one practice that he persistently followed while taking care of me. Father used to load me with a variety of homilies. But the positive side of that was his regular advice that even if what he was saying was not understood by me at the time, I should try to remember it. His concluding remark was 'As time moves on, you will face situations in life when many of my current sayings will be helpful in moving forward.'

"In our conjugal journey, I, too, sometimes may feel like uttering something that may appear to be out of context or irrelevant. As time passes, you may understand the inner relevance of those, and that may help both of us in life. One example of such an experience of that in my life was his oft-repeated saying, 'Life is not a bed of roses. Problems, challenges, and some failings are part of this journey where success and shortcomings are twin sisters. Bad experiences as well as failures should not derail us from our priorities and focus in life. We should remember them, but that does not mean that will be allowed to impair progression.'

"In my life's journey so far, that oft-repeated saying has proven to be so true encompassing his sad demise to getting you in my warm embrace now."

With that sort of understanding being fostered over time, the frequency of conjugal engagements slowly increased with happiness overtaking apprehension. Around the end of about six months from their first physical engagement, Zarina came out of the bedroom to greet Javed with, as a variation, a mix of shyness and happiness. Her body posture was evidently different than other days and her facial expressions were full of coyness.

That intrigued Javed, but he kept it internal for the moment, giving space to Zarina to say what she was holding back even though apparently that steered happiness within her.

Zarina withdrew momentarily and came back with a glass of *sharbat*, placed that on the mini side table placed by the side of the bed where Javed was resting, sat by the side of him, and collapsed on his chest, saying mellifluously, "You are going to be a father." Saying that she put his right hand on her lower belly with light pressure.

Javed was dumfounded with an ardent mix of absolute happiness and abundant dreams pertaining to future life. But his reaction process momentarily was indolent being alone with Fatipa-Bu and Rafisa-Bu as well as his mother like Tahera Khala far away to celebrate the news about the new guest.

Javeed covered her upper body with his chest, embraced her tenderly, kissed her passionately several times, and made a request to open her eyes. As she complied with ease and loving feelings, he kissed her open eyes anew and then said, "Why did you keep your eyes closed?"

Zarina's response was simple and sweet, saying, "I just wanted to absorb your feelings." After a pause, she said, "I was surprised when neighbor Shiuli Bhabi, based on the symptoms that I narrated, told me first that I am pregnant."

"On my expressing uncertainty, she said, 'Look. I am a mother of three children, all born here. I had no family support even though I grew up in a joint family back home where for any problem, we used to have numerous opinions/suggestions. I learned to be on my own and thus attuned to live in this setting. Initially, when you told me about not having a monthly menstruation cycle, I, too, took that as something normal. Then I started observing you—your behavior, choice of food, and other expressions. All these convinced me about your pregnancy.'

"However, before divulging it to anyone, more particularly to you, the consensus between us was about inconspicuously getting the much-desired professional opinion based on medical investigation. Shiuli Bhabi took me yesterday to the university family clinic and introduced me to RN Martha, whom Bhabi knew very well. As we needed to be back home at the earliest because of me living alone and Shiuli Bhabi having a one-year-old son under the care of her neighbor, we hurried back with the understanding with RN Martha that Bhabi would be back tomorrow to pick up the report.

"The following day, Bhabi showed up on due time, gregariously smiled, handed over the report, hugged me warmly, saying, 'My experience can't belie me. Enjoy the moment.'

"That was about an hour back. The minute indicator of the table clock was not moving. I looked at the clock several times to estimate your presence. I was engrossed in thinking about the best way to divulge the news. Closing eyes was the best option during the time."

Javed was overwhelmed. Emotionally heightened, he went on describing his internalized feelings because of sharing with close friends and trusted physicians his conjugal constraints. Most feedback emanating from the process was vague with hopes for natural remedy being a common conclusion. I thus reconciled with the assumed reality that my life would be without a progeny.

At that point in time, I remembered a repeated saying of my late father: "If one or any of his close associates has an unsolvable problem, the easy option is to distance from him, but the best course is to give him/her a shoulder to help the process of a meaningful living. One does not know what the Almighty kept in store."

He then continued, "That saying of Father, like many others, just shuttered so long in my inner self without understanding. Suddenly, that relevant one came to my thought. I quietly prayed to his noble soul, thanking him for teaching me like that, and decided to be a part of you even if I am likely to have no offspring.

"Against that backdrop, the relevance and the value of present reality is unconceivable. Let us pray together tonight, seeking the Almighty's blessings for a safe and hassle-free pregnancy, and the delivery of a normal, gifted, and intelligent child to excel in all respects, especially the qualities of Grandpa and Grandma that made them luminaries at their time and in their respective settings."

Bringing Zarina close to him and bestowing numerous affectionate kisses, Javed spontaneously floated the proposition of slightly changing her name to reflect the earnest adoration with a tint of modernity. The change proposed was very simple but a very far-reaching one in terms of social acceptance and joviality. And the occasion could not be much cheerier and germane than this one. Javed then said, "From now on, and to me and our social setting, you are to be known as Zarin." Responding to that, Zarina surrendered on the chest of Javed, signifying both concurrence and happiness.

The union of two different individuals so long being nourished more on social compulsions bonded both emotionally and eloquently. That good news made all concerned of Ghazipur, Dhaka, and Sydney happy and ecstatic. Communications suddenly swelled.

A follow-on communication from Super Sir of college hostel life (Mr. Ahmed Farid) brought to him pertinent news of his interests and related implications. In a rare but comprehensive letter, he delt with their past relationship, mentioning particularly his wife Rohani's happiness and good wishes for his getting married as well as the news of pregnancy.

But surprisingly, that letter also dealt with the status and conditions of Mr. Shariful Alam, Lady Khadija, and Lolita. It was Javed's recommendation that Super Sir had access to the family more as a guide and mentor to Lolita during her arduous and perplexing time ahead. Super Sir recalled that and just thought that Javed would appreciate an update.

In a brief notation, Super Sir stated, "I tried my best to live up to your expectation, became more of a mentor to Lolita, and convinced her to opt for a temporary stay in their Bagan Bari at Marindrapur enclave. Both of her parents visited her regularly, and for me, that was a periodical one based on my convenience. The caretaker of the guest house discharged his obligations fully and sincerely to warrant frequent mentioning by Lolita's parents. Equally creditable was Lolita's ability to adjust to a new setting of life developing intensive relations with the caretaker, his wife, and two sons.

"All medical cares were ensured in strict privacy, and the baby girl was born without hassle. The girl was immediately named Momota by Lolita, knowing fully well that her physical bond with Momota was very fleeting.

"That happiness was short-lived as Mama and Mami of Lolita were in Dhaka at the right time, all prepared to take the baby girl to New Jersey as per the earlier agreed adoption arrangement.

"Within the next few days, Lolita returned to their Dhaka abode and was trying to orient her with an unalike normal life, and in discussion with me, she mentioned that her expectation was never for a life the family was used to. Whatever happened is inescapable, but her present priority is to make the parents happy. In that connection, she often referred to your feelings for parents within the small frame of parental longevity. On my part, I, too, encouraged her to follow that path even though parental love and care can never be repaid.

Outwardly, the family locus was amiable but internally discomfort, and tension persisted. To obviate that, a decision was taken to get Lolita married soonest. That critical task was reposed on me. My responsibility was to orient Lolita with the proposition once the likely groom was identified. That was performed by me fully, and Lolita got married to one Rattan of Dhaka south, an upcoming political activist."

Super Sir Farid's letter ended with the following summation; " With that sort of family configuration and Lolita getting steadily settled in life, I decided to slowly phase out of their life but failed due to the persistence of Lolita and Father Shariful Alam. Due to the passionate entreat of Mr. Alam, I was stirred to accommodate the plea with a reflection. After a nippy thought, I quietly advised him about my likely promotion as vice principal, a new administrative position due to an unexpected increase in the workload of the principal's office."

Sir Farid then politely said, "I appreciate and am thankful to you all for taking me to trust in this delicate phase of your family life even though our association is recent. I will try my best to be by the side of dear Lolita and you both. But it may not be as frequent as currently is. Nevertheless, you both and Lolita are free to call me anytime you need my help. I will definitely respond positively."

He concluded the letter by informing Javed about the deteriorating health conditions of VP Azmat Beg.

Javed was delighted reading the letter of Super Sir Farid except for the news of the health of VP Sir. He was very happy to know about Momota's immigration to the USA and the subsequent wedding of Lolita with Rattan, and rushed to his abode to share all the positive news except the one relating to VP Azmat Beg. As he was approaching his residence after parking the vehicle, Javed felt lighter and burden-free for the first time in recent months.

Zarin was equally delighted and proposed to pray for the happy life of Lolita and the quick recovery of VP Sir.

Months passed. Zarin gave birth to a baby daughter who, based on earlier understanding, was named Arshi Javed. They were very exultant with the name so chosen as it reflects the guidance and contribution of Arshi Appa in mitigating initial conjugal constraints, and her father's identity being reflective through a mirror. But as she was out of home in a stroller, neighbors and their offsprings started calling her Ash.

As Arshi was about six months old, Zarin's apparent discomfort with handling both household chores as well as Arshi's growing-up needs became apparent to Javed. In his inquisitive mind, and after due thought, he concluded that unlike his sisters and fellow compatriots, Zarin spent most of her adolescent life in study coercions away from family and community. She thus had no chance or motivation to know the art of handling a child and taking care of them.

Realizing that, Javed was willing to assist Zarin with his limited expertise in occasionally handling or cuddling nephew Amin. That, however, was no substitute for discharging responsibility inherent in taking care, whether smiling or crying, whether due to hunger or acidity due to overfeeding, whether being wet or dry within the napkins and so on. Javed, despite intention otherwise, could not be of much help because of those limitations as well as preoccupations with teaching and research works.

At that moment of tribulations, an unanticipated communication from Javed's previous university in Dhaka took him by amazement with a mix of cheerfulness and appreciativeness. Even though he left Dhaka soon after finishing his masters, Javed maintained his relationship and link with his previous learning institution by sharing some elements of his research productivity.

The institution, in a program to enhance its academic excellence, offered Javed a variable teaching cum research assignment for one to three years with permissible optimum benefits.

Returning home, he shared the exceptional news with Zarin, whose immediate response was in the negative. She got used to the American way of family life and the individuality it adulates.

On being pursued, she finally concurred with a stipulation that the proposed relocation would be for a maximum period of three years to ensure Arshi's growing up and learning foundations be U.S.-based.

The initial few months were socially most demanding and entertaining for both, while academically, that was rewarding beyond expectation for Javed. Gradually, the warmth started stinging while the professional disputation crept.

After a few months, the real impulses of some so-called friends and well-wishers started emerging. Negative comments were copious, while some spread rumors about Javed's inability to balance with US academic standards. Their simple conclusion was, "Who else will leave the USA to come back to Bangladesh?'"

Though used to such behavioral traits, it was difficult for Zarin to live with all these as the inference was to her husband. She was thus dejected and morose. Javed ignored the whole occurrence initially but could no longer ignore to bear that. Instead of not openly contesting the misleading assertion of the mostly ignorant populace of related society, Javed sat down with Zarin to explain his mindset.

In the emotional paradigm, he referred to the sudden loss of power and prestige by the Muslims with the advent of British rule in India. Worst was the rise of the hitherto subjugated Hindu populace, particularly in economic consolidation and modern learning.

"The independence of 1947 and the liberation of 1971 aggravated those sensations. The worst is emerging high feelings about our knowledge, competence, and capability on all scores including the Nobel committee's inability to recognize our merit and inventiveness. We inclined ourselves to believe in our greatness. So US-based eminent seats of learning like mine have no relevance in the local context."

After a pause, Javed continued his assertion, saying, "I decided to be here on a fixed-term assignment to repay my debt to this remarkable root of mine. Let us sustain this for the time being. I am more than certain to go back to the USA to pursue a larger arena of academic excellence as well as proper grooming of our dearest Arshi. I have the job. We need immigration documents. So please do not worry.

"On my part, I am gradually complying with my obligations here. In consultations with Fatipa-Bu, Rafisa-Bu, and with the concurrence of Fyruz Bhai, actions are being taken to ensure the sustainability of AIT, including ownership and the use of the parental home for teachers' and students' need-based accommodation, granting of monthly allowance to Nazir Bhai and regular treatment of Hamid Ullah Sir out of income from the ancestral home at Shetra. In addition, I am in touch with Tahera Khala and guiding Amin in the new responsibility as the owner of the business since the demise of Bepari Chacha.

"Importantly, I could convince Fatipa-Bu to concur with Rafisa-Bu's decision to settle permanently in Australia with her husband and two children.

One good outcome of this impermanent stay is we could think through the future of the late Zakir Mia's family. The emerging consensus was that with the future being undefined and impulsive, we can prepare ourselves for a befitting response in terms of time and demand."

Zarin was content but not convinced about the essence of that assertion. She nevertheless opted to let it go for the time being as contesting the emerging opinion of seniors so soon may not be taken in good grace. She is disturbed as the avowal has no specifics.

Waiting a few days and being assured of the poised mood of Javed, she brought up her concern about the nature of their decision concerning the future of the family. With certitude as to the aptness of her thinking, Zarin raised the relevant issue of future education opportunities for Azeem (a name change initiated by Ameen himself, as he was growing up, with the consent of parents) and suggested that since the latter has the opportunity to pursue higher education abroad, one should explore that.

Javed was not only awestruck but thanked destiny for blessing his life with such a solicitous life partner. He passionately looked at Zarin and commented smilingly, "Do you cogitate that it is not a part of my thinking but our present location in Dhaka is the constrictive factor? I will act on that once we return to the USA."

Zarin quipped quickly, "To my understanding, we may not have a better time than this as it may involve a process requiring more time than we anticipate. This thus possibly the most appropriate time and opportunity to raise the issue as part of the package for the family as a whole we are considering. When I was thinking about Azeem's future, the constraining factor you indicated was also vigilant within me. I also thought about a possible way out of that.

"Having relative exposure to and experience of the public education system updated by feedback from friends engaged in recent delivery of the same, I am more than convinced that this is the optimum time to act so far Azeem and the future of the family are concerned.

"This impression of mine is due to the evident gulf of difference between school and higher education, the latter mostly being detached from family and surroundings in which one grows up. This along with the inevitable physiological change transforming a young into an adult with specific traits and a reversal later on is often both difficult and challenging.

"Based on such rationalization, I would suggest that you raise the issue with both Fatipa-Bu and Fyruz Bhai proposing the option for Azeem to go to Australia for higher studies after secondary school level with our support. If he likes it later, he can get a transfer to a nearby U.S. school and pursue the next level of education under our care. If agreed to, we may have a full discussion on the proposition with Rafisa-Bu in due course."

Javed agreed with her propositions and acted accordingly to the amazement of Fyruz Bhai notwithstanding initial reservations on the part of Fatipa-Bu. Her major apprehension was that it may be indicative of delinking from Ghazipur and the heritage of late Zakir Mia once gone as it happened with both Javed and Rafisa.

Javed intervened, saying, "Fatipa-Bu, the world is much bigger and larger than Ghazipur. Wherever one is in this global village, one can contribute to well-being of humanity. Father's broad objective was that. It no more matters where one is located so long objectives are clear and intentions are candid." To the delight of Fyruz, she eventually agreed contentedly.

With that frame of family congeniality, both Javed and Zarin were having a rewarding stay even though occasional thwarting was not uncommon. Both attuned themselves to live with that. Their happiness was illimitable noting one or two broken Bangla words uttered by Arshi in her slow induction to talking.

Nothing in life is sacrosanct. No comfort constituent is perpetual. The same applies to happiness too. Even though life has its concerns and challenges in its usual rotation of living process, some of the time becomes excruciating. That happened in Javed's case too.

It was the early part of November. In Bangladesh, that signifies the advent of winter after discomforting a few months of high temperature and elevated humidity. Apart from seasonal changes influencing the way of life, it also signifies a notable change in food intake items and their components. More noticeable was in nature and varieties of *pithas* (rice powder-based breakfast and snack items).

Javed just finished his late breakfast of *chital* (thick and mostly round-shaped snack item heated in a clay pot with a cover causing glosses) *pitha* with cooked spicy duck meat. The beauty of this snack item is that this pitha is equally tasty even with grated coconut mixed with *rub* (thick and sweet date juice).

With Zarin retired to the bedroom to pick up the landline-premised incoming call and Javed sipping his tea, the doorbell rang. The household help lady (generally called *Bua*) showed up informing about the presence of police visitors.

As three of them, one in civil dress and two in uniform were ushered in, Javed, hiding his discomfort and surprise, decently welcomed them while requesting them to be seated.

The one in civil dress introduced himself, saying, "I am Masood Aftab from the intelligence outfit of the special branch, and these two are my colleagues from the regular line force. We had no plan to disturb you without advance indication. We went to meet your vice chancellor and we came to see you at his behest.

"The government likes intelligentsia like you and would support them in every respect. It systematically monitors various writings and essays by significant people like you. The authorities concerned have so far been very appreciative of your writings on social and economic issues, but increasingly, it appears that you are crossing the lines the government has hypothetically earmarked.

"I would not say more on this issue. You are well educated, and I am thus certain that you got the message."

While standing up to go out, Mr. Masood Aftab said unconcernedly, "I went to Ghazipur to enquire about you and to check on your activities. I came to know that you do not have any real estate outside Ghazipur. If you are interested, you can touch base with me. I can be of help in getting allocated a reasonably sized plot in the Pulshan residential area for you. The time is very short. The availability is being increasingly constrained. Consider this as a genuine offer."

Saying those words and exercising due decency, all three stepped out, with Javed being stamped in his drawing room.

Zarin came back after a long chat with her mother and was astounded to observe a pale and disjointed Javed standing motionless. Knowing Javed very well by this time and without any inquisition on her part, she quietly walked to the kitchen and enquired from Bua about the people who rang the doorbell. She kept on waiting for Javed to open, but he maintained a grievous posture.

It was after dinner that he started showing reactions. The first relevant incident was a small fall sustained by Arshi. Javed was prompt in responding to the lachrymose of Arshi. After she assuaged and went to sleep, Javed finally stated all that was exchanged between visitors and him.

Javed, having a restless mindset since the morning meeting with law enforcement officials, could not have a pleasant sleep. He woke up thinking about his future life and that of the growing options for Arshi.

Hours passed. Finally, he silently sighed for Zarin's participation in that agonizing thought process. At Zarin's signal, both moved to the drawing room and took seat side by side.

But the following time was one akin to prolonged silence and indifference between them, signifying a lack of camaraderie with nothing common to share. Zarin was in a state of disarray but refrained from reacting, enthused by Javed's holding of one of her nonresponsive hands in a solid grip. In that stint, time's prolongation was unbearable but equally unavoidable. It is more discomforting for one like Zarin in a state of ambiguity.

The table clock ticked twelve, indicative of midnight. There was a mild mechanical notification. That possibly alerted Javed who, after significant time, showed some retort as he relaxed the grip voluntarily, looked at her fervidly, and drew her still close to him with all adoration.

By this time of conjugal living and based on past experiences, Zarin was certain about a likely philosophical avowal before he said what he wanted to. She kept calm but still warm in her relinquished posture.

Javed, caressing the disorganized long hair of Zarin more to ensure attention, slowly started saying, "If one does not have the freedom to think, he is archaic. If one cannot perform the task of a reconnoiter in establishing facts and truth, he is fusty. If one cannot express what one believes to be true, he is nonexistent. These, among many others, were repeatedly emphasized by my late father, Zakir Mia, with the common notation to remember for full understanding in due course. I was repeatedly advised to remain upright in the face of adversity and never to yield to pressure or threats.

"I could sense some restrictions in pursuing my thinking at the beginning but ignored those as rudimentary. I exercised patience, always hoping better setting for intellectual exercise. The impression that I harbored probably was it is easier to change practices and improve things from within than confronting that from outside. However, the visit by police officials made me aware of the real dimension and focus concerning the issue.

"Like most things and situations in life, patience has its limitations. Too much exercise of that may cause insuperable impairments in future. Thus, while keeping this morning's inexplicable experience in view and the possibility of its recurrence in the future, I spent most of the day and part of the night surveying my options as to the future course, keeping in view my professional preferences, family values, the way I grew up, the future of Arshi, and our family life. In the process, I unknowingly sometimes pressured my grip while holding your hand. That was to ensure emotionally not to lose you in the process in case of possible disagreement. I hope you will not say no to what I would say now."

With wide-open black eyes having the touch of *kajol* (shimmer), Zarin had a penetrating look at Javed but remained nonresponsive so as not to derail the latter from his current thinking. Her silence during that midnight parley and the quietness predominant in Javed's behavior and expressions did cast a shadow of haziness in that misty setting of the drawing room. Anxieties multiplied, provoking Zarin finally to say, "If we are to remain quiet as we are currently, then it is better for us to be in bed." Saying those few words without expression of apparent anger, Zarin wanted to move out but was courteously resisted by Javed.

Responding to that, she adopted a different strategy to provoke Javed. She took possession of his left hand, pressed it, and said, "A few minutes back, you told me that you took possession of my hand to ensure that I do not leave you after dissenting with you. Now, I am holding your hand to assure you that I will never harbor any inkling of leaving you. I will always be with you and agree with your decision, whatever that may entail. Rest assured about that."

Having that clarity about her thinking and assurance, Javed briefly said, "I have decided to go back to the States after this academic year to have a living of my preference and to pursue professional competence without any imposition or threat. This will also ensure the growing up of Arshi in an open and free environment."

Contrary to previous thinking of communicating his thinking in an elaborate induction process, the above communication was direct and precise. He was happy within himself but decided to share a bit more of his thinking.

Javed illuminated, stating, "It does not indicate that we are abandoning our birthplace. We will periodically maintain contact and visit Bangladesh. Moreover, whatever is needed to be done on the family and social fronts has almost been done. All the preferences of Abba have generally been complied with. The high school has been renamed after him. AIT is functioning properly with the financial support from the ancestral property and with the transfer of the parental home. A sense of social amity is prevailing.

On family-related matters: Fatipa-Bu, Masha Allah (by the Grace of Allah Pak), is well settled in family life with someone like Fyruz Bhai always by her side with a shoulder; Rafisa-Bu is well settled in Australia with her family; the parental home was purchased back and assigned to AIT; both Hamid Ullah Sir and Nazir Bhai are being adequately taken care of; maintaining desired contacts with cousins of Shetra; and so on. We are on the track parents would have preferred.

Also, the next generation is on its move forward, with nephew Azeem being in Australia pursuing higher education as well as developing a family bond with the two children of Rafisa-, all being groomed to play respective roles in a much greater field of challenge. Our dearest daughter, Arshi, is learning to communicate.

With that oration, Javed culminated his thinking and preference for future professional and conjugal life. On her part, Zarin, as an indication of concurrence, hugged him warmly and retired to bed, responding to signs of restlessness of Arshi.

Javed just whispered, "You go, and I will soon be joining you after sending an email to the chairman of my department in the USA, conveying the intention to come back one year earlier. I will only tell my present university when I get an affirmation from him."

That response from his university in the USA was very prompt, setting the ball in motion. In a communication to Rafisa-Bu, Javed narrated the backdrop referring to the earlier proposition to take care of Azeem's higher education in the USA. Contrary to expectation, he received a separate letter from nephew Azeem, indicating his current preference to stay in Australia as he likes the country and its social norms, that he is enjoying his study in the school and the company of cousins under the warm care of Khala, and that, as he understands, it is relatively easy to get citizenship once one obtains graduate-level education from an Australian educational institution.

So that chapter is temporarily closed. The couple who returned to Bangladesh with noble hope had to pack off prematurely to live in the States.

STUCK

THE COUPLE RETURNED to their adopted city with uncertainty about the physical settlement. Their discussions during the process, as a bypass of the sad experience of living home country earlier than what they had in mind, were about finding a good place like their old community, for affable growing up of Arshi.

Fortunately, during a social call with Shiuli Bhabi and her spouse, a science faculty staff of the same university, they came to know that their previous house coincidentally is in the market for fresh leasing. That caused cheerfulness in them.

Within a few days, the couple undertook a physical inspection and was happy about the upkeep of the house, including restoration works after the previous occupant vacated. The related moving-in and settlement processes were done without much hassle.

Arshi, to known community inhabitants, became once again their Ash. She, having the same house and almost similar settings, adjusted remarkably to the glee of her parents.

In the midst of related happiness, one thing has systematically troubled Javed—the failure to touch base with Lolita and her parents. He thought of that several times but refrained from acting due to the implications inherent. Moreover, their departure was sudden too. At the end of such thinking, his inner conclusion was always that perhaps it was better to enable the maintenance of peace and tranquility in that family.

Time passed. A surprise letter from Super Sir Ahmed Farid with the most unexpected information percussed all related feelings containing the life and family of Lolita. He, unlike his known self, was very brief and straight in conveying the sad news of the sudden death of Lolita followed by the unfortunate demise of Mr. Ashraful Alam, and the subsequent withdrawal of stylish Lady Khadija to the surroundings of their Bagan Bari at Marindrapur to help the poor community.

In response to follow-up communication at the behest of Chachi Rohani, Super Sir summarized what he knew. The essence was that in no time, it became apparent that Rattan married Lolita for property. He, like a shrewd operator, started with all politeness and love. As nothing was shaping up, he became rough and rude, including the occasional loud abuses to convey to in-laws the reason for his unhappiness. On the evening of the fatal incident, he physically assaulted her while the parents were distraught and stunned.

Sensing that the parents were approaching her bedroom with a previously tested proposition for a make-believe interim settlement in exchange for some cash for Rattan, Lolita while trying to escape that repetition, was hurrying to take shelter in her room on the ground floor while fixing her crumpled saree. In that rage and diverted focus, she missed steps, lost balance, and fell with her forehead hitting the much-adored imported marble wedges of Lady Khadija. Lolita collapsed instantaneously and succumbed even before the physician's arrival. Either sheer wariness or a sense of guilt, Rattan quietly left the house, not to return.

Days passed. Friends and some relations distanced themselves point-blank from Mr. Ashraful Alam and Lady Khadija while some others maintained infrequent contact and basically used that opening to share with others the couple's despondent breathing surroundings with a mix of agony and blemish.

The resultant agnostic conditions aggravated Mr. Ashraful Alam's flustered mindset and started assessing life, living, and possessions from a totally different perspective. As a possible consequence of that among likely many others torturing him within, Mr. Alam took the sole decision to divest all his property and assets and create a trust fund for supporting distressed girls while the family's much adored current residence of Pulshan to be a shelter for them.

Both success in social setting and accumulation of wealth were the fruits of the joint efforts of the couple where Lady Khadija was the mover and Mr. Ashraful Alam was the executor. But when it was the unforeseen time to take a decision about those, Mr. Alam acted individually oblivious of the consequences. At this point, he was a different person.

The sudden sad demise of their beloved daughter impacted Lady Khadija's thinking, reversing her priorities, values, and focus of life both outwardly and internally. She suddenly lost all her ego and focus on life and became subservient to the decisions of Mr. Alam.

Seventy-five percent of the annual trust income is to be spent on the upkeep, operation, and functioning of the boarding house named Nirob Bhavan (literally house of silence) and operational programs for the betterment of the quality of life of the distressed girls.

With all related arrangements in place, the couple moved quietly to a modest structure in the compound so far used as a farmhouse. That was suitably modified for a judicious living of two heartbroken individuals whose avowed priority so far was high-profile connection, accumulation of wealth, and visibility in society without directly bearing the responsibility of power. They were, therefore, always out of public scrutiny, an accountability obligation for public office holders. Occasional donations for charitable purposes kept them in the good book of power brokers and the government, irrespective of periodical changes.

That was easy for Mr. Alam to comprehend, but his inner self was probably not ready to accept the reality. Successive health-related complications were too much and too many for him to bear. Mr. Alam succumbed to that reality soon.

Lady Khadija steadily reoriented her life pattern after the sad and sudden demise of their dearest daughter. That process was quiet but sublime. She slowly conveyed to closed staff and associates not to use the salutation of Lady anymore. She started feeling more comfortable with traditional salutations like *amma* (mother) and *bu-jan* (local word for BuBu-Jan, elder sister close to heart).

Khadija shunned public appearances, cast off the habit of going for expensive hairstyles, discarded wearing trendy sarees and tops, and gradually tilted to secluded living. Her apparent preference for performing daily mandated *namaj* (Muslim prayers) was self-evident.

She slowly was getting used to secluded living, spending some of the time with close household staff about earthly things around their lives. But the unexpected death of Mr. Alam, soon after the tragic demise of her daughter, was too much for her to bear. She preferred an escape from that huge house. The related settings with memories of power, connections, and influence were haunting her. That was aggravated by frequent visits of presumed well-wishers and continuous ranting of their words of succor, more as a consonance reflection of past days.

Consistent with such feelings and no one to acquiesce, Amma Khadija decided to relocate to the natural and neutral setting of Bagan Bari, leaving her known place of dominance and eminence. But she took a practical step as she decided to keep up the properties of the compound they were living in since the house was assigned to the charitable trust.

After disposing of her fancy personal acquisitions of choice so far and as a preparation for her new functional life in and around Bagan Bari, she started attiring herself in a simple but elegant local *tanter* (handwoven) saree.

That gradual but sublime change was taken by staff as normal after successive shudders, but they were surprised to observe her on the final day of leaving the compound putting on a *hijab*.

As her car stopped in front of the renovated cottage, the caretaker of the Bagan Bari greeted her warmly with respect and prudence and invited her to have tea with his family and other support staff to make the transition both physically transient and psychologically smooth.

That happened too soon and very quietly. Within the Bagan Bari compound and its periphery, she carried the identity of Amma. To the community outside, especially ladies, she was known as Bu-jan—one with all sorts of help, ranging from the supply of needed vitamins, basic medicines, and other advice to enhance the quality of the life of the poor. Her high emphasis on the quality of drinking water, basic hygiene needs, especially of girls, and the need for sustained schooling with meaningful financial support made her a very likeable and popular person in the area. The establishment of the Ashraful Care Center and Lolita Birthing Center stand out prominently. Gradually, she engrossed herself in such activities, earning the name and fame equally without any objective.

Javed read the letter minutely, shared the contents with Zarin and left that letter on the table. He inadvertently forgot to take it along. Seeing the letter, Zarin picked it up and read it with all intensity.

When he returned from the university, Zarin told him about the letter on the table and said, "I have read the letter twice and learned a lot from its contents so nicely articulated by Super Sir."

In response, Javed said, "I inadvertently left the letter but drew solace from thinking that you may reread the letter at your convenience. I wanted to ensure that the vivid description enriches both of our living together."

That episode was supposed to end there. But that did not happen. Zarin continued, "As I had finished the second reading, an interesting thought crept into my mind. That is related to doing something to enrich others in the local setting. However, I was confused and could not enunciate anything in this developed society. I thus felt frustrated."

Javed noted that with positivity and pride but kept quiet as he, too, was unsure about what she could do in this society on a scale that would have some impact.

While discussing school options for Arshi, one thought suddenly struck his mind. He kept it within himself until the time was affable to share it with Zarin, she being the principal player in his tentative game plan. That opportunity came soon after Zarin put Arshi to sleep and they were sitting with their after-dinner tea.

Javed was prompt to share his idea as to what one like Zarin can do to help community assimilation even though in a limited way. He referred to mostly half-educated or some untrained Bangladeshi individuals coming annually under the much-publicized diversity visa (DV) program and facing initial problems, among others, in terms of language, behavior norms, social practices, education, health care, and so on.

In their supportive discourse, it was agreed that the paucity of needed resources, lack of support hands, on-the-ground contacts, the spread of immigrants needing such help, and multiple others like the above are immediate problems. The consensus was to try out the proposition on a small scale in their own homes and pursue it based on experience.

Zarin floated a very workable proposition. She opined that since new immigrants are relatively fresh from Bangladesh and are struggling, they are likely to be more religious and still oriented to the habits and culture of the past. So the masjid (Muslim prayer place) would be a good venue for the dissemination of news about the availability of needed services. Also, she highlighted the need to clarify that on being provided with related information, the advocate will visit the relevant home at no cost. That is the best way to talk to and help the process of assimilation.

Notwithstanding all efforts, the beginning was sluggish and quite disheartening. The couple was thinking of abandoning the idea. Right at the moment, the doorbell rang. As Zarin opened the door, a young and confident Bangladeshi girl standing opposite smiled with a mix of edginess and glee and introduced herself. She opened with a mix of politeness and confidence, saying, "I am Rubiya. Our family migrated to the USA about a month back under the now-popular DV lottery program, and I completed my ninth-class education in Bangladesh.

My family has no relation or contact in the USA. Father had little idea about living constraints and challenges here. He only knew that the USA is the country for enlightened education and learning. From associates and friends, he came to know that Boston in USA is the most enviable place for that purpose.

He aspired that his only daughter and younger son would be well-educated and learned individuals contributing to the well-being of society. With that dream in mind and the hope of excellence in his heart, he packed off and left Bangladesh with his family and some funds.

It is about a month and we are still uncertain and confused. Returning from local the masjid, he shared the contents of a post extending help in the settlement. I got your address from him and with some help reached your place. I hope I am speaking with Mrs. Zarin Javed."

Zarin stepped out, embraced Rubiya, got her inside, and made her easy, saying, "You have come to the right place, and what your father told you and your family from his reading of our post is correct."

Rubiya became instantly friendly with Arshi, and that pleased Zarin. She invited Rubiya's family to be in her place the day after which is Sunday.

Rubiya left with a ray of hope on her horizon, while Zarin was thrilled seeing the prospect of realization of her idea. On return in the evening, Javed was exhilarated to know about the development.

Zarin started visiting Rubiya's home to guide them in every respect of assimilation. The meaningful guidance she was giving became known in no time in the community concerned, and that soon became a full-time job. Not to jeopardize the work, Zarin organized small groups of adjacent families and continued her efforts to guide the new arrivals.

In a post-dinner conversation, Zarin was sharing her happiness and was enchanted to tell Javed about her new identity as Zarin Appa of the community.

Javed was very pleased and observed that all the progress she made has an inherent message, and that is, "If one wants to help the society, he or she can do that from any place. While physical presence is helpful, it is not an imperative. Your work is evidently proving that. You deserve to be happy."

Time passed by. Years roll down. Arshi started growing up, enrolled in school, and with successive progression, was recognized as a talented student of her class as Javed made a name and fame for his research work and teaching prudence. Zarin found solace in being the appa (sister) of the Bangladeshi and other communities needing support in the settlement process. The unique feature of her guidance effort was being at no cost and generally home-based, with herself moving from house to house, in some cases in lead homes, based on demand and need.

The only negative experience of Javed in this period was the contents of a letter from Fyruz Bhai conveying the sad news of the demise of respected Hamid Ullah Sir after a prolonged ailment. Javed, even though apprehensive about such development for quite some time, was shocked, bewildered, and continued lamenting.

Zarin, being conscious of his feelings, was at a bay about her course of action. Arshi, who just finished her ninth-grade education, stepped in. She, being aware of the full contents of the letter of uncle Fyruz, observed by saying, "We fully understand your feelings and share it equally. Since my early childhood, and as I recall, you mentioned in many expressions his respect for Dadaji (grandpa), support and guidance to the family since Dadaji's demise, and articulated in various lingos and private family discourses his contribution to what you so far achieved in life."

Having said so and surfacing the confused mother and saddened father's facial reactions, Arshi, in an untapped course of commentary, changed her deliberation focus by saying, "It ought to be the occasion for sober celebration. The inevitable has happened. His life's journey has followed those of billions of others, but the positive feature is that was at his prime age. But the best thing is that the school management has responded befittingly by naming the office room of the headmaster as Hamid Ullah Sir's office, and the community has shown its gratitude by renaming the enclave where the school is situated as Hamid Ullah Nogori.

Javed stood up instantaneously, came close to Arshi, hugged her, and said, "I am so happy. You are talking like Father. I am proud of you and would bless you profusely."

Zarin, the silent observer, was in tears as an expression of happiness and gratitude to the Almighty for blessing her with such an understanding girl.

With silent appellation and esteem, the family continued its passage to the happiness of Javed, a sense of fulfillment of Zarin, and a silent resolve within the mindset of Arshi. Things for the family could not be better.

In life, nothing is everlasting and nothing can be taken as guaranteed. And that precisely happened with Arshi's life.

Zarin, while preparing to go out for her social service commitment of that day, collapsed in front of her dressing counter and embraced death despite efforts by medical professionals.

That unexpected and profoundly tragic experience in the life of a happy and contended small but equally intimate family having their nest far away from roots shattered both husband and daughter.

Arshi, with her high school load of academic pressure, focused, though missing her dear mother at every turn of her life's journey, more on academic preparations with specific objectives in mind. Recalling frequent discussions that Father had with Dadu (grandpa) before the latter's sudden death and their insinuations in shaping the father's life, Arshi rivetted her attention and priority in spending all her available time in taking care of and having discourses with Father, apprehending something similar.

Time passed. Reality dictated adjustment, however painful that is. It happened with Javed too.

Referring to frequent queries pertaining to some of her inquisitions reflective of his exchanges with his father, Javed, on an opposite juncture, jokingly observed, "Look, Ma, I am not going to follow the footsteps of your Dadu. He could go leaving his son to sink or swim in the rough water of life. But I have a daughter whose solo journey in this world is full of peril. With that, I am not going to die so soon."

Javed laughed, having amusement engulfing his facial echoes.

While preparing the dining setting for two as usual, Arshi kept her ear alert and listened to what Father said and his follow-on reflexes. She moved close to her father and hugged him dearly as an expression of love and thanks for having the determination to live long as her shelter.

In a similar setting after some lapse of time, both father and daughter were exchanging their thoughts for Arshi's future focus and priority for higher studies. While Javed always preferred to see that his daughter follow his footsteps in pursuing liberal arts to earn laurels in life, he was taken aback when she determinedly expressed priority to become a doctor. Her very substantive justification was to have authoritative knowledge about the causes of her mother's death and to have knowledge and expertise to ensure that such deaths are minimized in future, at least.

Javed was both happy and ashamed. Happy because observing Arshi growing up as a responsive adult with an inclination to do service for society. He was ashamed as Arshi's feelings about Mother were totally misunderstood by him due to few outward references and expressions, even though internally. Those occasional outbursts were reflective of agonizing internal frustrations for not having the presence of mother in her life at that critical phase of growing up.

The most authoritative medical documents and expertise view so far concluded that the cause of sudden death in young people (age group of twenty to thirty-five) is hypertrophic cardiomyopathy (HCM), a genetic heart condition.

"In HCM, the muscles of the left ventricle get thickened with growing up and get enlarged, reducing the left ventricle flow of blood and impairing activity of the aortic valve. That causes sudden death. In essence, it is a genetic disease. I plan to research how to identify it early and what can be done to minimize, if not reverse it."

Javed was excited and thanked Allahpak for blessing Arshi with such a mindset.

Days passed. Father and daughter had similar discussions whenever Arshi had been home from her medical-study pursuits.

Time just elapsed. Arshi finished her medical education and internship in her medical school and was looking for a likeable professional opening with a preference to be close to Father in Chicago, his new place of work.

With a startling opportunity of having an internship at the famous Saint Fatima Research Hospital, she, too, moved to Chicago, living with Father after intermittent gaps of around the last four years of her medical studies. Both father and daughter were very happy even though Javed very much hoped that Arshi would get married and settle in life, an inborn urge of any father. That was more so as he, in the absence of Zarin, has the singular responsibility to see the daughter fully settled in life. He prepared himself several times but could not say what he had in mind, looking at the face of Arshi. For the first time in his cherished life, Javed found himself in the most flustered phase of life.

Arshi merrily joined her assignment and made efforts to cultivate professional and personal relationships with colleagues and coworkers.

She had a natural inclination to exchange looks and smiles while crossing colleagues in the workstations and even in the corridors.

In that process and while in the line of the hospital cafeteria holding her food tray to make payment, she noticed another Saree-clad coworker in the other line. Amazement and inquisitiveness overtook north American social etiquette, and Arshi stepped out of the line and approached the line where the Saree-clad lady was standing and politely enquired whether she was from Bangladesh.

The lady responded affirmatively but proceeded to the cashier as she was next to make payment. Even then, Arshi was happy and excitedly told Father about that in the evening.

The following day, Arshi went to the foodcourt well ahead and kept waiting for the Saree-clad lady. Even though somewhat delayed, she showed up, and seeing Arshi standing alone, went to her with a greeting of Salam. Both shook hands, took their respective food, and went to a far corner table hopefully to avoid others.

Saying her name and introducing herself as one who just joined the assistantship program, she had a loving look at the lady. The lady hesitantly said, "I am Momoto, though many call me either Mo or Mom. I feel comfortable with both, and you can choose either."

Arshi, without responding to choose either specific option and taking note of uncontrolled noise from adjacent tables, replied, "I will decide later how I address you, but the noise here is too much for a personal discourse. I suggest that we meet in a quieter place tomorrow after duty hours and can have a heartwarming conversation."

Momota, scanning her phone, commented, "Since tomorrow is a Friday, and fortunately this happens to be the one when I am free after 5 p.m., we can meet near the reception counter and then can decide as to options."

Arshi was very excited and narrated the precipitous experiences to Father on return home, especially highlighting her dress-up in Saree. Javed listened carefully, but for myriad reasons, opted to keep quiet.

They met on the following day and at the appointed venue. Walking out of the hospital complex, Momota took a turn to the right in silence and then headed to the small foodcourt on the opposite side. As she entered, it was apparent that she happened to be a known face. They took their seats at a corner counter, and Momata just walked back to the cash counter to place orders for both.

She came back with two trays having the same food items and two bottles of frozen Coke.

Drawing the attention of Arshi to chicken pieces on their service trays, Momota observed that these are not common fried chicken, normally marketed by different outlets under varied brands. Pollo Compero is a restaurant (food chain) originating in Guatemala, very popular throughout South America and presently parts of the USA. The most popular and succulent of their dish items is shallow-frying chicken that ensures a crispy golden-brown texture all over without the amount of oil needed for full deep frying. It, however, needs to be supplemented by a small dose of MSG to give the chicken a much-desired savory flavor. It tastes very well when layered with different types of spices and paired with tortillas, french fries, and dinner rolls.

Momota continued her avowal, stating, "I had to spend about five months in Guatemala as part of my professional training. I discovered Pollo Compero at that time and remained hooked. When Pollo Compero opened their outlet here about six months back, I was overjoyed. Since then and on any occasion of happiness, I visit them. As I am attired in a Saree always, they identify me easily. A few local words and expressions that I learned in Guatemala also helped in getting familiar with them."

She paused saying those words and politely said, "Bon appetit."

As Arshi was having her bite, she was wondering about the nature and traits of her new acquaintance. She had the agonizing pain of asking her the relevant questions or opting for some latitude for her to open. Arshi was conscious of the reality that specific questions would have specific answers but not genuine ones. She thus decided to try emotional blackmailing.

Without awaiting any more time, with dinner almost half through, Arshi framed her inquisitiveness by saying, "If I am not mistaken, you are likely to be elder compared to me. The tragedy of my life is I do not have either a sister or brother, growing up without the love and affection of a sibling. I was born and mostly grew up in the USA without any interaction with a family comprising of uncles, aunties, and cousins. I grew up in a setting where Arshi became Ash. If you appreciate my frustration, may I have your consent to address you as Appa instead of Mo or Mom?"

The emotive reaction of Momota took Arshi by both suddenness and surprise. The emotional impact of what she just said was beyond any comprehension of Arshi. The tear-filled eyes of Momota could not hold that anymore, and slowly drops of that plunged through her cheeks, simultaneously stopping the intake of food. Arshi was nervous, thinking her earlier unfolding might have hurt Momota unknowingly and was thinking of a proper statement to disparage that.

At that juncture of emotional irritation, Momota unleashed her assimilated frustration, saying, "You are relatively lucky to have a father. I even do not know who my father is! When my Nani was ailing seriously after the demise of Nana, I accidentally got a hold of a notebook, an apology for a diary recording my life within a strict framework of understanding with my real Nana and Nani leading to my adoption. Thus, I have only a peripheral idea as to who I am and why I am in America.

"In essence, I was adopted soon after my birth in Dhaka and was flown into the USA as a part of an adoption deal with a childless sister and brother-in-law of my direct Nani living in Virginia. That deal was premised on win-win syndrome for both parties: saving a prominent and successful couple in Dhaka from a likely social disgrace for having their only daughter pregnant before marriage with vagueness shrouding the relationship, and the professionally successful childless couple having a family member to take care of.

"The couple made every effort to take care of me but exercised strict confidentiality with matters pertaining to adoption. On my part, I had little interest in knowing the details. I was enjoying my growing up centering my studies and Nana and Nani. To me and at that point in life, that was the world coupled with my dream to become a physician, as ladies attired in white aprons always fascinated me while accompanying Nana and Nani to their periodical visits to respective chambers and hospitals.

I grew up merrily under the love and care of my adopted Nana and Nani. That beautiful journey suddenly got a major setback as I finished my ninth grade in high school. Both grandparents successively had major health issues: Nana had serious diabetes and Nani had a balance problem along with dysfunctional knees.

That was the turning point in the journey. My life centered, besides studies, on frequent visits to doctors and hospitals for consultations and investigations, mostly resulting in further referrals, and to CVS for varied medicines. The side change in that trajectory of life was that I unknowingly became a driver even though I was only a student in grade ten and started valuing care along with love in taking nursing of old and dependent, besides doctors and medicines.

"I tried my best to give the desired level of comfort to both, minimizing their sufferings as much as I could. My Nana left us when I was in grade eleven. That was very sad for my Nani. I fully devoted my time and energy, to ensuring the peace and happiness of Nani. In the process, we became very close but was astounded to notice her mental alertness as she did not respond to say anything about my birth and growing up.

After some calculative efforts, I gave up and opted to enjoy life in the company of Nani. But soon that, too, was snapped when she gave in to the dictum of life. I was finishing my grade twelve.

Coming back to an empty home, the feeling of loneliness impended me continuously with atrociousness, and for the first time in my life, I realized how lonely I was. In this world of about eight billion people, I do not have even one person who is of my link.

"I just used my home as a sleeping space, spent most of the time in varied activities outside, and meticulously started eating outside, mostly in fast food outlets.

"That realization reoriented my focus in life, and I opted consciously to become a professional nurse with dedication. That brings me here to attain that objective and coincidentally meet each other. Thanks to you for taking the initiative to interact with me."

As the food earlier served apparently lost its desired crispness, Momota ordered one fresh service of the same food without checking with Arshi.

Noting that, Arshi observed frivolously that by that solo authoritative act, "you have endorsed my earlier proposition of addressing you as Appa."

Sharing fresh service of food, both were on their way to their respective homes when Momota stopped for a while to lament, saying, "You are going home with Dad waiting for you. I am returning to my abode with bed and pillow in their respective shape and setting, reminding me of my Nana and Nani." She then continued saying, "I know from indicative sources about the death of my mother. I am certain about the demise of Nana and Nani who bequeathed all that they had to me. The sad part is I do not know whether my father is dead or alive. That haunts me every night as I go to sleep. That is where I am going."

Despite such tragic expressions of the pristine acquaintance, Arshi was all happy, sensing that she was about to hit the end of the dark tunnel that so far made Father's life a miserable one despite other all-around accomplishments and Momota's life an appalling one.

Right then, a fear-provoking thought overwhelmed her. She realized that her aspirations to identify and have conclusions pertaining to apparent missing links in their respective relationships are fraught with dares of impenetrable implications. Putting a cap on her enthusiasm, she decided to be steady in her pursuit of the truth, framing that not only emotions but perceptible evidence is a basic ingredient in such effort. She decided to move carefully with caution as warranted.

Arshi tried her revised strategy of generating an impression in the mind of Father having a premise of probability, if not of possibility.

In such a long conversation after one dinner discourse, Arshi gleefully noted that as she is concerned about Father's mental piece, among others, in search of a possible likely daughter, the father too was also having the burden to see his daughter settled in life.

Javed pointedly conveyed to her his mental agony caused by her lack of interest in marriage matters, and that triggered an answer so guardedly harbored by her till then.

Arshi responded, "I am overwhelmed knowing you are concerned about my marriage. I, too, have the same worry. But I am pursuing an independent project. In either situation of success or failure in about next six months, I will talk to you on the same issue again. I do not have anyone in mind, though there are several enthusiasts in my previous place of work. At an appropriate time, and that may be sooner than you expect, I will be ready to marry anyone of your choice."

She was relieved after saying that. He was happy to note that Arshi remains what Zarin expected her to be.

Arshi made a calculative move by having sustained dialogues with Momota within the general frame of life where expectations are to be separated from possibilities, more relying on probabilities.

In such a discourse, Arshi, with a specific objective in mind, mildly floated an indirect challenge within the frame of general terms, saying, "It is perhaps more prudent to test out anything that creates heaviness in mind and thinking rather than allowing that to cause continuous vexation."

After following up on that point on different days and in varied ways without any positive response from Momota, Arshi, fusing fried chicken and french fries dinner, opted for a direct approach. Shredding all pretensions and having a simultaneous objective of laying the needed backdrop, Arshi pointedly said, "Appa, I have something in mind and that is causing edginess within. I need your help and support in addressing that once and for all. Since we met about two-plus months back, we bonded very quickly and dearly, felt a closeness, and treated each of us as sisters besides having almost similar agonizing life histories and experiences. I am keen to test how close we are. Maybe we are not at all! But that will be good enough for me to have peace within."

Momota kept quiet for a while and then said, "What do you have in mind?"

Arshi was prepared for that sort of inquest and replied politely, "I have a school friend working in an ancestry test center relatively close to our hospital. When I joined the hospital, I started feeling lonely. Not only that, Abbu (Father) also needed to interact occasionally with someone else other than me. I started communicating with my school and college friends.

"I promptly got help from a few. A friend of the ancestry testing center, Shefa by the name is one of them. Because of financial constraints, Shefa's parents could not afford her formal higher education. She thus decided to become a technician. After a few changes, she liked the work related to ancestry, a new field of scientific inquisition.

"It was just not that she was of help to us only. Our association and home, especially interactions with Abbu, were beneficial to her as she misses her father. Both Father and I were having a discourse to work out an arrangement to help her without her knowledge in pursuing her abortive ambition for higher learning. In that quest, I started silent efforts to learn more details pertaining to the field of ancestry DNA. I found that to be enchanting and concluded that she likes that field of learning. Eventually, I shared that conclusion with Father.

"As I went to bed, a new thought cropped up in my mind. Shefa's presence and working in the hospital adjacent to Ancestry DNA Center is a golden opportunity for us to determine the closeness or distance in our relationships since we have so many similarities in our temperament, thinking, attitude, and preferences in life. All these could either be coincidental or a product of a very natural life phenomenon. Though conscious of that, I still have that burden.

"With the passage of time that became unbearable. It motivated me to share my feelings with Momota Appa without spelling my rationale of having almost identical life history. Of available options, I strongly opined for an ancestry test for both of us so that we can have time-tested conclusions without skepticism and misperception. Momota Appa consented after some persuasion. Appa finally agreed but put two conditions: the outcome should not have any impact on our present relationship and we should have a solemn commitment to keep this a secret.

"The process went through smoothly, but we had to wait for specialists to review the data. After some days, I received a call from my friend Shefa from the testing center. She said that the result had arrived, but the professional scientist in charge was only the authorized one to open the envelop in the presence of clients. In consultations with us and her higher-ups, the time and date of conveying the result were determined. That was the Friday, one day after the said telephone conversation.

"Those two nights and the following day were the most agonizing and excruciating time in my own life that far. It was not only that I could not talk to anybody about the test, but even I could not share the process I was in with uncertainty engulfing at the passing each moment."

During the joint walk from the hospital cafeteria toward the testing center on that fateful following Friday to be not unduly ahead of time according to the center's schedule, Arshi was astounded, noticing a very casual and carefree Momota for the first-time having doubts about the relevance of the relationship she has been chasing. But Arshi grew up with a strong and determined mindset. She concluded firmly that irrespective of the outcome, Momota will always be her sister. Possible negative outcomes will not have any impact on that.

Taking their seats in assigned chairs in the closed meeting room, the two young ladies jointly, and possibly for the first time, felt nervousness. That aggravated with every passing minute indicated by a long passing needle of the wall clock affixed to the wall facing the lonely ladies.

Right at that moment, the doors were opened, and three ladies, including the professional scientist in-charge, entered the meeting room and took their seats. Their grim faces were suggestive of something ominous. Arshi, as a defensive response, placed her hand under the table, holding the hand of her dear Momota Appa. The latter had a nonresponsive reaction as all through, she had doubts about this and its related outcome.

The professional scientist, following their operative practice, deliberatively followed a slow and steady approach, preparing parties concerned mentally ready and stable for its outcome, many a time contrary to expectations.

She glanced through the summary, and wearing a relieving smile, said, "Oh my God, what an outcome! Both of you have the same father. You are real sisters."

Hearing that, Arshi rushed to the other side of the table to have a look at the report, more to assure her that what the scientist was telling and what she heard was correct.

She then looked at Appa to confirm, only to find her in a semiconscious position reclining her head on the side cushion of her chair. Before anyone could react, Arshi took possession of the glass full of water placed in front of the scientist's chair and sprinkled some on the face of her dear sister. Momota slowly opened her eyes and said, "Is it true, what I heard?'"

On being assured that what she heard was what the report documented, Momota straightened herself and extended two hands to embrace Arshi. Everyone was happy, and both proven real sisters cheerily stepped out of the testing center after saying thanks profusely to all staff, particularly the school friend of Arshi who orchestrated the whole thing.

Being on the road, Arshi quickly thought and concluded that the lead she had would not be allowed to linger, being fearful of an unlikely twist and decided to act quickly. She picked up her cell and called Father. In her brief call, she first enquired about his performing Juma (Friday Muslims' congregation for prayer), keeping in view the father's new discomfort with his knee, and then said in the form of a command, "I am coming home now and have a colleague with me. So dress up nicely. As we will be approaching the home door, I will give you another call, and you then open the door." Without giving any chance to Father, she abruptly closed the call.

As the Uber car stopped in front of the designated address, both Arshi and Momota got out and started walking the approach after thanking the driver. Arshi made her promised call to Father. She then noticed the apparent nervousness in the physical reflexes of her dearest Appa and the resultant shivering. She got hold of Appa's one hand, placing her another on Appa's shoulder.

The doors opened soon. There was standing Prof. Javed looking elegant in his white Juma prayer outfit of Punjabi (white flowing long outfit) and pajama.

Arshi could not wait anymore. She loudly said, "Dad, I am at the end of the project I mentioned before. You can now make your move to find a groom for me."

She paused and continued saying, "The lady I am holding hand is my proven real sister and your first child, Momota, whom you have had been thinking of and looking for always, notwithstanding being excused of responsibilities by Mother Lolita."

Turning to almost unmoving Momota, she said, "Appa, this is our father whom you have been looking for every moment of life to recline on his shoulder saying 'Abba.'"

In the midst of pristine emotions, Javed took a step forward and then stopped involuntarily as unrestrained tears overwhelmed him. The frenzied tears through his cheeks drained to engulf his chest. Finally, he reacted by extending both hands to welcome the daughters.

Arshi moved quickly to help Momota in her move. The latter took a step and then collapsed. Javed instantaneously bent, took hold of the physique of Momota, and drew her close to his wet chest, saying, "Ma (mother), I am here for you both."

Saying those words, he extended his other hand, indicating Arshi to join. Her physical proximity caused a bewildering impact, and all three started crying for some more time.

Javed turned to move inside with the daughters, opening both his hands as their assured shelter from now onward with respective identities renewed and established.

As earlier said by Javed, life is nothing but a process. In that process, fragmentations are preordained and inevitable. Most of the time, such fragmentations cause immediate sadness and are equally shocking. But many of such fragmentations sometimes have hidden challenges, giving chances for new opportunities and beginning afresh. That perhaps is what life is all about.

With that dictum in mind and the challenges inherent, Javed started his life afresh in the loving company and care of Momota and Arshi.